A LOVE LIFE
LIKE
KARMIC DISASTER

a novel

casey pope

ISBN 978-0-9966966-0-9
eBook ISBN 978-0-9966966-1-6

Published in the United States

A LOVE LIFE
LIKE
KARMIC DISASTER

CHAPTER ONE
The Joy Over A Severed Head

Explosive thunder rattled Victor Gottenberg's larger than average brain within the confines of his literally thick skull. Sat upright from self-medicated coma and shouted out, "Francine! Francine! Francine! Francine! Francine!"

Torrential rain, a million tiny hammers pounded the apartment complex, slamming against the roof, clapboards, and against the windows, daring the glass not to break. A creation of severe white noise, enough to challenge Victor's sanity. Thunder after thunder crackled, trying to breach his atheism. Felt like a metaphysical baseball bat to the head. Like a message: don't do it, don't do it. Don't you dare. But he could not be swayed, would indeed dare. Had to. Knew no other way.

Victor checked his calculator watch. The LED screen indicated that the alarm which had been set for 10:00 p.m. was activated. But the sad little electronic beep was inaudible. Now 10:22 and he was running late. The damned white noise.

He pulled himself out of the depths of the couch. Lumbered to the dinky closet, looked for his rain slicker until his illegally-prescribed-drug-induced haze started to wear off and he realized he owned no such thing. Victor found an undersized hoodie and wrapped it around his lanky frame. Pulled the hood over his impressive white-guy 'fro. Snatched car keys, envelope of cash, gangled out the door.

Relentless rain as Victor pulled his subcompact into the parking lot of Goode & Gish's Bar & Grill tucked between an industrial park and a freeway overpass. Clipped a few parked cars due to impeded visibility and windshield wipers with crappy top-speed. Found a space under the failing neon sign, letters blinking and unblinking, some not lit at all. He stumbled out of the car, was savaged by the downpour, squinted up at the sign which for one second he thought flashed, "G o - d - - - is - - - - - -rill." Rubbed his eyes, shook his head, looked again: "Goo- - & -ish's Bar & G - ill."

He entered the bar, pulled the hood off and stood searching. Water dripped off him, pooled at his sneakered feet. The place was only a quarter-full but noisy. Clack of pool ball collisions; ping ping ping of the pinball machine; drunken raucous banter; the juke box playing a country song: a woman singing about a broken heart, sweet revenge.

Because of dim lighting and water-logged eyes, it took Victor until the end of the song to spot Percy Maplewerm sitting in the dank corner booth. Water stain from the ceiling spreading down the faux wood paneling. Half empty pitcher of draft on the table. Percy wore an '80s metal band T-shirt, the agreed upon sign of recognition.

He, Percy, was slight of build, bad-postured. Thin hair pasted against his bony skull. A greasy aura about him. He slurped at his mug of beer.

Victor sloshed over to the booth, asked, "Mr. Maplewerm?"

Percy put down the mug, burped, "You're late."

Victor slid into the booth, spouting apologies and explanation. Percy raised his palm, said, "Stop." Slurped beer, pointed his crooked finger at Victor's face. "What we're talking about here is a serious deal, man. Serious shit. See this?" He grabbed his own neck. "This is on the line for you."

"Mr. Maplewerm." Victor hyperventilated for a few seconds, then said, "I need. I need this to happen. I need I need I need—"

"Stop with the blubbering already. Jesus. Are you crying? Jesus."

Victor shook his head. "The rain in my eyes." Breathed in and out through his nose. "The rain."

"Okay, whatever. So. How well do you know Henry?"

"We're best friends. Known him since, forever. And we're in med school together now."

"Yeah? Well, him I know. You? Not so much. I can't have this come back to me, Vic-Tor. Can you understand that? It's not like bodies go disappearing everyday. Does it happen? You bet your ass it does. More often than you know. Henry may have vouched for you but I still have to be careful. Do we understand each other?"

Victor nodded briskly while saying, "Yes yes yes."

Reached inside his hoodie, pulled out the sopping envelope. "Here. The money. I've got it."

"Jesus! Not here." Eyes darted about, chameleon-like. "Put it away. I come here all the time, man."

"Maybe we shouldn't have met here then," said Victor, sincere about it, not at all being a smartass despite the opportunity.

But Percy responded, "What are you, some kind of smartass? Are you trying to piss me off? What are you— ah, hell, just hand it over." Snatched the envelope from Victor. Looked at his watch. "We don't have a lot of time, Victor. Let's move our asses."

A waitress walked up to their booth, demeanor and dress trying to ignore middle-age but only succeeding in amplifying the fact. She said to Percy, "Is that a wad of cash in the envelope or are you just happy to see me?"

Victor thought the reference was disjunctive. Percy: schoolboy giddy, voice went an octave higher. "Oh, ha ha, Maggie. Ha ha. I'm always happy. You know. I mean. To see you." Maggie waited. Maybe for a different answer. Percy forced a grin. Fat yellow teeth. Maggie still waiting. He couldn't hold her stare, looked at the sticky-stained table instead. "We'll take another pitcher, Mags."

"Okay then," said Mags. Walked off, trying too hard to shake her money-maker which stopped money-making about ten years ago.

But not according to Percy who grimaced as if it pained him to see her go. Eyes lit up as they soaked up the vision that was Mags. The spell broken when Victor blurted, "The time, Mr. Maplewerm, the time. We need to move our asses. Your words."

Percy mussed his hair, violent-like, un-pasting it.

Slammed his fist on the table. "Fuckssake!" Then searched for Maggie. When he spotted her, he said again, "Fuckssake," but softly, and to no one in particular.

Victor shivered, waterlogged. Couldn't understand Percy's sudden mood change. Pent up desperation pressed outwardly against Victor's thorax. Felt like his heart was about to detonate. Gritted his teeth, swallowed the sensation, pressed it down, down. Let it ooze out of his pores instead.

Percy stared at him as if smelling it, said, "Okay. Damn shit. We'll go, okay? We'll go."

***

At the morgue, Percy introduced Victor to the night intake person, a non-jovial fella who said flat-toned, "Hey, boss. Always a pleasure." Didn't sound like he meant it. And didn't blink an eye at Percy's guest. While the three looked at each other not making small talk, a body in a body bag was wheeled in on a gurney and so the intake guy said, "The fun never ends," and commenced to do his intake thing.

Victor and Percy fast-walked down the overly florescent-lighted hallway past rooms 1 and 2 to room 3. Victor asked, "Are all these rooms—"

"Yeah, you bet your ass they're filled with bodies. We're a high volume operation. It never ceases to amaze me that death never ceases. But who's complaining, eh?"

Victor, hands in pocket, gave an unconvincing shrug, trying to appease.

Percy led the way into Room 3, flicked on the lights. A blast of fluorescent hum. He grabbed a lab-coat off the stainless steel examination table and slithered into it and opened the thick door to the cooler. The hiss of refrigeration, the walls lined with body-drawers, three high. Walls and walls of them. Victor took it in, became discombobulated.

Percy walked up to one of the drawers, rapped a knuckle at the stainless steel exterior. "Here's your girl." Percy sucked air through his teeth, exaggerated a frown. "Look, I know we all have our preferences but you may want to re-think this. Maybe I could interest you in someone who's more put together. Literally." Walked two drawers over. "She came in early this morning. Also an auto versus auto fatality but came out less scathed than your friend there." Unlatched the door, slid out the drawer. Percy with a grin. "Voila."

The woman's naked body was indeed unscathed. Face looked about college-age. Left side of her head, slightly collapsed, the result of side-impact collision.

Percy bent over the woman, leaned close to her face, as if to kiss her but didn't. Put his hand on her belly, caressed her up the length of the torso, to her neck, to her face. "I could love a girl like you."

Victor was unmoved, didn't share Percy's necrophilic affection for this corpse. Impatience in his voice: "Can we get back to who I came here for?"

"Not your type, huh? Have it your way." Percy pushed the drawer back in, told her he would see her later. Went back to the first drawer, pulled it out.

Victor glanced at the body, then jerked his head as if violently jabbed in the eyes. Had to look away. The room tilted, this way and that. His vision faded to white. Deafening electric hum. Percy's voice, muffled, buzzing in the background, saying I told you so and keep your shit together. Legs like flimsy spring coils. Victor, bent over, wheezing.

"Hey, Vic-Tor. Get it together. I need a done deal before the next shift comes in. They tend to be more, uh, by the book and see bodies as a task to be dealt with. Wouldn't understand people like you and me."

"Just one minute, Mr. Maplewerm. Give me a minute." Victor fought against the wobble, stood straight, forced himself to breathe. The white haze dissolved, the world came back into view. Didn't look back at the body just yet, said, "Okay, okay, okay, okay." And then looked.

Her right leg was pulverized from mid-femur down, mangle of meat and bone. Torso misshapen, broken-looking and lumpy. Internal damage for sure. Cuts and abrasions abound but clean of bruises due to instantaneous death.

"They brought her in without the hand, couldn't find it at the scene," said Percy.

Victor checked the right arm. Hand still attached. Checked the left, appeared that the hand had been wrenched from the wrist. "Okay, okay." Quivering voice. "So the hand's lost. But where's her head?"

At the juncture between her clavicle and where the larynx should have been, was a pristine laceration.

Percy mused, "Remarkable, you know, to get a decapitation that clean in an auto accident. Pretty cool."

Victor yanked puny Percy by the lab-coat collar, shook him to where his bony head swung wildly back and forth, making his fat lips flap. Slammed him against the stainless steel wall of death drawers. "Where the fuck is her head?!"

Percy's eyes took a moment to regain focus. He coughed

out, "Jesus, man! Take a pill, man! The head's gotta be here somewhere. They brought it in with the body. It's gotta be here. Although some in the night crew have been known to, you know, take souvenirs."

Victor made a fist.

"Whoa, motherfucker. I have delicate bones."

POW! went Victor's fist into Percy's fat lips. A tooth fell out, blood was a given. Victor made another fist.

"No!" muffled Percy through the hand holding his busted mouth. "Stop. Please! We'll find it. Just understand that things get misplaced here, okay? We're just government workers, man. Don't hold us to such high standards."

Victor slammed his fist into Percy's forehead. Percy flopped to the floor. Cried out, "Ow, fucker, okay." He scrambled up, started opening and pulling out drawers. "Sometimes, parts detached from the body get checked in separately, depending on which idiot is manning the intake desk. Gets put into separate drawers."

Drawer after drawer, searching. Victor did the same from the other end of the wall. The cooler echoed with sounds of abused metal, hard and desperate breaths. Both men sweating despite the cold. Done with his share of the drawers, Victor watched Percy getting down to the last few.

As if feeling the stabbing stare, Percy stopped. Couldn't immediately meet Victor's eyes, perhaps expecting a gaze foretelling Percy's impending doom. But when he did look, he instead saw blinking away of tears. Eyes dimming, twin suns dying. Percy's fear seemingly replaced by vicarious desperation, he swung open the next door, pulled at the drawer. It was empty. Until the head came rolling from the far end to rest against the front of the drawer.

"Holy shit," whispered Percy. "Here she is." He picked up the head, raised it as if a trophy, bellowed, "Here she fucking is!"

Victor trudged to Percy, felt as if walking in hip-deep mud. Percy offered the head to him and Victor cradled it with shaking hands. Her frizzy, unruly hair, now flattened to the skull, caked with blood. A pugilist's nose - tall bridge, thick and busted. How he had missed that nose. A gash across one of her lush brows, the brows she thought "bushy" and despised yet never plucked. Her eyes, closed. Lost in dreams was all, he told himself. Slightly parted pale pink lips. He could hear that voice with the rasp she's had since childhood as if afflicted by a permanent sore throat say, "Hello, Victor."

"Hello, Francine." He held her to his chest, arms wrapped tightly. Laid his cheek atop her head, let out a sigh to beat all sighs. Had to sit down. Stayed on the floor, rocking, rocking.

Percy, with knuckle marks developing on his forehead, watched Victor, then wiped away tears with the sleeve of his lab coat. Through bloodied lips, he croaked, "Just so you know..." Sniffled. "...we have a no-return policy. It's a done deal. Ms. Francine Styne is all yours now."

They carried body-bagged Francine, and her head in a garbage bag, out the rear exit doors which said "Emergency Exit Only - Alarm Will Sound." The sign was a fallacy. No more alarm. Percy's long-ago handiwork. The exit led out to a narrow alleyway where they were immediately doused by the rain. They hustled Francine to Victor's awaiting subcompact. Into the hatchback she went.

Lightning like atomic flash. Cannon blast of thunder. Mere background noise to Victor as he drove away.

CHAPTER TWO
Origin Story (In Two Parts)

<u>Part One</u>

Summer! Family trip to the Magic Kingdom! Victor, surprisingly un-enthused about it all for a kid his age, going into the 3rd grade. Saw it as an inconvenience. Had wanted to use the summer downtime to get a head start on next year's curriculum. He aced 2nd grade without trying. So with concerted effort, he thought he could maybe skip a grade or two. Though Mom and Dad were proud of their son with the larger than average brain, they thought it was unnatural for a kid his age to be so driven as to study away his summer vacation.

The motel was so-so, but conveniently close to the Magic Kingdom. Free cable. Twenty-four hour diner next door, decent, practically gourmet, not greasy-spoon, liquor license. And there was a pool, a requisite against the subtropic sultriness.

They had arrived late-evening, took advantage of the still-open diner. The non-vacant motel hummed with full capacity of air-conditioners. Victor's Mom and Dad reclined on the bed, belly-full of meatloaf special and vino. Their eyes, glazed over from gastronomic satiation, reflecting the romantic comedy playing on the movie channel.

Victor sat at the small table by the window not watching the movie, reading the last volume of the latest trilogy of his favorite sci-fi writer. But not really reading because of his agitated state, high from the chocolate malted his parents, via intoxicant-warped decision-making process, granted to him for dessert. His vision skittered over the pages. Had to go back and re-read what he realized had not really been read. Skitter, turn page, go back, re-read. Skitter, turn page, etc., until he heard a splash, outside, from the pool maybe. He checked the clock on the nightstand: 10:47 p.m. Recalled the pool-side signs: *No lifeguard on duty. No running. No glass containers. No swimming after 9:30 p.m.* Must have been hearing things. Skitter, turn page. Splash.

He parted the curtains, craned to check the pool. No one there. But the water rippled. So he waited. Then she surfaced at the shallow end, climbed out of the water, her black hair draped wetly against her head and down her neck to just between her shoulder blades. Looked to be about someone within his peer group. And she wore a bikini. A bikini!

He checked his parents. A light snore from both, rhythmic and soothing. Victor rummaged through the suitcase hoping for, hoping for. Yes! The swim trunks. He slipped out of his cords, pulled on the trunks over his tighty whities. Took off his shirt. Thought about it. Put it back on.

Victor held his breath, eased the door open and slipped out. His bare feet pattered against the still warm concrete walkway. Passed by the pool. She didn't see him. Made a second pass, pattered a little louder this time. It worked.

She asked, "Are you coming to swim too?"

"Ummm. I was just going to, ummm. Yeah, okay." Pushed through the gate, made straight for the deep end and flopped into the water. When he surfaced, she was wheezing with laughter. He struggled to the ladder, swam like a speared fish.

Her laughter degenerated into a hacking cough. She fell to hands and knees, torso expanding and contracting violently.

Victor climbed out of the water, hurried and knelt next to her. Water dripped off him, pooled around them.

"Are you okay?"

She nodded, caught her breath after a minute. When she looked up at him, tears were gathering at the corners of her smile.

"You're funny, what you did," she panted. "That was like the worst dive ever. Oh, and do you wear your shirt in the shower too? Oh oh, and and, you swim like a fish out of water." A chortle.

Swim like a fish out of water.

Swim like a fish out of water.

Swim like a fish out of water.

He repeated it three times to himself so as not to forget. What a thing to say. Wonderful.

"Is there something wrong with you?" Touched his own chest, imagined the pain.

She stood, chose not to hear the question. "Come on."
Led him to the pool's edge, sat and dipped her legs into
the water. He followed.

"Look at our legs," she said.

Their legs wobbled and bent like flimsy rubber in strong
wind, an optical parody created by undulations of water
and light. She giggled. It made him dizzy. Then they just
stared, hypnotized.

The whir of the water filter. Swoosh of late night traffic
on the nearby highway.

Victor turned to her, noticed for the first time the
paleness of her skin. As if never seen the light of day.

She caught him staring, hugged herself, embarrassed.
Said, "I wish I could be a doctor."

"Wish? Why don't you just do it?"

She ignored him, got up. "Be right back." Left footprint
puddles leading to one of the parasoled tables. Lifted her
towel, found her Hello Kitty coin purse. "What kind do
you like," she asked as she headed to the kiosk illuminated
by vending machines. "Cola, lemon lime, orange, and a
cherry one?"

"Uhhh…"

Coins plinked. Ka-thunk ka-thunk, the soda-can
making its way out of the machine. "Cola it is." She sat
back down next to him. Popped the top, slurped a sip and
held the can out to him.

Victor stared at the opening of the can where her
mouth just was. Thought he could see the imprint of her
lips on the aluminum surface. Never had he wanted to
share a drink where someone else's saliva had preceded
his. Until now. Guzzled as if extracting more than the
sugary fizz.

They finished off the cola, had a burp contest. Slid into the water and stayed in until they started to shiver. They lay out on the warm poolside concrete, pointed out constellations, making up names for ones they didn't know.

Then a woman's voice. "Honey? Time to come in. It's very late."

They sat up. The woman stood at the gate to the pool. The girl said, "Just a little longer please, Mom?"

The mother looked at Victor, a smile in her eyes. Said to the daughter, "I let you stay out longer than usual. And we have an early start tomorrow."

"Ohhh, okay." To Victor, apologetic, "I have to go."

His throat clenched, chest felt constricted, a dread like never before. The girl retrieved her towel and coin purse. He followed. Felt like every bit of happiness was gushing out of him.

They stood in front of the mother. She asked, "What's your name?"

"Victor."

"Victor, we don't live in Florida. Just visiting. There's a doctor here that — well, anyway."

"Doctor?"

"What about you, Victor?"

In a small voice, "Just visiting."

The girl and boy hung their heads, looked at their feet. The mother said, "Say goodbye to Victor."

"Bye." Barely audible.

He went back and lay in the spot from where they had named constellations. Fell asleep repeating the names. In the morning, he found a Hello Kitty memo paper stuffed in his left hand with an address written on it along with the words, "This is my address. We can be pen pals okay?"

15

Victor wrote 4572 words to her. She responded with 4997. Then nothing more from her. He continued: 1288. Still nothing. Then 32 words from her mother.

"Victor: I'm sorry to have to tell you that Mary died last Tuesday. Her funeral was today. Thank you for being a friend to my daughter. She was very, very fond of you."

***

He wondered about being a doctor. Saving lives. But what if they died before he had a chance to save them? Maybe there was a career in bringing back the dead. Why not?

Part Two

It was a Tuesday, Sloppy Joe day at Washington-Lincoln Middle School. Victor's favorite, the Joe. Meat sauce on spongy buns. And sure to be accompanied by either tater tots or those zig zag fries. His stomach swashed and gurgled with anticipation. Could barely concentrate on math equations.

Then, just like that, there she was. Standing in front of the chalkboard. The teacher introduced her, the new student. Francine Styne. The name was sucked into Victor's brain, that part of it, just southwest of the hypothalamus, where nothing was forgotten, and where resided for the past five years, the face of Mary, the girl at the pool. There was only a vague resemblance between Francine and Mary but it was more than enough to spark the synaptic activity of memory-emotional transferral from the dusty archive to the day-to-day processing center. Electrical impulses commanded the glands to release molecular compounds equivalent of warm fuzzies into the blood stream. Victor's heart sang.

Two rows over sat Henry Clerval aka The Physical Presence. Towered over his peers most of whom could fit comfortably inside his barrel-like torso. The combination of his physicality with just enough paternal discord at home, along with a touch of sociopathy, made him an exemplar of bullies. So good was he at his vocation, he was able to open a savings account from extorted lunch money.

As for Victor, Henry considered him an archenemy but had never laid a hand on him. Everyone else was a victim. Victor, an archenemy. High praise for the skinny geek. They'd known each other since third grade. Henry was tops GPA-wise, until Victor arrived. Ever since then, Henry had been number two. His initial reaction? Beat the crap out of Victor. But what would've been the challenge? Henry could pummel all comers, especially the likes of Victor. Had been doing so for years. Instead, Henry's goal was to regain intellectual supremacy, after which he could shake off the precarious respect he's had for Victor and enable him to finally beat the crap out of him. Order would be restored.

But then there was this new girl. Francine. "Pretty" wasn't exactly her suit. Her nose outpaced the growth of her head by a 2 to 1 margin. Frizzy, unruly hair, ponytailed, exposing ears the size of wings of a small flying animal. Brows of such angle and bushy-ness, that if furrowed just so, gave her a sinister appearance. Her eyes the color of sludge. Lanky-looking despite below average height. Hunchy posture. Big head. Homemade haircut, crooked bangs. The teacher asked that Francine give a little backstory and the exposition rasped out of her mouth as if sandpapered.

But there was something there to keep one stay looking. The quirky features worked together to become a composition exceeding the sum of its parts. And something bone deep, an invisible beacon. Like a prism. Had to know how to look at it to get the translucent piece of glass to emit a rainbow.

Pastel colors reflected off Victor's eyes. Henry's too. Smiling stupidly, the both of them. The boys then turned to each other, discerned immediately the intention of the other. Henry glowered. Victor, by years of reinforcement, knew to give ground, his eyeballs felt about to falter, to shift gaze. But Victor did not allow it. Henry clenched his fist, snapped the pencil he held. Showdown now imminent.

High noon. The packed cafeteria murmured with Sloppy Joe and tater tots excitement. While in line, Victor searched for Henry who was hard to miss even in this crowd. Not there. Curious as to his absence, but relieved.

Victor carried his tray through the throng and headed to the nerds-loners-new-students sector where he was sure to find: Francine! Not surprisingly, Amy sat next to her, yacking away. Everyone knew of Amy who was avoided, friendless, oblivious.

Francine's brows were furrowed with unintentional sinisterness. Then she spotted Victor, cracked a grin. She waved. "Hi hello? You're in my class? Can you help me?" Side-eyed Amy. "With the math assignment?"

Amy said, "I can help you, I'm super good at math and planning to be a math teacher even or an accountant maybe possibly a pilot I don't know but you don't need Victor. He's kind of weird even."

"Oh but we're in the same class so…" Let it hang. Eyes imploring Victor to hurry.

He got the hint, made haste, but was stopped when a brick wall by the name of Henry stepped in his path.

"Hey, Vic. Mmm, hey, that lunch looks delish," said Henry, as if just making chit chat.

But Victor saw past the facade. Gleaned irritation and aggravation in the subtext. Henry's eyes betrayed his confidence, revealing incomprehension of a threat he could only control by violence and fear. Victor, a sudden urge to urinate.

"So, Vic, what're you doing, where you going? Oh, are you thinking of going to sit with the new girl?"

"Her name is Francine."

"I know her name, asshole."

"I, I know you know. I was just saying—"

"Shut up. That seat over there, next to her, to Francine? It's reserved for me. You just have to imagine Amy not being there. And me being there."

"You never sit there though."

"Stop being an asshole."

"Do you like her or something?"

"What?"

"You don't own her."

"What?!"

And "thump" went Henry's meaty knuckles into Victor's soft underbelly. He collapsed to the cafeteria floor, head smacking the cold concrete. He lay there, clutching his gut, trying to control the spiraling in his concussed brain. Suffering the pain of not being able to breathe, of being perplexed by human meanness. Tater tots, Sloppy Joe and soggy buns, single serving carton of milk, and apple crisp, splattered around him, framing his fetal position.

Francine shot up. Amy gasped. Victor's vision spun counter clockwise, a kaleidoscopic blurring. Heard, through ears seemingly stuffed with cotton, what sounded like arguing. Thought he saw Henry flop to the floor. Thought he saw him get back up, then a yelp maybe. Felt warm liquid dripping on his face. A crescendo of a marching army.

Fade to black.

***

Victor woke up in the nurse's office. Nurse Bleu. When he came to, she was standing over him. Came eye to eye with canyon-esque cleavage.

"Are you angels and am I in heaven?" he said groggily to the cherubic heavenlies trapped in the pushup bra.

Nurse Bleu lifted Victor's head via her index finger under his chin. "Victor, my eyes are up here. Be a gentleman and talk to me up here."

"Um. Hi, Nurse Bleu. So I guess I'm not dead?"

"You were always the astute one, Victor."

"My head hurts. Was I concussed?"

"Yes. 'Concussed.' That's it, that's the accurate diagnosis. What's the prognosis?"

"I feel a little dizzy, but no nausea. My vision is clear and I'm not slurring my speech." He moved his limbs stiffly, robot-like. "My arms and legs are working so no serious trauma."

"'Trauma.' Good use of the word."

"So the prognosis? I should recover fully as long as I avoid cracking my head on concrete floors."

"Excellent! Medical science seems to be right up your

alley. Just don't become one those doctors who copulate with nurses as a sport. It affects people, you know, the nurses I mean. I was head-nurse of an E.R. at one the most E.R.-friendly cities in the U.S. Now I'm here. Consequences."

She opened a cabinet door, looked at the array of by-the-book medication. "This won't do. You are in pain right, Victor?"

"Um."

"No. This won't do." Went to her desk, pulled opened the bottom drawer, reached deep and retrieved a ziplock bag full of pills and capsules in a range of rainbow colors. Located two mauve ones, popped them into her mouth, munched away. Gave a thick pale pink one to Victor. "Chew it slowly. Swallow. Enjoy."

He did. He did. And he did.

Minutes of medicated silence between them. Then Nurse Bleu piped up and recounted for him what had happened.

"The new girl Francine. The one with the busted nose?" said Nurse Bleu.

"Huh, what?" Alarmed. Seriously.

"She's a trouble maker in a good way." Slapped her thigh. Guffawed. "All for you, Victor. For you."

"What?"

While Victor had writhed on the cafeteria floor from the punched-in-the-gut agony and onset of a concussion, which would have been more serious if not for his literally thick skull, Francine had launched at Henry.

She said, "Why did you do that that was not cool why?"

Henry hesitated, unsure of what was happening. Never

been challenged before. So the lizard-core of his brain stepped up, apparently, and made him raise his hands as fists. But she beat him to the punch, thrust an uppercut to his jutting chin. He fell like a side of beef. The bully with a glass jaw. Several seconds of daze and confusion. Shook it off, lumbered onto his feet, knee-jerkedly punched her in the nose. Immediate regret.

To and fro, Francine staggered. Blood dribbled from her busted nose, some splashing onto semi-conscious Victor. Staggered staggered about to fall. But the student body rose up as an indignant collective, marched like an army, caught her, held her. Henry squealed apologies as he was about to be trampled. Fists and feet and elbows and knees pummeled him. Was heard telling himself not to be a pussy. He fought back, made an impressive effort in taking out a number of the students, most of whom ended up in Nurse Bleu's office telling the tale.

"Did he die?" Victor asked, hopeful maybe.

Nurse Bleu laid her palm on his cheek. "It's understandable that you would wish death upon him." Her voice, milky. "But you should keep that to yourself. And I would say that the sooner you forget about the girl with the busted nose—"

"Francine."

"Yes. Francine. The sooner you forget about her, the better off you'll be. That's what I would say but I won't because it will be of no use." She looked at the clock on the wall, then out the window. Postured as if looking for an escape. She shuddered smally. "We're birds of feather in that regard. So just let me tell you that there will be consequences."

"Okay. But, so, did he die?"

"No, Victor, he did not. But he was taken to the E.R., at County General. Sounds like he probably will survive."

Victor looked out the window. Postured as if. As if not knowing where to go.

"Would you like more medication?"

"Yes, please."

***

Two weeks after The Incident, Henry was back in school. Recovered from injuries within days but had been suspended for his assault on Francine. A deal was brokered by the school district and Henry's parents who had threatened a lawsuit should Henry's record not be expunged. Mob violence, even against a bully, did not play well in front of juries, even if the mob was made up of idealistic middle-schoolers.

Henry thought to resume his reign but knew he had lost bully-credibility. Their anger quashed fear. And his weakness had been exposed, as if flayed open, and they had seen the guts of his insecurities. Now, persona non grata. His career effectively over. Wasn't sure how to wrap his mind around it.

On his first day back, he saw Francine in the cafeteria sipping chocolate milk during mid-morning snack, her body english: listing away from seat-mate Amy with the pistoning jaw. Victor sat across from Francine and munched happily. Francine's gaze slipped over Victor's right shoulder, locked in on Henry. Against his expectation, her eyes did not shoot daggers. Her nose, a gnarled bridge mess which she kept touching, tracing the asymmetry, pinching it as if trying to straighten it. Flinched from the pain, the injury still tender. Henry's regret for busting her nose was replaced by pride.

Notwithstanding potential rhinoplasty, she might as well had "Henry" tattooed across her face.

Victor knew of Henry's return but was unaffected. Persona non grata and all that. And he and Francine had become like this: picture index finger and middle finger intertwined. But after mid-morning snack, there was a vibe. A vibe Victor couldn't ignore and could ignore even less when she was not in fourth period class. Hearsay upon hearsay reached him and so he skipped fifth period and fast-walked out past the special-ed trailer classrooms, past the soccer fields, past the 100-year old oak tree under which a pair of eighth-graders were smoking weed, and made his way to the baseball field, where under the bleachers, silhouettes writhed. When his vision adjusted to the shadowy under-bleacher world, he made out that they were making out. Henry's mouth on Francine's mouth. Tongues were involved.

Victor thought he was suffering a myocardial infarction. Knew it was a crazy thought but thought it anyway. He went through the symptoms: 1) Sweating: Yes. 2) Shortness of breath: Yes. 3) Sudden chest pain: The pain radiated more from his stomach than his chest but he counted it as a "yes." 4) Vomiting: Ran past the oak tree where he stumbled to his knees and indeed vomited. The stoners laughed. He turned over and lay on his back. The blue vastness of sky engulfed him. There were streaks of jet streams which were not immediately clear as to their beginning and ending. He went through the symptoms again. Believed he was dying.

Two days later, during lunch break, Henry tracked down Victor sharing a joint with the eighth-graders under the 100-year old oak tree.

Henry said to Victor, "Hey, man! Since when did you become a pothead?"

"Oh, hey, Henry, Henster, Henry-otski, my bestest friend."

"You are fucking high."

"I am sooooo high." He took a toke, coughed out smoke, and coughed some more until tears ran down his cheeks.

Henry snatched away the joint, snuffed it out in his fist. "This shit will eat your brain. And just because you have a larger than average one, doesn't mean you should waste it."

"Why would you even care?"

"Because that brain qualifies you as my archenemy. My one and only." And with that, Henry kicked one of the eighth graders in the chest and punched the other on top of the head. "Get the fuck outta here, you assholes!"

The stoners stumbled away crying and laughing at the same time.

Henry sat next to Victor. "I came to tell you that your girlfriend is a bitch."

"My who?"

"She let me get to second base but only over the shirt. How lame is that? And so after that, I was like, 'Hey, Francine, you wanna go make out again?' and she was like, 'No why would I?' That's like a total bitch, right?"

Victor waited a beat before answering. Had to make sure to contain the glee before saying, "Yeah, I guess so." Gave a good impression of a sagely nod. Expected to hear more put-downs about Francine but Henry said nothing and just looked skyward. Maybe Henry also wondered about the streaks of jet streams, where they began, where they ended.

They sat there in the silence of stoner daze and jet stream contemplations for something like five minutes. Until Henry said, "So hey. The chess club is signing up new members. You wanna go check it out?"

"Um. Really?"

"What? You think I can't hang?"

"I know you can hang. But you and chess club? What about your reputation?"

Henry slumped. "Who cares. Kicking ass is not the only way to kick ass."

Victor, another sagely nod, for real this time. Said, "Okay then."

"Cool. Let's go kick some chess-geek ass."

Victor laughed. The first time ever in Henry's presence.

CHAPTER THREE
Best Way To Stave Off Decomposition

Sheets of rain made Victor drive at a crawl, squinted and strained to check the numbers on the storage units. Row after row after row. A mad maze of sameness. He glanced back at the bodybag. The clock in his head sounding ominous ticks, counting down to when decomposition would set in. Slammed his palm against the steering wheel over and over. Let loose a string of incoherent obscenities.

Finally came upon storage unit number 815. Berated himself for remembering it as 518. He pounded the horn which bleated pathetically. The roll-up door of the unit slid open and bright light poured out around the tall, burly figure who had opened the door. Victor shielded his eyes from the sudden glare and leapt out of the subcompact, opened the rear hatch.

"Hurry, help me," he shouted over the din of falling water.

The big fella strode to the car, lifted the bodybag, placed it over his shoulder, hurried into the storage unit. Victor followed with the garbage bag.

The storage unit was lit by rented light stands, the concrete floor crowded with hastily opened crates and boxes, a litter of packing material. Against the back wall, a stainless steel rectangular box that could easily be mistaken as a coffin. Conduits linked it to a computer and two cylindrical tanks like those used to fill helium into balloons. But no lightweight gases here.

The big fella, about six-eight-ish, a semi-solid 320 pounds. Henry Clerval. Clean cut, handsome, unlike his former teenage self when he was big and clunky and a bully which had been an easy fallback position despite his self awareness, despite his intellect.

"Is it good to go?" Victor said, breathless.

Henry unzipped the bodybag. "Do you doubt me? Look at it. It's a thing of beauty." Indicated toward the stainless steel coffin-looking box. "You cut it close though. We need to get her cry-oed asap."

"The rain. It played havoc. This insane rain." Voice tinged with bewilderment.

"You've angered God."

"What?"

"You've stolen an angel. Or trying to anyway."

"Fuck off."

"Said the atheist," said Henry. Then looked at Francine's body, let out an involuntary yelp. But took a breath, calmed himself. "Uh. It seems like something is missing here."

Victor placed the garbage bag on the floor. As if performing a ceremony, he knelt beside it, purposefully folded the bag down and around Francine's head, picked her up, and turned her around to face Henry.

He blanched, Henry did, but only for a moment. Reached out, cupped her face and grinned, soothed by familiarity despite her utter deadness. The grin went upside down as he turned to Victor, said, "So can you do this? Can you really do this?"

"Cryogenic freezing? Of course."

"That's not what I'm asking. It's the next step that's the payoff, the money-shot, yeah? Something no one's done before."

"So you're doubting me now?"

"I'm just saying. I mean look at this. A body without a head. The head without the body. It's pretty extreme. If this isn't desecration—"

"Desecration? Are you serious?"

"I know you love the shit out of her but what we've got here is a serious mess. This is starting to look like a serious cluster-fuck, i.e., something not doable even for someone like you, my friend."

Slow drip of jaw-clenched words: "Hey, *friend*, if you don't want to help me—"

Henry grabbed thickly at Victor's sopping collar, inadvertently causing a water-shedding jolt. "Get this straight. I will do what I have to, to help you do this. But what concerns me is that you've brought the rains."

Victor looked out the doorway. Was it possible that it was raining harder still? Water gushed past, flowing down the roadway. Checked his subcompact, saw a million raindrop dents in the metal maybe. Shook the thought, said, "If you're going to help me, could you leave your superstitions at the door?"

Henry laughed, but it was forced and nervous. He fidgeted, play-slapped Victor, rocking his head. "Just tell me you can pull this off. Tell me that our dear friend Francine is not just lying in a dead heap here and with her cut-off head over there for no good reason. Tell me you know what you're doing."

Victor's gaze went back and forth from dead heap to the cut-off head. "No, I don't know what I'm doing but I have to do it. There isn't a choice."

Henry let go of Victor's collar. Picked up the body. "Okay then. Let's put her on ice." Henry placed her in the box, then typed commands into the computer.

Victor pulled the storage unit door down shut. Lifted Francine's head off the floor and into the box. He closed the lid but opened it back up. Told her, "This is not goodbye."

"Come on, Romeo. Close the lid. It's time to flash freeze her."

Victor closed the lid and the tanks hissed and hissed, and in a few minutes, Francine's death was halted. For the time being.

They shut down the rented lights, dismantled the stands. Gathered up the detritus in the glow of the single 100 watt light bulb that came with the storage unit, the flicker from the computer screen streaming data. They stepped out of the unit, stood under the starlit sky. No more rain. Not a drop, not a single cloud.

After a stunned-silence minute, Henry said, "Looks like it's your move, Romeo."

Victor inhaled the cool, moist air. Felt like he hadn't breathed in hours. Cracked a smile. His move indeed.

CHAPTER FOUR
Wreckage

The sunbeams through the half open blinds pounded at Francine, forcing her awake despite internal protestations. Mornings like this, being in dreams was better. Mornings like this, the real world pressed down upon her chest, crushing, dark matter coating her brain. Better to stay in dreams.

She mustered strength to push back, to force herself out of bed. When she wiped away the tears was when she noticed the naked guy with his back to her sleeping on the other side of the bed. Had to take a moment to think about it. Tom, her classmate from the masters program? Or was his name Tim? God, let it not be one of her professors. Again! University Ethics Board inquiries were a pain in the ass.

She tip-toed to the other side of the bed, peeked at his face. Nope. Not a clue. Sigh, relief.

Francine trudged out to the living room, checked her voicemail for the message she knew would be there. Victor wanting to meet, his voice tinged with lousily veiled annoyance. Her shoulders sagged even more. She felt the apartment shrink around her. They always ended up fighting on her birthday, an annual drunken airing of grievances. Mostly by Victor. Hence, the preemptive exit from last night's birthday bash, easily done in a crowded bar. And with an accomplice apparently.

Francine took her medication, got dressed, left a note taped to naked guy's forehead: Thanks for the memories, let's leave it at that.

She parked across the street from the coffee shop, Victor and Francine's meeting place, not in a strip mall but located at the periphery of a resuscitated neighborhood in the shadow of the city. Rejuvenated townhouses, moms with careers likely on hold pushing strollers, dads driving off in their used luxury brand cars to their jobs to try to achieve beyond-middle-class lifestyles. Young couples striving to build the American life. This meeting place was Victor's choice. She, ambivalent.

Francine got out of her car, a '68 Mustang Fastback, 302 V-8. She loved it, the car. Leaned with thighs against the fender, hands splayed on the warm hood that went tik, tik, tik, the metal trying to cool. She saw Victor sitting at a patio table, watched him guzzle coffee then slamming down the cup, practicing his angry face, rehearsing his invective laced speechification. There was another cup sitting on the table. The Americano he bought for her, cold now, because she was late.

On her good days, Francine would have laughed from

the giddiness welling in her belly of seeing Victor going through his stupid silly routine. Then she would go to him and play along because this is what they did. Because this is what made her dear friend feel better. She wasn't laughing now, but prodded herself. Had to do this one last time.

"Hey, Mr. Grumpy," she said as she walked up to the table, took a seat, reached for her Americano and sipped. "It's cold."

"You're late."

"Will you get me another one?"

"I don't think so." Victor with a smirk.

She smirked back, sucked down the Americano in a show of defiance. Enjoyed it regardless, caffeine tingling her eyeballs.

"So," said Victor, letting the word dangle for a moment. "You left your own birthday party. You don't think that was rude?"

"I left because you were about to start in. Am I wrong?"

"You robbed me of the moment."

"I know."

"You know?"

She sighed.

He sighed. Victor had great sighs, much more convincing than hers. She knew what was coming. Braced herself.

"Did you fuck that guy you left with last night?"

"Victor, can you not be mean to me today?"

"No, I think I can be."

A sinister furrow to her brows. Rasped out, "I've told you I'd spread my legs for you anytime."

He flinched. Said with thready voice, "Who's being

mean now?"

"Can we please not do this? We've been doing this since, since high school. Don't you think we've beaten the dead horse plenty?"

"Junior high."

"What?"

"It's been since junior high."

"Wow that's a long time," exhaled Francine.

"I'm sorry that our history doesn't exactly dazzle you."

"That's where you're wrong. I am dazzled. Very much, and proud even. Our friendship—"

"Right. 'Friendship'."

"You say it like it's a dirty word. I'm sorry that the history of our *friendship* doesn't exactly dazzle *you*. My lifelong unconditional love for you as a friend, I would think, would mean a whole lot more to you than, than—" She grimaced and pinched the bridge of her nose as if trying to straighten it, a telltale habit, sign of vexation. "I'm not capable of what you want, you know this." The words came out harsh, extra raspy.

An angry silence from Victor because he knew the truth of which he refused to accept. Francine ached to give him what he wanted but could not, absolutely not. But it wasn't him, it was her, and why that was, she didn't know. She loved her mother and father and kind of loved her spoiled brat sister and of course loved Victor as a friend and that kind of love she could give and accept. But love of the romantic kind was like a treatise on quantum physics embedded in a block of concrete sunk 10,000 leagues under the sea: incomprehensible, unobtainable. She had never been "in love" with anyone. Ever. Sure she had her share of sex partners but that, at least to her, was about fucking, not "making love," which by the way was a phrase she found cloying. Maybe someday when the mysteries of human DNA were finally unravelled, they would find a falling-in-love gene, and unofficially and un-ironically, call it the Romeo-Juliet gene. She could blame it all on that, some stupid missing gene named after a tragedy, and it would not be because she was some kind of unfeeling freak, or a cold bitch, or a sociopath. But frankly, maybe she was glad for missing that gene. One less human foible to deal with. Yeah, glad. Except for the part about what it did to Victor.

This was a game now, not even a real argument. It was theater. Because friendship from the time of childhood didn't translate well into their becoming lovers overnight. Because what he wanted would require traveling back in time and a genetic transfusion. But Victor didn't cope well with impossibilities. And there was the anger, frustration, jealousy, years of it. How did one tamp it down? One couldn't, really. Even a woman incapable of falling in love could empathize with the sadness of this. After all, she could love a car, but not him. Sad. So on a day like today, where wicked tendrils wrapped around her brain, squeezing the light out, Francine cried, which was another telltale sign because she was not a cryer. Flop of tears. Convulsion of sobs.

Victor snapped out of his sulk, went to her, held her. "I know, I know. I'm an asshole."

Francine nodded vigorously.

"Well maybe you didn't have to nod so vigorously?"

She coughed out a laugh. Then another. Her tears reduced to a trickle, sobs diminished to sniffles. Wiped her nose on his shirt resulting in an ironic thanks from him.

He said, "Did you stop taking your meds again?"

She shook her head. "The new stuff isn't working."

"I told you that your so-called doctor is a quack."

"You know the old stuff didn't work anymore. The change takes time he says."

"He's still a quack," Victor said mopishly.

Francine had to smile. Knew that Victor didn't mean it, given that he had vetted the doctor himself. She took his hand, held it to her wet cheek. "I love that you give a shit about me."

They stayed like that for a long moment then Victor let out one of his patented sighs, a contented one, and said, "This is nice."

She watched Victor drive away in his subcompact. Had to promise him that they could redo her birthday celebration, just the two of them, no theatrics. So she lied to him, said okay, that she would call him when she was done with classes today.

The dark matter weighed a ton now, could barely hold her neck straight to support her head. Ringing in her ears. Got back into her car, collapsed into the seat, let her head loll. She had actually been glad when the new prescription didn't take. Felt like she had an excuse now. Enough was enough already. Maybe she had hung on this long for Victor's sake. Could she truly have been that altruistic? She wasn't sure, but no matter, because she had no choice but to be selfish now. Enough was enough.

***

At around 3:00 a.m. was when Victor finally tracked her down. Police informed him that the Mustang was found slammed into the rear of a semi parked on the shoulder of the freeway. The tractor-trailer had pulled over due to engine problems. The driver had taken precautions: reflective safety triangles, hazards flashing like Christmas lights. The driver recalled that there had been no sound of skidding tires before he felt the impact and that it happened about 1:15 a.m. There were no other cars until the tow service that the truck driver had been waiting for arrived five minutes later. The cops were perplexed, said the cause was still being investigated. Oh, and that if it wasn't obvious, Francine was dead on the scene.

Victor gave himself five minutes. After he hung up the phone, he collapsed to the kitchen floor, a sledgehammer-to-knees kind of collapse. He writhed, beat the linoleum tiles till his knuckles went bloody. He was crying, but no sound came out of his mouth. Peeled himself off the floor at the five minute mark. Picked up the phone, dialed.

"Henry? It's me. I need your help. That guy you know. The Maplewerm guy? Set up a meeting, I need a meeting asap."

***

Victor paced until sunlight when Henry called back and told him that Percy would meet him at 10:30 p.m. at Goode & Gish's Bar & Grill. And to not be late. To bring plenty of cash money. So now he couldn't sleep, climbed the walls, clawed at them in fact. Too many hours before meeting Percy. Dead Francine beckoned. He climbed and clawed. Had to leave the apartment and walked and walked until:

9:33 a.m. He sat in a diner booth because he hadn't eaten in 20 hours and thought maybe he should grab a bite despite not being hungry. Ordered the blueberry pancakes with a side of bacon. A shared favorite with Francine. She used to put the bacon in between the pancakes. Called it her version of pigs in a blanket. He smiled at the thought, started to actually feel hungry. He heard excited chatter. Turned to look over his shoulder at the corner booth where a girl of about 12 years old was talking to a woman, the mom probably, and ready to dig into a stack of whipped cream covered waffles. His heart went arhythmic. She had frizzy, unruly hair, and a nose that outpaced the growth of her head by a 2 to 1 margin. Francine. Seventh grade.

When the waitress walked up with his order she asked, "Sir? Are you all right?"

Didn't know what she was talking about until he followed her gaze to where tears had pooled on the table. Then noticed for the first time that her name tag said "Francine."

"What the?" Reached for the name tag.

"Um, sir. The patrons are not to be touching the waitstaff, especially the way you are touching the region of my breast area just now."

He stared until the name tag turned from "Francine" to "Annabelle."

"You're not Francine."

"No, why would I be?"

"I'm not sure."

"The hand, sir."

Victor removed his hand from the region of Annabelle's breast area. Looked over his shoulder to check on 7th Grade Francine. Her hair was perfectly disciplined; nose, normal-sized.

He pushed out of the booth, tossed a twenty on the

table, said weakly, "I'm sorry, but I think I've lost my appetite."

Annabelle put down the plates. "Sir. Wait." She grabbed the napkin off the table, wiped his tear-soaked face.

"I thought we weren't suppose to touch each other."

She crumpled the napkin, stuffed it into her apron pocket. "Rules can be broken for good cause."

His eyes brightened as if she spoke revelation. "Annabelle. Thank you." Victor walked away muttering, "good cause, good cause, good cause."

CHAPTER FIVE
An Understandable Crime Of Passion, Nice Boobs, And The Childhood Fear Of Ghosts And Zombies

Detectives Lavenza and Hobin in an elevator, zipped upwards past floors of the high-rise condo complex. The interior of the elevator was a mirrored finish. As if being in a confined space with strangers wasn't bad enough. How the heck was one supposed to avert their gaze now? Look at their feet or the ceiling which would make it obvious as to the gaze-averting? Besides, the ceiling was mirrored too.

Elizabeth Lavenza. Ell. Her and Hobin, no strangers, but still. She glanced at his reflection, never realized how much she towered over his portly figure though she was only three inches taller than the female average. He stared at the ceiling, so she stared at herself, wanted to look away.

Her hair, ponytailed, because of, well, didn't have time to wash it, again. The hangover aura, again.

Unimaginatively wore a tank-top and black jeans. What was she thinking with the tank top? Her shoulders, my God her shoulders, which she had inherited from her father, the guy who played linebacker in the National Football League for 10 years. And her hips? She wore her badge and sidearm on her belt to give the illusion that she had a pair. Believed since puberty that her hip-to-waist ratio could be better, needed more jutting curviness.

Bloodshot eyes. The day-before patina of her unwashed face.

Besides, she wasn't a morning person. Ell could've put on the right clothes, poured in eyedrops, concocted and downed the hair of the dog, took a frickin' shower at least, if she hadn't been roused out of bed at the ungodly early morning hour, Hobin and her having been assigned back to the dayshift. Ell wasn't sure exactly which higher-up she had pissed off this time to deserve this.

Hobin's gaze slid down from ceiling to doors, stopped at her tank top tightly wrapped at chest level. His pupils dilated. At least she was proud of those, the ladies.

"Hobin. It would last longer if you just took a picture."

"Wha?" said Hobin, face flushing hotly.

They entered condo number 2515 of the 25th floor, just below penthouse level. The spacious square footage was sparsely furnished but appeared to have been a design intent. Furniture and decor conjured multiple dollar signs.

A guy from the Medical Examiner's office was zipping up one of the body bags. The other bag already zipped. A uniformed cop, looking bored, leaned against the living-room-length floor-to-ceiling window. Another guy who wore a windbreaker with fat yellow letters on the back which spelled out, "Police Investigator," stood watching the M.E. guy, then turned around, made an exaggerated checking of the watch gesture, said "Hey, Ell. Punctual as usual."

"Fuck you, Larry," she said.

"Your brand of humor tickles my cockles, Detective," said Larry then grinned at her chest and smacked his lips.

Hobin raised an eyebrow, the left one. Then the right.

"You wish," Ell said to Larry.

"Is that so wrong?" Larry's response.

"Chrissakes. Haven't you been married ˈfor like 52 years?"

"Twenty-five thanks for remembering. But all the more reason." A shit-eating grin.

"Chrissakes. To business already, Larry. To business."

Larry laughed, then pointed at the body bags. "You wanna take a look see?"

"No. Just tell it to me."

Larry stood, rubbed his gloved hands. A gleam in his eyes. "Well, as you have already surmised I'm sure, based on the brain and skull matter, here there everywhere, that a large caliber handgun at close range was involved."

"The gist, can we get to it?"

Larry walked to the leather sofa, a sectional with a lot of sections. Went to the corner one. "This is where the male victim sat when the female placed the large caliber handgun…" He pointed to the bagged and tagged weapon on the coffee table, "…to the back of his head and shot said male victim." Pointed to the blood spattered, gray-matter-gunk laden, carpet. "The bullet? Hollow point." Talked through a grin. "Holy shit the hole the bullet blew out of this guys's forehead. It's a work of art."

Ell scratched hard at her oily scalp, more from irritation than itch. Looked to Hobin who stared at the ceiling. Followed his stare, saw blood, brain, skull pieces up there too, and she said, "Wild guess. The girl shot herself under her delicate little jaw. I take it that the giant hole in the top her head is a work of art too."

Larry tittered.

Ell to Hobin. "Take a look around will you?"

"Roger that."

Ell back to Larry. "Is this the male victim's place?"

"It is indeed."

"His gun, his hollow points?"

"Check and check. That's why you get the big bucks I guess."

"Hollow points though? What's the point, pardon the pun?"

"A boy and his toy. Let me just evoke Freud for a moment."

"Please don't," grumbled Ell.

Larry with his patented shit-eating grin, about to provide the unwanted evocation, when Hobin, in a rare moment of good timing, sauntered back into the living room, read from his memo pad. "No personal affectations, i.e., family photos and such, and the furniture, though beautiful, looks barely lived in. The fridge has beer, wine, and leftover take-out, and nothing more. The cupboards: paper plates, nothing more. Medicine cabinet? Still-packaged toothbrushes."

Ell said, "Really? You needed to write that down?" But then saw the hurt in Hobin's eyes. Reined in her irritation, not really about Hobin anyway, so said, "I mean, yeah thanks. This was a love shack then, basically. Guess he was married and monied." Said to Larry, "There was a wedding band, yeah?"

"We should call you genius-big-money Lavenza."

Ell stopped with the scratching, clenched and pulled on a handful of hair instead. "Why can't you just answer my fucking question, you irritating bastard. How someone has tolerated being married to you for 25 years is beyond my comprehension."

Larry blushed, several shades of it.

Hobin whispered, "Holy jeez."

The Uniform who was previously not listening, was now pretending not to listen. The Medical Examiner guy too.

Larry snapped off his rubber gloves, balled them up, stuffed them into his windbreaker pocket. Tried to fake a grin but came out as a sneer. Said, in forced monotone, "Yeah, so, yeah. The male victim wore a wedding band."

She gave him a "no shit" look, asked Hobin, "What's it look like to you?"

"Uh, well. The bed's unused. And like I said, there's wine, but it's unopened, and no empties. The takeout smells like it's been here a while." Almost said to Larry, but instead said to the Uniform, "Were they wearing jackets?"

"Yeah, like they were about to leave. Or just got here, not planning to stay."

Ell said, "Ah yes. I can hear it now: 'Sweetheart, I can't stay. I've grown a conscience and I love my wife, I truly do. This was a mistake, I'm so sorry, darling, gotta go, got a date. With my wife of course. By the way, can you leave the spare key?'" To his body bag she said, "Prick."

The Uniform nodded slowly, agreeing as if gospel. Hobin worried a glance at Larry packing up his tools of the trade into a briefcase. An elbow-nudge by Hobin and Ell got the hint, cleared her throat. "Thanks, Lare, good job."

Larry opened the apartment door but didn't leave. Just stayed standing there.

"Lare?"

Kept his back to her as he said, "At least I didn't catch *my* spouse ass-fucking the neighbor's wife." Here, he turned around. "Wasn't this like your third failed marriage?"

Her eyes jiggled as if being pins and needled. "It was… he wasn't…we weren't married. So technically not a third failed marriage."

"Interesting though, huh? The common denominator being you?"

Hobin rushed Larry, shoved him out. "Get outta here!" Slammed the door. When he looked for Ell, she was digging through the dumped-out contents of the female victim's purse.

"Ell?"

"I knew it," she said, holding up a couple of prescription bottles. "A chick this fucked up had to be on something." Opened them both, walked into the kitchen. "You said there was wine?"

"Ell?"

Hobin drove the generic, government issue sedan into the parking lot of the Medical Examiner's office. He shut the engine. Ell was reclined in the passenger seat. Soft snores, drug/wine-induced. He stared at her lips, at the corner, where a little drool pooled. Leaned toward her, extended his hand, index finger first, was about an inch from wiping the saliva when she awoke and sat upright.

Blinking groggy eyes, she said, "You probably told me, but why are we here?"

"How are you feeling, Ell?"

"Am I grinning?"

He nodded.

"Then that's how I'm feeling." But she thought about it and stopped with the grinning. "God please let this not be another crime of passion."

"Safe bet it's not. It's the hand they found at the mall, in the middle of the food court. Remember?"

"The hand! Yes the hand."

"You're grinning again."

"You sir are a good man, Hobin, looking after me and all that shit."

"Aw jeez, Ell, you know," he said as he fingered his wedding band.

On the stainless steel examination table was a hand the color of late stage meat rot. Slender fingers, lovely long, like made for playing piano exquisitely. Chipped fingernail polish of a pinkish hue. Severed at the joint where hand met wrist. A clean sever, likely done on purpose and with some skill.

"What are those?" asked Ell pointing at the steel pins protruding from the bones at the base of the hand.

The lab-coated Assistant Medical Examiner, Kenny Blokenhaal, built like a giraffe, all neck and legs, barely a torso, fidgeted, expositing dire caffeine addiction. He whipped out a cheap ballpoint pen from the pocket protector and clinked the pen against the pins. "Surgical grade titanium, pretty pricey. Inserted into the scaphoid and the lunate bones. And you see, you see, perfectly aligned to connect with the styloid process of the radius of the wrist."

Ell drummed fingers on the stainless steel table. Buzz wearing off, irritation setting in. "Doc, I appreciate your qualifications as an M.E., but I don't know what you're saying, what are you saying?"

"Oh ho well, I'm not exactly *the* M.E., just one of the assistant M.E.s, but thanks, thanks for the vote of confidence."

"There's no vote here and my confidence level is suspect at best. What I need from you is to confirm or deny that what you're telling me is that someone lopped off this hand, reattached said hand, and, and what else exactly?"

"Exactamundo, Detective, pardon the less than professional parlance. He or she, the brilliant bastard, reattached, or at least attempted to reattach, this hand, and not just a run of the mill reattachment but the kind at the micro surgery level that reconnects each and every nerve ending for a fully functional hand, down to the sensation of the tug and pull of a fingernail being clipped. And the 'what else' is that the attachment didn't take."

"How could it not take? Hand off, hand on. Back to the wrist it came from," said Ell.

Blokenhaal paced, did an excited hop, paced some more. "That's the amazing part of it. It's not the hand of the person to whom it was attempted to be attached to, or was attached to."

Ell said to Hobin, "It's like he's speaking Japanese. Do you understand this?"

Hobin didn't seem to hear her, and instead said to Blokenhaal, pissy like, "Take a picture, it'll last longer."

Blokenhaal, embarrassed for being caught, said to Ell, "Your assistant is right. My staring at your breasts is quite unprofessional."

"I'm not an 'assistant'," said Hobin.

"The cold temperature in here is making your, well, uh, you know, protrude profoundly through your practically sheer, and a size too small, tank-top," said Blokenhaal.

Exasperation clenched vice-like around Ell's skull. She groaned out, "Maybe you should get off my chest and back on topic."

"Yeah, perv," said Hobin.

"I just miss them is all. I mean my girlfriend's. I mean my ex-girlfriend's. They weren't as voluminous as yours but when they're attached to the one you love, they are the best ever."

She went around the table where Blokenhaal stood and gave him a hug. "My condolences for your loss. Boobs can be like comfort food. I understand."

He pressed into her, not out of perviness as Hobin's raised eyebrows would have you believe, but out of his need for that kind of energy from a female and a fellow human being. Blokenhaal perked up. "Okay, okay then, let us get back on topic, because the topic will blow your mind. Blow it, absolutely blow it." He thanked Ell and started with his excited pacing. "And so. This here hand belonged to a Lanna Vodak."

"You mean 'belongs'," Hobin interjected.

"No, Detective Hobert, I don't."

"It's Hobin. Hobin."

Blokenhaal ignored Hobin and continued. "So the hand? It belonged to Lanna as I said. But the blood that coursed through it was that of—"

"Wait," said Ell. "Vodak, L., case number 5523 something something. The DOA disappearance from County General E.R. Case still pending. Remember, Hobin?"

He nodded as if he did, but his empty stare revealed his barely being able to keep track of one missing body from another.

Blokenhaal said, "That's impressive, Detective Lavenza. Do you typically keep a running inventory of your cases in your head?"

"Heck no, Doc. I remember her only because the case is relatively new but mostly because her last name reminds me of 'vodka'."

Blokenhaal laughed and laughed while Ell and Hobin remained straight-faced.

"Okay okay," Blokenhaal continued. "So? The blood that coursed through the hand? Can we get back to that now? Because it will blow you."

Hobin with condescending tone: "Oh please, do blow me." Winced immediately at the inadvertent double entendre.

Even Ell couldn't help but laugh. "Tell us about whose blood it is, then I'll leave you boys alone to your devices."

Didn't phase Blokenhaal, kept on talking. "It belonged to one Francine Styne."

"Say what?" said Ell.

"Blown, yes?"

"I think you're mistaken."

"She's in the system. DNA matches."

Hobin fidgeted, chewed at a nail. Like an inside joke he was not privy to.

Ell asked, "Is the blood from a transfusion maybe?"

"Nope, no way. The blood contains her markers only."

This fact, like trying to figure out calculus, her mathematical limitation, made the back of her eyeballs feel heavy from the strain to crack the code. She knew that an immense headache would follow because it always did. Rubbed temples with fingertips. Grimaced with agitation.

Hobin's seen the look before. "Ell, what are you not telling me?"

She located a chair, walked to it, plopped herself down. "Hobin. Francine Styne died 10 years ago."

Had to be a joke. He chuckled. Her expression said stop doing that, so he did. It hit him that this was for real. Childhood fears of ghosts and zombies crept out of his memory bank into the here and now. He was trained to deal with adult fears, not irrational, long buried, childhood ones. He shivered cold sweat.

Blokenhaal to Hobin: "Blown?"

"Yes," he croaked. "You have blown me."

CHAPTER SIX
A Love Life Like Karmic Disaster

There was knocking at the door. Pause. More knocking. Pause. Then pounding. Victor came stumbling out of the bedroom, wearing only tighty whities, checked the clock synchronized via radio waves with the atomic one: 11:02 a.m. How long had he been asleep? Was it just last night or the night before when they put Francine into deep freeze? He imagined frozen Francine having arctic dreams. How long had he been asleep?

Pounding. The goddamned pounding.

"Mrs. Boskowitz," he said at the door. "I slid the rent check under your door last night, or maybe it was the night before. Either way, it's there, so just please put on your glasses and—"

"Mr. Gottenberg." The voice from the other side of the door, sounding nothing like Mrs. Boskowitz. "I am detective Elizabeth Lavenza. Please open up."

Victor's response was Pavlovian. He flitted about the apartment. "Uh, just a moment, Detective, uh, I need to put on some clothes." And surveyed the apartment for the things that needed to be hidden under the sofa, between the mattress, for contraband to be thrown out the window or flushed down the toilet. Then realized he was being a cliché and chided himself. He'd been careful, nothing to worry about. In fact, he had anticipated that the police would show up as part of the investigation into the disappearance of Francine's body. The interviews with family members, then with friends and acquaintances, to determine if they knew who, if anyone, had the motive to steal her.

Victor opened the door. The detective, seemingly youngish to be a detective, wore an unimaginative, gray business suit. He was a bit disappointed by the attire. Had expected something more based on the voice he heard. Badge and sidearm worn prominently on her waist, and she jutted out that waist to show her authority for being there, for pounding and pounding on the door. "I thought you said you were putting on clothes," she said.

Victor looked down, realized he was still only wearing underwear. Happy trail bursting out of the waist band. He raised his head to meet the eyes of the detective, said as convincingly as he could, "Yeah I did put on clothes." He tugged at his underwear. "See?"

"I would expect that kind of act from some others of our clientele but not from you. Well-educated, a larger than average brain, no priors. So how about showing me some decorum."

"You've been checking up on me. Makes me wonder why."

She brushed past him into the living room. "Shirt and pants. A robe even?"

"Okay, okay." Victor headed into the bedroom. "Sorry. Didn't mean to disappoint."

"I didn't say anything about disappointment. Except maybe in your manners."

He stopped. Wanted to turn and look but felt the blush coming on, so he continued into the bedroom. Came back out wearing a polo shirt, cords, no socks. The detective was adjusting her watch relative to the clock connected via radio waves to the atomic one.

He asked, "So are you going to tell me why?"

"My watch is a piece of shit. Always slow. I hope your clock is right."

"It always is. But that's not what I'm asking."

She pulled her bland gray sleeve over her shitty watch. Straightened her posture. "I think I've been rude. No, I know I've been rude. Not to make excuses but there's been issues recently. I'm off my game."

Victor with inquiring eyes.

Her response: "I'm not at liberty to say, about the issues. But what I do want to say is that I am sorry for your loss. I know Francine was a lifelong friend of yours."

"You would only know that from talking to a select few. What is it that's happened to make you do that?"

"She's gone missing. Francine, her body. It's not where it was supposed to be."

"What what?!" Came out like a screech. Victor took a moment, realized he was over-acting. Tapped the brakes. "I don't think I understand what you're saying. Missing? How is such a thing possible?"

"Well it's like— Wait. Where are you going?"

He headed into the kitchen, she followed and watched him pull out a vodka bottle from the freezer, a coffee mug from the cupboard.

"Breakfast, is it?" she asked.

He poured. "For the past few days? Yeah. Now you're here. With more good news apparently." A swig. Waited for the soothing heat to reach his stomach to give him the artificial courage to lie to a cop who seemed dangerously disarming. Another swig and a refill.

There was a heel-stamp from her. Hands on narrow hips, eyes glaring. Caused Victor to ask, "Have I offended you with my cavalier attitude toward alcohol abuse?" Ready to drain it into the sink.

"No. You've offended me by not offering me a drink."

He waited for the punchline. It didn't come so he grabbed another mug. Poured. Offered. Watched her not exactly sip it. "Is this about your 'issues'?"

"Huh? Oh yeah, that too." She gave him back the mug. "More, please. And try not to be such a miser."

She took off her jacket, threw it on the small dining table. Standard issue white blouse straining against her decent rack. Victor trying to avoid eye contact with the pair as he handed back the brimming mug.

"Here you go, Detective."

"Call me Ell."

Ell, Ell, Ell, he repeated to himself. Didn't know why. Dangerously disarming. Keep it together, Gottenberg.

"So, Victor. Would you possibly know of anyone with a motive to steal Francine?"

And there it was. Entrapment question number one. "Stolen? Really? The police have determined that?"

After a tiny clearing of the throat, Ell said, "She

could've been misplaced, sure, but theft is not an impossibility."

"I can't believe someone could do such a thing. It's like, like, desecration. Or something." Tried to keep a straight face.

She stared at him, as if searching. Then said, "Uh-huh." Took a gulp of vodka. "You'd be surprised at how many bodies go missing. It's a mystery, like doing laundry and ending up with less socks than you started out with, leaving the unpaired ones alone and useless."

"Alone and useless," Victor said, pondering.

They drank in silence.

Then Ell said, "Must be hard to lose a lifelong friend. I can barely manage to hold onto to current friends, let alone someone since childhood. Must be unbearably lonely right now for you."

Was she actually getting teary-eyed? Was he? Drinking was a mistake. Keep it together.

"At least she didn't suffer, you know?" said Ell. "What with the decapitation and such. She went quick." A sorrowful head-shake.

The alcohol was slowing him down. Almost missed entrapment question number two. He wasn't supposed to know that Francine had been decapitated. The cops never told him the details about the accident. Yet he didn't react to what should have been horrifying news. Precious seconds ticked away. Could he still give a reaction and not seem obvious? She was watching him. What to do? Tick-tock, tick-tock.

Then Ell's demeanor changed suddenly. She was no longer watching him but instead was looking into his eyes.

"I'm so sorry," she said. "You didn't know. How could

you, right? It's just that, I, well…" Her voice trailed off, she looked away, embarrassed.

Victor touched his face. Wet with tears. Hadn't realized he'd been crying. Let out a quiet sigh.

She turned back to him, smiled weakly. "Like I said, I've been off my game lately." She checked her newly adjusted watch. "Look, so hey, it's like almost noon, lunch time. Or maybe for you, this is brunch, perhaps breakfast? Don't know, don't care. But I know this awesome steak place, The Carcass. It has a great basement bar, shit-kicking whiskey selection, low ceilings and wood beams and surly bartenders. Vodka makes me talk. A lot. So that's why I prefer the brown stuff, the bourbon? Anyway. Lunch is on me. What do you say?"

Now that he thought about it, he was starving. Steak sounded damn good. So. Was she just this cunning, this disarming, this dangerous? Or was she sincere now? She had her hook in him since the moment she uttered the words: "Must be unbearably lonely right now for you." Because he was and she made him need her that way. Couldn't let her go just yet. But couldn't trust her yet either.

"Steak for breakfast sounds awesome. Do I ride with you, take separate cars, how would you like to— Oh by the way? Just being curious. You know the reason for *my* pain. What's *yours*, the reason for your 'issues'?"

"I said I had issues, didn't say anything about pain."

"You seem young for a detective, so that must be about ambition, the type that can be a wedge-driver with those who are close to you." He pointed at her left ring finger with the tan line where a ring used to be. "And you're not just a cop who drinks. It's embedded in you. Started well before you ever became a cop, right? So what's the trigger this time, what's caused you to drink on the job and in front of one of your 'clients' no less? Is it about trying, but failing, to live up to your father's expectation, who probably is also a cop?"

Ell laughed genuinely, then said, "Are you trying to get the psychological upper hand? It's not bad actually. But I'm a little disappointed in your resorting to the cliché about the cop dad."

"He wasn't a cop?"

"Far from it. He was an all-pro linebacker in the NFL. Ten years."

"Are you an only child?"

"Yeah. What of it?"

"Are you kidding? The pro linebacker dad whose only child is a girl?"

"Okay, fine. That may be the ambition part of it but it's got nothing to do with the trigger. At least not the current trigger."

He coaxed her with his eyes to answer the question already but she wouldn't budge. So he asked her, "That thing you asked, about being unbearably lonely, is that about you?"

Ell laughed, but this time, not so genuinely. She gripped hard at the empty mug. Seemed to be thinking about something to say, a retort possibly. She mouthed words but there was no sound. Until finally she said, "It's stupid, it doesn't compare to what you're going through."

"It's okay. Misery loves company for a reason. So if you're in any way miserable, please, do share."

"So what, are we friends now?"

He grabbed the bottle off the counter, refilled her

empty mug. "I wouldn't go that far." A smile. "But I'm agreeable to calling it a détente."

She smiled back, gazed down at the aged linoleum tiles peeling at the edges. "Well let me tell you this, my partner in détente, don't fall in love with a boy who in your mind is the promise of a happy ending with a fairy tale in between. And don't marry that boy because you will find him one day when you did not at all expect it with his dick in your best friend's mouth, in the bed you two bought with money you had to scrape together because you were poor college kids, and doing it on top of the quilt your grandmother made and gave to you for a wedding gift." Her forearm tensed, squeezing hard at the mug. Could almost hear her teeth grinding. "It took all my strength not to cap the both of them right then."

Victor, voice quiet, asked, "When did this happen?"

"Thirty-one days and…" Checked her watch. "…21 hours ago."

Victor wondered which was worse: years of unrequited love or one moment of immense betrayal.

"You know what really sucks, is missing him, despite the fact that I truly, truly contemplated putting a bullet in his head. It's all so stupid though, so not worth it, so nothing."

"It's not nothing. It's everything."

Their watery eyes locked onto each other. Birds of a feather they seemed. Mugs fell and broke on the crappy linoleum. Speed records were broken: his cords and tighty whities down at his ankles, her skirt hiked up, bunched around her waist. Blouse hung from the light fixture, the bra somehow in the kitchen sink. Pubic pounding rocked the 70 square feet kitchen. The tiny dining table beneath them creaked in agony. Imminent explosive climax. Until,

"Oh oh oh. Oh, Francine."

A screeching halt.

"What did you say?" asked Ell in a tone ranging from surprise to hopeful-mistake to trigger-pulling rage.

Victor, confounded. "What? Did I say something? Out loud?"

"Get off of me," she seethed.

"Ell, wait, I—"

She gripped her gun. He backed away slowly, shuffle-stepping, hands raised, his member swaying sadly in contemplation of the botched opportunity.

"You weren't entirely forthcoming were you, Victor?" While he attempted to put together a coherent sentence, she snatched the blouse off the light fixture, put it on, wrapping up her package. "Chrissakes. This is unbelievable. I pour my soul out, spread out the goods, and you're busy fantasy-fucking a dead girl." She adjusted her panties back over her hot-spot, straightened out her skirt. "You can put your hands down now. And pull up your pants already."

"I…"

"What? Speechless are you?"

"I have no excuses." Couldn't meet her eyes. Pulled up his underwear and pants.

"Chrissakes. You don't even have the decency to lie to me?"

This time he did look her in the eyes. "I have no excuses. I'm sorry. So, are you going to cuff me, take me 'downtown,' interrogate me or something?"

Ell laughed as derisively as possible. "You are just so full of yourself, yeah? Victor, you were never a suspect."

"But then why are you here? On top of which you

asked entrapping questions."

"I asked what?"

He felt his internal gyroscope wobbling. Had he been wrong in his assessment of her? Of the situation? Of everything? Confusion and self-doubt were something new. He sensed a dizziness coming on.

"I'm here because you knew her very well and I thought maybe you could give me some information about others who may have had a motive to steal her body. And if not, then I could chalk it up to random malfeasance or incompetent government process. Obviously you had desires for Francine. But according to those I've spoken to already, her desire for you was only as a friend. A good friend. Kinda like a *girlfriend* is the impression I got."

Victor lurched over to the counter to brace himself. It took a moment before he could make words come out. "Well, Detective. I guess this makes us even."

She took in what he said, then asked, "That's it? I make you sound like a wuss and you're not going to dish it back?"

He shook his head.

Ell pounded her fist on the poor abused dining table, grabbed her ordinary gray jacket and stomped her way out of the apartment. He put his head down on the countertop, his face against the cool ceramic tiles. Noticed the bra in the sink. Picked it up, tamped down the nostalgia and threw the bra in the trash.

***

Victor pored over a medical textbook and guzzled coffee as he sat in the patio of the coffee shop, the place where he and Francine used to hang out.

"Hey," said a vaguely familiar woman's voice.

He looked up to see Ell still wearing the same boring outfit but not making the effort to brandish her badge and gun.

"Hey," he said. "Is this a coincidence or should I be asking how the heck did you know to find me here?"

"I detect for a living, so no, this is not a coincidence. Anyway, I think I maybe overreacted the other day. I mean—"

"No you didn't."

"Beg your pardon?"

Victor stared at the holstered sidearm peeking out from under her jacket. Cleared his throat. How was he to explain the feeling of infidelity over a woman with whom he had never consummated, let alone copped a feel. Usually he got over this feeling toot sweet, but now that Francine was dead, er, in suspended animation, the sense of guilt was compounded. Wasn't talking about being chaste. After all, he was only human, a male human at that. But it just seemed too soon. And Ell was a cop, hot on the trail. How was that supposed to work? Hi, honey, how was work, caught the body snatcher yet?

"Your reaction was what I deserved," he said. "I'm sorry. It's not a great way to treat someone."

"So what you're saying is that you're confirming the fact that you used me as a surrogate dead girl. That intense passion, nothing to do with me I guess. Maybe someday when I'm dead, someone will pine over me enough to go fuck the shit out of someone else while pretending it's me. One could only hope."

"But then how would you know?"

"Are you trying to get pistol whipped?"

"Sorry."

"Chrissakes. My love life is like a karmic disaster."

Victor wanted to say join the club but refrained. "Can I at least buy you some consolation coffee?"

"No you may not have that satisfaction, Mr. Gottenberg. Let's just hope for your sake that our paths don't cross where I actually have probable cause to arrest your ass." She sniffled, tried to control it but just could not. "I'm not crying over you, just so we're clear."

He nodded sincerely.

"Shut up," she said and heel-clacked outta there to her generic government issue sedan. The squeal of the tires sounded like, "Fuck you, Victor." He wondered how she did that.

Then, a pang of regret. But he thought of frozen Francine and it was like, Ell who? He stuck his nose back in the textbook, had to focus. Francine's life depended on it. His too.

CHAPTER SEVEN
Rules Can Be Broken For Good Cause

Deep-amber sunlight of the late afternoon filtered through the thickly dust-coated windows and illuminated the dimly lit, claustrophobic hallway of the science building located on the 152-year-old campus. The university was storied but only in terms of age. Never quite got the billing of the other aged universities, the academically elite ones. At this time of day in this part of campus in this part of the building in this hallway, the student traffic consisted of some grad students, hardcore undergrads, or the parent-pressured desperadoes, who took advantage of office hours of the professors who gave a crap to have office hours, to shoot the shit on the subject du jour, seek help, question test scores, maybe slide an envelope of bribe money under the table done usually by the parent-pressured desperadoes, usually those questioning test scores. And of course the kiss-asses who showed up to kiss ass, or those who showed up to offer ass, usually the hotties looking for a father figure or just turned on by a larger than average brain. Or both.

Through the door with the opaque glass stenciled with the name "Professor Gottenberg" on it, muffled moans and the creaking of a straining desk percolated.

Joseph Cruciate tried the door knob. Locked. He was sure he heard moaning and a creaking desk. Strained a look-see through the opaque glass. Nothing but blurs. He put down his approximately 48-pound-weighing backpack and pulled out the crumpled sheet of paper on which the office hours were indicated. Checked the hours then checked his calculator watch.

"What the heck?" Joseph asked himself. Then there was giggling for sure, blurry movement. He rapped his knuckles on the glass. "Professor Gottenberg? Professor Gottenberg? Professor? Professor? Professor?"

There was a clack of the ancient lock, door hinges squealed, and out came a slightly sweaty female student with flushed cheeks. Jeans, not quite zipped up, low on her hips, blouse buttoned out of sequence. Mane of unruly hair, ponytailed, exposing ears the size of wings of a small flying animal. Her nose was normal size but made prominent by the bridge which was a bit on the askew side.

She said to Joseph Cruciate, "Hey, Joe. You here for office hours too?"

"Um." He noticed she carried no bookbag. She clutched a bra in her left hand. What was her name again? Sasha? Samantha?

She pointed at the bulgy envelope Joseph gripped tightly, held against his chest. "Is that a wad of cash in the envelope or are you just happy to see me?"

"Huh?" Was confused by the disjunctive reference. Then quickly crammed the envelope into his back pocket. Stared open-mouthed at Sally, maybe Stacy, like he didn't know what the heck she was talking about.

"Well jeez, Joe, don't talk so much." And off she went with a skip in her step, a bounce in her boobs, bra a-twirling.

Joseph stuck his head into the office, saw Victor standing at an open window as if waiting for a breeze. The Prof was naked except for boxers and calf-high socks. He was slightly sweaty.

"Professor? This is office hours right?"

"Come on in, Joseph."

He did and stood over the who-knew-how-old sofa and checked for fresh stains. Seeing none, parked himself.

Victor walked from the window to the front of his cluttered desk, cleared a spot, parked himself.

Joseph tried to keep his sightline above Victor's happy trail which was bursting out at the waist band. Was impressed with the Prof's four-pack abs. Not bad for a thirty-something dude. But really, what was with the 'fro? The '70s were like 40 years ago. Maybe it was a retro thing. In which case the 'fro would be pretty cool actually. Joseph touched his own straight, flat hair. Felt suddenly inadequate. But what of the porn 'stache? No retro to that aspect. Or was there? Joseph touched his own face, the smooth-as-a-baby's-ass skin which at best grew sad little stubbles incapable of the full glory of an awesome mustache. Inadequate indeed.

Joseph pulled out the envelope, held it out with arm ramrod straight.

"That's quite a package you got there," said Victor as he reached for it.

"Professor, I've never gotten anything below an 'A' ever, and now and now and now—" Started to hyperventilate.

"Deep breaths, Joseph. Deep breaths."

"Okay, okay."

"By the way, thanks for not asking about, you know, about the locked door, my state of nudity, and about Sara with unzipped jeans and bra in hand and her post-orgasmic glow."

Joseph nodded, said to himself, yes Sara, that's her name. But he did not recall any post-orgasmic glow.

Victor weighed the envelope in his palm, put it up to his ear, shook it, listened. "Not 100's. Not even 20's. What's in here exactly? Monopoly money?"

"Um, um, mainly dollar bills, about 15% fives, and 1% 10's. Sorry. The parental units are little low on the funds this month. You know, the so-called current recession? I can get more eventually."

Tossed the envelope back to Joseph who had the catching ability of someone without arms. The wad of petty cash bounced off his forehead.

Victor said, "I'm sure you'll do better next time. I run a tough course. Don't get so down on yourself."

"I need to do better *now*," Joseph beseeched.

"It's not like you're flunking out. Tell your parents to lay off already."

Joseph lowered his head, grimaced as if in pain. "It's Hannah."

"Hannah?"

"Potemkin."

"Hannah Potemkin? Wow."

"I know."

"So she's the one that—"

"Size matters to her."

"Uh…"

"Brain-wise, I mean."

"Okay. So she's pressuring you to—"

"No. She's got nothing to do with this. I can't even tell her about my horrible grade."

"Joseph. You got a B+ on your paper."

Joseph sobbed, blubbered, "I can't lose her, Professor! It's like she's been expressing some doubts lately anyway. This will just push her over the edge I'm sure. I'll never score better than her. Even my parents are impressed. And they're never impressed with anything I do." More sobbing.

Victor went to him, hugged Joseph's head to his hairy belly. Snot and tears intermingled with happy trail. "I get it. I totally get it." Victor walked back to his desk, sat in the chair, typed something into the computer. "Okay. Done."

Sniffling, Joseph said, "Just like that?"

"Rules can be broken for good cause."

"Rules can be broken for good cause," Joseph repeated as if it were a decree from God.

***

Joseph on his hands and knees was blubbering. Again. He was good at that, the sobbing and the snot and the tears. His anguish bounced forcefully off the walls of the closet-size, near-campus apartment as he watched Hannah writhe on the beer-cum-salsa-potato-chip-grease-stained carpet. She was suffering extreme breathing difficulties, suffering from an onset of seizures, flexing from cardiac arrest. Died within minutes. And her skin turned pink. A peculiar effect of cyanide poisoning. Not the dying part but the pink skin thing.

"Sorry sorry sorry," slobbered Joseph.

**

The M.E. guy was wheeling out the gurney with body-bagged Hannah on it when Ell and Hobin walked up to the puny near-campus apartment. M.E. guy asked Ell, "Wanna take a look see, Detective?"

"No, just tell it to me."

And he did.

Ell hunched over, pinched the bridge of her nose, scowled. Hankered for the metallic-tinge taste of the screw-top of the flask half full with bourbon, the flask of which was in the secret compartment pocket of the jacket she stupidly left in the generic government issue sedan. She straightened herself, made a beeline to handcuffed Joseph curled up on the floor at the corner of the living room/bedroom/dining room.

"Ell," cautioned Hobin.

She kicked Joseph in the ribs.

"Oooooo," he moaned pathetically.

"So I've been told that you've confessed to killing your girlfriend who apparently is super hot even in death, whom you clearly lucked out in bagging and clearly did not deserve. Where did you get the cyanide from?"

"I made it."

"What are you, one those with a larger than average brain?"

"I thought I was."

"Don't be too proud. I knew one of your type once. He was an asshole."

More moaning from Joseph.

"Why, Joseph?"

"I got a B+ on my paper. And I had to tell her, even though it wasn't a B+ anymore, because she would've eventually found out that I was a phony and dump me anyway, so why prolong the agony you know? A preemptive strike I guess."

"Was she? Leaving you?"

"I gave her a glass of diet soda laced with the cyanide before I confessed about my shitty grade. She drank it then I told her and she laughed at me because she thought I was being stupid, worrying so much about a relatively decent grade in a tough class. So, no, she wasn't leaving me. And it was more than size that mattered to her."

"What?"

"A sage told me that rules could be broken for good cause. I thought I had good cause."

"A sage? A sage?! Are you fucking kidding me? Who is this asshole you're quoting?"

"Detective. I've confessed so can we just maybe skip the whole due process thing and have you execute me right here and now?" He pointed his chin at her sidearm attached to her waist.

She clenched-unclenched the grip of her gun.

"Ell," cautioned Hobin.

"No, no sir, Mr. Cruciate. You may not have the satisfaction of a bullet through the brain. No quick death for you. But maybe I'll have Hobin here take you in the back-alley and beat you purple."

"Wha?" said Hobin.

"Okay that's fair but after, will you do it, the bullet through the brain thing because I was so stupid not to plan for a contingency, an antidote." He got up on his knees, leaned against the wall, pressed himself upward, struggled but eventually got onto his feet.

Ell clenched-unclenched the grip of her gun. "Take it easy. I didn't say you could stand up."

"I was so sure she was going leave me. I just couldn't lose her," said Joseph ironically.

Their eyes locked for a second and that's all it took and she had to look away because she knew that he was sincere and understood exactly what he was saying about the loneliness. Her job required that she not have empathy for someone who just poisoned his girlfriend. Had to look away.

Joseph took advantage of the opportunity, sprinted at the window and threw himself through it. A dull, crunchy sound followed, the effect of a human body falling out of a window and onto a sidewalk three stories below.

Hobin stuck his torso out the broken window, ignoring the remaining shards of glass tearing through his suit jacket, through his Oxford button-up shirt, and slicing into him. "Holy holy shit, what just happened?" He turned to Ell. "What just happened?"

She touched her ears, could barely hear Hobin, kind of a ringing, an onset of a migraine maybe. Told him, "You're bleeding."

He looked out the window again, said, "Holy holy holy."

The back of her eyeballs felt heavy and strained. She pinched the bridge of her nose, grimaced. "Hobin. Take care of the bleeding."

***

The Joseph-Cruciate-buzz made the rounds at the university and then the detectives made the rounds at the university.

There was a knock-knock on the opaque glass, with "Professor Gottenberg" stenciled on it, of the slightly ajar door. Victor said come on in, and a dark-suited, somewhat portly, somewhat shortish fella walked in brandishing a badge, said, "Professor, I'm Detective Hobin."

Victor sat behind his desk, bare feet up. Tweed jacket and jeans. He was biting on the stem of an unlit pipe made for tobacco but actually used for other purposes. A convincing professorial-facade.

"You're here about Joseph Cruciate."

Hobin checked the sofa, decided against sitting on it, stayed standing. "How would you know that exactly, Professor, exactly how?"

This guy Hobin, not of piercing intellect. "The obvious buzz about campus is how, Detective," said Victor.

"The buzz, the buzz?" A forced incredulity.

"It's what happens when one of your own turns out to be so emotionally and mentally disturbed as to poison his hot girlfriend and jump from a three-story window."

"To an untimely death," said Hobin, attitude softening.

"Is it ever timely?" Victor's teeth clacked against the pipe stem.

Hobin seemed confused by the question, had to sit. On that sofa.

Victor gave him a minute. Clack, clack. Another clack, then asked, "It seems pretty open and shut so why the canvassing of the campus?"

"No it's not, it's not open and shut. We are looking for someone."

"'We'?"

"Me and Detective Lavenza."

"Ell, you mean?"

"You know her?"

"I didn't 'know her' know her, you know? She was investigating the disappearance of my best friend who had died and someone had stolen her, or misplaced her. Or something. She came to talk to me about her." Victor thought about it, shook his head, blurted, "That was like 10 years ago. Wow. Can you believe it? Ten years already."

"I don't have to believe anything. So you were a suspect then."

"No, she made it absolutely clear that I was not, absolutely not, a suspect." A dejected sigh. "Is she still doing that? Investigating missing dead people?"

"Do you think the world has gotten any better in the past 10 years? The answer is 'no it has not.' So of course she is. You'd be surprised at how many bodies go missing."

"So I've heard." Time to change the subject so he segued into, "You're looking for someone in this case, the Cruciate case? That's peculiar. Under the circumstance."

"No it's not. A sage put him up to it. So we are looking for that guy. Or gal. But statistically most likely a guy."

"When you say 'sage' do you mean someone with profound wisdom or do you really mean a cult leader type?"

"'Sage' was the perp's word, so what we, the police

mean when we say it, is the latter of your two choices. I mean, he told this mentally disturbed individual that it was all right to kill his girlfriend if he had good reason."

"Is that what he really said that this sage guy said?"

"Um no, but that's what he meant." Hobin pulled out his leather bound standard issue looking detective memo pad and flipped pages till he got to where he wanted. "Here we go. What he said was that he was told, 'rules can be broken for good cause.'"

"Wait, what?" Victor shot out his chair, stood there behind his desk, jaw going a bit slack, the pipe dangling.

"'Rules can be broken for good cause.'"

The pipe fell out of Victor's mouth, plopped into a mug full of cold old coffee. A tiny coffee droplet hit his left eyelid which he wiped off with the back of his hand absentmindedly.

Hobin found a clean page in the memo pad, had the pen at the ready. "Are you okay, Professor? Do you have something to tell me maybe?" Clicked clicked the pen.

"No, I uh…" He had about 2.5 seconds before Hobin would likely discern a purposeful hesitation of a guy trying to come up with a convincing lie. Two seconds later Victor said, "…it's just that, it's shockingly, well uh, shocking for someone, even a disturbed individual to be so swayed by a seemingly clichéd and practically innocuous saying that you'd find inside a fortune cookie."

"You're probably right about that." Hobin stuffed the memo pad and pen back in the inside pocket of his suit jacket. "I think I did see that in a fortune cookie in fact."

"Right. So then, anyway, I guess I can go to my next class if it's okay with you?"

"No, not until you answer whether you are that guy or

not."

"What? What guy? The sage you mean?" Victor wondered whether tenacity could overcome lack of piercing intellect. This Hobin, like a puny dog gnawing on your ankle. Wouldn't kill you but enough pain and irritation that made you eventually yell "uncle." It would take more than that to make Victor squeal though. "Detective? Do I look like a sage to you?"

Hobin acted as if he was thinking about it but his pretense was clear. Power of suggestion strung him up like a puppet, made him say, "A sage of the 'profound wisdom' type? No, can't see it. Of the 'cult leader' type? Not that either."

"So, I'm first-impression-wise, neither seemingly profound nor darkly charismatic. That's kind of a hurtful thing to say. Maybe I'm cultishly brainwashing you right now as we speak."

"Ha! Doubtful. Firstly, my brain is unwashable. And number two, and try not to take it personally, but you seem too unremarkable to be a sage who can mind-control people. Except though I have to admit I am impressed by your afro and that healthy mustache of yours. Otherwise, doubtful."

"You're right. I apologize for wasting your time."

"Apology accepted."

They stared at each other as if waiting for something to happen. Then Hobin finally asked, "Don't you have a class to get to?"

"Right you are. Thanks. And nice meeting you."

"Likewise," said Hobin, leaning back into the sofa, arms folded over his chest. He sported a broad smile, as if he believed he accomplished something.

Victor suppressed a smirk, said, "Feel free to hang out. Just lock up when you leave." Strolled away, down the hallway, free to pursue his destiny for another day.

CHAPTER EIGHT
Barging Into God's Realm

Victor stood clutching the sides of the podium, nodding, nodding, pretending to listen to one of the twelve grad students, this one a yammerer, so he took the opportunity to tune out. Looked to where Joseph Cruciate used to sit, the upper deck of the stadium style classroom. Imagined his ghost there muttering in echoey ghost voice: "I had good cause."

"I don't think the action you took should have been the byproduct of what I said to you about 'good cause.'"

"You have no right to judge me, Professor."

"I haven't killed anybody in my quest, Joseph."

"Not yet."

"What is that supposed mean?"

"How should I know? I'm being conjured by your sick and desperate mind."

Victor felt the pores of his forehead spew sweat. Tried

to think of meditation exercises to calm his heart rate, his racing mind.

And then the yammerer said, "Maybe we could try and experiment with Joseph Cruciate? Try to bring him back?"

Victor snapped out of his minor panic attack.

A chuckle from two students including the yammerer. Eight of the students gave a look of disdain, disgust, contempt and/or abhorrence re: the comment. One actually booed and hissed. Another seemed to be sleeping with eyes open.

Victor responded with, "Do you think this is a joke? Let's get serious here. Joseph has been dead for over a week. The M.E. has had their way with him and decomposition is setting in as we speak, got it? What do you think we're trying to do? Create the living dead or something? Zombies, maybe? This is not a gothic horror story or a B-movie from the '70s. What is required is viable, unadulterated tissue capable of being revived. Besides, human trials are currently verboten, ironically." The collective eyes of the class implored something more, so Victor said, "But of course, worst of all, it was a, uh, morally reprehensible thing to suggest experimentation on a, uh, fellow classmate. Whose death was tragic. And untimely." Victor winced, improv was not his thing. But the class seemed to have bought it.

"I, I actually *was* joking about Joseph," said student-on-the-spot. "It's not the same as saying what we're trying to accomplish is a joke. Right?"

Stares and silence.

"I'm so sorry," the student said, voice shaky.

Victor stroked his 'stache repeatedly and hard enough

to create friction-heat. Irritated, he said, "Okay then, folks. Are we serious now, are we ready to do this? Because if you're not with me, you are against me."

"Whoa with the drama, Professor," said the female student who kinda sorta looked like Francine.

"Point taken, Sara," said Victor "I'm just worked up over this thing, you know?"

"I bet you are," Sara said, her words dripping with college-girl-sex-lust, referencing something not at all to do with what Victor was trying to convey.

"Uhhh, ummm," mumbled Victor, at a loss for words. Caught a break when Kevin raised a forceful hand. Victor pointed at him. "Yes, Kevin, speak."

Kevin, nerdish and of the soft and pudgy ilk, tried to play against type by being confidently outspoken, though it was clear to everyone that it was just an act, what with his frequent flop-sweat and his ascending vocal tone which made him sound like a pre-pubescent girl, leaving his listeners unimpressed, eyes rolling. "Now that we're leaving the theoretical and going into experimentation, it seems, I mean it seems... I guess I'm not sure what the point is anymore?" Voice pitch rose, dribble of sweat streamed down the bridge of his nose. "Reanimation is fascinating, amazing even, but who are we serving exactly? Ourselves or the deceased?"

Sara rolled her eyes, hissed a sigh.

Victor shed his slouch, said, "I'm not understanding your sudden change of opinion. We're only experimenting on rats right now anyway."

"Rats are people too. In a manner of speaking."

"What's your problem, Kevin?" asked Sara, her mood no longer sexy.

"It's one thing to——" Kevin looked over his shoulder at scowling Sara. His shirt was soaked through. Turned attention back to the Prof. "It's one thing to improve medical procedure but it's something else entirely to try to defeat death. When someone dies, I mean when they've clinically checked out, nature has spoken"

"'Nature'? Is that what you really meant to say?" said Victor.

"It's one thing to talk about it in theory, like some fantastical tale, or to romanticize it even, but now that it may actually happen? It feels like we're barging into..."

"Just say it, Kevin. You need to just say it."

"It feels like we're barging into God's realm," squealed Kevin, then exhaled, relieved for having said what he did.

"God's realm?!" screeched Sara. "Why are you even studying science?"

"It's okay, Sara. Kevin makes a valid point really, I mean, what we are trying to accomplish here, I guess, is 'barging.' And because we're dealing with the realm of the unknown, or 'God's realm,' being afraid is normal."

"I'm not afraid, that's not what I said." Kevin's faux anger soon turned to genuine concern. "Why do say that anyway, Professor? Are *you* afraid?"

The slightest of hesitation detectable only by an exactingly calibrated scientific instrument before Victor said, "Nope."

"But but, you said it was normal to be——"

"Normal for most. It can't be for me, got no room for it. And it's cool that you have a well-formed opinion, but if you don't participate in lab, you'll likely receive a failing grade. Got it?"

Then the chalkboard, the size of a youth league football

field, fell off the wall, crashed to the floor, the sonic pandemonium of which made everybody almost crap their pants. As the chalkboard tipped forward, Victor dove out of the way to avoid being crushed. Several students simultaneously uttered "Ohmygod," unclear as to whether they meant it as an acknowledgement or to express concerned surprise.

Bit wobbly, Victor stood, checked the chalkboard which was cracked at four equidistant points. The podium, gone, lost somewhere beneath the rubble. He turned to the students. They were shocked and awed. The classroom fell silent, could hear dust settling. The air was charged with ions of fear and reverence for a power beyond human comprehension.

Victor said, "That was somehow you wasn't it, Joseph?" But actually only said it in his head because how would it sound coming out of the mouth of a man of science, a man who shunned the supernatural, an atheist even? Not too good is how. Instead he said, "Okay I've made a grading policy change, so if you decide not to participate in the lab experiment, I won't fail you, it'll just count as extra credit if you do do so. So. If you don't want take part, you can leave."

Kevin jetted outta there. A trembly voice from somewhere in the shadows of the upper deck asked, "Professor, does what you just said apply only to Kevin or the class as a whole?"

"Uh, well, to be fair—"

And so six more students bailed as if the building was being swallowed into the depths of the earth's core.

"Pussies," said Sara.

***

The five leftover students wore lab coats and protective eyewear and were setting up for the experiment. There was a stainless steel table, on top of which dead lab rats were placed. Latex-gloved fingers gently poked the white furries to make sure they'd thawed out. Strapped onto their tiny lifeless rodent heads was a helmet with little blinking lights flashing red; ten insulated wires connected to the aluminum shell and leading to a black metal box the size of a car battery, also with flashing lights, and leading via single cable to a computer tower. Electrodes sprouting from the black box were attached to fragile ribcages. Each rat had a number painted on it, one through ten respectively. Victor was busy tap tap tapping commands on the computer keyboard.

At the perimeter of the lab were a group of people: fellow professors, Business Suits, Uniformed Military, and in the center of them all, glad-handing and with neon smile, was Dean Hiram Brasz, snazzy suit, hair plugs, not exactly politician-slick but plenty earnest, perhaps masking desperation pent up through the decades and now festering in a guy still working past retirement age.

The dean, trembling with giddiness, sidled up to Victor. "How are we doing? Good? It all looks good. Ready to go, right?"

"Are you okay, Hiram? Sounds like you're about to hyperventilate."

"You might be right, right, right." Took a moment to control his breathing. Didn't seem to help. In a breathy whisper, said, "They are ready, so ready, to throw money at this thing."

Victor typed in final commands, and on the computer screen, popped up 10 EKG monitors all currently flatlined. The question "READY?" in large pulsing letters was superimposed on the screen. "That's awesome, Hiram, because this research is running on vapors. I really wanted 20 rats." A grin.

"Ha ha," said the dean, patting Victor's shoulder. "Come on. Say a few words to your future sponsors."

So Victor did the ass-kissing, hand-shaking, neon-smiling thing, as much as he could tolerate and tried to extricate himself from the group when one of the generals asked, "What I don't understand is, this all seems pretty fancy, and apparently costly, for what in my mind should be as easy as rubbing those paddle things together then yelling 'clear!' then zapping the dead guy to life. I'm no doctor but we've all watched those hospital dramas on TV haven't we?"

Nods and chuckles from the group.

The left corner of Victor's mouth twitched. Hiram gave him a just-take-it-in-stride look. Victor responded with a if-I-have-to-okay-then glance, then said, "The General's question is a valid one, a typical misconception made by the layperson. Only if it were that easy, General. Only if. There are two factors that have prevented the reviving of the dead, and when I say "dead," I mean not just legally dead but totally dead. One: the cure for what killed the person. That's an ongoing thing, but as to certain causes, there are remedies now. Such as heart transplants. So why can't we just throw your middle-aged, overweight, uncle, father or friend, who died of a heart attack, into a cryo deep freeze until a replacement heart is available, then thaw him out, slap that heart in there, zap him back to life as you say? The answer is: you can. At least get the heart beating again, but that's about it. No brain activity. So what you get is a dead guy but with a healthy, beating heart. Weird huh? Which leads us to the second factor: the Jump Start Conundrum. When a person dies, there's a window of opportunity to revive them. But once brain activity shuts down, zapping the heart isn't good enough."

"What you're saying is you gotta zap the brain."

"Exactamundo, General."

"I guess that is a little more complicated."

"Thanks for understanding. It's called a 'conundrum' for a reason. People have been trying to figure this out for a millennium really, because short of an alleged miracle, it hasn't been doable."

"And you've figured it out."

"Yes, sir, I have."

"If that's true, you'll certainly get a piece of the federal defense budget, which I don't think I have to remind you is quite substantial even at the minority percentage level."

"I appreciate that, we could use the funds."

"You could ultimately be a rich man, either in dollar terms or prestige or both."

"Didn't do it for either."

"Bullshit. It's always about either money or prestige. Or both. Or love I suppose, but that would make no sense whatsoever under this scenario."

Victor did an almost-smile, the General crinkled his brows. Then Victor gave the "go" signal to Sara who answered the question on the computer screen by hitting the enter-key for "yes" which made the black box buck and hum. The spectators closed in, tight quarters, shoulder to shoulder, some passive aggressive elbowing and nudging to get a gander at the miracle about to happen. The rats shimmied and shook. Number 3 exploded, sending shrapnel of rodent guts and bones into the gasping crowd. Someone who sounded like the General screamed. The EKGs of rats number 1, 2, 4, 5, 6, 8, 9 and 10 came to life. Numbers 1, 4, and 8 opened their eyes. The rat painted with number 7 exploded too. Then 2, 5, 6, 9 and 10 flashed their baby pinks.

A collective holding of breath.

The rats tried to get up and move but they were defeated by atrophy. But they kept trying and were definitely alive. Pink eyes twinkled, little limbs wiggled. And the audience clapped like crazy.

Champagne flowed, hors d'oeuvres were gobbled. Oldies but goodies music wafted from somewhere and one of the students had rigged a homemade disco ball that spun and glimmered. The lab now a house party.

The Suits, the Uniforms, the Academics, mingled the only way they could: shit-faced. Victor was wall-flowering it in the shadow of his bud, Henry, who had his own champagne bottle in one hand and a fistful of hors d'oeuvres in the other and looking unimpressed only because he'd known Victor for too long not to expect this day to come, hence his air of anti-climacticness. Dug the free food and booze though.

"Victor! Victor!" Hiram weaved and stumbled his way through the crowd. The dean red-faced with drunken delight. "Victor, my boy!"

"Hiram, I think you need another drink," said Victor.

Hiram hiccuped a laugh. Got close to Victor's ear, breathed moist air into it, said, "This will be the largest research funding anyone has ever received in the history of this university. Do you know what this means, Victor?"

"That you'll be opening up a Swiss bank account and retiring to an island in the South Pacific?"

"Ho ho, hee ha," said-laughed Hiram. "Such the comedian you are." He then stepped back, looked Victor up and down. "I knew it you know, when I hired you. That you were a boy wonder."

"Jesus," said Henry, eyes rolling.

"Not quite to that status yet," Hiram responded to Henry. "But maybe someday."

"This is my friend Henry," said Victor. "He's an M.D."

"Well hello, Henry M.D. and a large fellow at that."

"Nice to meet you, Dean Brasz. By the way, did you notice that the rats didn't look quite right? Do you think it's possible for rats to suffer from existential angst?"

The dean said, "Huh?"

"I mean, being dead, then suddenly not being dead, it's got to screw with you a little bit don't you think?"

The dean said again, "Huh?"

"Stop messing with the dean, Henry," said Victor. "Hiram. They're only rats. There is no angst."

"Oh ho ho, of course, of course." Then he bit his fist, and with face clenched, said, "Victor, this is a proud proud day and I am proud proud of you."

"Are you crying, Hiram?"

The dean hugged Victor then went searching for a full glass of champagne and more hands to shake funds from.

"That guy is a tool," said Henry.

"Takes one to know one. Anyway. I want to——"

"Don't say it."

"What?"

"That you're ready to take Francine out of deep freeze."

"I am ready."

"You had two rats explode on you. The process doesn't seem perfected. Are you willing to risk Francine's life?"

"That seems hardly possible."

"You know what I mean."

"It'll be fine. I'll make it fine."

"It's been 10 years, I mean, you've waited this long. What's the rush?"

"It's been 10 years."

Henry guzzled from the bottle. Didn't stop till it was empty. A lengthy belch. "So this is really happening?"

"You bet."

Henry postured as if trying to hear something.

"What, what is it?" asked Victor.

"Do you hear it? The distant thunder, sounds like, sounds like, God's disapproval."

"Don't start," said Victor secretly listening for it but hearing nothing. "So are you with me or not?"

"Don't insult me."

Victor smiled, punched Henry's thigh-sized upper arm. Felt a twinge in his wrist, a likely sprain.

While Victor grimaced, Henry said, "Are you finally going to dust off the 10-year old Moleskine with your diabolical plan in it?"

"Don't have to. It's all in here." Victor tapped his index finger to right temple. "Need to open a Swiss bank account. Set up facilities to do the deed. And we need to get parts. Is Maplewerm still around?"

"Are you fucking with me? He disappeared years ago when the FBI got all over his ass for his entrepreneurial ventures in the dead flesh trade biz."

"But you know where he is."

"No."

"What?"

"Okay yeah, I know where he is but he's not gonna want to do business with you, especially given your history with him, and by the way, age has made him more nuts than ever."

Victor went over to the specimen refrigeration unit, pulled out a bottle of champagne, tossed it to Henry. "Maybe more of this will loosen your lips."

In one swift motion, Henry caught the bottle, popped the top, swigged hard, spilling not a bit of bubbly. Took a moment to let the alcohol-warmth pass through his gullet, smacked his lips, and said, "Fine, I'll tell you where he is but you better be sporting a bulletproof vest when you go to see him. And be discreet. Maplewerm is on the Fibbie's 100 Most Wanted List, so if this thing goes sideways, we will both be screwed."

"Don't worry. Destiny is on our side."

"Please tell me you're joking."

Victor snatched the bottle from Henry, took a long draw, gave a wink and a smile.

CHAPTER NINE
The Butcher Counter

Victor sat cross-legged on top of a plastic wrapped crate marked *medical equipment*, one of several in the garage of his house. In the corner, hummed quietly, "the freezer" with Francine coffined within. Stack of lumber and drywall in the other corner, tools of the construction trade spread about. A flimsy DIY plywood table on top of which sat a computer connected to the freshly unpackaged MRI scanner that hunkered, like a giant doughnut dipped in white frosting, in the middle of the garage. He stared at the computer monitor which was running a slide show of recently MRI'd frozen Francine.

Pen to a legal pad, he scratched out a shopping list:
1. Left hand.
2. Right leg.
3. Liver.
4. Heart.

5. Right Lung.
6. Left kidney.
7. Cervical spine

Tore the page off the pad, stuffed it into the pocket of his cargo shorts. Headed out, slid into Francine's rebuilt '68 Mustang Fastback parked in the driveway. His flip-flopped foot slammed the gas, the car vroomed and tire-squealed down the oak-tree-lined unassuming suburban neighborhood. Three hours later, Victor was driving on a desolate two-lane highway sandwiched between vast, yet-to-be-replanted farmland, commercial grade tillers kicking up dust. Eventually, small pockets of civilization emerged, mirage like, in this middle of nowhere. He took the exit that announced "Downtown," drove purposefully, looking for, looking for, and there it was: a dinky strip mall which included a shuttered Italian restaurant, a massage parlor, chiropractor, and the County Coroner's office.

He parked the car. Walked through the Coroner's door, the attached bell cling-clanged. A big-wigged woman, well within her geriatric phase, sat behind a desk that looked about as capable as Victor's homemade plywood version, and was snuffing out a cigarette and lighting another at the same time. She sucked on the newly lit cigarette, inspected Victor, blew smoke towards the water-stained ceiling.

"Are you here to identify a body? Because if you are, you are not on the list." She held up a clipboard with a piece of paper on it. The piece of paper was entitled *Those Who Are Coming To Identify A Body*. The document was blank. "So you see, you will need to go through the proper administrative channels to—"

"No no. I'm here to see the Coroner."

"If you are here to see the Coroner, you are not on the list." She held up another clipboard with a document entitled *Those Who Are Coming To Meet With Coroner.* "So you see, you will need to—"

"Miss— I'm sorry, I didn't catch your name."

"Why would you? I didn't offer it."

"Okay well I have an offer for him. That he can't refuse."

She took a deep long drag of the cigarette as if salvation could be achieved by it. Reckless exhalation followed. A look of being unimpressed. "The Coroner is busy. You will need to go through proper administrative channels to set up an appointment with him."

Out of his pocket, Victor pulled out a thickly rolled-up wad of hundreds and peeled off several of the bills, slapped them on the desktop. She eyeballed the Benjamins. Long drag, exhale, punched the intercom button, said, "Your eleven o'clock is here." She thumbed the direction to Victor and he made a beeline. The intercom answered back, "What? What eleven o'clock? What the fuck is going on—" She turned the intercom off, put out the cigarette while lighting another.

Victor pressed the door open to Maplewerm's office, found him backed into a corner, jitteringly pointing a large caliber handgun at Victor's face. Ten years since he had seen Maplewerm. The greasy aura, greasier than before. Hunchy posture now to the point of being qualified as a hunchback. The only thing not more so was his pasty hair which was still pasty but only as to the few remaining strands.

"Whoa, Mr. Maplewerm! Whoa!"

"Who the fuck are you? You're not on the list. I will fuck you up man I don't care if you're the law I'm no longer in the business this is all legit I will fuck you up."

"Percy. Calm down, I'm not the cops. We've done business before."

"Bullshit."

"Henry sent me. You know Henry. He says you're still running the business."

Percy fell into a relaxed slouch, lowered the gun. "Yeah, I know Henry. That fucker. What's he doing telling you about my business?"

Victor tossed the cash-roll on the desk. The wad went thunk, didn't even bounce. The gun slipped out of Percy's hand, soft-landed on the carpet. He wiped a bit of drool from the corner of his mouth, said, "Okay then. But next time, be on the list."

Out behind the strip mall, past the dumpsters, was a field about an acre or so surrounded by wire mesh fence humming with electrification. Coiled razor wire topped it off. The field was barren except for weeds, a refrigeration trailer, and hogs penned at the rear of the property. At the entry gate, Victor watched Percy unlock a small metal lid of a box buried in the ground and flip a switch. The fence went silent, the magnetic lock released, and the gate squeaked open.

They walked up the ramp that led to a man-door on the side of the trailer. Before they went in, Victor asked, "So the hogs, are they pets, food, or garbage disposal units?"

"Who the fuck keeps hogs for pets?"

Inside were body drawers three-high, lined sideways

against one wall of the trailer.

"Lot of capacity for a rural county," said Victor. "Expecting an epidemic?"

"If I relied on local supply, I'd be out of business, man. Gotta outsource which means it ain't gonna be the standard fare you might be used to. High fuel prices, middlemen, storage fees, it's all bullshit but can't be helped."

Victor unfolded the shopping list, handed it to Percy.

"What's this?" said Percy, squinting at the piece of paper held at arm's length.

"It's a list of what I need."

"This ain't the butcher counter at your local supermarket. We don't sell parts here. You gotta buy the whole cow."

"I'll pay for the whole body, but I just need what's on the list."

"Are you not hearing me? What am I supposed to do with a one-legged, one-handed corpse with most of its vital organs missing?"

"And I'll need a second set of everything for spares, for contingency purposes."

"Why are you not hearing me? I'm a one-man operation. I can't inventory parts. Besides, my customers want the whole body. I can't sell leftovers, might as well feed 'em to the hogs."

Their eyes met, locked in on the same idea.

"Okay then," Percy said. "But it's gonna cost you extra."

"Done. By the way, for the leg and hand, she has to be a 20 to 25-year-old, approximately 5'2" to 5'4" tall, weighing somewhere around 110 to 120 pounds."

"Are you kidding me with this shit? It's not like there's uh, uh, 5'4", 120 pound, 20-year-olds coming through here everyday. Not exactly your typical morgue demographic, man."

"What's available then?"

Percy and Victor loaded the Mustang with the last of the coolers filled with two sets of what Victor came for, except for the leg and hand. Percy couldn't comprehend: so what if the leg wasn't of the exact age, or of the desired circumference or a few inches shorter than specified, and so what if the hand had stubby fingers or was a bit on the masculine side, proportion-wise?

"I usually don't ask but I gotta ask," said Percy. "What're you planning to do with all this anyway?"

"I'm rebuilding a dead friend. Francine Styne is going to live again."

"Okay, ha ha. Wait, what? Francine Styne? That chick. That chick without a head?"

Victor hopped into the Mustang, started her up. Said to Percy, "You remember me now?" Peeled out of the parking lot.

Percy pulled out his fake front tooth, waved it as he ran after Victor. "Yeah I remember you, motherfucker! You did this! *You* did this!" He ran and ran. "I will fuck you up, man. Come back here because I will fuck you up!" He dropped to his hands and knees in the middle of the street. Winded, wheezed and wheezed. The comb-over coming undone, strands of hair dangling like oil-slick seaweed. He watched the Mustang speed away. Looked back at the strip mall, saw his receptionist standing at the edge of the parking lot. She was scratching an itch under the wig with a pencil, one and a half cigarettes going at the same time. Percy turned his attention back down the road, the Mustang, a dot on the horizon.

After his breathing calmed, he said, "Yeah, I remember you. You loved the shit outta that dead girl. Francine Fucking Styne. And she didn't even have a head." He laughed, not because of anything being funny, but because he was trying to counteract his lament, the dribble of tears. "Rebuilding a dead friend, huh? Good luck, you stupid bastard. Don't you know that romance is for the birds?" Stood up, brushed himself off. Thought about his date later with a recent arrival, a stripper who died by way of head trauma, a tumble off the stage. A most pristine body of which he had been looking forward to violating, but now he could only see her as a cold clammy corpse who would not whisper in his ear about how wonderful he felt as she wrapped her legs around his waist, as she gently clawed his back. And she would not react with a kiss as he told her that he would love her until the end of time, which was what he used tell his wife when they were young and stupid and until she died of an overdose. Wondered what miracle Victor could perform with only the bones of his wife, 30-years-buried. Nothing is what, you stupid fuck, he told himself, then hunchily walked toward the strip mall, wiping his tears. Yelled at the receptionist to get her old, lazy ass back to work.

CHAPTER TEN
Piano Fingers And A Leg Quarter-Inch Too Short

Around midnight, moonless. TV-light flickered through some of the otherwise darkened windows of the prototypical, upper middle class, assembly-line homes. The TV-light from one of those windows emanated from a black and white 1940's Dracula movie. On the coffee table in front of that TV were cartons of Chinese takeout, food-strewn plates, two empty wine glasses. And on the couch, Victor and coed Sara were making out hot and heavy.

Wriggled of out her jeans, panties around Sara's ankles when Victor stood, grabbed the wine glasses, smiled and walked into the kitchen.

"Oh, Professor, where are you going?" purred drunken Sara as she palmed her crotch. "Kitty needs you. Come back, come back."

As soon as he was in the kitchen, the smile was gone.

Hurriedly snatched another bottle of wine from the cabinet, uncorked it, poured and missed the glass entirely. Bordeaux all over the ceramic tile counter. Controlled his shaky hand, poured again, hit the mark this time. Out of his pocket, he pulled out a tiny plastic baggie with a purple tablet in it.

The tablet went "plop" into the fuller glass and it fizzed and fizzed until it didn't anymore and Victor picked up the glasses and went back into the living room, forced that smile, handed the fuller glass to half-naked Sara. She sucked down the vino-plus, then doffed the T-shirt, the bra, doing a strip tease while humming a bluesy tune.

Victor clapped her along but there was a sadness in the resonance. Then he asked, "So hey, Sara, hey. Got a question. Are you a donor?"

"What do you mean? Like to charity?"

"No, I meant like organs, body parts. You know."

"That's not a sexy question." She stopped her dance, found her purse, dug through it, extracted the drivers license, said, "See?" On the license was printed the word "donor."

"That's good. You're a good person. But why wait?"

"What-wha?" uttered Sara as she swayed, woozily, to and fro. Fell onto the couch, flat-out unconscious.

Victor's garage was now in tip-top shape. No more detritus, packing material, lumber or drywall stacks. The garage door was converted into a permanent wall, and along the back, shelves were loaded with medical supplies, a counter spread out with surgical equipment, and a medical grade refrigeration unit holding the goodies procured from Percy. The MRI machine still hunkered in the middle of it all, the Francine-freezer on one side of the garage, and on the other side, a plexiglass partition kept separate a cozy state of the art operating room.

And in that cozy O.R., Victor in scrubs, stood over the operating table on which lay passed-out, stark naked Sara with a drug-induced smile. Took a tape measure to her right leg, length-wise and circumferentially. A knowing nod, then drew a line around her upper thigh with a red marker. He held her left hand, stroked each finger, kissed her palm, then marked a red line around her wrist.

Victor turned on the overhead surgical light, checked the instruments on the stainless steel table. Picked up the electrical bone saw, a large gun-looking thing, pressed the trigger to give it a test run. A high pitched whir, the blade moving in a blur, would cut through bone as if butter. Satisfied, he turned it off, put it down. Opened a box of garbage bags, large-size, extra strength, odor controlling. Pulled one bag out, then another. Eye-balled the length of Sara's body. Pulled out a third for good measure.

Victor grabbed a scalpel. "Okay, let's do this," he told himself. But just stood there. All he needed was her leg and hand, she could easily survive the procedure. But how does one explain to his girlfriend about the sudden disappearance of certain appendages? Even Victor couldn't come up with an answer to that one. So he wouldn't explain it, and instead would lop her into garbage-bag-fitting pieces for easy transport and disposal. Kind of a waste, but he would have to break up with her soon enough anyhow. Less heartbreak this way. He hoped at least that Percy's hogs would enjoy her.

"Okay, Gottenberg, get to it." Held the scalpel at the ready but his hand wouldn't move. "Dammit, just do it already." White-knuckled the scalpel. Went for the incision.

When Victor woke up, the room was still spinning. The pain pulsed outward in concentric circles from his brain's core to his temples. Struggled out of bed, dragged his ass, wearing only boxer shorts, into the living room where he observed the carnage splayed on the coffee table, on the couch, on the carpet: three empty wine bottles, five crushed cans of beer.

"Oy," he muttered and continued into the kitchen.

"Well hello, sleepy head," said Sara with Victor's oversized T-shirt draped over her bod. Stood at the stove, scrambling up some eggs or something. Still had all her parts. "Oh my gosh, I slept so well!" She kissed his cheek, stuck her hand down his boxers.

Flinching, he said, "I have a headache. Kitty's gonna have to wait." Plopped himself down at the table, laid his head down.

"You kinda do look like crap." She mussed his bed-headed 'fro, poured him some coffee. "By the way? What kind of kinky shit did we get into last night?"

"Huh?"

She lifted up the T-shirt, exposing her naked glory. Thrust her right thigh out, the red marker circle there. "And look." She pointed at the other red circle around her left wrist.

"Ummm."

"Whatever it was, let's do it again," she said, grinning, eyes twinkling. "Because I don't remember any of it."

"I don't think so." Suckled at the coffee.

"Please, Professor? Please-please-please?"

"Oy," he groaned.

***

"Truly, I don't think I want to do that. I mean, let's weigh the costs and benefits here. A potential five to seven in the Federal pen versus paying a few bucks for some prosthetics. They have some excellent stuff these days, man. I'll drop off the catalog," said Henry, his phone voice sounding muffled and scratchy. Bass-heavy thumping music in the background.

"Where are you?" said Victor, fetal-positioned in his bed, cellphone to his ear.

"My home away from home."

"You're at a strip club at..." Poked his head out from under the cover, checked the bedside clock. "...9:00 am?"

"Yeah, so?"

"They're open this early?"

"You mean this late."

"Don't you have surgery in a couple of hours?"

"Yeah, so?"

Victor took a meditative five seconds, then said, "Listen to me, Henry. Prosthetics? No way. Francine deserves better than artificial limbs. I will not, absolutely not, compromise on this. And if you cared anything about her, if you actually gave a shit—"

"Okay, damn, calm down."

A pause.

"Are you thinking about it?" asked Victor, "What's the plan, what're we doing?"

"No, man, I'm not thinking about it, you're the genius here, a freakin' 'boy wonder' apparently. I'm sure you can figure it out. I could lose my medical license over something like this, not to mention the five to seven in the pen, maybe reduced to two with good behavior, but still."

"That is rich, just rich. Since when have you been so concerned with legal proprieties?"

"I have zero concern with legal pro-pri-eties. You wanna know what I am concerned with? Your goal turning into an obsession turning into recklessness and exposing me as a co-conspirator."

Another pause.

"Vic? Hey, hello?"

Voice calm and true, Victor said, "Here's what I'm going to do. I'm going to find that hand. I'm going to get that leg. And all the king's men and all the king's horses *will* put Francine Styne back together again. And when we resurrect her and she says, thank you, Victor, for bringing me back to life, but golly gee where the heck is Henry? I'm going to say, Henry cared more about *potentially* losing his medical license than about you. He was more worried about the *potential* five to seven reduced to two for good behavior than having you back among us, among the living, among your loving friends. He did a cost-benefit analysis and you lost, Francine. You lost. And she would say, wow, Henry is kind of an asshole."

"You motherfucker. She would never say that."

"Wanna take that chance?" Victor heard heavy, rapid, seething breathing. "Is that a 'yes, Victor I will help you without being a pussy about it'?"

"I should have crushed your skull when it was still papery and soft back in the 3rd grade."

"I love you too, man."

***

Henry trolled the E.R., but not finding what he was looking for, took a break from the search, chatted up a wide-eyed and bewildered candy-striper. She probably should have been on the fifth floor, the geriatric ward, tending to the semi-conscious old folks rather than assisting in traumatic injuries, vile diseases of unknown origin, cardiac arrests, wrongful insertion of objects in orifices where they should not have been inserted, and cranky patients who were not actual emergency cases made to wait hours for actual emergency cases to be treated. She must have taken a wrong turn somewhere. But the E.R. was busy tonight and there was no way they were going let this Cherry get away.

Henry asked Candy-Striper if she wanted to grab a cup of shitty cafeteria coffee. She told him that sounded maybe like it was against regulations or something and besides she didn't drink coffee.

"Maybe you prefer some pretty spectacular bourbon? Got a bottle in my office."

"Um…"

"I'm a doctor. You can trust me."

Nurse Rejjitt, long and tensile and in the sunset of her athletic good looks, sporting a razor-sharp, fake smile, walked up to Henry and the Cherry. "Doctor Clerval, what an honor it is to have you visit us down here on our humble little floor of horrors. Are you here on a consult?" A purposeful glance at the Candy-Striper, then back to him and she said, "Or are you hunting down lovely young virgins to sacrifice upon the altar of Clerval the Insatiable?"

"Ho ho, ha ha, hee hee," Henry said, devoid of any humor. "Good one, Nurse. I am actually, or was, on a surgical consult."

"Really? Were you? Excellent. We are better for it, I

am sure."

The Candy-Striper said, "Um, maybe I should—"

"Yes you should," said Nurse Rejjitt.

And off she went, the Cherry, and was quickly snatched up by another nurse to have her help with a newly arrived patient with a butter knife stuck in his left ear.

With Nurse Rejjitt still all up in his business, Henry was about to launch into invectives when he noticed, over her right shoulder, in the narrow hallway which led to the stairwell, three gurneys with sheet-covered bodies.

She followed his stare. "They're DOAs brought in together. We had to park them there for the time being. We're somewhat backed up as you can see."

"What happened to them?"

"Friday night, teenage girls. Parties and free flowing alcohol and no designated driver. Take a guess what happened."

"*Girls*, you said?"

Nurse Rejjitt, slowly and dramatic-like, turned back to Henry. She squinted at him and her jaws moved as if chewing on her tongue. A moment later she said, "I suppose maybe one, or all of them, may suit your need. After all, their being dead is not an impediment to you, right? Although the odds of any one of them being a virgin are probably not very good."

"Fuck you."

"Right back at ya, doc," said Nurse Rejjitt, shoulder-bumping him as she rushed off to assist with the now screaming butter knife guy.

Henry pulled out his phone, made the call. "It's me. I think I've found the motherlode. Be here in fifteen minutes." Hung up, went to look under the sheets. All three of them were fairly mangled but the parts he needed were intact, uninjured. The first girl was too big though. The second one too small. But the third one was just right. Henry checked the plastic-sheeted paperwork.

"Lanna Vodak, you're coming with me."

Henry pushed the wheelchair, with Lanna limply situated in it, out of the dense-air E.R., past the sliding glass doors, and into the cool night. He had covered her bloody-clothed torso with a jacket from the lost and found. Her hair was arranged as to make her crumpled skull less obvious.

He stopped in the ambulance bay, looked for the Mustang that wasn't there. "Where are you?" His watch indicated 12 minutes had elapsed since the phone call. "Where the fuck are you?!"

Despite the chaos inside, outside was an exemplar of serenity. Quiet enough to hear a cricket chirping. Stars twinkled. The moon smiled upon Henry who was feeling naked and exposed, imagining FBI agents with guns pointed, materializing from the shadows, all courtesy of that snitch, Nurse Rejjitt. He then heard the rumble of the engine, the squealing tires, and finally, Victor pulled into the bay with the Mustang. Henry checked his watch: 14 minutes, 58 seconds since the call.

"Are you fucking kidding me?" Henry said as Victor got out of the car. "I've been standing out here for three minutes like a damn virgin ready to be sacrificed."

"A virgin? What are you talking about?"

"Never mind."

"You said to be here in 15 minutes and here I am. If you wanted me to be here before then, what you should have said was, be here as soon as you can but no later than 15 minutes. And that's not what you said."

"Did anywhere in that fat brain of yours, occur the thought of the getaway car being ready to go from the word 'go?'"

"What *occurred* in my brain, was that you must have told me to be here in 15 minutes for good reason, such as you having a strategy planned to the precise minute and my showing up even a minute earlier would have disrupted that perfectly timed plan."

"You clearly don't know shit about pulling off a heist."

"And *you* clearly didn't have a perfectly timed plan. On top of which, are you trying to tell me that in the history of so-called heists, there's never been an instance of where the getaway car had to be there at a precise moment and not a minute before and not a minute after?"

"No, there hasn't been because pulling off a heist requires flexibility. Even if you get your plan to where the probabilities are in your favor, things can get fucked up."

"I can name you seven movies that support my position," said Victor.

"I can name you eight," retorted Henry.

"Okay. Name them."

As Henry thought about it and as Victor watched Henry think about it, they came to a mutual realization of the stupidity of this discourse. Then they realized that while they were obliviously confabbing, two ambulances and a cop car had pulled into the bay. The paramedics, the cop, the orderlies, and nurses, unloading what were likely victims of a multi-vehicle accident.

"Shit," said Henry and Victor at the same time, then Henry said, "Come on, hurry, help me with her."

Victor opened the passenger side door. Henry lifted the

dead girl out of the wheelchair, tossed her onto the seat and she splayed like a rag doll. Victor propped her straight, seat-belted her in and asked, "What's her name?"

Henry peered over his shoulder at the personnel gathering at the ambulances, Nurse Rejjitt among them. Henry hunched, trying to make himself small. "Her name is, uh, Janet, maybe Jenny." Turned back to look at the girl. "No, it's Lanna. Lanna Vodak. Partied hardy and now she's dead."

Victor checked the hand, the leg. "Her leg is a perfect match, except it's a quarter inch shorter, but okay I guess." He grasped her left hand, massaged open her rigor-mortised fingers sporting chipped nail polish of a pinkish hue. "She has piano fingers."

"Say what?"

He held her hand up to Henry. "See? Long and slender fingers. Perfect for playing piano. But a little too long for Francine, I think."

"Don't even fucking tell me you're not going to use her hand," said Henry, shaking a clenched fist. "I am not going back for seconds."

Victor went over to the driver's side, got in. "Piano fingers will have to do." Buckled up. "What *you* need to do is go back up to your office, unlock that locked drawer, pull out your premium booze, knock it back, relax."

"That's the most sensible thing you've said tonight. But relax? I don't think so. I haven't relaxed since the day your skinny ass showed up in my 3rd grade class." He snuck a glance at the commotion by the ambulances. Nurse Rejjitt, hands on hips, was looking his way. "Come on, man. You gotta get her out of here."

Victor started the car, then head-bobbed thataway

toward Nurse Rejjitt making towards them.

Henry said, "Yeah, I know. I'll put her off the scent." He watched Victor ease the Mustang out of the ambulance bay, back onto the main drag, melding with traffic. Muttered, "The shit you get me into."

Nurse Rejjitt sidled up closely next to him, could practically feel her body heat. She exhaled, sounded like a balloon quickly losing air, said, "I'm sorry, Doctor. I was kind of a bitch to you earlier."

Her apology took the spunk out of what was going to be his putting-her-off-the-scent tirade for her being a bitch to him earlier. To top it off, the apologizing of this stern, former hottie was a turn-on. So instead he said, "Wanna come up to my office for some spectacular bourbon?"

Her expression was of anger-tinged perplexity. "Why the invite now? Never got one before."

"Didn't realize there was so much sass packed into that tight bod of yours. It's got me all worked up."

"Sweet-talker, you," she said, then looked up at the smiling moon, let out a grumbly sigh. "Sadly, that's the best offer I've had in a while."

"Wanna meet me in five?"

"Make it ten. I need to make sure to cover my tracks. Can't really be seen going into your office. Know what I mean?"

"Who's being the sweet-talker now?"

She laughed. He laughed. They laughed together. But without much conviction.

CHAPTER ELEVEN
Operation Humpty Dumpty

The meetings took place over the course of three days. The first was at the hospital cafeteria. Shitty coffee, amazing peach cobbler. Not the ideal place but Henry had a number of surgeries lined up, couldn't get away, and Victor was anxious to get the process started.

There would be three phases in the rebuilding of Francine and the entirety of the those phases would take five days. Vacation days were to be put in with their respective employers. Their cover stories: Victor, going to a writer's retreat to start his novel about a college professor obsessed with a dead girlfriend and driven to insanity. Henry, as per usual, going back to Amsterdam.

They would have to work in shifts for most of those days because they would not be able to stop until—

"Wait," said Henry. "We should decide on a name."

"A name for what?"

"This project. Let's call it Humpty Dumpty."

"This 'project' doesn't need a name. I don't like that name anyway."

"It's based on your own reference the other day to all the king's men, et cetera."

"That phrase, in the context of my reference, made sense, but the use of the term Humpty Dumpty in the context of this project, makes it sound like it's going to be a failure."

"That's what's cool about it. The irony makes it the perfect code name."

Victor chugged the coffee, grimaced. "Anyway…"

They would have to work in shifts for most of those days because they would not be able to stop once the thawing-out process began. The cozy operating room in Victor's garage would be maintained at low temperatures keeping Francine semi-thawed to prevent the onset of decomposition because refreezing her would be too risky. Victory's theory was that a human being could be subjected to a freeze/thaw cycle once, but doing so multiple times could cause unacceptable cellular degradation. They had to get it right the first time and five days was the outer limit of keeping her semi-thawed before she would basically start to rot.

Phase One would be the least risky. Removal of damaged parts, easily done within a day. Victor gave Henry a copy of the outline of the Phase One procedures along with the MRI images. Henry barely glanced at the outline and the images, tossed them onto the table.

"This is gonna be cake," he said with a mouthful of cobbler.

The next night, they had Meeting Number Two. Took

place at the basement bar of The Carcass Steakhouse. Victor had the Rib-Eye, Henry the Porterhouse. By the end of the meeting, they had downed a goodly amount of Kentucky rye. For good reason. Phase Two was ambitiously estimated to take three days. The procedures for this phase were too complex to be just an outline. It took a three-ring binder to hold the instructional manual created by Victor. There were four major organs to be transplanted, a hand and a leg to be replaced, and there was the minor procedure of reattaching Francine's head. After Henry studied the contents of the binder, he uttered, "Holy Mother." When they were finally booted out of the steakhouse bar, they had yet to broach the cervical fusion.

The final discussion of operation Humpty Dumpty happened two days later at the university, after-hours. Had to shoo the janitorial staff from the classroom with the state of the art video projection system. After their meeting at The Carcass, Victor had rethought the cervical fusion presentation — 3D and huge would now be the order of the day to properly prepare for the alignment of the spinal cord tracts. This, the reconnection of the spinal cord, would take one of the three days of Phase Two.

Henry choked and gagged on the mouthful of chips he'd been munching on. Made for a can of beer out of the 12-pack, cracked it open, chugged it down, cleared his gullet. Blurted out, "One day? Are you totaling fucking with me? To reestablish the connections of the spinal cord, we're supposed to get it done in one day?"

Victor's shrug implied: what's the big deal? And: are you going to share that 12-pack?

Henry tossed him a beer, held out the bag of chips, and gathered himself. "Are you aware of anyone reattaching a severed human head?"

"Yes," said Victor.

"Successfully, I mean."

"Of a complete head-off-the-body decapitation? Then, no."

"So because there has yet to be a successful human head reattachment, and because even the repair of an attached-head spinal cord injury is labor intensive and complicated, shouldn't we conservatively estimate at least two days for this procedure alone?"

"Don't have the time. But we don't need it." Victor sipped the beer and continued sipping, whittling away at Henry's patience. "I've got something to help with the procedure."

"Something? What something?"

"A contraption."

"You're not going tell me?"

"On a need-to-know basis I will. Not before, because I know how you're going to react and I don't want to deal with it right now."

"That's just rude, man," Henry said, stuffing more chips into his pie hole. "You know what? I don't care, you judgmental prick. By the way, you want me to score some pharmaceutical grade amphetamines, some 'A'-quality coke, to get us through the stretch run of Phase Two?"

"That's probably not a good idea. It may affect performance."

"Never affected me."

Victor thought about it, said, "We are talking about the same thing aren't we?" Henry about to utter a response, Victor put up a hand signifying "stop, never mind, I don't want to know."

"Whatever," said Henry. "So, Phase Three. You have perfected the process, right?"

"It's never not been perfected." A tinge of irritation in Victor's voice.

Henry, chomping on the chips, crunchily responded, "I guess you forgot about your little experiment. When the rats exploded? That was a hoot, yeah?"

"It was only two out of ten that exploded, which by the way was a calculated and acceptable failure rate at the time. Any and all bugs have been worked out now." Victor's irritation now more than a tinge. "There will be no glitches, no explosions. Got it?" Victor downed his beer, gripped the empty can, crushed it the best he could, and hurled it at Henry who caught it and crushed the can appropriately.

Henry, laughing, said, "Stick to what you're good at."

Operation Humpty Dumpty: Day One (Phase One)

Francine's body was laid out on the operating table, thawed enough to be able to operate on. The room was cold, keeping her at optimal temperature to hold decay at bay. Henry and Victor stood over the body, just staring at her, their breaths frosty and visible. Ten years since they had seen the hue and texture of her skin resemble anything human. So they gave the moment a moment.

Henry grabbed the red marker and wrote an upside down "Y" on her torso, the stem of the "Y" running from the base of the neck to the bottom of the sternum, the inverted top of the "Y" tracing the base of the ribcage. Victor said, "That's going to be a gnarly scar."

"You think so, doctor?" said Henry as he placed the protective face shield over his head.

"I don't like it."

"Get over it. There's no room for delicacy in a wholesale operation like this." Tested the electrical bone saw. The high pitched whir made Henry smile.

Victor worried a look, said, "Maybe I'll stay and help."

An aggravated sigh from Henry. "What're you going to help with? Scratching my balls? This is going to be a walk in the park, a one-man job, and you know it. You need to be rested for Phase Two. So scram already."

Victor nodded, then slowly backed out of the operating room, closed the door. But stayed standing there, watching through the plexiglass wall. Henry flipped him off and Victor finally skulked out of the garage.

Day Two of Operation Humpty Dumpty (Day One of Phase Two)

The inverted "Y" incision had been made, and the ribcage, sawcut down the sternum, was held gaping open via rib spreaders revealing the thoracic cavity from where Henry had removed the damaged heart, right lung, liver, and left kidney. The thigh, amputated at mid-femur. Because the left hand had originally been wrenched from wrist, Henry reshaped the area to make for a clean reattachment point. Since he had time to spare, Henry inserted surgical grade titanium pins into the bones at the end points of the thigh and wrist to make for a secure connection of Lanna Vodak's leg and hand.

Though he really didn't need to, Victor went ahead and made a close inspection of Henry's work. As expected, the work was precise and clean and evidenced high craftsmanship. Victor always marveled at how Henry, with his grizzly-bear-paw size hands, could have the touch to perform surgical techniques bordering on art.

Victor started with the orthopedic stuff, the hand, the leg, the bone work, which involved rods, clamps, plates, and screws. More like carpentry than surgery, a way to ease into it. When the hand was done, he checked the large digital clock on the wall counting down the time until irreversible cellular decay would set in. He was behind schedule. Told himself to stop thinking of the body as Francine's and think of it as just another body: You're doing fine Gottenberg, you are not going to fuck this up, it's just another body. He started on the leg, done in record time. Was able to fit in the liver. Record time.

Day Three of Operation Humpty Dumpty (Day Two of Phase Two)

Henry knocked on the plexiglass, came in, walked around the body. "Are you kidding? The hand, the leg? Expected. But you got the liver done too?" Henry congratulated him with a smack to the shoulder, making Victor bounce off the plexiglass.

And when Victor regained his balance he said, "God I'm tired."

Henry laughed. "So is that how it works? When the going gets tough, the atheist starts talking to God?"

Victor trudged out of the operating room. Said over his shoulder, "It's just a saying, that's all. Just a saying."

"Sure it is," said Henry, then got right to it.

The lung and kidney were a relative cinch but the heart was a bear, seemed as if the replacement heart and the body were of the same magnetic polarity having the effect of mutually repelling forces. Henry knew this was nuts, believed he was suffering from fatigue. So he took a snort to clear his head then forced the issue and sutured her torso shut with artisan flair.

With jittering eyes, Henry glanced at the clock. Satisfactory nod and a smile. Then his attention shifted to the stainless steel box sitting on the floor, tucked in the corner of the operating room. The box was just the right size for holding a human head. He knelt at the box, grasped the lid with both hands, about to open it, but stopped. Checked the garage outside of the plexiglass partition. Dark and still. Turned back to the box, opened it, scooped out Francine's head with one hand. Was it just him or did she actually look pretty good for someone lacking a body and being dead and frozen for 10 years? With his free hand, he stroked her cheek until he heard the O.R. door open. Startled, he jumped to his feet and Francine's head slipped from his grip. But caught her by the hair, inches from the floor.

Victor barged in. "Are you crazy? What are you doing?!"

Henry, drenched with panic-sweat, said, "What? It's all cool." Voice uncharacteristically trembly. "I caught her didn't I? And it's not like she's gonna be any more dead than she already is."

Victor, with fist cocked back, charged at Henry. But Henry stiff-armed him in the forehead, sending Victor crashing into the instrument tray. "Calm down, dammit," said Henry. "I was joking. It was a stupid joke, okay? It was stupid."

Victor pushed off the floor, took possession of Francine's head from Henry. Cradled it. "What exactly *were* you doing?"

"Nothing. Getting her prepped for you."

"No, really. Just tell me. What were you doing?"

"I told you," said Henry as he tore off his scrubs. "Now get the fuck off my back."

They glared at each other until the glare reduced into a stare which turned into shifting glances which eventually, sheepishly, landed at their feet. Victor then put Francine's head back into the box, told Henry, "Try to get some sleep. This part of the phase is going to be a bitch."

"Right. Okay."

Day Four of Operation Humpty Dumpty (Day Three of Phase Two)

A high-powered surgical magnifying scope was strapped to Victor's sweaty stubble-bearded face. His 'fro and 'stache droopy from unwashedness. Grimaced as he worked on the cervical procedure. Francine's body had been turned over and her head rested face down on a specially made device for the purpose of supporting a decapitated head for reattachment to the neck. So tired he was, this bitch of a procedure to align the bundles of spinal cord tracts. The clock mocked him with every second that ticked down: Failure, failure, won't finish on time, she doesn't love you. And she never will.

"Shut up!"

"Who are you talking to?" said Henry standing at the doorway. "And why didn't you come wake me?"

"The clock, was uh…"

"The clock? What're you saying?" He got up into Victor's face. "You sleep-deprived, hallucinating bastard. This is what you get for thinking that you can do this without me. No matter how much you try to ignore the fact, I am integral. So get over yourself."

"I'm fine fuck you very much and don't ever expect me to get over myself." He turned back to the clock, stared it down, challenging its perceived mockery of him. The clock didn't budge. So he said to Henry, "By the way, got any of that coke left?"

"Now you're talking."

After they completed the alignment of the spinal cord bundles, Henry took off his magnifying scope, sniffled hard, asked, "Okay, here we are, time to fuse the nerves and you said you had something up your sleeve, some damn contraption, but now that we're here at this juncture I'm not seeing that 'something' that 'anything,' I mean we're making a reconnection of the spinal cord. Right? It's an imperfect and difficult-at-best procedure. Right?" With dilated pupils, he stared down Victor. "So what is it, the solution? Because I'm more than a little concerned for our friend's soon-to-be rotting head which may or may not be able to be reattached successfully."

Victor let go a sigh, sounded like a growl. Left the O.R., retrieved a metal collar off one of the garage shelves and grabbed the laptop from the plywood desk. The collar was about an inch thick made of polished steel with a hinge to open and close it so as to fit around one's neck. Long tails of two cables connected to the collar dragged behind him as he came back into the O.R. He set up the laptop, plugged in one of the cables, held up the collar and proclaimed, "This will make quick work of the procedure and drop the failure rate to zero."

"Get the fuck outta here."

Victor furiously typed commands into the computer. "The problem with cervical fusion procedures is that the current level of micro surgery doesn't have the technological capacity to make a proper reconnection of the nerve endings." He then took the other cable and linked it into the coupling protruding from the side of a lunchbox-sized, lead-lined, heavy gauge, steel case. "So what needs to happen is for the nerve connection to be made at the atomic level." Took the collar, clamped it around Francine's neck. "And this device, which I've been calling the V-Gott Fuser, will do the trick."

"It sounds nuclear."

"A gold star to Henry."

"Are you telling me there's radioactive shit going on in that lunchbox-looking thing?"

"Two gold stars to you."

Henry covered his nads with both hands. "Shouldn't we be wearing lead-lined jocks or something? And by the way, how did you score the, uh, enriched uranium is it?"

"Got somebody in the Physics Department, owed me a favor," said Victor as he initiated the V-Gott Fuser. A bumble-bee-decibel buzz filled the O.R. Henry grabbed a metal tray, used it to cover his crotch, backed himself into a corner.

The twitching started at her upper arms. Then her fingers, chest, her ass, thighs, calves, and toes. A sure sign that the nerves were reconnecting, firing signals down the spinal cord. Victor shut the Fuser down. Took off the collar.

"Come on. Help me close her up."

Henry didn't budge.

"Come on already," said Victor.

Henry still didn't budge. Finally said, "Are you telling me that with this thing, the V-Gott Fuser, you've basically found a way to cure paralysis, the various 'peligia resulting from spinal cord injuries?"

"Quick. We need to close her up."

"Hey, man! Can you just answer my question?"

Victor rubbed his temples with the heels of his hands and said, "I knew this was how you would react."

"But—"

"I did this for her and no one else."

"Just hold on. Think about the value of this," implored Henry. "This is worth millions. Billions maybe!"

Victor ignored Henry, started the stitch-up procedure. Henry, stunned into silence, could only watch. Victor's method was in-artful but there was grace and gentleness to it, as if Francine were wide awake and he was trying his damnedest to minimize discomfort and pain. His focus was white hot. His focus didn't give a shit about millions possibly billions.

Henry shook his head, trying to dislodge the disbelief. Didn't work, gave in and said, "You're going to make it look like a zipper necklace. Playtime is over so make room for the grown-up to do his thing." Held out his hand for the instruments. Victor begrudgingly acknowledged his limitations, acquiesced without argument.

When Henry was done, a brace was put in place to keep her head from moving. Then they stood shoulder to shoulder. No words passed their lips, only frosty vapors of breath. So there she was, all put back together again. For Victor, an absolute eternity to get here. But no sense of relief, not yet. But almost there. Almost there.

CHAPTER TWELVE

The Super Duper Magical Miracle Kiss From A Woman Named Eunice
(Final Day of Operation Humpty Dumpty)

10:28 a.m.

Ten hours and 32 minutes until 9:00 p.m., the theoretical deadline before irreversible cellular degradation set in, rendering Francine truly dead and gone if she was not resurrected before then.

Victor, sprawled out on his bed, hadn't bothered to take off his scrubs from last night, still dead asleep. Henry, wearing only bikini briefs, lay face down on the couch, his snores muffled by the cushion. Empty beer cans littered about along with grease-stained pizza boxes.

11:17 a.m.

Victor and Henry sat at the kitchen table, going to town

on a bagful of breakfast burritos. Victor still in soiled scrubs, Henry still only wearing his bikini briefs. Despite their sleeping in, a pall of exhaustion filled the kitchen. Days of being unwashed, unshaven, contributed to their scruffy hairiness and a farm-animally smell.

12:31 p.m.

The garage O.R., now set to room temperature. Francine on the operating table wearing boxer shorts and a bra.

"How long till she's fully thawed out?" said Henry.

"She should be ready to go by about 7:30."

"Cutting it close, aren't you?"

"Not really. Prepping her and hooking her up to the black box and initiating and completing the process is only going to take at most 30 minutes."

"If things go without a hitch."

"There will be no hitches."

"Uh-huh. By the way, why is she wearing underwear?"

3:22 p.m.

Victor and Henry sat at the kitchen table, going to town on a bagful of cheeseburgers. They'd showered and shaved. No more smell. Strategized about post-resurrection, about how she would need to be kept in a drug-induced coma until her body healed, otherwise she would have to deal with a shit-storm of post surgical pain as Henry put it. And while she was in a coma, it would be a good idea to hook her up to electrode therapy to keep her muscles stimulated to mitigate the atrophy of being 10-years frozen.

"Where are we going to keep her?"

"Here," Victor said, astonished, as if she would stay anywhere else.

"Don't you have a day job?"

"I'll take a sabbatical."

"How are you going to get away with that when you're supposed to be in the throes of your 'research' for the university? I would think that the sponsors will be all over the dean's ass asking about results. Then you'd have the dean all over your ass—"

"Fine. I won't take a sabbatical. I'll just reduce my hours, give them some bullshit about how I need to stop teaching classes for a while to focus on 'the research.'"

"Or. I can take time off and take care of her."

Victor squirmed in his seat. Pretended to study his cheeseburger, said to Henry, "You don't need to do that. I can handle it." A half-hearted grin.

Henry let go a sarcastic snort. "It's not like you have ownership rights over her."

"Didn't say I did."

"You didn't have to." Henry stuffed the last bite of cheeseburger into his mouth. Pushed away from the table. "I was shitting you when I said I could take time off."

"Why are you raining on my parade?"

"*Your* parade. See what I'm talking about?" As Henry left the kitchen, he said, "You can have the rest of the cheeseburgers."

Victor checked the bag. Empty.

5:58 p.m.

Victor stood at the living room window, looking skyward. Cloud-cover, out of nowhere, the color of which was an ominous dark purple. A distant telltale rumble of potential ferocity. He turned to Henry who was curled up on the couch. "Was there anything about a storm-front coming in?" Henry responded with an incoherent grumble. Victor returned his gaze to the clouds, whispered, "Why are you raining on my parade?"

8:02 p.m.

Francine, fully thawed out. Strapped to her head was a helmet of aluminum shell from which 10 insulated cables led to the black metal box which in turn was connected via single cable to the laptop. Electrodes sprouting from the box were attached to Francine's ribcage. The EKG monitor on the computer screen currently flatlined. Victor typed final commands into the computer, the tapping on the keyboard drowned out by the pounding rain. When he was done, the question "READY?" pulsed on the computer screen.

Victor's lungs felt heavy, impeded his breathing. A jackhammering heart. Over the "Y" key, his shaky index finger at the ready. Henry, ramrod stiff, stood on the other side of the O.R., his forehead beaded with sweat. Their eyes met, Henry's asking the question. Victor swallowed hard and nodded smally. His finger about to press the key when thunder detonated, the sonic force of which made Victor and Henry hit the deck, crouch for cover.

"What the?!"

"Holy shit!"

The lights flickered.

Victor shot up off the floor, lunged for the "Y" key. But the garage went pitch black before Victor reached the keyboard.

"No, no, no, no, no!" howled Victor as he rushed out of

the O.R., through the garage, groping in the dark, running into things, tripping, falling. Finally made it into the house then out the front door. Henry on Victor's heels. They were instantly drenched by the rain. Lighting lit up the neighborhood flash-white, immediate explosion of thunder made them flinch hard. No lights on in the neighborhood. The transformer, a block away, on fire from a lighting strike.

"No…" said Victor slack-jawed, barely audible.

"I don't get it, man," Henry yelled to be heard over the torrent.

"The black box runs off of household current."

"Okay so? Just bust out the backup generator."

Victor lowered his head. "There isn't one."

"Wait what? It sounded like you said there isn't one."

Victor responded with a glare.

"You didn't account for this contingency did you? You were in such a damn hurry, you didn't even think about it."

Victor headed back into the house. Henry followed, said, "Hey, man. Hey!"

Victor stopped abruptly, grabbed Henry by the collar, tried to shake the big fucker but couldn't budge him. "Can you just get off my back and help me? Please?" Voice cracked. "Just help me."

"All right. So what're we doing?"

8:22 p.m.

The living room was illuminated with one of those large, brick-like flashlights placed upright on the coffee table. Victor paced. Henry on the couch, ate stale pizza, jittery bites. Pacing, pacing. Eating, eating. And then,

"Hey, whoa!" said Victor. "Do you still have the portable defibrillator?"

Henry with a mouthful of cold slice of pepperoni-mushroom-Italian sausage thought about it, stopped mid-chew, said, "Yeah, I do. It's in the trunk." Hopped up, sprinted to the front door, was about to step back out into the torrent when he stopped and said, "But wait. Defibrillation is not going to help."

"I know I know. But all we need is to start with fibrillation and I can get that with chest compressions and pumping her full of Epinephrine. And once we're there, we jolt the heart to get regular rhythm."

"No, I get that. What I'm saying is, starting her heart without brain activity is still technically dead."

"If we get her body functions going, the decay-cascade can be prevented," said Victor as he pressed Henry out the door. "We'll deal with starting up the brain later."

8:31 p.m.

When rain-drenched Henry walked into the garage O.R., there was an empty Epi injector on the floor along with Francine, and Victor kneeling at her side doing chest compressions, which were forceful but precise and efficient to avoid tearing the sutures. Henry set the portable next to them. He opened up the small case made of high-impact, white plastic. Pulled out the paddles, turned a knob, flipped a switch. A high-pitched sound of the unit charging up.

Victor counted each compression: ...28, 29, 30. He stopped. Caught his breath, checked the EKG monitor. Still flatlined. Started again: 1, 2, 3...

Henry stood watching Victor, then the monitor. Back

and forth. Kept shifting his weight, one foot to the other. Back and forth. Under his breath, said, "This is impossible, this impossible, this impossible."

"...28, 29, 30." He looked up at Henry. "Dammit shut up with your negativity. Can't you just—" Victor was interrupted by Henry's index finger pointing at the monitor. He followed the pointing, saw that the line was no longer flat. "Shit yeah," said Victor. "V-fib. We got V-fib!" Not a normal heart rhythm but it was a start. Reached for the paddles, placed them at Francine's ribcage. Shocked her, body tensed rigid, then relaxed. No change. Re-charged and shocked. Still no change. Charged, shocked, nothing. Charged, shocked, nothing. Tried to charge again but the defibrillator was out of juice. He checked the EKG: flatlined again. "It's back to asystole. Fuck!" He looked at Francine. Her skin had taken on a splotchy complexion akin to rotting fruit. "Shit." He slumped, head in hands. Rocked on his haunches.

8:40 p.m.

"This is not the way it ends," said Victor.

"Who's to say, except, you know." Henry raised his eyebrows heaven-ward.

Victor thought about the 3,788 days that had passed since Francine's purported demise. Each one of those 3,788 days he never deviated from having her on his mind, the vision of her not fading whatsoever from memory, and he had toiled those days to make a miracle into scientific reality. Imagined her alive every day. Every day, he had spoken to her.

"Who's to say? I'm to say." Victor fetched a carrying

board and asked Henry to tilt Francine a bit so as to slide the board under her. Then Victor placed the laptop on her chest, the black box placed across her thighs. Draped a cut-open garbage bag over her.

Henry piped up. "Okay, I give. Where are we taking her?"

8:46 p.m.

The Mustang's engine rumbled impatiently as the car sat in the driveway, getting pelted by the deluge and waiting for the two of them to make up their minds.

"East. We should go east," said Henry behind the wheel.

"No. West is the way to go," Victor replied from the backseat where he sat with Francine laid out lengthwise, her only-recently-put-on head gingerly cradled upon his lap.

Henry looked westward down the street. Pitch black. Victor checked east. The same.

"Might as well flip a coin," said Henry.

"No way. We're not relying on randomness. Go west and it'll get us on the freeway, above surface and on higher ground to be able to see where the light is. Besides, west, past 54th street, they're going to be on a different grid."

"What I want to say is, how do you even know that, but what I really want to say is, getting to 54th takes probably 15 minutes with full illumination and clear weather. And dry roads. Francine's going to exceed the expiration date before we get there."

"Well then. You need to make like Speed Racer and get us to our destination asap!"

Henry looked over his shoulder, gave Victor the what-the-fuck? look.

Victor gave back to Henry the why-are-you-giving-me-the-what-the-fuck-look-for look and said, "Go already go!"

Henry slammed the gas, the Mustang roared, tire-screeched out of the driveway, went out of control on the rain slick street and side-swiped a neighbor's Beemer parked at the curb. The engine sputtered to a stop. Henry tried to restart the Mustang but she just went "ur-ur-ur-ur-ur."

"Dammit, bitch, start already, start!" said Henry.

"Hey!" said Victor. "You need to be cool with her."

"Are you shitting me right now?"

"Just be cool."

Henry flailed fists at air for a couple of seconds, then gripped the steering wheel, calmed himself, said to the Mustang, "Okay, baby. Do daddy a solid and turn over for me." Pumped the gas, tried the key, and she went Va-Room! and he punched it and they shot down the street.

8:51 p.m.

As Henry jetted down the sparsely trafficked freeway, they saw the light all right as Victor predicted, west of 54th street. They made for the closest lit establishment, an off-brand convenience store at the edge of the industrial district. The Mustang slid into the empty parking lot, came just yay short of crashing through the storefront doors. They hopped out and hauled Francine into the store. Drenched, dripping wet, laid her down on the linoleum tile floor in the puddle that formed beneath them. And then, Henry got cold-cocked with the butt end of a shotgun and he flopped to the floor like a sopping towel. Pretty much comatose.

The not-butt-end of the shotgun was pointed at Victor's face. He felt the sudden urge to urinate, possibly a bowel movement too. But despite the fact that he was staring down the gaping single barrel that was about to blast buckshot into his forehead, Victor was mesmerized by the woman toting said shotgun. She was built like a supermodel, long and lean, 5'11" at least, with perfect curves in perfect places that could only have been purposefully placed there by the hand of God. Her face, sculpted by Michelangelo's ghost. Except, that is, for a missing canine, a keloid scar that ran from her cheek, the right one, to the tip of her pointy chin, and the glass eye, the left one, that stared at you a little bit crooked. Her pitch black hair, the consistency and thickness of a lion's mane, poured out from under the gnarly-stained trucker cap and streamed down to the cleft of her ass. She wore short shorts that revealed camel toes, and a tube top trying valiantly to keep the ladies in place. A name tag that hung from a cheap chain around her neck said, "Eunice." A tiny smiley-face sticker next to her name.

And so Eunice said, "Do you think I haven't seen couple of jerk-wads like yourselves come in here before, trying to unload a dead body? Well I have, jerk-wad, so just take this dead little lady friend of yours outta here before I blow your head off of that spindly little neck."

Victor held out his hand, palm up, as if making some kind of offering. "It's not what you think."

"Oh, it's not is it?" Sarcasm coated Eunice's words. Click-clack went the shotgun as she cocked it.

While Victor's throat choked with dryness, he noticed

on the wall behind the counter and just above the porno mags, one of those novelty kitty clocks with the shifting eyes, swinging tail, looking more ominous than cute just then.

8:56 p.m.

"Eunice. Eunice? Have you ever been in love, I mean like head over heels, like, like, implosion and explosion happening at the same time in the core of where you feel stuff like that, wherever that is, and you cannot, absolutely not, go on living without that person, and if that person died, you would die, unless you found a way to not let her be dead, i.e., bring her back to life?"

"Of course. How do you think I got this glass eye and came to own this place?" Unpointed the shotgun, leaned it upright against her clavicle. "So let me understand this. You love this girl, this dead girl, or not quite dead girl whose condition is about to be irreversible from the look of her." The color of Francine was about the shade of just-ripening eggplant, her texture was that of a rotting tomato. "And you've found a way to bring her back. Her name?"

"Francine."

"This girl that you love and want to bring back to life whose name is Francine, was it you that killed her?" Eunice jammed the tip of the gun barrel into Victor's right cheek.

"No! She, uh, was in an accident? A car accident. I swear."

"What's *your* name?"

"Victor."

She pressed the barrel even harder into his face. "Look

me in the eyes, Victor." He did, and she said, "Tell me you love her and that your intentions are true and good and that your actions are that of selflessness."

Victor's throat was closing up from being ultra parched. His eyeballs wobbled, struggled to maintain eye contact. Sweat poured out of him but who could tell what with him being soaked from the rain. And then there was the bowel movement business. With ass clenched tightly, he said, "I love her and my intentions are true. And good." About the "selflessness" part, he was a lousy liar and didn't want to chance being caught in a lie, so said nothing and hoped for the best. But still. He shut his eyes tightly, imagined it would be quick, though probably not painless.

The barrel was pulled away from his face and Eunice asked, "So what is it that you need from me?"

He opened his eyes and breathed out the words, "I need a 120 volt outlet. For a three-prong plug."

9:04 p.m.

Francine had been laid out on the counter, the head/neck brace removed. The black box was plugged into the outlet beneath the cash register. Her head was helmeted with the aluminum shell. The laptop screen showed an EKG flatline over which the word "READY?" flashed. Victor worried the kitty clock.

Eunice noticed and said, "I know what you said about the 9:00 o'clock deadline, but it was a theoretical deadline right? Her name is Francine, not Cinderella. Right?"

"It *was* theoretical. I'm hardly ever wrong though. But if you say otherwise I'll believe you because I just really need to right now."

"I am saying otherwise." She scooped up his hand, held it, gripped tightly. "Now press that key, Victor. Time's a-wasting."

He pressed the "Y" key on the laptop and the black box hummed and bucked and the lights lit up on the aluminum helmet. Francine shimmied and shook but she was still flatlined. Victor and Eunice stared at the EKG monitor. And stared. And stared. Nothing changed. Victor held his breath, felt himself turning a wrong shade of human. His body convulsed with little tremors.

Following an impatient sigh, Eunice asked, "Is this it? Is this all that you do?"

"Wha?" Victor said weakly.

"Men. You're all about technique. Where's the heart, you know?"

She bent over and whispered into Francine's ear, then kissed her, a passionate lip-lock for a good minute, maybe some tongue too. Couple of the lights on the helmet blew out.

There was a blip on the EKG monitor.

Then another. Another and another. Regular heart rhythm. Francine's color normalized instantly. Slight rise and fall of her chest. Eunice, with an I-told-you-so smile, stood off to the side making room for Victor.

He turned off the black box, lifted the helmet from her head. Blank-faced, he stared at Francine. Her eyes slowly opened. The gaze was unfocussed until her pupils dilated suddenly like a starburst, as if from blindness to sight. Her vision roamed, then found his face, locked in on him. She seemed to mouth the word "hi." Struggled out a tiny smile as Victor's tears plopped all over her face.

"Hi," he said back to her with hoarse voice. "Hi."

CHAPTER THIRTEEN
Monster...Of A Situation

Ell's taut thighs tightly wrapped in a pair of jeans rubbed against each other at the inner part and went swish swish as she walked down the late-evening-quiet hospital hallway checking the name plates on the office doors. She stopped in front of "Dr. Clerval." Took off her leather jacket, tucked the V-neck tee in tightly. Checked cleavage, good to go. Badge on right hip, sidearm holstered threateningly just around the bend. She knocked.

"Dr. Clerval? Detective Lavenza." Waited a beat, then another. She knocked harder. "Hello?" Nothing. He was in there, she knew, having been told so by one of the nurses. "Screw this," she said. Clenched the gun grip, pushed open the door, made her way in.

Whom she presumed to be Dr. Clerval, sat at his desk, penning at paperwork. Had headphones on, torso rocking to the beat, didn't notice her just yet. She made a quick survey of the office: a sleeper love-seat in the pulled-out position, tucked in the corner; an un-sexy bra nestled on the floor just underneath the love seat; a mini fridge in the other corner; the book shelf mostly of medical texts except for the one on Kama Sutra, the one called "Oedipal Complex For Beginners," and the one on "How To Make Love To A Woman While Fooling Her Into Believing You Actually Give A Shit."

The good doctor looked up, didn't seem too fazed to see a stranger with a badge and a gun standing in his office. He checked her out in this order: Boobs, badge, eyes, crotch, gun, boobs, eyes.

"Detective. Welcome." He took off his headphones, stood up and his open lab coat revealed that he was wearing only bikini briefs. Tacky, certainly, but his not-too-shabby-a-bulge was a redeeming factor. He offered a hand. She took it, shook it. "You're here about Lanna Vodak, right? Can I offer you a beer, or is that against the law or something?" He waltzed over to the mini fridge.

"It's against the law if you *don't* offer me a beer."

"Well, then," he said with his face in the fridge. "It looks like I am in deep shit because I am out of brewskies."

"No shit you're in deep shit." She put her leather jacket back on.

"You're not leaving are you?" Doc's brows genuinely furrowed.

"That dive-bar-looking place on the corner. You know it?"

"Too well."

"They serve any food?"

"Awesome burgers."

"You're buying," Ell said.

They sat at the bar, the dark corner end of it. A pitcher of beer between them. Henry still wore his lab coat but buttoned up, had pants on now, a shirt too. The second-shift personnel from the hospital crowded the place, their collective energy was of drunken solemnity. Music in the background: the thump thump thump of an electronica backbeat, the latest pop queen trilling about a broken heart, sweet revenge.

"So, doc, you know about Lanna Vodak how?" said Ell, sipping at the mug of beer.

"A cop comes sniffing around asking about a missing body and people tend not to stay quiet. Is he your partner, this Hobert guy who, I heard, has been doing the sniffing?"

"Hobin. His name is Hobin."

"And now *you're* here."

"Yup, for clean-up work." The barkeep brought the burger over along with a basket of onion rings. "That is quite a hunk of meat," said Ell.

"Thanks," said the barkeep. "The burger is of a generous portion too. Har har."

"'Har har' right back atcha." She chomped down on the fat burger, juice dribbling down her chin. She made "mmmmm" noises as she chewed.

Henry stared while nibbling on an onion ring, said, "I don't know what I can tell you that you don't already know, but I'll tell you what I do know and then maybe we can go back to my office and I can tell you some more of what I know, carnally speaking."

She tossed the burger onto the plate, looked for napkins

and finding none, wiped her chin with the back of her hand. "That's the best you can offer, the cum-stained love nest in your office? Why don't we go one better and just head into bathroom stall, I'll get on my knees on the piss-puddled floor and give you a blow-job."

He raised his hands in a sign of retreat. "Sorry." He leaned in, said with a romantic purr, "My place then, much nicer, and clean sheets. I promise."

She took another bite of the burger, chewed and glared and let him hang, then said, "You know what ends a career of a cop quicker than you can say 'chlamydia?' Bedding a prime suspect. You agree?"

"Prime suspect?" He squished an onion ring in his fist. "It was Nurse Rejjitt wasn't it, who said something?"

"Yeah she said something. She told me you were in the E.R. the night of Lanna's disappearance and made inquiries about her and her dead friends. Oh and she also mentioned that you guys screwed that night and that the tales of your sexual prowess were highly exaggerated."

"I knew it. That fucking—!" He caught himself mid-seethe and laughed it off none too convincingly. "She's a kidder she is."

Ell's response was via polishing off the burger and letting there be an awkward silence. Henry squished another onion ring and Ell said, "Please don't waste the onion rings. They're dang good."

"A serial necrophiliac. Have you considered that?" said Henry, wiping his greasy palm on the lab coat.

"What do you think we are? Bunch of amateurs? Of course we considered that and we know who that is, and it's Percy Maplewerm who apparently has disappeared from the face of the Big Blue according to the Fibbies who now have jurisdiction over the case." She spat on the floor. "Let me just say that I highly disagree with their assessment as to the extent of his so called disappearance. Whatever. But he skedaddled well before Lanna's disappearance so it's got to be someone else, and you know what? I think it's you."

"Say what?"

"It's okay. So you have a thing for bangin' dead women. It's gross but not the worst type of crime out there. They're dead after all, but it's gross, man. Just cop to it, pun intended, and it'll make you feel better, cleanse your soul, give you good karma and all that good shit."

Henry slammed his fist on the bar, caught the lip of the onion ring basket, sending the dang good greasy rings tumbling head over heels onto the floor. Pointed his index finger, with seeming violent intent, at her face.

"You don't have shit on me, lady, that's why you haven't cuffed me and that's why you've been pushing your tits in my face all night and why we're now sitting here having drinks."

Ell patted her holster. "I'm a dead-shot, Dr. Clerval. And at this range, what do you think your chances are, huh? So calm your ass down. I may not have probable cause just yet but I have enough to keep you on a short leash. Maybe if you name names, we can come to some kind of understanding."

"Nurse Rejjitt. That's a name."

"Look, Henry, this type of crime is not necessarily high on the list of priorities for the D.A., but you will do time and I'm pretty sure that the Medical Board will yank your license. And if this thing becomes a federal jurisdiction matter, you're most likely going to get hit with a max sentence."

He poured himself a refill of beer. Ignored Ell's empty mug. The bar was a shade on the warm side but not so much so to make one perspire to the extent Henry was. His eyes, which had been rage-focused, were now shifting in thought.

Ell filled her own glass. "That night, you were seen picking up a patient out of a wheelchair and placing said patient into the passenger seat of a vintage Mustang. I think we know who this patient was. So what I want to know is, who was the driver? What did he do with Lanna?" No answer. "Talk to me, Henry."

He re-found his focus and said, "First of all, I don't know who that patient was. I was just passing by, they needed help, and my middle name is Good Samaritan. I have zero clue who the driver was."

"Really? That's what you're going with? Come on, Henry, play ball."

"Actually, Detective, I don't want to play anymore." He stepped off the bar stool, walked purposefully on the onion rings and headed out.

Ell eyeballed the rings, said, "What a jerk."

***

"He's hiding something for sure," said Ell. It was well past midnight, nobody left on their floor except her and Hobin who sat at the desk across from her. "A few more turns of the screw and he will be unlawyering-up soon enough."

"Why so sure?" said Hobin. "Did you see the fear?"

"Yeah, he had fear. But that wasn't all I saw. When the shit hits the fan, it will be every man for himself where this guy is concerned. I almost feel sorry for his cohorts because the doc will definitely be ratting them out."

Hobin opened up a file folder, sifted through pages until he found what he was looking for and read off the page. "There were 22 bodies reported missing from the time Dr. Clerval started at the hospital to the present. Fourteen were found within 72 hours, just misplaced. Three turned out not to be dead at all, apparently left the hospital under their own power. Five have never been found, including Lanna Vodak. Do you think he's black-marketing body parts?"

"That's what's most likely. But he did get a bit touchy when I suggested that maybe he was giving corpses the hot beef injection."

Hobin shuddered. "Who wouldn't get touchy? That's just…"

"Gross?"

"Yeah. Gross."

"But actually, I don't think he's doing that. A serial necrophiliac's set in his way, he's rationalized his actions. He's not going to take offense by someone suggesting that he is what he is."

"He maybe was faking it, the anger?"

"No, it was for real. I almost had to shoot him in the face."

"Oh." The wheels turning creakily in Hobin's head could be heard. "Well then, could he have just started with Lanna?"

"Maybe. But one-timers or first-timers tend to have a connection to the person, the body. Dr. Clerval couldn't give a rat's ass whether this girl was Lanna, Laura, Lena, or Lilybelle."

"Huhn." Hobin looked sleepy. "Hey. I knew a Lilybelle

in high school. I was in love with her. She was hot. I wasn't."

"Would you do her now—"

"Totally."

"—if she were dead?"

"Jeez, Ell. Gross. On top of which, I'm married."

Ell picked up a styrofoam cup filled with coffee gone icy. Cold and pitch black, just the way she liked it. Guzzled and said, "I had a case once where a woman was brought into the E.R., O.D.'d on pills, a suicide case. She was DOA. It turned out she was the young mistress of one of the doctors there. So he stole the body, had her preserved and stashed her away in a rented condo where he'd go and visit her every so often."

"That is disgusting," said Hobin, double-shuddering this time. "It must have been like screwing beef jerky."

"No, Hobin. He wasn't humping her. He just missed her, couldn't let her go. Kind of romantic if you think about it. I mean it's a crazy thing to do but how many people would risk such a thing to hold onto their loved one?"

"Certainly not my wife."

"Maybe it's because you're here so late. Go home to her already and bang her like she was high-school Lilybelle."

Hobin thought about it. Became suddenly perky and hopped up from the chair. As he was vamoosing, he said over his shoulder, "Maybe you should take your own advice and go home too."

"But I don't have a wife," Ell said to the door swinging shut on Hobin's vapor trail.

***

The cozy spring breeze came through the office windows and wafted over Victor, enhancing his current state of being. He sat behind his desk, leaning back into his old-school non-ergonomic plush chair. Eyes half closed, a stupid grin on his face. On the desktop, in the makeshift ashtray of a coffee mug, was a roach of a joint he scored from one of his grad students. A legal pad with drawings of naked stick figures representing himself and Francine getting it on, certain appendages enhanced unrealistically. His grin got bigger and stupider, the anticipation of Francine's post-resurrection-drug-induced-coma coming-out party.

Victor's bliss was disturbed by the ratatat knocking on the door.

"Entrez vous!" he said.

Dean Hiram Brasz burst in, no suit jacket, dress shirt slightly untucked, hair strands out of place. Very un-Hiram like. He walked two tight circles and then planted himself in front of the desk. In his right fist, crumpled sheets of paper, slightly moist from palm sweat.

"What's up, boss?" said Victor. "Is it the Apocalypse or something equivalent?"

Not laughing, not even cracking a smile, the dean said, "I'm sorry for not properly responding to your attempt at humor, Victor, but we have serious matters to discuss." Before Victor could say okay sure whatever, the dean continued: "You were having sexual relations with one of your graduate students."

"Oh, that." Victor had broken up with Sara a week ago. Sara did not understand his purposefully vague basis for the breakup. She did not take it well and not in the sad-despondent-crying kind of not taking it well but more in the manner of anger-rage-revenge kind of not taking it well. "I'm sorry, Hiram, I know it's against university policy—"

"I don't care about that. What I care about is what she told me in regard to the research project."

Victor sat up straight. Definite buzz-kill.

"She said there's been nothing going on and that you've had your students working on unrelated side projects." He held up the crumpled sheets. "But you've been spending the research funds. Quite a bit of it."

"Sure. Right. Uh, the research has stalled. Only temporarily though. I'm working on, uh, trying to find a solution to the sticking point."

"But the rats! You resurrected them, they were alive! What happened to them?"

"They ate each other."

"What?!"

"Relax, man. It's what rats do, sometimes. Besides, going from rodents to jump-starting higher life forms, i.e., people, is not exactly a walk in the park. Hence the sticking point."

Which was not a lie after all. Victor thought about the Eunice-kiss factor. How does one replicate that? He wasn't sure but ultimately didn't care. He'd gotten what he needed out of this research project. Francine was alive. He could now dispense with the cover story and declare the project a failure. Hiram would probably throw himself off the clock tower. Victor had to string him along a little longer to leave a trail of plausible experiments gone awry, stagnant, or dead on arrival, so to speak.

"Are you saying human experiments are next, because that's what it sounds like you're saying, and if that's the case, and then, and then..." Choked up, Hiram couldn't get the rest of the words out.

So Victor threw him a bone. "Sure, Hiram, sure. Human experiments."

"Oh, thank God, thank God. You had me worried there, my boy. Whew! So we are almost there, of securing a great legacy."

Victor pondered: Yours, mine or the University's?

Hiram pulled out a handkerchief, dabbed at the tears of joy, blew his nose. Proceeded to cup Victor's face, the damp hanky pressing moistly against his cheek.

"Never lost faith in you, my boy," he said to grimacing Victor. "Press on, Victor! Onward to Vic-tory! Ha ha."

After Hiram skipped out of the office, Victor wiped the dean's wetness from his cheek, and was about to light up the roach when Hiram popped back in.

"Forgot to tell you," he said waving the haggard sheets of paper. "The Defense Department is sending an investigator to look into the project expenditures."

Victor reflexively spat out the roach, which ricocheted off of Hiram's crotch unnoticed. "What why?!"

"To borrow your term, 'relax, man.' It's just one of those bureaucratic necessities or headaches, depending on one's point of view, when one garners funds from a branch of the federal government."

"But but," Victor said, pointing at the sheets of paper. "I kept track of it, the spending."

"Ha ha. Such sense of humor. Non-itemized, lump sum expenditures, with no backup documentation, and no account information, even for a modicum of sums, will trigger an audit every time. If I didn't know you so well, I would say you were trying to cover your tracks, you know, like the Swiss or Bahamian account to funnel funds to, the new luxury home, the yacht. And was that a brand new Ferrari parked in your space? Ha ha! Why aren't you laughing, that was a good one, I thought."

After Hiram left this time, Victor locked the door. On hands and knees, he searched for the roach. Found it, stuffed it into his pipe, sparked up, and sweated over how to explain the Swiss *and* Bahamian bank accounts; the spending on remodeling of his garage into a state of the art operating room; the extensive, high grade medical equipment and supplies; the MRI machine; a week's worth of pizza and beers; illegally begotten body parts and organs. He sucked on the pipe until the bowl was smoked spotless.

A partnership meeting was called. Henry brought over take-out from The Carcass Steakhouse. Victor busted out the good Scotch. They drank, stuffed their faces, and drank some more. Henry bitched about the cop who was a total bitch to him but who made him want to do her nonetheless. Don't worry about it, she's got nothing, was Henry's response though his atypical weak voice and shifty eyes seemed to say otherwise. Victor explained about the Defense Department audit while not looking Henry in the eyes, didn't tell him not to worry about it.

They sipped their after-dinner drinks as they stood over comatose Francine. So peaceful she looked, so ready to live again she seemed. But the fellas were tense-jawed and quiet. Until Henry, staring straight and hard at Francine's face, said, "I think we've created a monster...of a situation."

CHAPTER FOURTEEN
Dream Life

At last.

***

The day Francine said yes, Victor, though on the low end of the spectrum of athleticism of the general population, literally did a back flip off the park bench, almost nailed the landing but it was slightly askew. Popped various ligaments of his knee, a severe injury from which he would eventually recover but would become one those injuries that could foretell impending storms by the onset of telltale-pain, and this pain would not make him grimace as one would expect, but instead, made him gleam with pleasure as a reminder of the day she said what she said.

Once Victor got off the crutches, they sped to Vegas in the Mustang where they were married in a quaint faux chapel that used to be a fast food place that still had a functioning drive-thru for the quickie ceremony package if one so chose. The young minister was black-frocked, earnest, and of an unknown denomination. Victor wore one of those pseudo-tux T-shirts and a pair of black cords and classic Chucks as shoe-wear. A heavy-duty brace clamped around the still recovering knee. Francine, ever lovely, wore a white sundress with spaghetti straps, a pattern of nubile orchids covered the delicate fabric. She too wore a pair of Chucks, but in pink. On her head, a pristine-looking trucker cap, turned backwards. Victor put the 20-carat gold ring on her finger and kissed the bride and got their photos taken in front of a backdrop of what was alleged to be Niagara Falls.

The next three days, they didn't leave their hotel room despite the awesome buffets, the tempting casino action with what was claimed to be the loosest slots on the strip. The two lovebirds, Victor and Francine, were like a couple of teenagers discovering the new world of naked pleasures, reveling in copulatory delights. Drunk on love, life, and room service that catered to their every gastronomical whim.

On their way out of town, at the outskirts of the outskirts, they passed a travel trailer parked in the massive, barren parking lot of an abandoned outlet mall. Installed atop the trailer was a neon sign that blazed prominently in the fading light of dusk. "Tattoos," announced the sign. No words were exchanged but they knew what had to be done. Brakes were slammed, the Mustang was U-turned, and into the lot they pulled. Francine got her ass tattooed with "Property of Victor" in the font of Monotype Corsiva. Victor wanted one put on his butt too but the tattoo artist, upon observation of his hind quarters, told him that it was not as an appealing canvas as that of Francine's, no offense, and frankly, she did not want to go near the tangle of curly ass-hair.

He reluctantly agreed with the assessment and went ahead and took her recommendation and had the tattoo placed spiraling down and around his forearm. When the tattoo artist finished, she beamed, not only in pride of her freshly inked work, but also in appreciation of the words Victor had chosen from the works of Nabokov, something about fire in the loins, sin and soul.

After leaving the tattoo trailer and while driving through the stretch of desert, Victor's knee felt of a thousand daggers and sure enough, 30 minutes later, metric tons of water fell out of the sky and there was a flash flood and they almost died in this instant river that carried them into the desolate desert but an empty, oarless rowboat came floating along in the nick of time. The torrent deposited the boat and its harried passengers on a sand dune 30 miles later. Francine thanked God for their surviving the flood. Victor thanked the inventor of boats. By morning, the clouds had cleared, drying out the terrain, and so they commenced their trek toward the highway in order to flag down a ride, but the sun pounded them and they almost died from exposure and dehydration but they ultimately made it to the highway where a trucker picked them up. Francine thanked God for their surviving the desert. Victor thanked evolution for programming living beings with the will to survive for the sake of perpetuating the species. They promised each other that next time, their mode of transportation to Vegas would be via airplane.

***

Francine gave birth to Jack eight months and 14 days later. Victor had loved nothing and no one except for Francine, but now, here was a thing called a child popping out of his beloved, and this child, his son, gave him bone-deep warm fuzzies, the sheer joy of which made Victor cry a little bit. Love amazed him once again. Then a daughter, Jill, came 30 months later and love amazed him again, once again. He knew that there was shit going down in the world so it almost seemed unfair that he of all people should be blessed with such utter happiness. Oh well.

They lived in Victor's house until it burned to a crisp in the middle of the night after being struck by lightning during a storm that produced no precipitation but packed an electrical wallop. The family almost died that night but didn't because Victor was awake in anticipation of potential doom due to the sledgehammering pain of his bum knee. He came to associate the knee pain less and less with the day Francine said yes, and more and more with imminent death by natural disaster.

Though they could have afforded a McMansion, the Gottenbergs opted for a split-level Ranch style with four bedrooms, two and a half baths. There was no fence around the front yard so Victor put one up, which was of the white picket variety. He refurbished the remnants of a tree house left in the oak tree by the previous owners. Hung a tire swing from the thickest branch. The lawn was perfectly shorn, the color of lagoon-green. On summery Sundays, the neighborhood filled with the scent of fresh-cut grass, the sound of children at play, and birdsongs sounding very much like the country tune he'd first heard years ago: a woman singing about a broken heart, sweet revenge.

Jack was now 7 years old. He had inherited Dad's lankness and slouch, the 'fro too, as well as the larger than average brain — he'd already skipped a grade. Jill was 4 years old, and like her mom, had frizzy, unruly hair, under which were ears growing into those of the size of wings of a small flying animal. But her nose was maintaining normal size, so far. Jill, too, possessed mental dexterity, reading at the 3rd grade level and able to beat her brother at chess, which was a source of tantrum-making consternation for Jack.

Victor had retired from his teaching job after licensing the rights to the patent of his V-Gott Fuser to a Chinese auto parts manufacturer desperate to get into the medical supply business. Henry had been right when he proclaimed that the V-Gott Fuser could be "worth millions, possibly billions!" It was a shame that Henry was currently serving time in the Federal Penitentiary for various drug related and organ/body-parts trade violations.

With his free time, Victor finished his novel about the college professor obsessed with a dead girlfriend and driven to insanity. The manuscript got the attention of an agent who got it published. Obtained a three-book deal. Sold the film rights. Told Victor to not rest on his laurels and to get crackin' on the novel series when the going was hot.

With her free time, Francine started an all-girl band with the women in her neighborhood. She played bass and was the lead singer and songwriter. The band's sound was of grunge-revival infused with '60s inspiration. On guitar was Katy, who also had free time because she'd been fired from the school district for her radical teaching philosophy despite the uptick in student test scores. The keyboard was played by Monica, a 40-something former supermodel whose husband was doing time for his indiscretion re: a prostitute who happened to be an undercover cop. And on drums was a woman named Eunice whose background was unknown because she didn't say much but she sure could beat the living shit out of the kit.

Francine and her bandmates practiced in the garage while Victor wrote his novels. How he loved hearing Francine rasp out her poetic lyrics. And the music energized him, during which time he cranked out his best work. Though he did wonder about where that tinge of anger tucked in between the lines of her songs came from.

The band became tight and seasoned as they made the rounds of local gigs and they soon were approached by an A&R guy with an indie label who signed them to a deal and released their first album which topped the college charts and cracked Billboard's Top 25.

All was good in the land of Gottenberg.

***

It had been one those summery Sundays: the scent of fresh cut grass was smelled, sound of children playing was heard, birdsongs bounced off eardrums. At dinnertime, Victor was in the backyard barbecuing up some steaks, fresh corn on the cob from the farmers market. Francine in the kitchen, whipped up her famous coleslaw and potato salad. On the windowsill, two apple pies cooling. The kids in the living room watching TV, totally absorbed in a PBS series about String Theory. And after the family gleefully polished off dinner, they did their nightly assembly line routine of clearing the table and washing the dishes while singing songs of Gilbert and Sullivan.

Once the kids were put to bed, Francine and Victor went skinny-dipping in the pool, and afterward they spread out on a towel on the lawn and took turns reading Rumi's love poems to each other under the happy-face moon. They went to bed, watched some late night programming then proceeded to do some love-making. And when Victor woke up during the night, ready for a second time, Francine was not in bed. He found her in the living room lit only by the moonlight filtering through the blinds. She sat naked on the sofa, handling a 9mm handgun.

She looked up and asked, "Do you know how to work one of these?"

"Aim, pull trigger."

"Smart-ass," she said, smirking. "How do you load it is what I'm asking. Do you know? Of course you do, right?"

Victor picked up the box of ammo off the coffee table and sat next to her. She handed him the gun and he released the magazine, loaded it, snapped it back in place, put one more bullet in the chamber and handed the gun back to her.

Francine placed the tip of the gun barrel underneath her chin. "What do you think?"

"I don't know." Victor contemplated. "I don't think I would chance it. What if you mis-aimed and only blew off a part of your jaw?"

"Okay then, what about this?" She stuck the barrel into her mouth.

"No. For the same reason. You could end up shooting

yourself through the cheek or something and there you are, still alive, gagging and choking on your blood."

Pulling the barrel out of her mouth, she said, "Sounds painful."

"Totally."

"What's your suggestion?"

"Point it flush against the flat surface of the temple. That should give you the highest probability of success." Victor got up and headed toward the kitchen. "I'm gonna get some water. Want some?"

"No thanks," she said, pointing the gun to her right temple.

Victor pulled out a glass from the cupboard and filled it from the tap. As he was about to take a swig, Francine called out.

"Victor? Will you love me forever?"

"I am genetically predisposed to loving you forever." He drank. "Mmm. Good stuff."

"Victor? Will you tell the kids I love them?"

"Okay," he said. After a few more gulps of water, a thought came to him. "You know what would really work?" he excitedly yelled out to Francine. "Forget the gun. Instead, drive the Mustang at a hundred miles per hour into the back end of a flatbed tractor trailer, you know the ones where the ass end of it is basically shaped like a guillotine? Not only will that shear the roof off the car, it'll take your head right along with it." He smiled, proud of his suggestion. But then something started to feel very wrong and his telltale knee pulsated, felt about to explode, and he asked himself, "What did you just say to her?" Dread body-slammed Victor, made him tremble and he dropped the glass which bounced off the ceramic tile floor. Tried sprinting to the living room but it was like running in sand. He finally made it but the gunshot had rang out and he fell to his knees at Francine's side where she slumped, having fallen off of the sofa. Tried to lift her but his grip kept slipping from all the blood gushing out of her shot-through head. Then there was the low volume screaming coming from who knew where. Sounded like a man's voice saying, Francine, Francine, Francine, and it kept getting louder until Victor screamed himself awake.

He jolted upright in bed yelling out her name. Stopped and was panting and shivering from cold-soaked sweat. Leapt out of bed but his legs gave out and he face-planted onto the carpet. Get up goddammit, get up, he chastised himself and he did and ran to the other bedroom. When he got there, he collapsed, let go a long groan of relief. She was still alive, in bed and in a drug-induced coma, intubated and breathing with the help of the ventilator. The monitor showed her vital signs to be a-okay. Three weeks since her rebirth and she was doing fine, just fine, healing nicely while he was coming apart at the seams apparently. He laughed at himself, then crawled over to the bed, pulled himself up, got in and snuggled next to her.

Tried to sleep but couldn't and soon the dawn light seeped through the fabric of the curtain and the room glowed a faint orange. He thought about Jack and Jill, mourned them, the loss of his dream children. He missed the split-level Ranch, the tree house, the white picket fence. The pool for skinny-dipping. The dish washing routine accompanied by songs from the Pirates of Penzance. The nightly love-making. The band. Writing the novel series. He checked his forearm. No tattoo. He lamented not having that tattoo.

Francine as his wife.

It had to happen. He would make it happen no matter what.

Victor eventually fell asleep while mumbling, prayer-like, "Happily ever after, happily ever after, happily ever after…"

CHAPTER FIFTEEN
Lies Swallowed With A Morphine Chaser
(or in the alternative)
The Vagina Situation

And then, she awoke.

It hurt to breathe, hurt to have blood coursing through her, and in fact, everything hurt and she was flat on her back and couldn't move, and when she opened her eyes, the light hammered the nerve endings deep into her brain. Some guy stood over her and she wanted to say to him, hey, man, I'm hurting like a mother-effer here and by the way, where am I? But she could barely control her mouth and it came out sounding like she was saying "hi," and then this guy was like crying and his tears plopped all over her face and she tried to say, dude, maybe you should grab a hanky or something, but again her mouth barely functioned so it probably looked like she was giving him a slight smile instead.

154

A woman whose jaw-dropping beauty was offset by a crooked glass eye and a gnarly scar down her cheek came into the frame. Her non-crooked eye sparkled with glee as if she just brought a dead person back to life or something. Then the guy was saying he was going to administer an injection to put her into a coma so she could recover comfortably and he would see her again in about 6 to 8 weeks and that he was beyond super glad to have her back.

The next time she awoke, there was a lot less pain than before, and the guy, whom she eventually found out to be Victor, was saying welcome back and this will only take a second as he withdrew what he called an endotracheal tube. He tossed the tube aside and said how do you feel, Francine, and she thought, oh, I guess she is me.

She coughed coughed coughed until she could finally say, "I'm really thirsty." Her voice extra raspy as if from rust. "For a gin and tonic."

Victor laughed and said, "Awesome."

She tried to sit up but her body felt like sludge and was unresponsive and the pain that was a lot less than before was now making some noise. "Ow, shit, sweet mother of pain." She gave up and lay back down. "Make that a gin and tonic with a morphine chaser." After a lengthy groan, she asked, "What happened to me and why is my memory of you, myself, and the past, like looking through smoky glass, and who was that woman with the crooked eye and the scar, and finally, why are you sporting an erection?" He wore a faded-out rock concert T-shirt and flower-print boxers and there was the telltale tentpole effect upon his underwear. "Please tell me we were at least lovers because, otherwise, you having an hard-on for a convalescent woman craving a stiff drink and painkillers is kind of weird."

He did a squiggly-line smile, said, "Yeah, uh-uh-uh, for sure, we were that. Lovers, I mean."

She weakly raised her left arm to look at her hand, checked for a ring to see if the term "lovers" might mean something more in this context. No ring. Disappointed and relieved at the same time. But what was with this scar around her wrist and why was her hand looking mealy and folded up claw-like. She compared it to the right hand. Not even the same. She pointed her left hand at Victor, shooting him the question with her eyes.

"Uh-uh, yeah. That. I really tried to find a perfect match but we were pressed for time. But it's close, right? And it seems that maybe there are issues with the nerve graft, hence the weird claw thing going on with the fingers."

Francine re-shot her question with emphasis on the fact that he perhaps missed a step in his answer.

"Right," Victor acknowledged. Took a moment. And as his tent deflated, he said, "You were in a car accident. A pretty bad one and stuff happened to parts of your body, for example, the loss of your left hand."

"What happened to the original?"

"Nobody knows."

"And whose lovely, shriveled up, replacement hand is this?"

"An anonymous donor," he said straight-faced.

"A hand donor? Anonymous? You make it sound like someone walking into a sperm bank, but instead it's a hand bank, and she says I'm right-handed anyway and I could use a few bucks so please lop it off and give it to someone in need." Her words came out pissy, she wasn't sure why.

"Francine—"

"So what else isn't me?" She flung off the bed sheet and saw that she wore the same looking boxers as his and an ill-fitting bra. A massive scar, as if someone had carved an upside down "Y" on her torso. She whispered ohmygod. Turned to Victor. "Tell me."

He swallowed difficultly. "Like I said, it was a bad accident."

"Tell me."

And he did, first telling about her being in a coma from the accident and going through the list of replacement organs plus the right leg. She then asked, I was in a coma really? and were all these frickin' parts from the same "anonymous" donor? and he said no not really except for the leg. As for the other stuff, "from various" was how he put it. She stared at the ceiling thinking I am but the sum of my parts then tried to get up again, not caring about the pain, forcing her sludgy body to work already dammit while Victor told her this was not a good idea just yet. But she did the if-you-truly-love-me-you'll-help-me thing, forcing Victor to comply. Once she got onto her feet with his help, she had him take (basically carry) her to the bathroom where she leaned against the sink, in front of the mirror, eyes closed for the moment, preparing herself. She eventually opened her eyes and looked at her face. She'd seen better she was sure, but this one was not too shabby despite the crooked nose and ears the size of wings of a small flying animal. Checked out her body. Her legs trembled and all she could see were the scars. Then she noticed something in the shadow of her chin. Tilted her head slightly and gasped. Just to confirm, she turned a little to the right, little to the left. Sure enough, the scar circled her neck. Francine asked Victor's reflection, "Exactly how bad was this accident?"

"It's not what you're thinking," he said trying to laugh it off. "Just a bit of neck surgery was all."

"So in all seriousness you're telling me that this zipper necklace is not the result of my head being re-attached to my neck from having been chopped off in what you keep calling a 'bad' accident?"

"Hahahahaha, Francine, you're a riot. Haha, I mean because, well, as I'm sure you know, successfully reattaching a completely severed head is basically impossible even in this day and age, and if your head was chopped off, you would be, like, dead. Ha. And do you know what's more impossible than successfully reattaching a severed head? Bringing a dead person back to life. Unless of course there was some super genius talented person out there in the world somewhere trying to do those things but that person I'm sure does not exist. Most likely."

"Okay. Stop sweating already and knock off the talking-weird thing. I believe you." She checked out the rest of her body aside from the scars. Her skin was practically translucent, as if she hadn't seen the light of day in a decade. She grimaced. Her muscle tone was non-existent, basically a skin-bag of sagginess. She scowled. Then there was that smell that lingered which she tried to ignore because, really, could that possibly be her? But she could no longer dismiss it. Sniffed herself deeply: a skunkish funk with a mix of month old gym-locker-towel smell and a hint of something like intense foot odor. Francine cried.

Victor held her, and after a moment of mutual lovey-doveyness, she felt it pressing against her abdomen, said, "Are you having a hard-on again?" Happy nods from Victor. "But why? I'm disgusting-looking, and the stench! And I feel like I'm contagious somehow." He ground his crotch against her reciprocal area. "Whoa there, stud," she said. "I don't think my body's quite ready to be open for business just yet. I'll definitely need that morphine chaser at least. And by the way? Is this vagina original, is it even mine?"

Victor cracked up.

"Stop," she said, trying not to crack herself up. "I am being serious about this vagina situation. Stop it, stop laughing." He didn't, and his eyeballs were pouring out laugh-tears which made his eyes sparkle like lollipops the flavor of sunshine. And then there was something trying to come out from the depths of her brain, these images, wait no, not images, something ephemeral, like a dream you just dreamt but woke up from and couldn't remember anything about it except the aura of it, and the aura she was getting about Victor was of a lovingness, sweetness, braininess, and a would-do-anything-for-her-ness. There was also a touch of something else to this aura, like thinking you're biting into milk chocolate but instead it turned out to be dark chocolate, slightly bitter, not as sweet as hoped. But that part seemed to be outweighed by the other parts, and boy, did she know then and there that this guy, this dude called Victor, loved the living shit out of her, so she told him, "I love you too."

And Victor said, "Whaaat?" Then passed out, a smile on his unconscious face.

When he came to, Victor gave Francine the morphine chaser and she slept for a while and when she woke up, she craved a good scrub and asked Victor to help her because she could barely reach around to scour her own stinky ass. So he drew a perfectly temperate bath, soaped her up, scrubbed her down. Afterward, Francine said she felt sparkly-new, energized, thank you very much. And then she started asking a lot of frickin' questions:

Q: If I was already in a coma from the accident, why did you put me into a drug-induced one?

A: Huh?

Q: It's what I remember you saying, the first time I woke up. And you never did answer my question about who that amazingly beautiful woman with the crooked eye and scar down her cheek was.

A: I think that's the morphine talking because that makes no sense. Speaking of which, would you like more? Of the morphine?

Q: Of course I want more. But for now, can you answer my question?

A: [Victor did an exaggerated shrug accompanied by an expression of accusing someone of conjuring up such a nutty scene from tripping on acid or from being in a super deep coma, though of course he knew that the woman named Eunice was for real]

Q: So you're saying I dreamt it up.

A: Yeee-ess.

Q: [A hard squint]

A: [Hard squint back]

Q: Whatever. Anyway. When I told you "I love you too," why did you pass out?

A: Low blood sugar. I skipped breakfast. And lunch.

Q: So it wasn't because you were super surprised to hear me say that?

A: No no, you used to say it all the time. All the time. I mean, all the time.

Q: Why do you keep repeating that?

A: ...

Q: How did we meet?

A: We've known each other since we were kids.

Q: Really? Because you're older looking than me.

A: Here's the explanation: a coma stops the aging process, so, there you go.

Q: [Quizzically raised eyebrow]

A: What? It's totally true. [It wasn't. And frankly, a pretty lame lie at that]

Q: [Still with the quizzically raised eyebrow]

A: Okay. It was about 10 years, your coma.

Q: [a dramatic pause, a dropping of the jaw, and then:] Can you pour me that stiff drink now?

***

Backyard patio, Victor barbecuing steaks, fresh corn on the cob. Henry splayed out on the lawn chair nearby tossing back a beer. They watched Francine gingerly walking back and forth on the lawn, part of her daily exercise and recovery routine. Still needed the use of a cane but she had gained weight, muscle tone, and her skin looked not so see-through anymore. Good progress in the 10 days since her "awakening."

Henry had been seriously pissed when he heard Victor brought Francine out of her coma without him and that Victor told her a bunch of lies that Henry now had to go along with lest he rock her world in a bad way. But Henry chilled out once he saw Francine alive for real and got reacquainted with her and she sweetly sassed him which made him act goofy, the big lug.

"What kind of bullshit did you feed her about her family?" asked Henry.

"That she was an only child and her parents disappeared just before she started on her masters program. They were an adventurous couple, her parents, but their trip to the Amazon was their undoing."

"Not bad." Henry popped a cap off another beer. "It sounds like her memory still hasn't shown up."

"You're right about that."

"That was a pretty convenient side effect, yeah? Like a clean slate. A huge break for you, man, what with the primrose path you've paved for her." Henry laughed like he was joking though clearly he was not.

Victor held his tongue. But Henry was right. Victor had taken a huge chance lying to her, betting on Francine never recollecting her past, especially the memory of her not ever having loved him and having told him that she couldn't love him except as a friend. He flipped the steaks, a good sizzle going. Rolled the corn over. "It's not like I planned the memory loss," Victor finally said.

"Uh-huh." Henry didn't take his eyes off Francine. "Are you sure that's even her?"

Victor didn't get the joke, but laughed anyway. "Who do you think she is?"

"Look, man. Physically, we can see she's Francine. But what left her body and what's now come back, may be two different things."

"Like a 'soul,' you mean? Doctor, please. Enough with this existential bullshit. Nothing *left* her. The electrical impulses of her brain were shut down, her consciousness was put on temporary hiatus. All we did was re-ignite those impulses, and now, the Francine of yore is back."

"The condition you just described is called 'totally dead' for a reason."

As Victor watched Francine hobble her way toward them, he said to Henry, "I think I've proven that terminology wrong."

"Hey, boys," she said. Eyed the grill. "Mmm. Me hungry. Me want meat."

"You're making real progress," said Henry and handed her a beer.

"Thanks. The replacement leg's starting to feel like my own. In fact, my own leg is starting to feel like my own."

"Good one."

"Gotta pee." She headed into the house.

"I don't think she used to have a sense humor," said Henry.

"Of course she did."

"Not like that."

"Stop."

She came back out, sidled up to Victor, gave him the empty beer bottle. "Do I have time for a quick shower? I walked like a whole 50 feet today. I'm sweating like a sow, don't want to be smelling like one."

"Go for it," said Victor, checking the steaks. "There's a few more minutes till these are cooked up just the way you like it."

"Thanks, love," she said, faking a British accent badly, and planted a juicy kiss on his receptive lips.

There was the clang-clang of Henry's beer bottle bouncing off the concrete patio. Francine limped back into the house. Victor stared at the bottle not being picked up, spilling out its malty content.

"Are you fucking her?" Tenor of belligerence in Henry's question.

"What? Why are you even asking me that?" To which Henry answered with a glare and Victor responded with, "It's none of your damn business, but whatever. The answer is no."

"Right. I'm glad someone's reaping the benefits of *our* crime spree. I did tell you about that cop right, that fucking cop who wanted to arrest *my* ass for *our* acts?"

"Why do you even care? You were ready to give up on Francine, how many times? Remember that?"

"Fuck you. She's my friend too. But I'm not the one lying to her. I'm not the one taking advantage of her. And I didn't defy God's will just so I could bring her back to be my fuck-toy."

Victor threw down the tongs, made for Henry, but Henry leapt out of the lawn chair, stood huge with his 6'8", 320 pound frame, daring Victor to keep coming at him and to experience death by giant fist. Victor got smart and made a detour to the cooler and fetched a beer instead. Headed back to the grill, mumbling, "That was a fucked-up thing to say."

Henry grabbed another bottle too, said, "I'll take this one to go," and made a rancorous exit.

***

Henry sat hunched on his bed, the only light coming from the cellphone in his palm. He punched in the phone number.

It rang 10 times before she answered, "Detective

Lavenza."

"What are you wearing?" said Henry in a drowsy voice.

After a beat she said, "A thong and tassels."

"Very hot."

"Now if you're done getting yourself off, I've got a shitload of paperwork to get back to."

"Don't go. This is Henry Clerval."

"Henry?"

"Yup. It is I, Detective."

"This is a surprise."

"Is it? Good. Wanna come over?"

"Henry, we had this conversation already, didn't we?"

"Maybe I have some information you want."

"Maybe you should tell me then."

"Tsk tsk, Detective. You have to come over and have drinks with me before I can tell you. We had fun the last time we had drinks, didn't we?"

"I was this close to shooting you in the face."

"That's right!" He laughed. "See? Good times."

"Henry, I'm going to hang up now."

"No no, wait! Don't hang up. Please?"

An air-leak sigh, then, "If it's company you want, I can refer you to some decent hookers. Strictly high class."

"No, that's not what I... Never mind."

He shivered, hugged himself and lay fetal-positioned on the bed. Dropped the phone onto the floor, the Detective's voice still coming through: "Henry? Henry? Henry..."

CHAPTER SIXTEEN
Intense Smell Of Rotting Baloney Sandwich And Copious Amount of Goo

Francine was in a funk. Having lost 10 years to a coma made her angsty. And although physically, Francine seemed to be recovering, her surgical scars still looked as fresh as the day they were sewn up. "A hideous human quilt," is how she described herself. And the left hand? Why was it not healing, not functioning? It hung from her wrist limply, a dead claw. The attachment point seeped periodically, smelled like lunch-bag baloney sandwich that had been left in a school locker for a semester.

"It's depressing, this thing, like a rotting corpse of a small and weird looking rodent that is fused to my wrist. Ugh!"

"I think maybe we need to get you a new one."

"Where from? The hand store?" said Francine with a note of derision.

Needed to change the subject, a lifting of the mood, wanted to avoid this whole depression business, so, "Wanna go to the mall?" suggested Victor.

Francine traced the neck scar with her index finger. This would be her first public outing since her awakening. She thought about it. Asked, "Don't you have to work?"

"I can do whatever I want."

She thought about it some more, then shrugged. "Okay, whatever."

At the mall, first and foremost, new underwear was what she wanted. Sick of wearing his stupid boxers and the ill-fitting bra. He let her go to town, delighted he was. Then, clothes of the non-underwear variety. She ignored Victor's lame suggestions and relied on her own taste. Was in fact relieved that she did indeed have taste. She indulged Victor in trying on a sun dress with a print of nubile orchids, and when she came out of the dressing room to show him that maybe it was not such a bad idea, a 5-year-oldish punk of a kid at the side of his shopping mother, stared at her, lingered on the neck, the left hand. He grimaced, acted like he was barfing. She flipped the kid off and the little pissant cried to Mommy who ignored him, then Francine disappointed Victor by telling him the dress was a no-go.

Victor, a little sweaty. Worrisome smile. "Forget the dress. If it makes you unhappy."

She side-eyed the little punk.

"That kid's an asshole," said Victor. "You're beautiful no matter what. Got it?"

She let out an assenting sigh, peeled the dress off right then, stood there in her quilt-work glory. Handed him the dress. "Okay. The dress is a go."

They were headed toward the coffee shop when a couple of girls with the piercings, the tattoos, the black color scheme including leather for wardrobe, stared at Francine but in a good way, one of them giving a smile and a thumbs-up and the other doing a hand motion at her own neck then at Francine's and said, "That shit is too cool. I'm tempted to do a cut-and-stitch on my own damn self."

Francine said to Victor, "My shit *is* too cool."

"Don't get cocky," he said.

She couldn't stop grinning.

At the coffee shop, he ordered a regular coffee and she got the frilly type "coffee" concoction drink with whipped cream and sucked it down in amazement as if such a tasty treat had not existed prior to her going "comatose" ten years ago which correctly did not exist at the time. Then they went to the specialty lingerie store, her suggestion, to get undies not so practical, wink wink. And afterwards they walked past a jewelry store and she stopped so he stopped. He looked at what she was looking at: a pricey piece of hardware, the kind with the retina-shatteringly brilliant rock, the kind given to a woman by a man who wanted to marry her for real.

Francine gazed at Victor. "You loved me so much that you never gave up on bringing me out of that coma and getting me put back together while anyone else would have just pulled the plug. So, what I want to ask is, were we ever...did you ever ask me to—"

"I did," said Victor, surprising himself with the quick lie. But he was in so deep already, what was the harm in telling another momentous one?

"You asked me to marry you?"

"Yes."

"What did I say?"

Guilt tapped him on the shoulder and said, whoa there, fella, maybe you might want to think this through. Victor elbowed Guilt in the face, told Francine, "'Yes' is what you said."

Francine glowed for a moment then got back to business. "The ring? I assume there was one?"

Being all gaga had put Victor two steps behind, stupidly did not anticipate this utterly obvious question. Quickly went through the permutations to assess the most plausible response, then the bell went "ting" and the lightbulb went whatever sound a lightbulb makes when it flashes on.

"The ring was on your left hand, the one that was lost in the accident." He smiled inside.

"Oh. Right," she said, melancholy-like, and turned back to the display window. "That accident sucked ass. It made me lose the ring and it robbed me of the memory of your proposal. And of course it almost killed me."

"We can always get another ring," he said, knowing that there was a sufficient amount of the research fund left to embezzle from, while ignoring the impending audit of the spending of said funds.

"And the proposal?" she said to the display window. Victor got down on one knee, prompting a grin from Francine but she said, "No, wait. Not here. Let's find the right time, right place. Surprise me again."

"Okay. It's a deal."

They hit the food court, decided on Chinese. Then to the frozen yogurt place on the second floor for dessert. They ate the fat-free creamy yumminess while leaning against the railing and watching the patrons feeding at the trough in the food court below. Then, there was an intense smell of rotting baloney sandwich, copious amount of goo leaking from Francine's left wrist.

"Oh shit," she said, seeing the goo-leak. "Victor, look. This is not going to—" As she was saying these words, she made a gesture with her left arm as if flinging her hand to emphasize the point of the crappy situation with said hand, not meaning at all to literally fling it, but that was exactly what happened. The hand detached from the wrist and flew about 15 feet out into the food court airspace then fell and landed into a kids-meal chicken teriyaki bowl. The bowl belonged to a toddler in a high chair who picked up the hand, giggled, and proceeded to suck on the index finger. The mother of the infant didn't notice right away, being too busy yacking on her phone, but when she did notice, she screamed ohmygod is that an actual severed hand you have in your mouth?! This freaked out the toddler and made the kid suck the finger harder, the clawy, oozy hand dangling from the mouth, and the mother let go a howl of horror, and soon the surrounding people noticed, which started a scream cascade, which was followed by a barf cascade, then a panicked-mob exodus. The weak and infirm were trampled in the process.

Victor and Francine gawked at the scene until he noticed that the goo mixed with blood was oozing out of her handless wrist and dribbling onto the floor, a gross puddle forming.

He said to her, "We need to get that under control," and led her back into the frozen yogurt place and snagged a thick wad of napkins and pressed the wad to her gruesome wrist stump. "Here. Hold this firm against your wrist."

She nodded and did just so. Asked, "Shouldn't we be calling 9-1-1? I mean, losing one's hand is probably not a good thing, on top of which, stuff is like gushing out of my wrist here."

"I really, really prefer not to do that. They'll ask questions. Loads of them."

"Why? What's the big deal with questions? It's not like anything illegal is happening. Right?"

"Um... I just need to get you home. I'll take care of it."

"You know what?" she said tossing the gunk-soaked wad of napkins and replacing it with a fresh wad. "Despite profuse amounts of stuff coming out of my wrist, and me getting kind of lightheaded because of it, I totally have utter faith in you."

He was about to say that is so awesome of you to say when there was a squirrel-ish squeal. They turned, saw the teenage girl standing behind the cash register staring at them with bugged out eyes.

Victor said, "Oh hi." Noticed her quivering hands. "Gee, your hands are lovely. Can we maybe have the left one?" Her eyes rolled white and she fainted. Hit the floor like a sack of doorknobs.

"Victor!"

"Sorry, just kidding, kind of," he said, then watched Francine replace the soaked wad of napkins yet again, the seepage not slowing down. "Francine. We need to get your ass back home asap."

They stepped out of the frozen yogurt shop, checked out the scene below. There was a convergence of the mall security personnel on those two-wheeled, self balancing, personal transportation scooter type things. The food court was cordoned off with the non-official version of crime-scene tape. The hand, confiscated from the toddler and placed and secured as evidence in a doggy bag from the Chinese food place.

And then one of the scooters came at Victor and Francine. The scooter whined, being pushed to its full-speed limit. "Halt!" screamed the security person driving the scooter.

"Oh shit," said Victor and Francine at the same time.

Victor took her existing right hand into his left and she took his left hand into her existing right. They asked each other, "Are you ready for this?" They said yes then high-tailed it through the semi-light traffic of the mid weekday mall-goers.

The security person screamed, "Halt!" one more time, at which point the scooter hit the puddle of Francine's gross goo and slid only slightly but the security person panicked and abandoned ship by leaping off the scooter, only to bellyflop atop of the railing and bounce and flip then plummet to the food court below. Landed atop the cheese-on-a-stick-eating guy who was idly watching the mayhem. The security person survived the fall, rolled off the cheese guy who did not fare as well. The security person stuck a palm to the guy's neck feeling for a pulse, and after a moment, shouted, "Man down! Man down!"

In the meantime, the scooter, no worse for wear, came to a halt beside Victor and Francine who had stopped running when they heard the Doppler effect of the wail of the security person taking a plunge. Victor hopped on the scooter and started her up. Francine followed, strapped her arms around him. The scooter scooted outta there, wheeling down the mall. Victor looked over his shoulder. No sign of the security personnel.

"We made it, Francine."

She smooched him on the cheek. "My hero."

He savored the kiss, and in his head, he replayed the audio: my hero my hero my hero. As he spotted the sign pointing them to the Super Gigantic Parking Structure, he tried to remember whether they parked in the Blue Sector, Level 6, Area S, or in the Pink Sector, Level 9, Area Z. Shrugged as if not a big deal. It would all work out.

***

What an utter cluster fuck, Ell thought, as she and Hobin left the Medical Examiner's office. The intense headache made her squint from the daylight despite her wearing shades. When they reached their generic government issue sedan, she grabbed her jacket from the back seat, pulled out a flask from the secret compartment pocket and knocked it back, finished it off the remnant. Hoisted herself onto the hood. Needed to make sense of what Assistant M.E. Kenny Blokenhaal had just conveyed.

Okay, so, this food court hand that used to belong to Lanna Vodak was being used by someone else who also happened to have Francine Styne's blood coursing through her apparently. The "Lanna" part of it was at least plausible. But Francine was long dead. What the fuck? Ell at least had a semblance of a lead on Lanna. But this Francine thing, like a bad penny. The case dead-ended 10 years ago, chalked it up to administrative incompetence and bungling. Francine was likely tagged as a "Jane Doe" and shipped off to a cadaver reseller or, more likely, given that her body was goodly decimated, she was cremated and her ashes swept under the rug so to speak.

When Percy Maplewerm's shenanigans came to light, some, including Ell, tried to pin Francine's disappearance on him but that ultimately made no sense because Percy specialized in selling dead hotties to his fellow necrophiliacs of the world. And in order to be considered a "hottie," parts of your body couldn't look like contents of sausage casing and you certainly had to be sporting a head. Couldn't have given Francine away gratis even. Or could he?

Ell's headache worsened. Watched Hobin pace, mumbling to himself about zombies and ghosts. She hopped off the hood, tossed the keys to Hobin. He was like, "Uh?" and the keys bounced out of his hand and into his face, then clanged on the pavement. He picked them up, shuffled quickly to Ell.

"So what do you make of this, Ell? I mean it's weird, totally weird. The hand situation is bad enough. But this whole Francine Styne situation? It's as if she came back from the dead and is going around stealing body parts for her own use because her parts are rotting from being dead for 10 years! And eating the brains of the victims for sustenance!"

Ell rolled her eyes. "Don't start freaking out on me."

"It's too late." He hugged himself like he was cold. "Doesn't the department have a division that deals with stuff like this?"

"As a matter fact, yes. It's called the Lavenza and Hobin division."

Hobin slumped, looked like he was going to cry.

"Jeez, Hobin. Do you need a hug or something?"

He answered in the affirmative by clamping onto Ell's torso like a frightened baby monkey on mama monkey.

"Uhhh, I was actually kind of joking about the hugging thing," said Ell as she stood there, not hugging back.

"This helps. Thank you, Ell," he muttered.

She let it go for a minute, until: "Hobin? If that's not your gun pressing into my thigh, I will seriously be pissed off." And at the moment she finished that sentence, he planted a slobbery kiss on her open mouth, most of the contact taking place on her lower lip and chin. She slammed her knee into his crotch and he released from Ell and assumed the bent-over position, clutching at the damaged goods, whimpering. Ell didn't bother saying what the fuck is wrong with you and just grabbed him by the scruff, opened the back door to the sedan, and shoved him in, giving a heel-kick to his ass for good measure, and cussed up a storm about her magnetic polarity which only seemed to attract assholes, idiots, jerkwads, etc.

CHAPTER SEVENTEEN
A Spiteful Pile Of Raw Meat

Victor sat at his usual corner table in the on-campus mini food mall that had a beer bar, a Mexican food place, the Italian-mostly-pizza place, the burger joint, and the quickie mart. He chewed on a bean and cheese burrito and drank from a frosted mug of beer while listening to couple of seniors and soon to be grad students asking him to please, please, please, start teaching classes again, though they knew he needed to focus his energy primarily on the vitally important research project they had heard about. But they still insisted. The duet of these two students, these two young women, was ironically not based on intellectual discourse, but on their perceived cuteness: the smiles, the body-english accentuating their areas of strength, the hair fling, the banter, the not too trendy trendy clothes, flashes of cute tiny tattoos of cute tiny things.

Victor ate, drank, gave a sporting grin. "Maybe, ladies. We'll see what the new semester holds." He garnered this type of attention more that occasionally from the women of this ilk, though it perplexed him as to why. Perhaps it was his unattainability, whether of flesh or conviction, not so easily swayed by "cute." Reputed to be an immovable object. Immovable except when under the influence of a certain type. "Peculiar" was how some described this "type."

As the ladies were doing their aw-shucks cute pouts, a woman, mid-50ish, made toward Victor. The throng of lunch-going students, Pavlovian-response-like, parted to make way for her. She wore a very businessy business suit, her dye-job head of hair shorn short. Carried some of that middle-age weight gain, but not so bad, gave her curves some heft was all. She looked her age but her face resonated with the comeliness of her youth. Eyes steely with intellect and experience and wisdom. And weariness. She was the Anti-Cute.

"Ladies," she said to the Cutes. "I need to have a chat with Professor Gottenberg. Perhaps you can continue pestering him with your youthful coquettishness later, at office hours maybe, as would be more appropriate."

The Cutes' expression was of a glare saying who-the-fuck-do-you-think-you-are but their resolve soon dissolved, buckling under the matriarchal brawn. With averted eyes, bowed heads, the ladies shuffled away.

The woman took a seat across from Victor, unshouldered the shoulder bag, a heavy thunk as it landed on the tabletop. She looked over her freed shoulder at the Cutes walking away.

"It's a shame you know," she said. "They often won't

realize until it's too late that relying on their interior qualities and having a sense of self-worth is what really counts and what gets you through the day ultimately. But it's too easy for them, isn't it? I mean look at them, all of them. They're beautiful, oozing with youth, vitality and sex, bodies that have yet to be ravaged by gravity and cellulite." She turned to face Victor. "I should know. I was *the* hot piece of ass in my time." Her eyes lit up. The sparkle though, quickly faded. "But look at me now." Gestured with her arm as if to indicate her current, less than desirable place in the universe. "Anyhow. I would apologize for chasing away your fan club but I won't because I suspect that your agenda is filled with more substantive matters."

Amused, Victor almost laughed. "Who are you?"

She held out her hand. "Blake Lemmonshire." After they shook, she pulled out a pack of cigarettes from the shoulder bag, propped a cigarette between her lips. "Is it okay to smoke in here?" Victor shook his head. "Oh for godssake." Tossed the cigarette on the table. "This may be hypocritical of me but the law can be a pain in the ass sometimes."

Victor asked, "I'm sorry, did we have a meeting planned that I forgot about?"

"No. I should be the one apologizing for dropping in on you, but frankly, the element of surprise is to my advantage." She slid a business card across the table. The card said:

United States Department of the Treasury
Blake Lemmonshire
Special Investigator

Victor's armpits went instantly moist. Felt as if the ingested burrito was reversing course, heartbeat not so mellow anymore. Longed for the Cutes to come back.

Blake pushed the mug of beer over, placed it right in front of him. "Typically, people I investigate tend to need some form of this. Go ahead."

He took several gulps, didn't help much, but at least got the burrito going back in the right direction. "I thought the Department of Defense was doing the audit."

"Oh please. The DOD is about how best to blow things up, not about keeping track of expenditures."

"Okay, so, I suppose you want to take a look at my accounting files?"

"Funny how those in your position always say that," she said, politely laughing. "No, Professor. I do not need to see your files. It's a perk of working for one of the most powerful governments in the world, and also of having connections at the CIA, NSA, among others. I have a lot of resources at my disposal. So I do not need to see your doctored files. My investigation is done."

The burrito was still headed in the right direction but now, was moving too fast, attempting to make a quick exit. Victor tried to think of where the nearest restrooms were but his internal Global Positioning System was scrambled by waves of panic. He imagined being locked away at Club Fed, being kept from Francine, probably for a long-ass time. Blake said something but it was hard to hear with the drumbeat of his racing pulse in his ear.

"Professor, come back to me. Nod if you hear me. Good." She picked the cigarette up off the table, the shoulder bag too, stood and took him by the arm. "Come.

Let's get you some fresh air and me my nicotine fix."

They walked down the main pedestrian mall which was surrounded by expansive lawn type areas where ample amounts of students lounged mainly in the horizontal position under the clear blue sky. Blake sucked deeply on the cigarette, exhaled long and hard, doing the act with relish. Victor felt entirely clenched, waiting for shoes to drop. But had to deal. Suck it up Gottenberg, suck it up.

"You've been a naughty boy haven't you, Professor?"

"Uh, my honest opinion? No."

"Those in your position always say that too. But I think in your case, you actually believe it. You didn't spend the funds on lavish goods, and the sheer sloppiness of your method of trying to cover up the embezzlement seems an act not of a deviant criminal but more like a kid in a candy store, overwhelmed by the possibilities, overcome by emotion, the easy rationalization of who possibly could be harmed by pocketing a handful of lollipops."

She sucked and exhaled. A happy smile, not clear if from the nicotine or from the cat-with-wriggling-mouse-under-paw rush.

"When I was first handed this file, I thought, this is it, I've hit bottom. The total sum of the funds involved here is less than the amount spent by the military flying their jets over a stadium holding a sporting event. A pittance in the context of DOD spending. This is the kind of file that gets handed to interns or to those being gently pushed into retirement. Or to those who used to be the hot piece of ass and got her pick of assignments until she wasn't the hot piece of ass and then had to actually speak up and prove she was worthy of choice assignments, and after which, she was labeled a pushy bitch."

She sucked deeply, exhaled remorselessly.

"I was stationed in London for ten years before this gig," she said, air-quoting "gig." "CIA branch there, though you didn't hear it from me. It was a decent position but year by year my assignments became more nominal to the point where I was basically a desk jockey. You know, I reflexively drive on the other side of the street sometimes still. American drivers tend to get peeved when you do that. The karmic consequences of being a bitch I suppose."

"You don't seem like a bitch," said Victor, playing the game.

She laughed a little. "Thank you."

Victor started to unclench. This file was a "pittance" to Blake, not worthy of her time. And her seeming disdain for her employer was to his advantage. So pepper her with questions of her heyday as the hot piece of ass, he thought. Work that angle well enough and it could be the ticket to having her look the other way on this pathetic file.

"I've never known a hot piece of ass before. Maybe you can regale me with your tales."

"You are a horrible liar, Professor. You teach at a university. You are surrounded by hot pieces."

"Okay. Then let me say it this way: I have never known *the* hot piece of ass."

"That's more like it. But nothing to tell really. Lavished with attention and praise, sometimes with material goods, getting your way frequently, such as choice of assignments as mentioned earlier, especially if you've developed a drop dead pout. And there were the promises of a better life by a slew of Alphas, some of whom were at the top of the tower of power. Three failed marriages later, I finally realized they were never in love with me, but in love with a coveted product. And once the product reached its expiration date, well…"

Her voice faded, seemingly burdened with lament. But her gaze became steelier, jaw clenched firm enough to crack a tooth.

Victor tried to appease. "It's tough out there, in the real world, for a romantic." He reached out to pat her shoulder for an added touch.

"Don't be absurd," said Blake as she swatted away his hand. "Romantic notions are for little girls who believe in unicorns. Do I look like someone who believes in unicorns?"

The anger loaded in her words made Victor wince. So much for that tactic.

Blake stopped walking and flung her cigarette to the pavement, ground it down under her heel. Tried to light another but the breeze kept blowing the lighter out. "Dammit!" Finally got it lit, sucked on it until she relaxed, until she got her smiley face back, as if the anger had been a mirage. "Where were we?" she said, resuming forward progress.

"Something about unicorns," mumbled Victor.

"Oh, I know what I wanted to say. Thank you. Thank you for making this file worthwhile after all. When I started investigating this file with utter disinterest and then discovered what this file was really about, it had my juices flowing again. By the way, that's a magnificent medical facility you've constructed in your garage."

"Thanks?"

"And the risk you took, going to an unstable and known

serial necrophiliac for the procurement of organs." She chuckled. "Your friend, Mr. Maplewerm, is a fellow indeed worthy of being on the FBI's 100 Most Wanted List. I'm afraid I had to let the boys from the Bureau in on this information. They are in fact on their way to convince him to surrender into their custody as we speak." She coughed and hacked from smoke and laughter then said, "It's not going to go well, is it?"

"There probably will be blood."

"Oh, I know, I know. It makes me miss the old days, my days on the front lines instead of being stuck behind a goddamned desk." Blake took a drag, spewed smoke out of her nostrils, dragon-esque.

Victor cleared his throat. "Did you also inform the FBI of—"

"No, Professor, I did not. I have no intention of giving you up to the Bureau. I prefer to keep you for myself."

Victor was not sure what to make of that so he said, "I'm not sure what to make of that."

She didn't hear him or very possibly ignored him and continued on a totally different track. "The absconding of Lanna Vodak's body with the help of your friend, Henry Clerval, was a ballsy move, wasn't it? The local police are baffled by her hand turning up in a shopping center food court." More laughing followed by a torrent of coughs. When the hacking dissipated, she said, "And they are utterly at a loss about finding DNA markers in the hand from someone who is not Lanna. Of someone ten-years-dead. Someone named Francine Styne."

There was no more laughing. A hard stare at Victor. He felt sweat beads on the tip of his nose and just above his eyebrows.

"Tell me please, Professor. The thing, the one thing I have not been able to figure out is your motive. You've sacrificed time and effort, broken laws, stolen from the federal government, crossed moral and ethical boundaries, toiled to make a miracle happen. If it weren't for the fact that you've known Francine since childhood, the answer would have been simple, wouldn't it? Now, I'm not so sure. But I am still willing to bet it was ambition."

Victor reciprocated her steely stare as he proclaimed, "I am in love with Francine Styne. Sorry, you lose."

Blake's expression, as if slapped in the face. Disbelief and stinging pain. They halted, stood at the edge of campus where, across a two-way street, was a parking structure. She pulled out car keys from her bag. Checked her watch, the glint of sunlight reflecting off of the glass face jabbed Victor in the eye.

She said, "I have a plane to catch." Patted her shoulder bag. "I think I have everything I need to finalize my report. Thank you."

"Wait. What are you saying?"

"What I am saying is, this is the type of nonsense that must be stopped."

The situation fast slipped out of his grasp. The dread came in heavy doses. "When you say 'must be stopped,' I'm not sure what you mean."

"I will be filing the report. You will be prosecuted for embezzlement, among the other crimes you have committed."

She turned to walk away but he grabbed her arm, spun her around.

"Why? This file is a pittance to you. You said my actions were not of a deviant criminal. I told you I did this out of love and not out of—" Right then was when he got it. "Look, Blake. I can empathize. You are very much human, not a 'product' obviously, and so it's okay to have feelings. Of hurt and loneliness."

She pointed at his face and told him to, "Stop! You need to stop this now. The actions you took, your blatant defiance of federal law, shows me that you have lost all self-restraint. This is the type of behavior that leads to a high body count, figuratively speaking. Although, who knows, perhaps it could turn out to be literal, because, you sir, are out of control!"

The body-count comment gave Victor pause, remembered his student Joseph Cruciate who had poisoned his girlfriend and then jumped out of a third story window just because of a passing comment Victor made. Could Victor really be blamed for that? Was Joseph Cruciate a "body count?" And how about Joseph's girlfriend Hannah Potemkin? Would she count too? This seemed totally unfair.

Blake ranted on. "I could have at least respected a motive based on ambition. But doing what you did in the name of love? You must be insane." Blake yanked her arm out of Victor's grasp. "I may think that this file is a pittance and not worthy of my time, and although it may have had some entertainment value, I am still an agent of the federal government and I have a duty and obligation to report violations of the law."

"You're not doing this out some kind of adherence to duty. It's spite is what it is. You are old and lonely. You are bitter. And you are taking it out on Francine and me."

Blake cackled. "Believe what you want, Professor. But please listen carefully to these words: You are in deep shit.

It's time for you to accept that fact."

Victor watched her backpedal toward the street as she deeply inhaled on her cigarette. She practically spat the smoke out at him, then smirked, wicked-like. Throttle her, is what the heat of the moment told him to do. He could practically feel her fleshy neck against his palms, her tobacco-ravaged windpipe crushing easily under his rage-driven grip. But he talked himself down. Doing that in public was crazy, would solve nothing. Besides, could he even do such a thing? His testicles shriveled in response. So all he could do was watch. Watched, as she stepped off the curb, still backpedaling, looking the wrong way, to her left for oncoming traffic, like someone who had spent a lot time in a place that had opposite traffic direction and who had yet to readjust. Seeing no traffic, she kept backpedaling into the street.

About three seconds from impact with Blake was a commuter bus approaching from the direction she should have been checking. The bus was not traveling too fast, maybe 30 mph, but at about ten tons, the bus, even at that speed, would cause pretty decent damage to a human body.

Three seconds. Probably just enough time to warn her, to save her spiteful ass.

One-one-thousand.

Two-one-thousand.

Three-one-thousand.

A metallic thud, surprisingly loud. She disappeared beneath the bus, under the left front tire she went. The bus lurched upward slightly, like going over a speed bump, then skidded to a stop. Blake was under the left rear tire when the brakes were slammed. The result: Ground

Chuck came to mind.

Screams from the bystanders.

Then there was the business with Blake's shoulder bag. Victor assumed there was more than her stupid pack of cigarettes in there, most likely Blake's laptop computer containing all the digitized evidence against him. It, the bag, had gone flying on its own trajectory, freed from Blake's body, and came to rest under one of the cars parked on the street.

Victor with a darn good imitation of nonchalance strolled to that car, retrieved the shoulder bag, turned and walked in the opposite direction against the chaotic onrush of the blood-lust-curious with maybe a minority of hero types who would do their utmost to try and save the spiteful pile of raw meat fka Blake Lemmonshire. Victor tried suppressing it but he could not: Oh joy, oh joy! His walk turned into a skip, his smile gleamed beacon-like, tried even to high-five some of the on-rushers, only one of whom reciprocated. He then veered toward the nearest hedgerow, the one against the Business Admin building, fell to his hands and knees, convulsed and sweated coldly and promptly upchucked the bean and cheese burrito and whatever else that was left inside of him.

Body Count Tally: 4.

1. Joseph Cruciate.
2. Joseph's girlfriend Hannah Potemkin.
3. Cheese-on-a-stick-eating guy.
4. Special Investigator Blake Lemmonshire.

CHAPTER EIGHTEEN
The Pigs Have Flown

Ever since the swift knee to Hobin's nads for his trying to stick his tongue down Ell's throat, he'd been making amends to her. Or maybe it just seemed like amends and it was really Hobin trying to stay in her good graces so he could once again try to stick his tongue, or whatever else, in her. No matter though. Perks was perks. The catering of gourmet coffee, the name brand doughnuts, and the gourmet lunches. Gift cards from the warehouse store where she could stock up on the industrial-size bottles of booze. He knew her well.

While debating with herself about whether she should go for the giant bottle of the Russian brand vodka or the Swedish one, Hobin landed at her desk, box of doughnuts in tow. Gave her this tidbit to beat all perks: "So, Ell. My wife, whom, as you know, works as a secretary for the FBI field office here in our neck of the woods, told me that they got a lead on our serial necrophiliac, Percy Maplewerm, and they are going to attempt to arrest his ass." Waved one of the name brand doughnuts excitedly as he said this.

The first thought for Ell was, it's about goddamn time they tracked him down, and the second thought was, how does a person with a low level position and limited clearance like Hobin's wife gain access to such information unless she was giving BJs to someone with higher clearance who spewed more than just spunk. The wife's behavior, if the situation were true, was nothing exactly shocking given Hobin's schlubbiness, but still, Ell kinda sorta felt sorry for him. Which led to what-if thoughts, such as, what if she could bring comfort to the lonesome-feeling schlub while deriving certain benefits herself from a human touch rather than from her vibrator for a change? She watched Hobin chomp on a doughnut, sugary crust at the corners of his mouth, crumbs clinging to his tie. He grinned at her, chewed-up doughnut clumps stuck to his teeth. Ell shuddered inside. Her high-density plastic, battery-operated companion didn't seem so bad after all. She shook loose the what-if thoughts and told herself, your vagina is not a pity receptacle.

"For fuckssake, Hobin. Can you maybe not chew with your mouth open?"

"Sorry. Good doughnuts make me wanna show and tell. You should have some. I've got some nice cream-filled ones here."

I bet you do she thought with more internal shudderings. "Forget the damn doughnuts. How reliable is wifey's information?"

"Very. It comes from the top. She has way of sucking

information out of people."

"Interesting choice of words."

"Huh?"

"Nothing." She flipped through her Rolodex, picked up the phone. Dialed. "Detective Lavenza for Special Agent Proll."

"One moment please," said the creepily nice lady-voice on the other end.

Jazzy on-hold music, then, "Detective. It's been a while," said Special Agent Proll, drolly. "What do you want?"

"Jesus, Proll. So much for pleasantries, I guess."

"Gosh, sorry," he said, his tone suggesting otherwise. "So, how they hangin'?"

"I'll take that as an uncouth double entendre, but you are after all only a man, so I'll let it slide. Anyway, they are hanging beautifully."

"That's just swell." Words dry, bereft of actual enthusiasm. "Now. What do you want?"

"You still doing sex crimes?"

"Maybe you can rephrase that."

"Are you still working the sex crime files? Is that better?"

"Yes and yes."

"I want to be there when you bust Percy Maplewerm."

"How you came across that information I don't know, but it doesn't matter. This is out of your jurisdiction so forget about it."

"I don't care about getting in on the arrest. You guys take all the credit you want. I just need to ask questions of that fucker. An ancient file has bubbled back to the surface and I think he may be directly connected. So how about giving a girl a break?"

Proll guffawed. "You're no 'girl.' What are you, like, pushing 40 now? And the answer is still no. You small fries stick to your shitty little cases and leave the important ones to the big boys."

"'Big Boys?' You wish. By the way, why did you a-holes take 10 years to track down Maplewerm, huh?"

"Be nice, Ell."

"You know what I'm thinking? I'm thinking that Maplewerm was probably tipped off to you by some other more competent department, maybe, like who? Homeland Security, CIA, ATF, FDA."

"FDA? That's a low blow. You want the straight shit on this? He sells dead chicks to others of his ilk. It's otherwise known as a victimless crime and not exactly newsworthy. Limited resources plus a non-sexy case equals we got better things to do. So yeah, if some other department wants to gives us a heads-up, I'm not going to be too proud, and I'll tell them thank you very much."

"Spoken like a dedicated officer of the law."

"I'm almost certain you're being a hypocrite right now with your judgmental tone."

"I want access to Maplewerm. Tell me when and where."

"No can do. I can't be perceived as being soft on the locals."

"All right, Proll. You win. I'm going to hang up now but oh wait. Do you happen to remember Candy Zhorandy aka Candice Zhorandivich?"

"Are you shitting me? You're going to cash in that chip now, after what, 15 years? Come on, Ell. I was young and stupid, and okay, maybe a little bit arrogant, but come on.

You're just being mean now."

"Are you still married to the woman who you said was the love of your life and that you would do anything not to have her find out about you partaking in the services of a prolific prostitute and you said please please please as a fellow officer of the law please look the other way on this one? And I said okay but that I was only doing this because of your wife and that you owed me big time, you sonofabitch."

"You are mean, Ell."

A long beat. "Proll? You still there? Come on already. Just swallow your pride and tell me what I want to hear."

Proll muttered something indecipherable, then said, "Okay, fine. But you better be wearing a vest. And bring heavy artillery because this guy has been assessed as somewhat of a wildcard. I mean, I wouldn't want you to die after all."

"That's the nicest fake bullshit thing that anyone has ever said to me."

"So are we good?"

"Very."

***

A generic government-issue sedan parked behind another generic government-issue sedan which was not as new, not as sparkly clean. The cars were about 100 yards down the street from the dinky strip mall, which included a shuttered Italian restaurant, a massage parlor, chiropractor, and the office of the County Coroner. It was a tad past 9:00 in the a.m. and this rural "downtown" was relatively quiet still, not much in the way of the hustle and/or bustle of the beginning of a business day.

Leaning against the not as nice sedan were detectives

Lavenza and Hobin. Out of the nicer sedan stepped out Special Agent Proll. Two other male agents followed. They wore the obligatory navy-blue windbreakers with fat yellow letters of "FBI" on them. Identical aviator shades. Out of the trunk, shotguns and vests. Windbreakers off, vests on, windbreakers back on. Checked their sidearm. Strutted like they were hot shit toward Ell and Hobin.

Agent Proll sporting a cocky grin said, "Good-day, ladies."

"I don't appreciate that," said Hobin. "I am a man as you can see."

The agents laughed. Proll introduced his buddies: Special Agents Vhacka and Tourr. "Hope you're ready for action, detectives, because we ain't here to babysit you. And remember, this is our show so try not to get in the way."

Ell rolled her eyes. "Not a problem, Proll. I'm sure you boys are perfectly capable of fucking this up all on your own."

"Ha ha, Ell," Proll said with a look like he wanted to cold cock her in the jaw.

Agents Proll, Vhacka, Tourr, jogged away, mumbling and tittering, likely calling her a bitch and such.

"I hope I don't 'accidentally' shoot one of them in the ass," she said.

"Not a chance, Ell. You're an excellent shot."

She shook her head, thought: Oh, Hobin, try not to die today.

Percy was putting the final touches on the parcel packed with dry ice and a freshly severed left hand for special delivery when his intercom buzzed and he was about to say whaddya want to his big-wigged, chain-smoking, geriatric receptionist, when she said, "The pigs have flown."

Percy responded with, "Have you been stealing your grandson's OCD meds again?"

"The pigs have flown," she said, very deliberately this time.

"What are you—" Then he remembered. It was one of the first things he had trained her on. The day the Feds tracked him down would be the day pigs took flight, or so it was Percy's thinking. Hence, the phrase. It was code for "The Feds have tracked you down, motherfucker!"

First, Percy made a few mouse clicks on his computer. The screen revealed a countdown timer of 30 seconds and a message asking whether he was sure he really wanted to delete what he was about to delete. He clicked on "yes," then shoved his desk out of the way to access the floor panel. From the subterranean storage space, he retrieved a bulletproof vest, a Kalashnikov, a pouch of AK-47 magazines, and a machete. The receptionist burst through his office door. Her head in a cloud of smoke from the two cigarettes going at the same time, could barely make out her wild eyes. Must have lost her wig somewhere along the way.

Percy asked, "How many?"

"Two men, one woman out front," she said with cigarettes bobbing between her lips, bits of ash being flung. "Don't know if anyone's out back."

From the reception area came the sound of pounding at the front door. Shattering of glass. A male voice announced the FBI's arrival. Percy put on his vest, stuck the machete through his belt, hung the shoulder strap of the AK around his neck. From a desk drawer, he pulled out a large-bore handgun.

"Ready to play hostage, you old bitch?"

"Is our deal still in place?"

"Yeah yeah. If you survive and keep your trap shut, you'll have access to the account in the Caymans. Your shriveled ancient ass can retire in high fashion."

"I cannot say it was a pleasure working for you but I shall enjoy the fruits of my labor."

Percy grabbed her hostage-style, cracked the door open, peeked out. There was a long hallway between his office and the reception area. Saw no one just yet in the hallway. Shadows of movement in the reception area. Stepped away from the door to take a moment. He glimpsed the special delivery parcel on his desk. It was unlikely he could get it delivered now and this pissed him off.

Victor had called him two days ago at the phone number given out only to the best customers and Percy asked how the fuck did he get this number and Victor said the receptionist knew a good thing when she saw it. With the threat to fire the receptionist and to hang up on him, Victor pleaded for him not to and told him he desperately needed a left hand if one was available, with money being no object, because Francine lost hers at a food court and she was desperately in need of one right now. Percy didn't say what the fuck are you talking about, do you expect me to believe you brought her back to life after her being dead for something like 10 years, and instead, he believed Victor instantly, had somehow known all along that this fucker was one in a million, the one who would perform miracles.

Percy told Victor he was expecting a shipment of high

school students that afternoon. School bus versus commercial grade tractor, number of fatalities. One of the girls would likely be a physical match. Then Percy said to Victor, maybe you can help me, if I bring you the bones of my long dead wife, you could perform one of your miracles for her too. Please. Victor didn't say yes but he didn't say no. What he said was I'm not sure if that's doable, but… That was all the encouragement Percy needed, and now, the Feds were going to try and fuck it up. No way was Percy going to let that happen.

Special Agent Vhacka took the lead, broke through the glass of the storefront door, unlocked it, and with shotgun cocked and aimed, entered yelling "FBI!" Agent Tourr followed. Then Ell. No one in the reception area, only the smell of mildew and cigarette smoke. Vhacka headed down the hallway toward the back office when the door flew open and out came Percy Maplewerm pointing a big-ass handgun, his arm around the neck of an elderly woman, presumably a hostage, smoking what looked like two cigarettes at the same time. Before anyone could say drop the gun, motherfucker, Percy shot Vhacka in the right knee which duly exploded. As Vhacka fell, his shotgun discharged, maybe by accident, maybe not, and blew a hole in the torso of the elderly woman. Percy held onto the hostage, continued to use her as a shield. Vhacka hollered incoherencies, clutched at what was left of his knee.

Tourr closed in on Percy. "The old lady's dead, Maplewerm. And now *you're* gonna be unless you—" The bullet nicked Tourr's shoulder, piece of navy-blue windbreaker and bits of shoulder meat flew. An enraged

Tourr rushed Percy while emptying out the shotgun, managed only to hit the hostage whose body was now a dangling mass of pulverized flesh. The bloodied body slid out of Percy's grip, his handgun too. Tourr tossed the spent shotgun, reached for his sidearm but he was no quickdraw so Percy beat him to it and whipped out the machete and clean-cut Tourr's hand off just below the wrist. The hand dropped to the dirty carpet, fingers still clutching his too-late drawn sidearm. Tourr stared at his handless wrist as if it weren't true. Percy retrieved his handgun as he watched Tourr stumble around, bounce off the wall and collapse.

Ell leaned into the wall at the end of the hallway, and when she took her next peek, Percy was pointing the handgun in her direction. He unloaded shot after shot, causing the drywall to blow up around her, shards of plaster bouncing off her head. She regained balance as quickly as possible. Pointed her gun toward where she thought the hallway was, which was hard to tell, what with the plaster dust cloud.

Then she heard, "Hey, baby," from behind her, and when she whipped around, all she saw was the muzzle-flash in the dusty haze. Couldn't remember how she ended up on her back, not able to breathe, pain the size of Canada crushing her chest. Out of the haze came the gun barrel, then bony knuckles around the gun grip, which led to spindly arms, then his crazed-eye face, yellow-toothed grin.

"You're a head taller than I thought," said Percy. "Otherwise it would have been a bullseye. Lucky for you I guess, for the time being." He checked the gun-chamber. Empty. Tossed the handgun, grasped the AK.

In the meantime, Ell felt around for her dropped gun, found it, but Percy stepped on her wrist, putting an end to that.

He asked, "How many more?"

She shook her head.

"What, like two, three more out back?"

She shook her head.

"Whatever." Pointed the AK at her face. "I'll give you a few seconds to let your life flash before your eyes. Then we're gonna have to say bye-bye."

Ell wasn't afraid, just pissed off that she let this happen. Had been prepared for this ever since rookie year when her mentoring partner told her to be, because if you approached this job with fear, you'd die anyway.

What she wasn't prepared for was the thought that knocked around in her head just then: Was there anyone out there who would give a rat's ass that she was dead and gone, and not like how her mom and dad would most likely miss her, but someone who wasn't obligated by blood relation to give a shit, someone who would miss her profoundly and be affected forever and a day. Could not think of anyone, except possibly Hobin, and this caused some understandable distress.

And *this* was how it was going to end.

Then she remembered the reason for being here, a reason not worth dying for, but here she was, because she just had to know. Was Francine really alive? This question was formed when Hobin was yammering about Francine maybe coming back from the dead and stealing body parts, eating brains of the living, and such. It wasn't as if she bought into Hobin's zombie theory but maybe Francine was a true blue resurrected non-zombie human being, because how else to explain Francine's blood being found in Lanna Vodak's hand, which by the way would make sense in terms of using Lanna's left hand to replace Francine's which was lost in the fatal car accident. Ell had shelved that crazy fucking thought because it was a crazy fucking thought. But crazy didn't necessarily mean impossible, and by the way, who would attempt such a feat? Someone who missed Francine profoundly and would have been affected forever and a day if she weren't resurrected which was more than anything anyone would have done for Ell if she died. Obviously.

Percy jammed the barrel of the AK into Ell's forehead. "Time's up, baby."

She gasped out, "Francine Styne!"

Percy unpointed the AK. "You know her?"

"Is she...alive?"

Percy flashed his fat yellow teeth, not as a devious grin, but as a genuine smile. "That fucker did it, you know? Ten years ago, he comes to me looking for her and we can't find her goddamned head and he goes nuts, man, and he punches my tooth out." Pulled out his fake front tooth. "See? He was totally fucking nuts and I didn't know what kind of shit he was up to then and I was pissed off about the whole tooth situation but ultimately, it made me wanna believe, you know?" He put his tooth back in. "And now, I do."

"Who is he?"

"He's a sage. A maker of miracles, man! That's who he is."

"Give me a name, Percy."

He knelt next to her, looked her up and down. "You're not FBI." Snatched the badge off her belt. "You're far away from home, aren't you? What's your name, Detective?"

"Elizabeth Lavenza. Ell."

"Ell, Ell, Ell. It's gotta nice ring to it. What are you doing here, detective with a name with a nice ring to it?"

"I'm here to arrest your ass."

Percy cackled. "No you're not." He clutched her by the jaw, got in real close to her face, his breath surprisingly minty fresh. "Your question about if Francine's alive? Why would anyone ask that about some chick that's been dead for 10 years? You don't have to answer that, it's what's called rhetorical. You're here because you want to believe too, Ell. We're the same, you and me."

She yanked her head from his grip. "Fuck you. I'm nothing like you, you sick fuck."

"That's not nice, Ell, passing judgment on me like that. I'm not passing judgment on you."

"Fuck! Off!"

And off he went, down the hallway, cackling away. A moment later, a report sounded of the AK being unleashed.

The pain the size of Canada was now about California size but it was still not so easy to get her ass off the carpet. "Get up goddammit, Ell, get your ass up!" And she did in about 30 seconds but felt like an hour. Checked her chest. The bullet was a splatter embedded in the vest, smack dab in the middle of her sternum. Picked up the gun, went to Tourr, cinched a makeshift tourniquet around his arm, did the same for Vhacka's leg. Called for backup, medivac, and went after Percy.

She burst through the back door, gun pointed fiercely. Found Proll face down by the dumpsters, blood seeping out from under him. She turned him over, saw that he had fallen on his shotgun, the tip of the barrel tucked under where his jaw should have been. No other apparent wounds. Death by tripping, a shitty way to die. Ell imagined karma having held a grudge against Proll for 15 years.

She searched for Hobin's body, but wasn't there, thank God. There was a field about an acre or so surrounded by wire mesh fence with razor coil topping it off. The field was barren except for weeds, a refrigeration trailer, and Percy running toward what looked like hogs penned at the rear of the property. Hobin, hot on Percy's heels. Ell sprinted after them. When Percy reached the hog pen, he took the machete and sliced the fence down, slapped some hog ass, causing a stampede under which Hobin disappeared. Ell dodged and weaved through the piggy onslaught and when she reached Hobin, she saw hoof marks on his face, blood oozing from nose and mouth, eyes closed, the right one looking a bit crushed in.

"Hobin?!"

He opened his uncrushed eye. "Ell! I heard shots, I thought you might be dead and I was really unhappy about that, but here you are!"

"You okay?"

"Yeah yeah. Just go get him. By the way, I think for sure Proll's dead." Hobin then coughed up a bit of puke and passed out.

She told unconscious Hobin to hang tight and that she'd be back for him. Chased after Percy through the hog pen, through the sliced opening of the wire mesh fence, through another weed-covered field and then a vacant parking lot that was there for no apparent reason, and up a knoll where Percy tugged at a camouflage tarp under which was one of those kit helicopters with passenger space for one.

Ell breathed like she just sprinted a mile because she actually did. "Are you kidding me with this?" she said, stunned, exasperated.

"Ha ha," he said and reached into the copter, started the engine.

With gun pointed, she shuffled closer, and at about 10 yards, she stopped. "Percy Maplewerm, drop your weapons, get on your knees and place your hands behind your head."

He laughed. "You're not going to take me in."

"I wouldn't fuck with me just now if I were you."

"It's not that you can't take me in, it's just that you really don't want to. I told you, we're compadres and you know it and you want me to succeed."

"Succeed at what?"

"I'm going to retrieve the bones of my dead wife, hand them over to the miracle worker and beg and plead and beg him to bring her back to life like he did with Francine Styne because I miss the goddamn shit out of my wife."

"Don't you dare. Don't even tell me that kind of crap." Her eyes got misty despite every attempt to control it.

Percy dropped the AK, tossed the machete. "You're gonna have to shoot me dead to stop me." Turned, proceeded to get into the cockpit.

Ell took aim, pulled the trigger. Blew the top half of his right ear off. Made him ricochet off the copter and stumble to the ground. Got up slowly, brushed at the grass stains on his knees and elbows. An expression of trying to make sense of what just happened. He touched the empty space where the upper part of his right ear used to be. Blood streamed down the side of his face and dripped off at the chin. Started up his cackle, reaching a crescendo.

Ell held her aim firm.

"That is some class-A shooting, sister. And thanks for not killing me." Without looking away from her, he once again tried for the cockpit.

Ell still held her aim firm. "Don't do it, asshole!"

There was a "pop" followed by a jolt to her left thigh, and just as her legs turned to jello, she spotted the Derringer in Percy's hand. "Motherfucker!" she said while rolling back-asswards down the hill with a slug in her leg.

The copter engine revved, sounding like a high-pitched lawnmower. The aircraft gingerly lifted off. "I'll send you a postcard, let you know how things turned out," he yelled over the din. "Bye bye, compadre."

At the bottom of the knoll, Ell checked the blood stain on her jeans which was growing but under control, a manageable injury, though it hurt like a bitch. She watched Percy and his copter fade into the sky. She holstered her weapon and asked herself, what the fuck is wrong with you?

More government-issue sedans arrived, a gaggle of Special Agents, a medivac helicopter. Agents Vhacka and Tourr survived despite the hideous injuries, shitload of blood loss. Hobin was okay too, seemed proud of the fact of having been trampled by a herd of hogs and lived to tell the tale. The receptionist and Proll, still dead. But before the arrival of the sedans, the agents, the helicopter, she had surveyed Percy's office. Found no documentation of his customers. The information most likely was only in digital form, hence his computer hard-drive wiped clean of any and all ones and zeros.

There was a parcel the size of a kid's lunchbox on the desk with an address, a P.O. Box, for priority delivery. It was officially FBI evidence so she couldn't technically tamper with it but she justified doing so because the address was within her jurisdiction. She tore into it and what she saw gave her a knee-jerk shock, dropped the box. Packets of dry ice and a hand, a left one, spilled out onto the floor. Also, there was a folded piece of notebook paper, the handwriting on it, as if palsy-affected: "Congrats about F-Styne. This hand should fit. No charge. Hope you can return the favor like we talked about."

Ell ripped off the part of the parcel with the P.O. Box on it, stuffed it into her back pocket. The piece of cardboard felt electric against her ass. That piece of cardboard was her ticket to possibly giving her some goddamned meaning to what she thought was meaningless, a pipe dream. And because Percy was right. She wanted to believe.

Body Count Tally: 6.
1. Joseph Cruciate.
2. Joseph's girlfriend Hannah Potemkin.
3. Cheese-on-a-stick-eating guy.
4. Special Investigator Blake Lemmonshire.
5. Percy's receptionist.
6. Special Agent Proll.

CHAPTER NINETEEN
"Bring it, asshole."

The deep-red Ferrari sluiced through the marginal freeway traffic. At 100 mph, the car barely broke a sweat. She was topless, the car, revealing Henry and Francine tucked into the cockpit. They wore pricey shades and roller-coaster-riding smiles. Francine's mane, frenzy-whipped. Henry's tightly gelled hair barely budged.

Henry had agreed to pick up the package at the designated P.O. box but insisted Francine come along, to get her out of the house, let her hang out with someone not so dull as Victor. Though peeved, Victor said all right whatever for Francine's sake, let her enjoy a day out, although it would be limited to the best Henry could offer, which were fleeting cheap thrills. Henry's response: better cheap ones than none at all. Besides, Francine was curious and excited about the package, her new left hand, to replace the current temporary prosthetic version.

Although Francine thought the mechanical hand was pretty cool, she had some reservations about being part machine.

"You ready to ditch the machine-hand?" said Henry.

"I guess, but I think Victor might be a little disappointed." A raspy giggle. "He won't cop to it, but he has a robot-girl fetish."

Henry made a face, scoffed, "Are you serious? What a freak." But then he thought about it, imagined the scenario. His johnson stirred. Maybe not so freakish after all.

***

This was Day Two of Ell and Hobin surveilling the Post Office. The package had "arrived" early yesterday, and given the perishable nature of said package, they were sure Percy's customer would show up to retrieve it before close of business today. A relief to Ell not having to spend any more time stuck in the car in this humid weather and with Hobin whose B.O. increased exponentially as the day wore on. But it helped not being on her feet, what with the fresh bullet wound still pulsating in her thigh.

Hobin thought he was cool now with his stupid eyepatch over his hoof-crushed eye. Just over a day and a half, and his side of the car, the passenger side, was already buried in fast-food detritus. Currently, he was wolfing down his afternoon snack of chili dogs. With onions. Extra onions.

"Seriously, Hobin? Did you not notice we're in close quarters here?"

"I'll try not to breathe on you. But come on, chili dogs with onions? It's worth the stink-breath."

"Only to those who are stinking it up."

"Then join the stink." He offered one of the dogs. "Take my wiener."

"Watch it," she said with severe tone.

"Unintended bad pun, Ell. For real, not on purpose."

"Uh-huh." She turned to focus on the Post Office. Wondered who it would be, the one who Percy called the sage, the miracle worker. The "package" was a decoy, the real thing confiscated by the FBI. The fake was rigged with a motion sensor device, so when it was moved in any way whatsoever, it would send a radio signal to the remote device, the pager-looking thing sitting on the dash, which would flash a red light, buzz and beep.

Sounds of hotdog-chomping, crunching of the onions. Soda being slurped through a straw. A burp.

"So, uh, um, Ell?"

No response.

"Ell?"

Still nothing.

"Ell?"

"What?!"

"Did you know that women find me low to moderately attractive but highly huggable. Huggability counts higher as an element of love. A more important variable than pure physical attraction."

The statement took her attention away from the Post Office. She said, "First of all, how do you even know that? Secondly, why are you telling me this? And third, you're assuming I give a shit?"

"Okay, I'll answer your questions in order. No. 1: In college, I volunteered for a sociology Ph.D. candidate's thesis/experiment of determining the priority of elements of what she called the 'Love Ponderability'."

"A Ph.D. candidate you say."

"It's a real area of study."

"You 'volunteered' to get a taste of her goods, didn't you?"

"That's not really relevant here."

"Were you successful at least?"

"That's not really relevant here."

"Whatever. What's your answer to my second question?"

"So, No. 2. I'm telling you this because you clearly are repulsed by what you perceive of my exterior qualities. But if you can get past that and acknowledge my huggability, maybe you can learn to love me."

"Not gonna happen. No. 3?"

"The answer is yes, I assume you do care. Because that's the kind of person you are. And before you react to what I just said, you should know that my wife is leaving me."

"What?! No she's not."

"Yeah-huh, she is."

An engine-roar of Italian origin caught Ell's attention. She saw the ass end of a Ferrari as it pulled into the Post Office parking lot. Turned back to Hobin playing up the sad-sack face.

He asked, "Don't you feel bad for me?"

"You totally manipulated me into that corner, you fucker."

"I could use a hug, Ell. I am huggable after all."

Hobin and his bastardly way of pulling on heart strings. What-if thoughts crept back into Ell's frontal lobe. But then the pager thingy on the dashboard flashed, beeped, buzzed. Like cold water to the face, snapped Ell out her pity-stupor.

"You're not doing this to me," she told Hobin, and exited the sedan, made toward the Post Office with hand on holster.

Hobin followed, fast-walked after her. "Okay, it seems you've called my bluff but don't be mad. My feelings are sincere."

In the middle of the street, she abruptly stopped, slugged him in the chest, causing spasmodic coughs from Hobin.

"Your wife leaving was a bullshit lie?"

"But my feelings are sincere," he wheezed out.

Ell about to slam her fist into his sternum again but Hobin held up his hand to protect himself and said, "The task at hand?" Pointed at the Post Office.

When they reached the entrance, Ell stuck her head in, checked the hallway lined with P.O. boxes. There were four mail-goers checking their boxes. Only one of them held the fake package, which was wrapped in pink paper for easy identification.

"Shit!" She immediately withdrew, leaned into the wall just outside the storefront doors. "It's Clerval."

"The doctor?"

"Yup."

"Isn't he like, huge?"

"Yup."

They both fingered their holstered guns.

"He's not who I expected," Ell said. "Can't imagine a guy like Percy calling this bozo a sage, a miracle worker."

"Looks can be deceiving."

"I don't think so."

"Maybe he's a huggable type."

"Doubtful, doesn't matter."

"Why can't you love me?"

"Don't start."

"Ell?"

"Seriously? It's like you wanna be hurt. No wonder your wife is leaving you."

"She's leaving me?!"

"Chrissakes, Hobin. Are you going to hold your shit together or do I need to call for backup?"

"It's just despondency, I'm used it, I can manage."

So they waited.

Hobin sighed. And sighed. And—

"A little advice?" offered Ell. "As soon as you accept that Love is a fickle bitch and that trying to attain the romantic ideal is like winning the lottery, you'll appreciate what you have and stop chasing pipe dreams."

"Hmmm." Hobin mulled. "Hmmm. That sounds philosophically wise, but I wonder if it's pragmatically sound."

"It's sound."

"Have *you* accepted it?"

Ell acted as if audio-impaired. If one heard no question, how could one provide an answer? Checked her watch instead. "He's taking too long." Stepped back into the Post Office. On the floor was the fake pink package torn asunder and stomped upon. No Clerval.

"Dammit! That fucking neon-bright pink wrapper tipped him off." Ell seethed. "Whose goddamn stupid idea was that anyway?"

Now Hobin acted as if audio-impaired.

Henry tore into the package knowing for sure that the hand wouldn't be in it. Because Percy didn't do pink.

Found the not-exactly-state-of-the-art transmitter and crushed it under his heel. At least it wasn't the Feds. They tended not to use off-the-shelf P.O.S. surveillance equipment. Out the window he spotted the unmarked cop car parked on the other side of the street, no one in it.

He ignored the postal workers advising him that this area was for employees only as he walked behind the counter, through the sorting area, to the loading dock, and out into the back alley. Eyeballed both directions, saw no cops. Turned the corner of the building into the parking lot, looked for his Italian beauty but found a .38 pointed at his face instead. The gun was held by a somewhat portly, somewhat shortish fella wearing a black suit on a humid day like this. The guy's B.O. was a good indicator that maybe he should have at least ditched the suit jacket.

"Doctor Clerval, I am Detective Hobin. I need you to place your hands behind your head and get down on your knees."

"You know me?"

"Detective Lavenza filled me in."

"Ell is here?"

"Never you mind. Assume the position."

Henry pointed at Hobin's eyepatch. "Detective Hobert __"

"Hobin. My name is Hobin."

"Apologies for that, Detective *Hobin*." He pointed again at the eyepatch. "You only have one eye."

"Well. It's an interesting story really." A proud smile. "There was this herd of hogs."

"Hogs?"

Hobin, with his stupid grin, ready to give an exposition about the purported hogs it seemed, when POW! went

Henry's giant fist into Hobin's good eye.

"Yarrrgh!" And down went Hobin.

Henry snagged and pocketed the badge, the .38. Thought it best to avoid the parking lot, reversed course back into the alleyway. As he passed the Post Office loading dock, there was a woman's bellow.

"Henry Clerval! Halt!"

He knew the voice. Turned around and made like he was suave or something and said, "What light through yonder window breaks? It is the east, and Ell is the sun."

"Clever," Ell said and gingerly stepped down from the loading dock, gun pointed.

"Thanks. I thought you'd like it."

"Didn't say anything about liking it." She took her time walking to Henry. Clearly favored her left leg, though she tried not to show it.

"So the elusive Percy Maplewerm was finally tracked down I guess."

"That's right. We busted his sorry ass and he ratted out his cohorts, including you."

"You actually captured him?"

"Hands on head, Doctor."

He complied. "Percy told you I was making this pickup huh?"

"That's right. Now, on your knees."

"Actually, that's really interesting, because I had nothing to do with setting up this deal. So he couldn't have known I was making the pickup." He smirked. "Methinks you're telling little white lies, Detective."

"Shut up and get on your knees."

Henry chuckled, did as told. Ell took a quick peek over her shoulder, toward the parking lot.

"Looking for reinforcements maybe?" said Henry. "I don't blame you. Taking me in is at least a two-man job. Oops sorry. Two-*person* job."

She kept the gun trained on him with her right hand, while with her left hand, she reached behind her back, pulled out the cuffs. She stayed standing there though, as if assessing the cost-benefit factors of trying to cuff a 6'8", 320-pounder who potentially might not come along peacefully.

"By the way, Detective. What happened to your leg?"

She reflexively touched her left thigh. "What? Nothing."

"Didn't have anything to do with hogs, did it?"

"What did you say?"

"Oh, hey," he said, looking past Ell. "Here comes Detective Hobin now."

Hobin came around the corner of the Post Office, clinging to the wall, feeling his way like a blindman without a cane. And when Ell followed Henry's gaze, he hammered his knuckles into her left thigh. With a groan she crumpled to the pavement. Henry wrested the gun from her, tossed it onto the roof of the building, jogged away. But no way was he going to hoof it out of there. Needed to call a cab or something and so he reached for his cellphone but it wasn't in his pocket. Left it in the car. Shit! What to do what to do. Ducked into a coffee shop through the alleyway door. Flashed Hobin's badge, bummed a cellphone call from a sufficiently impressed teenage girl. The taxi co. person told him the cab should be there in about 10 minutes.

Henry ordered a cappuccino and coffee cake. Found a discarded Sports Section of the Tribune. Took a load off. He believed that the cops for sure would think that he tried to get away as far and fast as possible rather than sitting in a coffee shop few stores down from the Post Office. He smiled a got-away-with-it smile. Relaxed, checked the box scores. Hold up though, what about Francine and their "date" and the — this was where the white noise washed over him to get his mind back on the task at hand because, after all, priorities were priorities. So back to the box scores. But then.

Here came Ell, into the coffee shop, highly gimpy, her pants blood-stained at the injured thigh. Hobin squinted hard to see with his good eye swollen purple. When Ell spotted Henry, she pulled up a pant leg, un-velcroed the retractable baton strapped to her ankle. Whipped the baton out to its full length.

Henry put down the paper, finished off the remaining crumbs of the coffee cake. Slurped down the cappuccino. So let's think about this. He had Hobin's gun, could shoot his way out. But be serious. Shoot a cop? For what? What exactly did they have on him? At best, they pin conspiracy charges for trafficking human body parts which probably was not a high priority in terms of the Penal Code. The D.A. would barely give a crap. But Henry would have to do some time given the connection to the notorious Percy Maplewerm. And there was the other stuff, the non-Victor/Francine related stuff that went back a ways which might be dug up once they started looking and would likely lead to multiple prison terms. Screw that. Time to wheel and deal.

"Detectives! Welcome. How about some caffeinated beverages? They have good coffee cake here too. My treat."

The teenage girl who lent the cellphone to Henry said,

"He's right, their coffee cake is pretty awesome, but wait," turned to Henry. "I thought *you* were a detective, what with your badge and all that, along with your hunky confidence."

Ell raised her badge overhead, said, "Folks, listen up. This man over here is not actual police. He is considered a fugitive and is armed and dangerous."

Henry laughed.

Ell continued. "Therefore, I advise all of you to vacate the premises at this time in an orderly manner."

Of the seven patrons, including Henry, only an expensive-suit-wearing guy, yapping on his cellphone and oblivious to the goings-on and scooping up his just made coffee concoction, left the premises. The two behind the counter with their name-tags indicating Timmy and Tammy stayed put. The spectators, all poised with smartphones in camera mode.

"So be it," Ell said. She then pointed her baton at Henry. "Clerval. What are we doing?"

"Here's what I propose. I can give you names, events, documentation. I can give you the so-called mastermind. I mean, you really didn't think *I* was the guy behind all this, with Maplewerm, the body parts—"

"Or Lanna Vodak?"

"*Nor* Lanna Vodak."

"Francine Styne?"

"You guys know a lot. Kudos."

"Is she…is she really…"

"I'll tell you everything you want to know. But you need to let me walk."

"I'm sure the D.A. will cut you a good deal."

"You're not understanding me. The deal needs to

happen now. The executive decision's got to be made now. I'm going nowhere except where I want to go."

"That's not how it works, Doc. And you know what? I'm taking you in anyway, deal or no."

Ah, The Standoff. All right, so he'd lose his medical license for sure but he wasn't about to do any time. Had enough fuck-you money for him to retire comfortably in a country in another hemisphere and/or timezone. He was a cornered animal now. Had to do what he had to do. Besides, he was still pissed off about Ell having turned down his advances. That too was sufficient motivation for what he was about to do.

He made a move for the .38 tucked behind him in his waistband, but gimpy Ell was super quick with the baton and cracked, literally, his right collar bone. Before he could groan in agony, she let loose the second swing at his right elbow. Direct hit. The pain made him almost swoon, fell off the chair, onto his knees, knew another blow was coming so he blasted a left cross to her crotch. She gasped, folded over on top of him. The baton went cling clang onto the concrete tile floor.

Henry brushed her off into the next table, the teenage girl's table, which toppled over with Ell on top, along with a laptop computer, an unfinished coffee drink. "Hey!" said the teenage girl to Henry. "That was totally not cool!"

Hobin launched at Henry before he could grab the baton but barely budged him. Henry peeled Hobin off, picked him up by the collar with one hand and by the waistband with the other, tossed him into the refrigeration case with the juices, the lowfat chocolate milk, pre-made sandwiches, fruit cups, and yogurt. Hobin wriggled like an upturned turtle, trying to get loose.

When Henry reached for the baton, all he grabbed was floor instead.

"Shit."

So he pulled out the .38, but by the time he turned to confront her, the baton had been unleashed. A gigawatt jolt of pain, his left knee smashed by a baseball bat is what it felt like. As he collapsed, Henry squeezed off several rounds, not really on purpose, but more in reaction to the wicked wicked pain. A source of release, the shooting. Blew out the pastry display. The delicious coffee cakes, muffins, croissants, among others, were decimated. Timmy and Tammy ducked behind the counter. Patrons took cover under tables.

While Henry was splayed out on the floor, Ell went to town on his right hand, the hand holding the .38. Broke the proximal phalanx of all four fingers, smashed a goodly portion of the metacarpal bones, and the third swing shattered the radius and ulna. In other words, his hand and wrist were fucked to shit. He flipped over onto his back, the next swing was en route toward his forehead. Grabbed a chair by the leg, bashed it into Ell's shin, made her fall hard on her side, her hip, shoulder. She winced, let go a grunt. The baton fell out of her grip, rolled out of sight somewhere, who knew where. As Henry stood, he felt the barrel of a gun pressing into the lumbar region of his spine. Raised his hands, surrender mode, turned around. Hobin held the .38.

Hobin stood too close to Henry. Adrenaline tended to get the best of Hobin, made him do stupid things like that. Ell tried to warn him but all that came out of her mouth was nothing, what with the wind having been knocked out of her from the fall. Sure enough, Henry swatted the gun out of Hobin's puny fist and the .38 skittered across the floor. Henry feinted his busted right hand to Hobin's barely good eye, made him flinch, landed a left to his kidney. Whoosh of air escaped Hobin as he bent in half, tipped over. Henry sat on his chest, pounded at Hobin's soft skull.

Ell discerned Henry's half smile as he beat Hobin bloody, pulpy, clearly knocked unconscious several punches ago. Henry's joy from the unrestrained rage, the impressive physicality, made Ell surmise that he was likely a bully in his schoolboy days, terrorizing the weak and innocent, amassing a fortune in forcibly procured lunch money.

Ell hated bullies.

She leapt onto his massive back, got his burly neck into a chokehold. He let loose a few more hits on Hobin until maybe realizing that he was on the verge of losing consciousness. Pried loose her hold, shed her off his back as if taking off a shirt, head over heels slammed her onto the floor. As he was about to sit on her chest, she head-butted his nads, made him howl. She wriggled out from under him, took to her feet. He remained on hands and knees, recovering, watching her.

"You need to surrender," she told him, breathing hard.

"Or else what?"

Ell assumed a boxer's stance, held fists out with arms extended, an old-school style.

Henry convulsed with laughter. Stood, towered over her. "This is going to be fun," he said.

"Bring it, asshole."

He too got into a fighting stance, the more conventional style. But he could only ball up his left hand into a fist, the right was a mangle of busted bones. He faked with his right but Ell didn't fall for it. After all, it wasn't as if he could do anything with that hand. He followed with a left hook under which she ducked, and on her way back up, she landed an uppercut to his chin. It didn't stagger him but he spat out bits of enamel.

He grinned a bloody, chipped-tooth grin, was about to say something when she snuck another to the chin. Actually heard teeth crack this time. Henry no longer grinned. Swung his right again but it was no feint this time and she got clubbed to the head with his meaty forearm. Face first she went, bounced off the counter's edge. Saw a few stars. Okay, so he could use the right in that manner. Lesson learned.

Ell just managed to sidestep a punch which glanced off her right ear and bashed into the cash register. She popped a one-two combination to Henry's nose and the bridge went crooked, blood dripping out of both nostrils. This time, he did stagger and she took advantage: combos to the head, the body, back to the head. He reeled. But she couldn't keep this up. Her hands and wrists felt brutally abused and a knockout blow to this beefy bastard wasn't likely. So she did her utmost to quickly get the cuffs out but the effort was still too slow. It gave him enough time to unreel and he bull-rushed her. She got body-slammed and the world turned off.

When the lights came back on, Henry was straddling her torso, his left arm cocked with bowling ball fist locked in on the target which was her face. She positioned her arms in a protective posture covering her head, elbows pointed toward him. The blow ricocheted off her right elbow and slammed the concrete floor and Henry yelped.

Not much of left-side dexterity for this guy apparently. He wound up his fist again, eyes shooting rage laser beams at her, his intention to pulverize her skull most likely. She held her protective position firm. He'd have to splinter her arms before bashing her head in. But the blow never came. Instead there was a "twhap" and a groan and he was no longer on top of her.

And there he was, good ol' Hobin with her baton in hand, standing over writhing Henry. But of course Hobin had to fuck things up by losing focus, beaming at Ell with a yes-I-am-your-knight-in-shining-armor grin. During that lack-of-focus moment, Henry leg-swiped him. Hobin flopped to the floor, his head bouncing off the concrete tile. Nighty-night, Hobin.

Henry, with some effort, got back on his feet. Wobbled to and fro. She too struggled to her feet. Wobbled to and fro. Her mind said, raise your fists! but her beat-up body told her, you must be kidding.

There was a honk-honk. The cab out front. Henry didn't contemplate for long how to end this. He gave a salute and limped out of the coffee shop, hunched over, right arm hanging lamely. Driblets of nose-blood in his wake.

Ell fell to her knees. Crawled to Hobin. Smacked at his goodly bashed-in face. "Hobin? Hobin!"

He came to. "Did he get away?" he asked through bloody lips.

"With Maplewerm's escape, and now Clerval? We are 0 for 2."

"I'm sorry."

Ell lay down next to Hobin. A long sigh. Maybe a minute of silence until,

"Ell?"

"You're not going to start again, are you?"

"I was."

"Please don't."

"Okay."

Maybe another minute of silence until she asked, "Why don't you love your wife anymore?"

"I don't think she loves *me*."

"Oh."

The sounds of patrons coming out of their hiding places, murmurs of recounting the tale. Sirens in the distance, closing ground.

"Ell? We had a moment here. Didn't we?"

"If 'moment' means we got our asses kicked, then yeah."

"I mean like a bonding of our partnership through this travail."

"Okay yeah, I guess."

"So, Ell?"

"Hobin, don't start."

"Okay," he said, not exactly disguising his melancholy, which seemed more so than the physical pain.

CHAPTER TWENTY
Machine Hand

Victor sat at his desk, staring catatonic-like out the second story window of his office. The sunset-sky was alight, deep orange with a touch of ruby seeping in. The light-molecules pricked at his retina, made him blink, tear ducts reacting. Had scored some weed earlier from his go-to student but was unable to spark up. An unopened bottle of liquor in the bottom drawer. The easy solution of drugs and booze wasn't going to cut it.

Last night, he kept waking up from the recurring nightmare of being force fed hamburgers cooked rare, made from ground-up Blake Lemmonshire. Best burgers he ever ate, which was maybe the point of the nightmare. He gave up on sleep, woke Francine up to confess everything, then changed his mind as soon as her dream-addled eyes found focus and met his. Sorry, he said, I was tossing and turning, didn't mean to wake you. With a groggy rasp, she asked if he was okay and after a pause he said yeah and she said you sure? and he said yeah. She fell back asleep, girly snores.

In the morning, instead of going straight to the university, Victor pulled into an alley behind a strip mall and parked among the dumpsters. Took out the laptop from the shoulder bag that belonged to Blake Lemmonshire. Surprised to be able to access the files without being asked for a password. Not surprised that the contents of the files were encrypted. Trying to figure out a password was one thing. But decoding encryption? Forget about it. How about just deleting the files then? No go per the on-screen message: You are not authorized to activate this function.

So he found a hardware store and bought a sledgehammer and a burlap sack. Suspicion-loaded raising of eyebrows by the cashier. Victor went back to the alley, stuffed the laptop into the burlap sack, smashed it, zealot-like, with the hammer. He distributed the pulverized contents among the dumpsters. All he could do was hypothesize that the trail ended there. His basis? Blake had been ready to cut him loose until he gave the wrong answer, so it made sense she would have withheld from distributing the incriminating evidence. God, let that be the case.

Caught himself just then saying "God" like he meant it, like he was asking Him for a real favor. Had to retract that part of the sentence as a good atheist should. But really, how good an atheist was he at this point? By his fingernails he clung to the cliff wall, about ready to fall to the next level, down to agnosticism at least. For Victor, the desperation and confusion was beginning to trump science and empiricism. Faith felt like a warm blanket. Resistance was futile. Keep it together Gottenberg, keep it together.

He had arrived at his office with the dime bag and alcohol, ready for a pity party, to try and deaden the nagging notion that he basically killed Blake. No, of course he didn't kill her. Well, maybe, if seen through the lens of cynicism and/or guilt and/or remorse, etc. Victor had these elements in spades right now, but these elements were a foreign concept to him. There was only one thing that could shift his gears, get him from low to high, and she coincidentally happened to show up just then.

"Knock, knock," she said from the other side of the locked office door.

As if sunshine had been forcefully stuffed up his ass, Victor perked up, jumped out of his chair. "Francine? That you? Franny, Franster, Franca-licious?"

"I didn't realize you had so many nicknames for me," came Francine's muffled voice through the opaque glass of the door. "It's kind of weird, but endearing I guess?" She stuck her face to the glass. Lovely she was, even in blurriness. "What are you doing? Why is the door locked? Are you doing something weird in there?"

Victor unlocked the door, swung it open, bear-hugged Francine, picked her up, squeezed out a giddy squeal from her. When she landed on her feet, she asked, "Miss me much?"

"Let me count the ways."

"You're gonna like me more after you see this," she said, holding up the carry-out bag. Emptied out the contents on his desk. Beaucoup take-out cartons, a jug of vino. "Thought you might be in need of nourishment after a long day of your professorial duties, which I guess consists of doing what appears to be nothing behind a locked door. So they pay you for this, huh, Prof? Great gig you got here."

"Despite your smart-asseriness, you are awesome." He unscrewed the cap of the jug wine. Took a swig. "By the way, how'd you end up here? Did Henry drop you off?"

"No. I got ditched during our errand."

"He ditched you?"

"Or something. All I know is that he left me sitting in the car forever at the Post Office. I looked for him, but no trace. So I took the car, went for a joyride. Now I'm here." She opened up cartons, ate like she was famished. "Abandonment apparently causes hunger," she said. "Who knew."

Victor pulled out his cellphone, speed-dialed a number. Francine said, "If you're trying to call him, you should know that he left his phone in the car."

"Oh." Pocketed his phone. "This is just weird."

"Not if he's a jerk."

"Yeah, but still." He went to her, held her left hand, currently of the prosthetic type, a fancy type though, the one where it reacted to electrical impulses to open and close mechanical digits. The hand was hastily crafted by Victor from an amalgam of his shelved projects. "So you wouldn't know if he retrieved the package or not?"

"Not a clue."

"Shit."

"Victor. It's okay. If he got it, he got it, if not, then, whatever. I mean, who needs a real hand when I have a cool mechanical one like this?" She stroked his face with it. "And I think this turns you on, what with your robot-girl fetish."

"I have no such fetish," he said, laughing but kinda defensive at the same time.

Francine stuck her prosthetic hand down his pants. "Well, Professor, our *friend* seems to think otherwise." She fondled and stroked with impressive dexterity and had Victor's eyes rolling back, had him moaning and groaning. Until,

"Ooh, ah, ow! Um, Francine, the grip, the grip, the grip. A little tight."

"Oops, sorry." Closed her eyes, concentrating.

"Getting tighter!"

"What?! But I'm trying to make it let go. It's not working!"

Fortunately, Victor's member soon deflated and slipped easily out of the grip. Sighs of relief all around. He fell into his chair, put a palm to his panic-sweat drenched forehead, then suckled at the mouth of the wine jug.

Francine got the hand working again, as if it had never not worked. Plopped her ass onto his lap. "Well, mister, I hope this close call disabuses you of your robot-girl fetish."

They busted out laughing.

After a few more shared swigs of wine, they pretended to be on a space station. Francine, the doctor on call. He, the space mercenary recently attacked by robot-girls and in need of medical attention in the area of his crotch. Lucky for space mercenary guy, the doctor just happened to be a crotch care specialist.

After space sex and polishing off the takeout, Victor and Francine left his office, hands held, waltzed down the hallway of the ancient science department building. The dusty windows were dark now, the sun having set. The outdated lighting system barely lit the way, which was deserted, except for couple of students walking by. Then,

"Victor! My boy!" The voice from a silhouette down the hallway.

"Crap," said Victor.

"Who is it?" said Francine.

"My boss."

"Are you concerned because the most productive thing you did today was screwing your girlfriend?"

"Such the comedienne you are."

The silhouette approached, materialized into Hiram. "Well hello," he said to Francine, took her by her real hand, shaking it. "I'm Dean Hiram Brasz."

"Hello, Dean Brasz. It's nice to meet my man's boss. By the way, do you know what the most productive thing our dear Professor did today?"

"Francine."

"Never mind."

"It's nice to meet you too, Francine. You look familiar. You're not a student here are you?" She shook her head. "Fine, then fine. It's good to know that we've weaned Victor here of that habit. Ha ha."

She turned to her man. "You dated students?"

"Um. So Hiram, you probably needed to talk to me about something, right?"

"You dated while I was in a coma?"

"Hiram?"

"Well, my boy, I was going to meet with you in the morning, but we can talk now I suppose. Firstly, this whole Blake Lemmonshire business…"

"Another one of your girlfriends?"

"No, she was auditing our boy here in regard to the

DOD funds for his project. You do know about the project, yes?"

"Only as a vague and ambiguous notion."

"Well I don't know why he's being so modest. Let me tell you that what he's trying to accomplish is—"

"Hiram? You were saying about Blake?"

"Right, right. Tragic, just tragic. She told me she was going to provide me with her report after she met with you. Did you get a chance to meet her?"

"Yes."

"And?"

"She told me, that uh, everything looked good, that it was all a-okay."

"A-okay," repeated Hiram, nodding solemnly. "That's good news at least, though not unexpected."

Francine asked, "Did something happen to her?"

"Hit by a bus. Truly tragic."

"A bus? How does that happen?"

Victor interjected, "She was stationed in London— I mean, I don't know. It happened after we had our meeting. She went her way, I went mine." He too did the solemn nod. "Yeah, tragic."

Victor and Hiram, heads lowered, taking a moment, a mournful pose. Francine not participating, glared at Victor instead.

Hiram raised his head. "All right then, let's try to get past this tragedy by getting back to the business at hand. Victor, the meeting with the Board of Trustees is going to take place in two days. I would really like to be able trumpet some news about our department. If you know what I mean."

Yeah of course Victor knew what he meant but it wasn't

going to happen. It was time to kibosh the project. Victor had planned to take Hiram somewhere public, like say The Carcass Steakhouse, get him soused, then drop the news. But why wait? Save a few bucks on steak and shots and tell him already. With Francine here, Hiram would likely keep his tantrum and/or crying under control. Victor's smile muscles twitched responding to his thought of the irony of the situation, i.e., informing Hiram that the project was a failure and needed to be terminated, while the bona fide success was standing right in front of the dean's face.

"Actually, Hiram, I do have some news. Not exactly what the Trustees will want to hear though."

But it was Hiram who wasn't hearing it. He was undisturbable, focus-locked on Francine.

"What?" said Francine to Hiram, noticing his stare. She felt around her face. "Is there food on me or something? We were pigging out on takeout earlier, so."

"No my dear, Francine. Your face is perfect," said Hiram, all breathy-like. "Francine?"

"Yes?"

"Francine."

"Yes?"

"Your last name is Styne."

"You know me?"

"Yes."

"Shit," said Victor.

Hiram patted his chest, as if trying to calm himself, his pounding heart. He beamed at Victor. "My God. You've done it." Grabbed Victor by the shoulders, shook him back and forth. Then clamped his palms on Victor's cheeks, drew him in and kissed him smack dab on the mouth.

"What's going on here?" said Francine. Hiram turned to Francine, grabbed her by the shoulders. She responded with, "Don't you dare try to kiss *me*, you old pervert."

Hiram laughed and laughed. "Francine! Oh, Francine! I've never met a miracle in person before." More laughter, then stopped suddenly. "No wait. Not a miracle. Not anymore. You are a scientific reality. Miracles are for universities without the likes of your genius boyfriend."

"Hiram, please," implored Victor.

"Stop with the modesty, my boy. This is beyond anything anybody has ever done. I mean, you've found a cure for death."

"You assholes better start telling me what's going on," she said.

"You haven't told her, Victor?" asked Hiram, then turned to Francine. "You are the first of your kind. At least in known recorded history. I know you because—"

"Goddammit, Hiram, stop."

"Relax, Victor. Take a pill, as the kids say. She deserves to know this. Francine, you were a student here, 10 years ago I think it was."

"Yeah, so?"

"Your death was tragically spectacular."

"Death? Spectacular?" She touched her neck, the circumferential scar. "So spectacular that I lost my head maybe?"

Hiram said, "High-speed death is almost always newsworthy, isn't it? But look at you now. All put back together. Newsworthy in death. Now newsworthy in life. *This* is spectacular."

"Francine cannot be revealed, Hiram."

"Oh, of course, we won't use her real name when we go to publication."

"No! You need to hear me, Hiram. She is not to be revealed in any way whatsoever as being related to the project. She does not exist where the rest of the world is concerned. Got me?"

"*I* was the project?" She looked to Victor, as if for confirmation, but didn't really need it. "I was the project."

"Victor. Having you been smoking too many marijuana cigarettes with your students or something? This will be published," said Hiram, pointing at Francine. "It will be patented. It will be revealed to the world for purposes of licensing rights to be sold."

"Licensing rights?" Victor, indignant.

"Your research is the property of the university and of the funding partners. And when I say 'research,' it includes your girlfriend."

Victor tried for an ironic laugh but it snagged in his throat. "I know you don't mean that, Hiram. You're a little excited right now, but— Wait. Where are you going?"

Hiram fast-walked toward the stairwell, talking to himself. "A Nobel maybe? It would be a first for the university. Yes, a definite possibility."

Victor started after him, but stopped. Francine wasn't budging, arms crossed, brows sinisterly furrowed.

"Mea culpa, okay?" said Victor and extended his hand to her. "If he does what he says he's going to do, it's the end. So for now, please just be with me, help me talk him out of this."

Begrudgingly, "All right." She took his hand. "But hear me, Professor, you are going to be so pussy-whipped."

"I think I already am."

When they reached him, Hiram was two steps down the stairs. Victor grabbed him by the shirtsleeve. "Hiram! I am begging you. If you reveal her...she's not some freak of science to be paraded around. Please. This is personal. I am in love with her, always have been."

"Dean Brasz, please listen to him. Because I really would prefer not to be a freak. And it's true, the jerk really does love me."

Hiram looked at her, them him. Back to her, back to him. His eyes got glossy. He asked Victor, "If you don't want to give up Francine, perhaps you can reanimate someone else?"

"What? Sure, yes. Yes!"

"How soon?"

"Well, uh——"

"Within days, I would hope. Shouldn't be too difficult finding a volunteer, yes?"

"Yes, good one, Hiram. But, you see, uh, there is a situation where, uh——"

"You haven't perfected the process, have you?"

"Yes I have perfected it. About 99% of it."

Hiram leaned in close to Victor's face, spoke through clenched teeth. "I can't let you walk away with this. This is all I have. This is all I am ever going to have. We have the 100% success standing right here, right now. Success is success, even if by dumb luck. It's likely you'll perfect the process eventually. But what if you don't? This it for me, my boy. I have to run with it." He jerked his arm from Victor's hold. Said to Francine, "I'm sorry. But you're young yet, and you've survived death, so I know you will survive this. I, on the other hand, will not." Hiram's face sagged with the weight of his sad little history. "So I ask you to let this old man have his indulgence."

As Hiram took the next step down, he lost a little balance, wobbled. Francine jutted her left hand out, giving him something to hold onto. He grasped it, gave a thank-you nod and a smile. Then he grimaced.

"The grip, the grip!" yelped Hiram. The mechanical fingers were crushing Hiram's feeble human fingers.

"Omygod!" said Francine. Closed her eyes, concentrating.

"Arrrgh!" was Hiram's reaction, followed by popping and cracking sounds of his finger bones."

"Francine! You need to let him go."

"I'm trying, I swear! It's not working."

Hiram's fingers thoroughly squashed, no more popping and cracking, but the flesh was now torn open, blood squirting. He tried to scream but his throat only produced squeaking sounds. Hiram tugged and tugged in desperation at the mechanical hand until it popped off of Francine's wrist stump. The momentum made him fall backwards, head over heels, down the stairs. He bounced and twisted and came to a rest on the landing. His body looked like a flung rag doll, contorted in ways a human body probably should not be.

"Holy crap."

"Stupid mechanical hand."

"Dammit!"

"Is he dead, you think?"

"I would say yes."

"What if he's not?"

"Shit," said Victor. Went down to the landing, felt for a pulse. Looked up at Francine, shook his head. He tried prying loose the mechanical hand but it wouldn't budge. Someone screamed from the shadowy depths of the first floor.

"Ah, shit-fuck-shit." Victor yanked at the hand. Just would not come loose.

"Leave the hand," said Francine. "It wouldn't be the first time."

Victor ran up to Francine, took her by the remaining hand, ran toward the set of stairs at the opposite end of the building.

Francine asked, "Do you feel bad?"

"Yes. But it was an accident. Right?"

"Yeah, an accident. And he seemed nice except for his greed and insecurity."

"I liked him too."

"And so why are we running if we liked him and it was an accident?"

"It seemed like the right thing to do. Things are complicated now."

"No shit they're complicated. And you've got a lot of explaining to do, mister."

"I know. But you don't disagree with the running, do you?"

"No."

"Okay."

"Okay," she said as the patter of their footsteps echoed through the hallway.

Body Count Tally: 7.
1. Joseph Cruciate.
2. Joseph's girlfriend Hannah Potemkin.
3. Cheese-on-a-stick-eating guy.

4. Special Investigator Blake Lemmonshire.
5. Percy's receptionist.
6. Special Agent Proll.
7. Dean Hiram Brasz.

CHAPTER TWENTY-ONE
The False Promise Of A Good Steak; A Tear-Soaked Thumb

Victor and Francine, both with a patina of panic, sheen of sweat from having sprinted from the soon-to-be crime scene, stood before the Ferrari. A citation was pinned under a windshield wiper for parking in the faculty lot without the permit sticker. Victor tore up the ticket, tossed the pieces to the night breeze.

"The keys?" he said.

"The keys to what?" sassed Francine.

"Come on, please? We need to scram."

"So you just assume you're going to drive, because why exactly? Because you're the man? That you're more capable? Or that maybe you just do as you please regardless of the consequences?"

"Let's not fight."

"No, let's. Take your own goddamn car!"

Victor glanced two lots down to where the Mustang was parked. His eyes shifted back to the Ferrari which, even in the unflattering illumination of the low-pressure sodium streetlight, screamed, I'm a diva and proud of it!

"A Ferrari abandoned at a college parking lot just might draw attention that could lead to dot-connecting that we don't want connecting. We can't leave this car here."

"What's the problem then, Professor?" Her rasp became more gritty from the growing irritation. "I drive this one and you drive the other one. It's kinda like 2+2=4. Duh."

"Actually, it's a little more complex than that, sort of like algebra."

"Is being an asshole something you wanna be doing to me right now?"

Victor pointed at his left hand. "I just thought it might be difficult to drive a six-speed and handle a steering wheel for someone in your condition."

She looked at her own left hand. Which wasn't there anymore. "Fuck."

Victor drove the Ferrari at geriatric speed, held to surface streets, wanting to avoid the freeway. It seemed like the thing to do given their potential status as fugitives. He could practically feel the vibe of Francine's eye-rolls. She hadn't said anything since they left the campus but he sensed she was ready to detonate. Didn't want to broach it but knew he had to defuse her.

"So are we cool now, you think?" he attempted.

She shifted in her seat, turned to face him. Her glare, like a clobber to his skull. Then the words gushed forth, steaming with hot anger. "Why didn't you tell me I'd been dead, instead of this bullshit story of a bullshit coma!"

"Well. It's not the kind of information that someone reacts to favorably. About having been dead. You know?"

"No fuckin' shit. I can't even begin to wrap my head around the fact that I was dead and gone, and now, somehow, here I am, back from the beyond."

"You were never in any 'beyond.' There is no 'beyond.' You were always in the here and now. As long as your brain was preserved and remained viable for future potential restoration, there you were."

"Gee, that's romantic," she said with fake glee then resumed the glower. "Stop talking about my death so matter-of-factly." A growl, not certain if from her or the engine. "Where exactly did you have me stored away for a decade? And if you tell me I was a block of human ice in your freezer in the garage with the steaks and weenies, I will bitch-slap you."

"No, no, a conventional freezer wouldn't work. You would have definitely experienced degradation at the cellular level. You needed to be in a cryogenic chamber. Which you were. Which actually is in the garage. But there were never any steaks or weenies in the cryogenic chamber, I promise."

"Hence the locked door, the inaccessible garage. It's your mad-scientist laboratory isn't it?"

"Come on, Francine. I wouldn't go so far as calling me a mad scientist. Hurts my feelings a little."

She leaned back into the high-quality leather seat. "So I really was in a deep freeze for ten years. Holy shit."

"Hey, it sounds like you've come to terms with the situation. I can practically see your angst evaporate into the ether. And I can definitely see a happily-ever-after here, yeah?"

She literally did clobber his skull this time.

"Ouch."

"And that's just the beginning unless you quickly fill me with many stiff drinks."

They planted their asses on stools of the crowded basement bar of The Carcass Steakhouse. Dimly lit. Surly bartenders. Francine said just leave the bottle right here. And when one of the barkeeps stared at her handless wrist, she held up the stump and flipped the dude off with her phantom middle finger. Dude got the hint, not so surly after that.

She knocked back two shots toot sweet. "Is this where you brought your girlfriends while I was dead?"

"Is there a right answer?"

"You catch on quick."

"Will it make a difference if—"

"No."

"Will it make a difference if they were just sad substitutes for you? Literal lookalikes in fact."

"No, God no, that doesn't help at all. It's creepy, is what it is."

Victor blanched. A mad scientist, a creep. Proclamations from the love of his life. He made for the bottle, she slid it out of reach. Ordered a draft instead, took a long draw. Foam fizzled on his upper lip. A heavy sigh.

"Aside from humping clones of me, and of the minor detail of me having been dead, what else have you lied to me about?"

This was it, time to come clean. You can do it, Victor,

yes you can! But he pussed out. "You now know everything that you didn't know before. Scout's honor." Gave the three-finger salute. Contemptible.

Her soused eyeballs didn't show belief.

His phone rang. It was Henry. Victor mostly listened, at times wondered if he heard things right, what with the noise in the bar. Hung up.

"What did your partner in crime have to say for himself?" asked Francine.

Victor told her that Henry didn't mean to ditch her at the Post Office, it was just that he was distracted when the cops showed up and tried to arrest him for the ill-begotten left hand among other things. Oh and by the way, Henry went by Victor's place but kept on going because cops were there now. Victor braced for the impending ire. Which came in staccato bursts of cussing and accusations and the woes of being assembled from body parts in violation of various laws and of now being for sure a suspect in the death of Dean Brasz. And of the fact that he was still being a lying sonofabitch.

Francine slumped a little, tired-looking from blowing her anger-wad. She no longer bothered with the glass, drank directly from the bottle.

Victor thought he'd give it shot, asked her gingerly, "So do you think you might be done now with your rage?"

"No." Sounded half-hearted. Or just weary.

"You sure? How about if I buy you a steak? Call it even."

"Right. Because that's the same, a steak."

Victor pounded down the rest of the beer. Clunked the mug down hard on the bar. "Can I say this? Wait, you know what? Actually, I'm not asking, I'm just going to say it, and what I want to say is that, all of what I did was because—" A contemplative pause. "It was because I was selfish, that's true, but I just could not let you go. I don't care about the scientific achievement or about being 'published,' I don't care about licensing rights, I don't care about Hiram's legacy, may he rest in peace. What I care about is that you're back. I have you back and that is everything, and I've never ever been happier than I am now. I love you and I love you on top of that. You are the sun around which I orbit, and without you, my universe is just a black hole. Can you please possibly understand that?"

Francine wouldn't look at him, but seemed like she wanted to. Chewed on her lower lip, swirled her fingertip in a little booze-puddle on the bar. She said, "That speech of yours just now, was not too bad. Except the part about the sun and black hole. Kinda drama-queenish." She finally looked at him. "Have you told me all truths now?"

The lies that still existed flashed before his eyes. You can do it, Victor, come on already.

"Um, yes, I have told all truths now."

What a pussy.

"Have you really?"

"Absotively."

"Okay then. You can buy me the damn steak."

***

The coffee shop showdown with Henry had left Ell beat but not broken, though she made sure to have the doc write a script for decent pain meds. Hobin on the other hand was indeed broken, like a bull-in-a-china-shop kind of broken. Say what you will about that fucker though, he was a trooper through and through. Wanted to tag along with Ell re: the call about the dead dean but the E.R. doc wanted to "keep him overnight for observations." Hobin's pummeled face had swelled to where he now looked like an angry blowfish, could barely make out the words coming from his fat busted-up lips.

"Erll, ub jonning u abfer gonn ouffer herf."

"Okay, Hobin, I'll see you later. Enjoy the stay. And make sure to ask for the good stuff, the morphine drip."

He gave a thumbs-up, his digit looking crooked. Not clear if he was smiling or grimacing.

***

University, Science Building, about 8:30 p.m. Ell, floating high on meds, the pain from the plethora of her bashes and bruises lovingly muted, her hobble barely noticeable now as she made her way to the crime scene. Her boss had told her not to bother, that another team could handle this one and that her and her beaten ass should take couple days of R&R. Ell's attitude was, gee thanks, boss, for the generous offer but another severed left hand shows up and you expect me to sit this out? Get real. Besides, this would be the third of the severed hands that had come into her purview, and the third time was supposed to be the charm, right?

A crime scene investigator guy she didn't know was packing up his wares. The Uniform watching over the scene, she knew. Jeremy? Jerry? No, Jeremy for sure. A youngster, but competent, an ass she could sink her teeth into. Married and with a kid already. What a waste.

"Detective Lavenza. Good to see you again. Where's your better half?"

"Please don't say that."

The Uniform grinned, his perfect teeth sparkling. "I'm just joshing with you. *You're* obviously the better half."

A tingle to the groin. "So, Jeremy. Tell me what's what here."

"Uh, it's Jerry actually. But it's all right. Jeremy, Jerry, what's the diff, right?" His smile went twinkle twinkle.

Humility even in disparagement. That smile. That ass. The dude was the whole package it seemed. Speaking of package, it took extraordinary willpower to keep her gaze from wandering below his belt.

He pointed at the body, tagged and bagged. "You wanna take a look?"

"No no. Just tell it to me."

So he did. Hiram Brasz, long time dean of the Science Department. His aged skull, like a cracked egg in a sock, from taking a header down the stairs. Jerry having difficulty getting the rest of it out.

"Detective. My words aren't going to do justice with this one. So you're just going to have to take a look."

He unzipped the body bag, pulled out the long scrawny arm of the dean, the right hand attached to it was crushed to shit, blood-caked, and in the vise-like grip of a severed left hand.

"When I heard 'severed hand,' I thought it was the victim's," said Ell. "Whose fuckin' hand is this?"

"Well first, we don't know whose hand it is. Second, it's not a real hand."

"Say what?"

"It's appears to be a homemade, mechanical, prosthetic piece. The kind that takes electrical impulses to make the hand function."

"Sounds fancy and it gladdens me to a certain extent that it's not real, but at the same time, it tends to confuse things a bit, doesn't it?" Pinched the bridge of her nose. Grimaced with agitation. "Got any theories?"

"I've gotta say, this is a tough nut to crack. All I have are harebrained theories so far."

"As long as it doesn't involve zombies."

"No zombies. But there is a mad scientist and a cyborg who—"

"Stop. Don't ruin the ideal image in my head."

"Come again?"

"Nothing, never mind. Just speak no more of your theory."

"How about if I offer you up a witness instead?"

"That might have been helpful information to have at the git-go, Officer."

He made an aw-shucks so-sorry face and absentmindedly adjusted his boys, like guys with a certain virility tended to do, and all was forgiven.

The witness, a junior, who was on her way out of the lab after working on some extra credit stuff, had heard crunchy, thudding sounds coming from the stairwell and saw a figure come to rest on the landing, crumpled like a rag doll. Couldn't make out who it was due to the less than ample lighting of the crappy old building. As she made her way to the stairs, she saw another figure come into the picture and bend over the rag doll person and it looked like he was feeling for a neck-pulse. Then this person looked up the stairs and shook his head, as if saying, no luck, the dude is dead. Then pulse-checking guy started yanking on the arm of the dead guy and that's when the witness screamed, she wasn't sure why, and sprinted out of there, afraid for her own life, she wasn't sure why.

Ell asked, "This guy, the pulse-checking guy, could you at least make out what he looked like?"

"At the time, no," said the college kid. "But in hindsight, his silhouette was unmistakably distinct? He was lanky, tallish, and the giveaway was the 'fro."

"The what?"

"Yeah, he's got like the kick-ass 'fro? Who but a geeky yet actually kinda cool prof could pull that off? Know what I mean? And have you seen his 'stache? I'm usually not into facial hair, but I would totally be okay with him going down on me with that thing. Can you imagine, those bristles rubbing against your—"

"Okay, so. You recognized this silhouette, this man."

"Yeah. It was Gott."

"God?"

"G-O-T-T. Gott, the Gottster. Professor Gottenberg."

"Gottenberg? As in *Victor* Gottenberg?"

"Oh, um, hey. Now that I think about it, it would probably be pure speculation to say it was the Gottster because of the very poor lighting, and speculation can't count as evidence can it? And besides, now that I know that the so-called victim was Dean Brasz, maybe the Gottster had good reason to throw him down the stairs. The dean was kinda creepy. Not that I actually saw anyone throw anyone down any stairs, so…"

The kid's words started the slow fade-out from "Oh, um, hey," until Ell was in full flashback mode. Reversed tape 10 years or so. Freshly minted detective she was, the Hot Shit she thought she was. And she was. Investigating the case of the missing coed, the dead coed, decapitated by way of high-speed collision with the back end of a semi. Knocked on the door of the shitty apartment of a med student with the larger than average brain. Victor Fucking Gottenberg. The purported best bud of the victim. He answered the door with his geek-chic swagger, in his tighty-whities even. Made him get dressed to avoid seeming like she was enjoying the view, which she was. Didn't matter because they ended up screwing anyway like couple of horny maniacs on his dinky dining table in the cubicle-size kitchen. And man oh man was that shit good, was that shit rockin'. Until he called out the dead girl's name, Francine's name, the woman he really wanted to be doing. And man oh man did that shit sting. But then she went back for more, apologizing for chrissakes for her overreaction, only to get kicked to the curb again.

All these years later, the memory of that botched attempt at sexual indiscretion still stabbed at the exposed underbelly of her heart. Why was that exactly? They had known each other only for about 30 minutes, carnally for 10, give or take. And yet, and yet. Maybe it was that moment where he didn't demean her for lamenting her lost marriage, the cheating bastard husband. He told her it was *not* nothing, what she felt, but "everything." That's what he said. That it was everything. She never forgot that. Was it possible? Had it been love at first fuck? Quickly shoved aside the thought, didn't fancy herself the lovesick teenager type. Keep it together Lavenza, keep it together.

Once she pushed past the lovey-dovey stuff, the array of pieces came together. The sage, the miracle worker. Of course it was Victor. He stole Francine's body 10 years ago and lay in wait, used his larger than average brain and university resources to somehow someway bring her back. Collected body parts, lost body parts, tried collecting some more. Lanna Vodak, Percy Maplewerm, Henry the henchman and medico-conspirator. Like stringing pearls, it all fell into place. And she believed it too, that Victor was perfectly capable of being that guy who missed a dead girl so profoundly and would have been affected forever and a day if she weren't resurrected, that he would pillage, destroy, sell his soul to undo the pain, to become a miracle worker, to bring her back.

Ell knew now, Francine was alive for sure. Paraphrasing Percy, she said, "That fucking Victor really did do it."

"Excuse me?" said the college kid.

Ell snapped to, as if awoken. Said, "Oh. You're still here."

"Um, this is my place? So you're the one that's still here. Right?"

"Yes, right."

Then the kid reached for Ell's face, wiped a cheek with her thumb. "Look. A tear," said the kid. "Was it something I said?"

Ell scrutinized the tear-soaked thumb, said, "I think it might have been."

CHAPTER TWENTY-TWO
The Gospel of Gottenberg

Victor and Francine drove into the parking lot of a motel, saw Henry in a T-shirt and PJ pants leaning against the railing of the second floor walkway watching them park in the space directly below. As they stepped out of the Ferrari, Henry said to them, "I'm glad my girl's still in one piece."

"Thanks," said Francine. "But I've lost my left hand. Again!"

"Sorry to hear that but I was actually talking about the car. Thanks for taking of care of her."

"What an asshole," she mumbled to Victor.

"You're realizing this only now?" Victor with a sly grin.

When they got to Henry's room, saw him up close, Victor uttered, "What happened to you?" Victor was referencing the crooked nose, dark circles under the eyes, busted fat lips, bruised cut cheeks, chipped tooth. His neck

with purple marks around it as if having been wrung.
Right arm in a sling and ample length of Ace Bandage
wrapped around the wrist and hand. A pronounced limp.

"I told you, I ran into cops."

"Was it the SWAT team or something?"

"There's no call to be a smartass here. The cops were
couple of thick-necked ruffians. With an assortment of
weapons, okay? I was lucky to get out of there alive."

Francine did an attention-getting clearing of the throat
and said, "While you co-conspirators continue with the
co-conspiring, I'm going to take a shower and wash the
grime of this day off of me." Slammed the flimsy
bathroom door behind her.

"She seems to be in a mood," said Henry. "And how did
she lose her hand anyway?"

Victor fidgeted. "We, uh, ran into Dean Brasz, and
killed him accidentally."

"You know, if we were normal type people, what you
just said would be shocking to me."

"Yeah."

"Witnesses?"

"Possibly."

"Fuckssake, man."

"I know."

"That explains the cops at your place."

"Was it the SWAT team or something?"

"Don't flatter yourself. It was one black-and-white and
an unmarked."

"Really? That's it?" said Victor. His attention then went
to the table in the corner, on top of which was an open
box of one those giant NY-style pizzas, few slices left, a
half-drank 12-pack of brew. Various pain meds laid out,

arranged in a smiley face.

"You hungry, thirsty, in pain and/or wanna get high?"

"No, yes, not necessarily, but."

Victor drank, popped pills. Henry walked over to the bedside table, picked up the motel-issue pen and memo pad, sat on the bed, slowly scribbled with his non-dominant uninjured hand. Tore off the page, stuck it out to Victor and asked, "Hey, you think you can go pick up some things for me? My hand and wrist are shot to shit and I need to make a real deal cast here. I'd go get the stuff myself but that ain't happening as you can see."

Victor eyed the bathroom door. Heard the shower going full blast. "Okay, but look," he said. "She knows stuff now, most of it anyway, for example, the fact that she was dead and not in a coma. But try to keep to the script the best you can."

"Sure, buddy, sure."

Again, Victor eyed the bathroom door. Then Henry drew his attention by unrolling the Ace Bandage, revealing the purpley-blackish ballooned-up, seriously busted-up hand and wrist.

"Egads," said Victor.

"That about sums it up, my friend. So whaddya say? Do me this solid, I'll watch over Francine not that she needs any watching over. Whaddya say?"

Victor snagged the memo pad paper from Henry, stuffed it into his back pocket. "Okay, but I'll be right back. Stick to the script."

"Yeah, yeah, of course. Thanks, buddy. Oh, and make sure you go to that one mega-store, for the good prices and such."

As soon as Victor made his exit, Henry picked up his

prepaid cellphone, pressed three digits. The phone responded with a woman's voice sounding professionally urgent and calm at the same time that said,

"9-1-1, what's your emergency?"

"I am a concerned citizen reporting the whereabouts of a fugitive wanted by the police. Got a pen and paper handy?"

"Sir, I will need your name and address."

"The fugitive's name is Victor Gottenberg. He has embezzled funds from the Federal government, he has traded in black-market human body parts and an actual human body. He also admitted to killing one Dean Hiram Brasz tonight, the incident of which I am sure has already been reported."

"Sir, I will need your name and location before I can forward this information to the pertinent law enforcement agency of the jurisdiction."

"Just contact Detective Elizabeth Lavenza of said pertinent law enforcement agency. She'll know what I'm talking about. But do hurry because this Gottenberg fellow has a larger than average brain and can be quite wily and has an agenda to beat all agendas. Okay, so, this is where the police can find him…"

When Victor entered the discount retailer, was the first time he read Henry's scribbled list of stuff to buy:
- Oatmeal raisin cookies
- More beer
- Chips and salsa
- B-day card for mom
- The stuff you need for a homemade cast

Victor made grumbly noises and put back the hand-basket and snagged a shopping cart instead. Made haste, zipped through the aisles, got bogged down in the "express" lane, paid in cash. Fast-walked to the car, tossed the plastic shopping bags of stuff on the passenger-side seat. Drove past the mega-store that Henry had suggested, saw three black-and-whites pull into the parking lot with lights blazing. Victor didn't have a membership card for this store, hence had gone to the alternative. Those cop cars, a curious coincidence that occupied 2.3 seconds of Victor's brain until his brain re-engaged in assessing said coincidence three minutes later when the telltale flashing red lights bounced off the rearview mirror into his squinting eyes. This cop car was not a cruiser but of the generic sedan variety. Curiouser and curiouser.

Waited to see if the car would pass, maybe was after someone else. Nope. The sedan rode his ass even harder. Victor's threat assessment flagged red. To pull over or not to pull over. The worst-case scenario was that he'd be cuffed, hauled off, charged and convicted of the various offenses, locked away, kept from Francine for a very long time. Or maybe it was just a busted taillight.

What to do what to do what to do. Fuck it. He put the pedal to the metal, confident that the Italian pocket rocket could dust the cop car. Sure enough, the sedan receded in the rearview. But not so fast. Victor hadn't accounted for the fact that he was on a highly travelled surface street, which of course had a number of traffic lights and other fellow drivers. So, a quarter mile later, as he was stopped at a red light, hemmed in-lane by surrounding traffic and contemplating his current heart-lung aerobic capacity to evaluate the feasibility of an on-foot getaway, a woman's voice said,

"Congratulations, Professor. You now hold the record for the shortest car chase ever."

He looked over his left shoulder from whence the voice came and got an eyeful of gun barrel. Then, her face came into focus.

"Ell! It's you."

"Hi, Victor. I have to say, when I have my gun pointed at someone, they're usually not so happy to see me."

"My eyes are sore. And you are a sight for them."

Her mouth twitched like she was suppressing a smile.

"So, Ell? Wanna get some coffee or something?"

Ell wanted to nosh so they settled for a nearby pizza joint tucked in between a dry cleaners and a bank, the same pizza joint from where Henry's NY-style had come from. They served no coffee but had decent iced tea. Ell ordered a slice of pepperoni. The place was empty except for a college kid waiting for his takeout order and a geriatric hippie getting his body-English on at the pinball machine. Ell and Victor took to the booth in the back next to the grimy-door restroom.

"You sure you don't want a slice?" asked Ell.

"Had some steak earlier."

"The Carcass?"

"Yup. You've been?"

"Of course. I was the one who suggested the place to you. Remember?"

Victor blinked, thinking, then the realization. "Oh! Yeah you did. Best steak/bourbon place suggestion ever."

"Ah, the bourbon, the bourbon." Licked her lips. "Well, I'm going to partake of this slice and you're just going to have to watch." Took a bite and another. Chewed. And he did watch, like he was studying her, and she went on chomping and chewing without a hint of feeling self-conscious which was weird given the close scrutiny.

He reached over with a napkin in hand, wiped her chin, the orangey pepperoni grease. He said, "Whatever happened to that a-hole husband of yours?"

"Which one?"

"There's been more that one?"

She shrugged.

"I'm talking about your first, the one you told me about back in the day."

"Oh, that one. The bastard married that bitch."

"What, really? Your best friend that you caught blowing him?"

"Yup. Two kids. Got divorced though. Not that I was keeping track."

"So what's going on otherwise? Relationship-wise, I mean."

She let out a grunty sigh. Decided to finish off the slice, except for the crust 'cause she was a not a crust-eater, before she answered. "Nothing to tell. Mostly a string of losers and assholes and near-misses and only-sometimes-good-sex." And she smiled a little. "That includes you."

"Oh ho. I hope you mean the sometimes-good-sex part."

She said nothing, kept that slight smile, walked to the counter to get another slice. When she returned with a mushroom-anchovy, she said, "This is not normal, is it, this conversation we're having? Ten years since our ill-fated tryst and we're, just like that, talking about our sex-fest?"

"For you and me? Yeah, it's totally normal. Birds of a feather and all that."

She harrumphed.

"So look," said Victor. "I'm sorry about what happened. I am, really. But I wouldn't have tapped your goods if I didn't think highly of you in that moment."

"Right, because every girl wants to grow up to be a dead-girl substitute."

"Wow, this is great, rehashing good times. Yeah?"

Sure he said it as sarcasm but he also had an expression of a little boy trying to get away with something. Cute. Damn him.

"Victor, I don't want you to get the wrong idea about —"

"I know why you're here. But what happened to the dean, it was an accident."

"There's the other stuff too."

"I know. But it was all for a good cause."

"Then let me just take you in. I need to take you in."

"It's complicated."

Of course it was. What to say to that? She ate away at the pizza slice, got to the crust, tossed it onto the grease-stained paper plate.

Victor continued: "I don't mean to be a smartass, but —"

"But you're going to be anyway."

"But I'm going to be anyway and say, when was the last time you arrested someone for bringing a dead person back to life?"

Ell had already surmised that Francine was resurrected. But to hear Victor say it, for it to be finally confirmed, was a dizzying revelation, like God whispering in her ear, letting her in on a secret.

"Ell? You still with me?"

"..."

"Ell?"

"Yeah yeah, I'm good."

"I assumed you figured it out."

"I did."

"Let me ask you. When you were investigating her disappearance years back, did you ever know what she looked like?"

"Yeah, but her image now is pretty fuzzy, I was mainly focussed on her vital stats. Didn't really need more than that for a corpse."

Victor pulled out his smartphone, tapped the screen a few times, showed her the display, a photo. "This is her, my Francine, alive and well."

What would a chick have to look like to engender the love, the determination, the insanity, to make someone, anyone, expend the brain power and effort over the course of ten years to accomplish the impossible, not to mention breaking of laws, both State and Federal, like Victor had? Okay yeah, looks weren't supposed to be everything, but still. So Francine had damn well better look like what Ell imagined she looked like, which was someone built like a supermodel, long and lean, 5'11" at least, with perfect curves in perfect places that could only have been purposefully placed there by the hand of God. Her face, sculpted by Michelangelo's ghost.

The photo of Francine revealed nothing like Ell had imagined, and frankly, kinda anticlimactic, and she wasn't thinking that way just to quell the tinge of jealousy. "Pretty" wasn't exactly Francine's suit, quirkishly cute at best. The initial unfiltered question that came from the id side of things was, why go through the trouble of a jewel heist just to get at cubic zirconia? But the ego side understood better and said, whoa there, and explained that this guy was really truly batshit head over heels in love with the essence of Francine Styne.

This "thing" was what Percy Maplewerm had espoused. This really-truly-batshit-head-over-heels-in-love thing and the possibilities it held in keeping loneliness at bay was Percy's religion and Victor was the sage. And how about you, Ell? Were thee now a disciple? Was the Gospel of Gottenberg potent enough to crack through your shield of cynicism?

Ell knew she was grinning stupidly but couldn't make it stop. Victor reciprocated, inspired him to talk about his dream, or what used to be his dream, but was now a to-do list: the split-level ranch-style with the white picket fence and the oak tree in the front yard (or could be in the back) where he would hang the tire-swing and build the tree-house, and—

"A swing and a tree house? For you and Francine, or can I assume you're planning on kids?"

"A boy and a girl."

"I would ask how you can be so sure about that, but you're 'you' so I'm sure you'll find a way. I bet you already have names for them don't you?"

"Jack and Jill."

"Jack and Jill," she repeated, choking on the names a little.

"What? No good?"

"No, it's not that. The names are lovely."

"How about you then? Any kids in your future?"

Not something anyone ever asked her about except her dad who lamented the fact that she hadn't popped out a few potential linebackers by now. But sure, she'd thought about it. Ell answered Victor thusly: "The docs tell me that my uterus is a piece of crap." She exhaled, shakily said, "So no kids in my future. I guess God's got the lone-wolf theme going for me." A shrug.

"Have you seen a specialist?"

"Several."

"Maybe you need to see more."

"I think I've seen all that I need to see."

"You haven't seen me."

"Wha?"

"Like you said, I'm 'me,' so I can find a way to make it work."

Ell could only gawk, as words were not forthcoming. She let her head be in the clouds for just a few seconds, then forced herself to get her feet back down onto terra firma. Pulled out the cuffs, laid them out on the table and asked,

"Why did you tell me all this? Do you have some kind of expectation that I'm going to just let you walk?"

He had that little boy look again, but this time expressing hurt, totally making her feel like shit. Damn him.

He said, "I don't know if I had any such expectation, maybe what I had was hope? Mainly I was having a nice conversation with someone I thought I had a kinship with."

"You're a fucker," she said under her breath.

He bent his right ear forward with the index finger, asked with a grin, "Pardon me?"

She scooped up the cuffs as she pushed out of the booth. "I'm going to the restroom now, and when I come back out, I'm making like I came here by myself to have some affordable, delicious dinner. Got me?"

"Got ya. And I'll be contacting you for our appointment re: your uterus. Don't forget your insurance card. I'm kidding."

"Thanks," she said and was about to enter the restroom when she turned back to him. "By the way? I think you have a snitch on your team."

Took him only a second to get it. "Henry?"

Ell nodded.

Victor responded with a terror-stricken look and bolted out of the pizzeria. Didn't even say good-bye.

CHAPTER TWENTY-THREE
From Somewhere Long Ago Of A Dark History

With a towel wrapped around her torso, freshly-scrubbed Francine stepped out of the bathroom. Looked for Victor but saw only Henry sitting on the edge of the bed cramming pills, sucking down beer. She started back-pedaling into the bathroom when Henry said,

"Hey, you. Come on out. Join me. I've got some grade-A pain meds here."

"Uh, um, sounds good, I guess. I'm just going to get dressed first."

"Nah, it's okay. I wanna take a look at you."

"Excuse me?" Another step back.

"Your scars. They're not healing well, are they?"

She touched her neck, the scar, tender and raw. Had known it was getting worse but ignored it. Denial, maybe? No "maybes" about it.

"Victor asked me to take a look at you."

"He did? Really?" Searched the motel room again. "Where is he?"

Henry stood, grabbed a beer, popped the top and offered it, said, "Quench your thirst."

"Where is he?"

"Running an errand. Here, drink up."

She was indeed thirsty. Took the beer, glugged and glugged. Relaxed her a little. Henry reached for her neck scar, caressed, then pressed hard.

"Ow!"

Henry showed her his fingers on which was a fair amount pus-goo squeezed from her neck scar. "Damn that guy," he said. "You're falling apart and he's neglecting you."

"First of all, gross. Secondly, he loves me, Henry."

He chugged his beer, belched. "I don't deny that, but what kind of love are we talking about? The self-serving kind, or the giving kind?"

"How can you even accuse him like that? He proposed to me didn't he?"

"Huh?"

"Don't act stupid. The ring was lost in the accident. It was on my severed left hand."

Henry thought about it for a second then laughed. "I'm sorry," he said between guffaws. "I'm sorry for everything. When I agreed to help bring you back, I didn't realize to what lengths he'd go to make you his. He took advantage of an opportunity."

"Stop talking like that. You're supposed to be his friend."

"He's gone too far, Francine. There was no ring, he never asked you to—"

"Stop! Please!" She clamped her wrist stub and hand over her ears, not wanting to hear it, not wanting to know that Victor maybe was still keeping truths from her.

Henry put his beer down and with his non-busted-up hand, gently massaged Francine's shoulders, alternating between right side and left. She tensed to his touch until she couldn't anymore. The guy had some mad massage skills.

"Francine. I'm telling you what I'm telling you because Victor's got you fooled and I refuse to be a party to this anymore. I'm making amends here, okay? So you need to know that there was no ring. He asked you to marry him, not that he wouldn't have. But you would have said no and he knew that." Done massaging, Henry picked up a slice of cold pizza. "He chased you all his life. You loved him but only as a friend." He bit into the slice, and with a mouthful, he said, "Then you died. Or should I say, committed suicide."

Francine dropped the beer. A foamy puddle formed on the shit-brown carpet. Her breathing labored. "Why would I do such a thing?"

"You suffered from Major Depressive Disorder. And yes, of course he knew."

She suddenly contracted room-spins. Dizzily, she went to the floor, on hands and knees. Puked up the beer. Henry helped her up, laid her down on the bed.

"Hair of the dog," he said, picking up and handing her the beer.

Francine sipped, rinsed, swallowed, ridding the acridity. Drank some more, dropped the empty on said shit-brown carpet.

Henry said, "I totally get it. You offed yourself for good

reason and he brings you back without your consent, knowing full well that you left us on purpose. That is some fucked up shit to do to someone."

She tried to say, can you stop talking, why do you keep talking, but the words stopped short of coming out of her mouth, caught in her throat. Tried again and said for real this time, "But you helped him do it."

"Can't refute that. But he was very convincing that he could bring you back and how could I resist such a thing, a freakin' miracle? To see you alive again, my very good friend? How could I resist? So again, trying to make amends here."

He handed her another beer and she downed it. Closed her eyes, sought perspective. Couldn't find it just then. Felt Henry's hand slip under her towel, slid up her thigh to where the scar was, squeezed, made her yelp. He showed her his palm. More puss-goo.

"Are you trying to hint at something, Henry? Maybe like an organ transplant gone wrong, my body is rejecting this 'donor' life kinda thing? First it was my left hand, and next, my right leg, then my head rots off? Is that it, is that what you're so inconsiderately suggesting?"

"I won't let that happen. Let me take care of you."

Wouldn't that be fantastic? Just to spite Victor. But she had to ask, "Why didn't I love him?"

"It wasn't your thing."

"What is that supposed to mean?"

"You didn't love anybody."

"Ever?"

"Never."

A sense of horrification made her shiver. "Was I a sociopath or something?"

He shrugged. "Probably not. It's not like you went around chopping up your neighbors' pets, that I know of."

"Henry, if it was your intention to make me feel like absolute shit, you succeeded fantastically."

"Look, Francine, I don't care if you were or are a sociopath or whether you can or cannot 'love' someone. And just because you couldn't 'love,' didn't mean you couldn't 'like' and you managed pretty well with that. *We* managed pretty well with that."

"You and I?"

"Don't be so surprised. We rocked as a couple."

She gave a doubtful look. "Really?"

"Okay so maybe we were only in the 7th grade and maybe the extent our relationship was kissing and groping under the bleachers but I like to think that I was the first 'like' of your life."

She had a mouthful of beer when she laughed, some sprayed out, some sloshed in her sinus and dribbled out of her nostrils. A mixture of snorts, coughs, cackles. Her towel slipped open, a fit of naked convulsions, probably not too attractive, but Henry clearly did not mind.

He pounced and lay out full-body on top of her. Jammed his mouth against hers, slid in the tongue. His large mitt pawed at her nudity. Hot and heavy it went until he pulled out his thang and made for her sweet spot.

"Whoa, Henry, wait. We need to stop."

He didn't.

"Henry, please?" He vise-gripped her thigh-scar. "Ow! What are you doing? Ow! Get off of me."

"You need to listen up, Francine. He doesn't *love* you, he *covets* you. You're just an object to him to fulfill his ego. You are his prize science project." His eyes smoldered with hatred. "I've got the real thing to offer. True love."

"Victor's love brought me back to life. Your kind will end up killing me. Now get the fuck off of me!"

He punched her scarred thigh, made her whimper. Still trying to force his way in, she squirmed, struggled, but fighting against his body weight and his strength was exhausting, couldn't last much longer.

Francine's right arm, the one with the remaining hand, was free. Reached out for something, anything. Felt the bedside table, but nothing. Henry now had a forearm against her throat and she sucked for air but no use, suffocation just around the corner. Kept feeling around on the bedside table.

Still nothing.

But then there was a memo pad. Then a motel-issue pen. Francine gripped the pen like a dagger. Plunged it into Henry's neck. His eyes went wide, mouth gaping but no sound. She yanked the pen out, blood dribbled. With a wind-up, she stabbed his neck again. When she pulled out the pen this time, the blood squirted like a fountain. Henry sat up, holding his wound but the blood poured out between his fingers, streaming down his arm. He staggered off the bed, yanked Francine's towel away and pressed it against his neck. Stumbled backwards into the table, knocking it over, maintained his balance by bracing against the wall. The white towel quickly saturated red. He focus-locked on her, let the towel drop, trudged at her. His face, his body, seethed with fury which did not seem to originate from the now but from somewhere long ago of a dark history.

He kept moving toward Francine but plodded as if shouldering a boulder. By the time he reached the bed, the blood no longer spurted, but only trickled from the lack of pressure. His eyes, no longer rageful, fading out, closing up shop. He teetered, fell face first onto the bed, bounced hard off the mattress and thudded onto the carpet in a heap. Francine scooted off the bed, stood over him. Didn't need to check for a pulse. The giveaways were the dead-fish eyes, the dry-tap neck wound.

She headed into the bathroom, checked her naked body in the mirror. Paw prints everywhere, bruised neck, the scar there bleeding with a mix of puss. Same with her thigh-scar. Her face and torso splattered with the would-be rapist's blood. She knelt before the toilet, dry-heaved into the bowl. Then noticed that she was still gripping the pen of death, dropped it in the water and flushed.

Francine crawled into the tub and turned the shower on and she lay out on her back the length of the tub. Watched the blood wash off, the draining water turning pink. The shower-spray pelted her and the water was very cold but she welcomed it and she stayed that way until she was shivering, until she was numb.

Body Count Tally: 8.
1. Joseph Cruciate.
2. Joseph's girlfriend Hannah Potemkin.
3. Cheese-on-a-stick-eating guy.
4. Special Investigator Blake Lemmonshire.
5. Percy's receptionist.
6. Special Agent Proll.
7. Dean Hiram Brasz.
8. Henry Clerval.

CHAPTER TWENTY-FOUR
A Reasoning Entirely Improper

Ell hated it when she showed up to a crime scene and the body was not yet tagged and bagged. Preferred human brutality to be dealt with behind the veil of a body bag. She especially hated it when the victim was someone she knew, a situation which had never happened until now.

Henry Clerval for chrissakes.

A trail of blood-crust from puncture wounds in his neck, his T-shirt caked with profuse dried blood. The upended table, the blood-soaked towel, the blood-soaked bed, the blood-soaked shit-brown carpet. Dead eyes wide open. Tongue lolling out between his teeth. An overall pathetic-ness to his death. But Ell would bet her left nut if she had one that Henry probably had this coming.

"We've got prints galore," said the crime scene investigator guy with some merriment. "Three sets, fresh and sparkly new, others not as good, smudged, likely from prior guests and staff. The prints have been scanned and being processed as we speak." He pointed at his laptop sitting on the bedside table. "The Wi-Fi here is pretty lame so the upload-download is taking some time." He walked to the computer to take a look. "Here we go, got results now. We've got a Henry Clerval, a Francine Styne, and the third is a 'no data found.'"

Ell didn't really need to see the third, knew who it was already. On the inside she said, "Goddammit, Victor. What did you do?" On the outside she said, "Oh. Darn."

"No no, it's okay. I think we've got the third. Here, look." Showed an artist's rendering of Victor Gottenberg.

"…"

"Detective? You recognize him or something?"

"Um, no. No I do not." Ell swallowed. "So there was a witness I take it."

"Yup. Said he saw this guy with the 'fro and porn 'stache sitting on the floor next to the victim. The victim looked 'pretty dead,' his words."

"Fan-fucking-tastic," she said, struggling to manage a fake smile.

Ell slept like crazy that night. No alcohol, no pain meds, just sheer exhaustion. Hadn't set the alarm and woke up late but not refreshed whatsoever. Maybe should have done the booze and meds after all.

When Ell finally got to work, she saw Hobin back at his desk. He still looked battered and bruised but was healing well. Seemed skinnier. A half-empty dozen-donut box sat open on his desk, Hobin apparently trying to un-skinny himself.

"My man," she said. High-fived him.

"Hi, Ell." Donut-glaze roosted at the corners of his grinning mouth. Same ol' Hobin. "Jeez, Ell, it's good to be back. Jeez!"

"Are you trying to tell me that you prefer being in this hole rather than flat on your back on a state of the art hospital bed being zonked out on morphine drip?"

"Ha ha, Ell. I missed that, your humor."

"I'm being serious."

"Ha." He swiveled his chair around, pointed at the info on his computer screen. "You've been busy. The dead dean. The dead doctor. And positive I.D. of the professor for both crimes."

"Hold on. There's no positives about it."

"Okay, if you want to get technical, let's call it 'implicated.' That's fair, right?"

She fidgeted.

"Ell?"

Faked a couple of coughs.

"Ell?"

She picked up a donut, a sprinkle-coated one. Took a hefty bite. Sat at her desk, typed at the keyboard though the computer wasn't on.

"Are you hungover again, Ell?"

"I resent that comment."

"Ha ha, good one." He started working on a chocolate-covered. "So is that the first of our agenda today, bringing in the professor?" Like a dog with a bone he was, wouldn't let it go.

"Hobin. Did you notice something peculiar about the prints found at the motel where Henry got his?"

"Nope."

"Are you lying to me?"

"Maybe."

"You do realize Francine Styne is——"

"No."

"Yes, she is."

He shuddered. Twice. Turned paler. "So you actually saw the zombie freak?"

"Well——"

"Oh God, oh God."

Looked like he was going to crap his pants. She felt kind of bad for capitalizing on his childhood fears of ghosts and zombies. But what to do? She believed in Victor, or at least she still wanted to, but with Henry showing up dead with Victor's fingerprints all over the place, she needed time to sort things out. When she next looked at Hobin, he had finished the chocolate donut and now was double-fisting the twisty glazed ones, alternately chomping between the two. He had the look of a baby suckling on mama's teat, seemed to relax him. And for the next hour or so, he mentioned nothing about going after Victor, and instead, worked on the backlog of paperwork. Until,

"Oh hey, Ell? We have a meeting by the way with a Special Investigator."

"Say what?"

"Some guy from the Treasury Department." Hobin ruffled through the detritus of his desktop, found the semi-crumpled napkin with his scribbles on it. "The guy's name is Patent Pending."

"I think you heard wrong."

"No, I asked him to repeat it." Squinted at the napkin. "He said it the same way."

"What does he want?"

"The professor."

Ell took an uneasy breath. "What for?"

"For the *implication* of the professor's involvement in the death of his fellow investigator..." Checked the napkin again. "...Blake Lemon-Sure."

She let go a weary sigh. Then searched and scrounged through desk drawers but only came across one empty flask after another. "Crap."

The proposed meeting was for lunch at a buffet-style Chinese food place, but per Ell's suggestion, they instead met in front of a liquor store, next to which was a hole-in-the-wall cafe that served the best gyros. The Special Investigator's name was not Patent Pending but Patton Bennding. He looked older that the mandatory Federal retirement age by 10 years, his lids sagging, heavy with gravitas, giving an appearance of perpetual sadness.

Bennding watched Hobin help Ell fill her empty flasks with the just-purchased bottle of peaty Scotch while he gave his spiel. His co-worker, Blake Lemmonshire, had been tasked with auditing Victor regarding the funds provided by the Department of Defense for his vaunted project. She never made it back. All that was known was that she had completed her investigation, met Victor, then died terribly. She had filed no report, which was unusual. Also unusual, her standard-issue laptop was missing. So the embedded tracer was remotely activated and the computer turned out to be located at the residential property owned by one Victor Gottenberg.

Ell suppressed a groan.

The signal then led to a nearby strip mall where the transmission ceased, where the laptop was likely smashed to smithereens and disposed of. Bennding checked the database of local activity and got a number of hits of recent "Gottenberg sightings." Found out that Ell and Hobin were the team handling said sightings. Based on Victor's latest shenanigans, Bennding now believed that there maybe was some funny-business involving Blake's death.

The flasks topped off, Ell capped them shut. A gulp's worth left in the bottle. Bennding pointed at the bottle, showed a receptive palm. Ell handed it over and he drained the contents down his throat.

He went, "Ahhhh!" Said, "All right then. You hungry? I am. The guy-roes are on me." Tossed the bottle in the nearby trash can, led the way to the cafe.

The gyros were delectable. The conversation was not, and it went something like this:

Ell: Victor's involvement in the dean's death is questionable, the witness unreliable.

Bennding: Are you on a first name basis with the professor?

Ell: (ignored the comment) As for the death of Henr— Dr. Clerval, my preliminary assessment is, it was caused in self-defense.

Bennding: Let's leave the 'preliminary assessment' to the D.A. There's more than enough probable cause to bring in your friend regarding all three incidents.

Hobin: (a dribble of cucumber sauce on his chin) Four-plus incidents actually. He stole a dead body, procured black market body parts from a necrophiliac, and now, he's got a zombie named Francine Styne wreaking havoc on the good citizens.

Bennding: Don't know exactly what the heck you're talking about, Detective Hobin, but it sounds like more

P.C. to me, doesn't it, Detective Lavenza? In fact, this professor sounds like a mad one, an insane one, someone who needs to be locked away.

Ell: Come on Bennding, I checked the file, and there's zero evidence of foul play in regard to *your* friend, Blake Lemmonshire. Why bother, why are you even here?

Bennding: Detective Lavenza, how about doing your elder a favor and pass along one of those flasks to me?

Ell: (gave him a jaundiced look for propriety's sake but handed over a flask anyway)

Bennding: (took the flask, unscrewed the cap, took a few swigs) I'm in mourning, Detective. In mourning for my friend, in mourning for what could have been. Maybe Blake was out of my league, maybe that's why it took me some time to muster up courage to pursue her. But I ultimately did make up my mind, and I was going to let her know how I felt when she got back. Though of course she never came back and I blame Professor Gottenberg for that, whether he actually pushed her into that oncoming bus or not, and I want him to suffer rightly for it. I know that this reasoning is entirely improper from a law enforcement point of view but I just don't give a damn.

Hobin: (impressed)

Ell: (felt one of her intense headaches coming on)

Bennding: So boys and girls, let's go do some professor hunting.

Hobin: Yes! And let's mow down that zombie freak bitch while we're at it!

After Bennding picked up the check and he and Hobin headed to the restroom, Ell fast-walked out of the cafe to the car, got in and laid her head against the steering wheel and stayed that way while Bennding and Hobin were finishing their respective piss. Bennding was a dickhead but some of what he said gave her pause. *Was* Victor "mad," *was* he "insane?" Ell thought about the dead dean, dead-Henry, Percy Maplewerm and his contributions to the "shenanigans" of Victor. Blake's stolen and destroyed laptop. If it had been anyone else, Ell would have cuffed his sorry ass and brought him in. So why exactly was she giving a pass to Victor? Was her judgment clouded by the Gospel of Gottenberg? Hadn't studies shown that there was a fine line between the emotion of love and the condition of insanity?

She wasn't any good at love but was damn competent when it came to her job. So, what's it going to be, Ell? Were you indeed a disciple? Or were you going to do your job and smite a fraudulent sage?

CHAPTER TWENTY-FIVE
Bonnie And Clyde

Victor arrived at the motel room just as copious amounts of blood was coagulating. Hoped it was only Henry's. Traced the source to two puncture wounds in Henry's neck, one obviously having penetrated the jugular.

No sign of Francine.

Victor stood over Henry. His purported best bud, now a corpse. Didn't give a shit though. "You sonofabitch." Quaked as he said it. "If you so much as touched her…"

He walked over to the toppled table and picked up a chair by the legs, raised it over his head to bash it into Henry's. But didn't do it because what would be the point of pummeling the skull of a dead guy? Tossed the chair aside, sat down next to the asshole. Many thoughts, none good, swirled in Victor's mind like razor blades. Except the one thought where he should have realized that he left the room door open for potential witnesses to gander. And sure enough, standing at the open doorway was a bug-eyed middle-aged dude in swim trunks, probably coming from a soak in the spa, his "fur coat" matted to his man-breasts and impressive paunch. Mr. Witness padded away, his horror-filled squeal ascending with each step.

"That's just great, Victor," said Victor.

Before he vacated yet another potential crime scene, Victor searched for anything that could incriminate Francine, for example, the implement by which she killed Henry. He found nothing because Francine was forward-thinking like that, even in a heat-of-the-moment stabbing of which he was sure was a justified taking of a life. While he was at it, he looked to dispose of Henry's wallet to delay his identification but couldn't find that either. Francine again taking advantage of available resources because she was forward-looking like that.

But where could Francine have possibly gone? Henry's wallet provided her with cash and his I.D. with which she could garner his home address. So Victor sped the Ferrari toward Henry's place believing she had taken a cab there, a place to collect herself, to hide out.

But wait a minute.

Would she really do that knowing Henry's would be the first place the cops would head to after finding his body? Victor went from fast-lane to ramp exit without much concern for his fellow drivers who honked and flashed brights for his inconsiderateness. Pulled into the parking lot of an off-brand convenience store. Half-expected, and hoped, to see a woman named Eunice behind the counter. But, no. Victor bought some teriyaki-flavored beef jerky and a cherry slushie and sat in the Ferrari, chewing, slurping, agonizing.

It took a meditative half hour of the chewing and slurping to slow his mind, tamp down the anxiety, and then, "Eureka!" he actually said.

Started the car, engine revving aggressively. Rocketed out of the parking lot, raced back onto the freeway. Several lamb-tail shakes later, he was at the motel, not the one where he'd left dead Henry but the one across the street, the only other motel within reasonable walking distance, a place where one would collect herself, a place to hide out and where someone as forward-thinking like Francine would choose so Victor could track her down eventually without her having to call his cellphone in order to avoid leaving a digital trail.

"Hello," he said to the wired and wirey young woman manning the check-in desk. "I'm supposed to meet my friend but I think she gave me the wrong room number?"

"Oh yeah really, a 'friend'? Sir, we are a respectable establishment and don't allow for the patronizing of patrons."

"She's not—"

"I'm kidding. It's totally allowed."

"Can I just give you her name?"

"Yeah yeah great idea." She typed on the keyboard, her wide-open pupils staring at the computer screen. Still seemingly confounded.

"I haven't given you her name yet," said Victor.

She laughed. "No wonder her info's not coming up!" Victor gave her the name and she clicked-clacked some more on the keyboard, read the room number off the screen.

He hurried out of the office, noticed the cop car across the street. Paused only for a moment, didn't give a rat's ass, then happily skipped to Francine's room. A gentle knock-knocking he did.

"Franny, Franster, Franca-licious—"

The door flew open, a tightly clenched cute fist launched and KA-POWED! his chin, sent electric shivers to that place just behind the kneecaps, giving him momentary wobble-legs. She walked away but left the door open. A good sign, the left-open door, he supposed. Rubbed his chin goodly, stepped into the room, into the potential fracas. Stayed standing close to the threshold and watched her lie down on the bed, assuming the fetal position with her back to him.

"I'm more than a little disappointed it took you this long to find me," she said.

"Henry being dead and you being gone and likely having been violated and/or hurt, my mind wasn't in the place of rational thinking. It took a meditative half hour with an icy drink and dried meat before I figured it out."

No one said anything for like a minute. Little tremors trembled Francine. Then she said, "What are you doing still standing there? You need to get your ass over here and comfort me."

He ran the 11 feet, slid onto the bed, spooned her. "Please tell me you're okay at least, please tell me Henry didn't, didn't, didn't—"

"I don't want to talk about that."

"But but—"

"Shut up."

"But—"

"Shut it."

"Okay. I love you."

"Just hold me for now."

And he did hold her and she continued to tremble and there were sirens from the second wave of law enforcement and emergency vehicles arriving across the street and when the sirens finally went quiet, she no longer trembled and he heard her girly snores and followed suit. When he awoke, morning light seeped in between the blinds and Francine sat at the table with arms crossed, legs crossed, just plain looking cross.

"Good morning, Sunshine," she said, voice gravelly, tone humorless.

A feeble "Hi" from Victor as he sat up, clinging to the blanket.

"Let's get the first order of business out of the way. It was self-defense. Your friend was an asshole of the worst kind. He maybe didn't deserve to die but it was one of the hazards of being who he was and he knew it. So. I can justify *my* actions. Which segues nicely into the second order of business: *Your* actions."

Victor's internal organs felt to be shuddering.

She let him stew, then asked, "What, no witty retort? How about more lies to cover for the lies you told about the other lies?"

No. No witty retort. No more lies. All he could do was cower like a beaten dog. And pray, yes pray, please, dear God, please please please, she can beat me up all she wants, physically, verbally, emotionally, but please, let her not stop loving me. He made the last-ditch promise of desperate souls: I will do whatever you want me to do if you grant me this, I will believe, my Faith shall not waiver.

Francine stood, walked to the bed and leaned toward Victor, lifted his chin with her index finger. "I didn't even love you in my former life. Not even an iota."

Those words, like ice-pick-stabbings to his eardrums. His metaphoric heart hemorrhaged.

Francine leaned in closer and he couldn't hold her stare and so she said, look at me, Victor, and he still couldn't and she commanded again. This time he complied, returning her gaze with a wince.

And then, she kissed him.

Because he was in utter shock, it took a moment before he thought to kiss her back. Her mouth, supple and warm, tasted like love, like from the kisses of his most cherished dreams.

When Francine pulled back, she told him, "You're a sly bastard and you're going to be in the doghouse for a good long time. But I love you."

The word "sicrylaaf" (Old English, Germanic origin) is defined in the dictionary as: 1) the intense, joyful reaction of an individual in the doghouse who gets a reprieve; 2) A reaction of such immense merriment that results in the simultaneous expression of sighing, crying, and laughing. Example: *Victor sicrylaaffed after Francine told him she loved him despite the fact he was a no good sly bastard.*

Francine and Victor hugged it out, rollicked and rolled on the bed. When there was a pause in the action, Victor had to ask,

"Did Henry tell you everything?"

"Yes he did."

"I mean everything."

"Yeah."

"And you really still love me?"

She clamped her right hand and left wrist stub on his cheeks, looked deep into his weepy peepers. "Okay, maybe I have a problem with the fact that I committed suicide and you resurrected me, which is basically bringing me back against my will, although I remember nothing about my suicidal state of mind so you lucked out in that sense. And I don't necessarily regret being alive right now except maybe the fact that I've now been involved in the death of more than one person and the cops are on the chase and also the fact that if the truth of my existence is revealed, I will be the ultimate freak of science and we will never, ever, know a day of peace from there on out. But aside from that? I didn't even love you and I abandoned you, but you persisted because you loved the holy shit out of me and who else in the universe would do what you did, risked what you risked, to bring me back not even knowing the outcome of how I would feel about you? That's some bat-shit crazy love, Professor, and what girl wouldn't dream of that? So, to bottom-line it for you, the answer is yes, after all that was revealed to me by Henry, I really do still love you."

"That was like, the best monologue ever. So do you see? Why I love you?"

"Of course. I am totally lovable," she said with eyes a-twinkling, lips a-smiling.

Victor hopped to his feet atop the bed, started up on a weird jig.

"What the heck is that, Victor, what are you doing?"

"My happy dance."

"Please stop, you're hurting my eyes."

She swept his feet out from under him and he bounced off the mattress and they laughed, clutched each other, kissed and kissed. She clamped his face again and said, "Take me away from here, Professor Gottenberg. Sweep me off *my* feet."

***

The Ferrari sped down the freeway, a red blur, doing her utmost to deliver the passengers to freedom. With the top down and in the light of day, Victor could no longer ignore Francine's condition, the ominous dark under her eyes, sallow and sunken cheeks, the neck-scar raw and wet, a gauntness as if she were dwindling, getting ready to disappear. Francine caught him staring and told him to keep his eyes on the road.

"But, Francine."

"I know. I'm okay for now."

"I'll make you better. I will."

"Eyes on the road please."

Victor abided, shifted gears angrily, the engine responding with a vicious whine.

She placed her hand on his thigh. "Victor. Maybe you need to accept that you can't control everything, that there are limits even for you."

"Francine—"

"Listen to me. If God wants me back, there's not a whole hell of a lot we can do about it. Let's enjoy the time we have left."

Shook his head hard. "No! God cannot have you back. I won't let that happen."

Less than 24 hours since he made his promise to God and already Victor was going back on his word. Victor knew this but felt justified because what God wanted was unfair and contradictory. To have been granted Francine's love only to have her taken away? Downright cruel. No way, not gonna happen.

She leaned her head against his shoulder and told him okay, but said it without much conviction.

***

Firstly, they needed replacement identities. And although it pained them, they knew the diva, i.e., the Ferrari, had to be ditched as well. Despite Henry's corporeal state, he had some utility left. Victor contacted Henry's "guy" for the I.D. makeover who responded that any referral of Henry's was a-okay by him.

His place was located in the heart of the downtown revitalization project, downtrodden being converted to upscale. The guy was a largish fellow in his late 60s maybe. Imagine Santa Claus with a close-trimmed beard, dye-job hair in a ponytail, wearing a striped polo shirt, cargo shorts, flip-flops. The large square frames of the designer nerd-glasses worked nicely in conjunction with his rotund face. The place of "business" was his residence, a swanky 3-bedroom condo. The decor, nothing out of the ordinary, bachelor-chic. They walked past the master bedroom and past the second one to the last bedroom. Guy unlocked the door and said come on into my office.

The first thing noticed, in the corner over there of his "office," was a glass case of handguns. A long table against the other wall, on top of which were three monitors, and underneath, several computer towers. There was a commercial grade copier/printer nudged against the end of that table. At the other end was what appeared to be a work area littered with hand tools and various electronic type components.

Guy said, as he sat in front of one of the computer monitors, "It's been a while since I heard from Henry. Has he finally been thrown in jail? Or dead maybe?"

"Uh, he's uh, little under the weather right now," said Victor.

"Henry's been a good customer but he's got the aura of someone who's gonna get shivved in the jugular one day," said Guy, prophetically. "Know what I mean?"

Francine said, "Oh yeah, totally."

Victor nodded uneasily.

"All right, then." Guy opened up programs on the computer. "New I.D.s and Socials, a clean slate." He scrolled through what looked to be a list of names on the monitor. Told them they should go with the names Bonnie and Clyde, then laughed, explained that he got a kick out of seeing couples' expressions when he said that. In seriousness, he suggested they be a married couple going by the names of Heloise and Abelard Smythe, even showed them an array of wedding rings with an option of fake or real bling. Francine whispered to Victor that it better damn well be the real bling because no way was she settling for cubic-Z and any non-precious metals. But Victor was in agreement even before she made her "suggestion," and in fact, asked Guy whether he could just marry them for real given his full-service operation.

"Interesting you should ask," Guy said. "I am an ordained minister of the gospel and in good standing the last time I checked." Thumb-pointed at a framed certificate on the wall next to the Ph.D degree. The certificate indicated that Guy was indeed a Minister Of The Gospel In Good Standing. "From my long ago past," said Guy.

He then opened a desk drawer and pulled out a photo album, opened it, giddily showed pictures of happy couples with Guy in between flashing a grin. "Looky here. Your predecessors, all of whom entered into holy matrimony under the authority vested in me. And to think my daddy thought I wouldn't amount to be anything but a social menace. So what do you say, kids? I can get you hitched for an additional nominal fee."

Of course they said yes and picked out rings of the real bling kind and Guy pronounced them man and wife and Victor and Francine kissed the kiss of eternal love and Guy dabbed his damp eyes with a hanky.

Victor, staring at the glass case of guns, asked, "Are those available for purchase?"

Guy said, "You're in luck. I have a sale going on right now on his-and-hers 9-mil handguns."

Francine asked Victor the question with a look and he responded,

"Till death do us part."

She understood, nodded.

They went to the parking lot, stood before the Ferrari and Guy whistled a whistle of appreciation then led them into the underground garage. Took the car-cover off of a pristine 1965 metallic blue Mustang.

Guy said, "I know she doesn't have the trade-in value of your Ferrari but she's a beaut as you can see, and her pretty little ass can haul. You two have chosen the path of fugitives, so speed and cool are now necessary tools of the trade and this baby will give you that. So what do you say? Do we have a deal?"

Victor and Francine looked at each other and grinned knowingly. Guy being an ordained minister and now the classic Mustang? This had to be more than mere serendipity and coincidence. This was a fate sandwich with destiny and providence being Wonder Bread.

"It's a deal," said Victor.

CHAPTER TWENTY-SIX
Fugitive Juice

Five days since Special Investigator Bennding's proclamation of the commencement of the hunt for Victor, and of Hobin's battle-cry of "let's mow down that zombie freak bitch," and they had zilch in terms of a lead. They'd gone to Henry's condo, found "exotic" porn; a supply of sought-after type meds in an amount sufficient to stock a small pharmacy; stash of cash and a passport (under an alias) tucked in the freezer and wrapped in butcher paper marked "sweetbreads;" a .22 under the mattress; a .38 stuffed in an unused running shoe in the closet. Otherwise nothing pertinent to the investigation. Then off they went to Victor's place where there was pertinent-a-plenty, including the state of the art operating room in the garage and well-preserved body parts and organs which Hobin surmised were spare parts or possibly snacks for the zombie girl. But nothing there in regard to the couple's whereabouts. Checked with the University, Victor hadn't been seen since Dean Brasz was found dead.

Next, they headed to the Styne residence, Bennding's idea of a good idea. He was insistent despite Ell's protestations that Francine's parents probably had no idea of their daughter's resurrection and that two detectives and a federal investigator showing up at their door asking whether they knew the location of their dead daughter would meet with disaster.

"When someone's desperate, got nowhere else to go, they head back to mommy and daddy," said Bennding.

"Even if their kid is a zombie?" asked Ell with sarcastic jab.

"*Especially* if the kid is a zombie," said Hobin, relying on his suspect zombie lore.

Bennding ended up with a black eye from a decent right jab by Mr. Styne. Hobin ran for his life, away from an andiron-wielding Mrs. Styne. Ell, safe in the sedan, watched the whole debacle unfold then had to explain to the cops called by the Stynes that the whole thing was an embarrassing mistake.

The trio retreated to a bar in the hotel Bennding was staying at. They huddled in a booth, mulled their next step. Bennding held a glass of Scotch-rocks to his swollen eye, studied Ell with the good one, asked,

"You seem to be cogitating particularly hard over there. Got any ideas?"

She picked at the label on the beer bottle. Almost glad that Bennding had asked the question, otherwise she maybe wouldn't have volunteered the information that had been volunteered by Victor himself. That night at the pizzeria, their 10-year reunion, he told her about his dream, his life with Francine, not only in terms of his aspirations but of the REM-sleep-produced kind where a particular location played prominently for whatever reason. He told her this because she was someone he had a kinship with, someone whom he could trust. But how could it be a betrayal on her part if he was a criminal after all?

Ell finished the beer, plunked the bottle down on the table. "I think I know where they're headed."

"How do you know that, Ell?" Hobin's inquiry.

Bennding interjected. "I don't give a crap where or how you got the information. All I need to know is, how sure are you?"

Victor had a way of making his dreams come true. So Ell said, "Very."

"Okay then. Where are they going?"

She told herself to say it already, just say it, say it, say it, because you can't be on the fence forever and you had to do your damn job and this pie-in-the-sky bullshit you're holding onto re: Grand Love was not your thing and you needed to fall back on your default position of being a hater of all things lovey-dovey. So she finally spat it out. "Vegas. They're headed to Vegas."

*****

The speedometer of the pristine 1965 metallic blue Mustang hit 98 mph as she blazed down the desolate desert stretch of the Interstate headed toward Las Vegas. Victor's idea, his grand vision, part of the dream life, the place where they were supposed to have their honeymoon. Francine said what the heck, sounds romantic. But they had to get tats, he said, because that was part of the dream too and the dream was their gospel. She asked what tattoo the dream insisted she get and he answered, "Property of Victor" in the font of Monotype Corsiva. Francine said I love you but sorry no, I'll give you the font, but I don't think so otherwise, instead, howsabout a "FS&VG" with a heart-shape around it? He asked whether it could be inked on her ass and she responded, no, a tramp-stamp is my best offer. Victor brooded some and she said chin up, mister, and he was like, oh-all-right, and she was like, damn straight "oh-all-right."

The first tattoo place they came across was situated next to one of them legal brothels. The tattooist admitted that the font of Monotype Corsiva was not his strength and suggested Apple Chancery instead. Victor made a face. Francine told tattoo dude that would be fine. Along with the face, Victor made grumbling noises à la truculent child.

"Okay, okay. Don't be such a baby," she told Victor and pulled down her pants and told tattoo dude to put it on her ass, the left cheek, her good side. Victor beamed.

Then it was Victor's turn. He had the truncated version of Nabokov's words from his dream placed on his wrists. He put his wrists together and Francine read the sentence, said, "Huhn. Famous last words, so to speak. Hope it ends better for you."

***

For three days they didn't leave their hotel room despite the awesome buffets, the tempting casino action with what was claimed to be the loosest slots on the strip. The two lovebirds, Victor and Francine, were like a couple of teenagers discovering the new world of naked pleasures, reveling in copulatory delights. Drunk on love, life, and room service that catered to their every gastronomical whim.

On the fourth day, while eating breakfast for lunch because lunch was when they dragged themselves out of bed, Francine asked, "Where do we end up?"

"You mean like the house with the white picket fence?"

She nodded, chomping on a croissant.

"Um, actually, the place was never clear in my dream."

"So we have room to maneuver then?"

"What's on your mind?"

They finally left their room to check out the sights, but before leaving the hotel, Victor and Francine moseyed on over to the concierge desk and asked said concierge whether he knew of a certain type of property for sale, or at least point them in the direction of a reliable realtor.

"I can give you a name of a realtor who will charge you the industry standard whereas I will only charge you one Mr. Benjamin," said the concierge.

Victor checked his wallet. "Will it be all right if it's five Mr. Jacksons instead?"

The concierge blinked in assent. "What is it that you and the Mrs. are looking for?"

Francine stepped up to the desk, leaned close, said, "A place where couple of fugitives can settle down, home-base it, somewhere on the outskirts but not so much so where it'll take an hour and a half to get a pizza delivered. Me and the Mister like our pizzas."

He, the concierge, raised an eyebrow, the left one, while one side of his mouth, the right side, cracked a smile. "Honey, do I have the perfect fixer-upper for you."

The place was 28 minutes from the Strip. Took the

interstate, then veered off and followed a two lane road, took a left, another left, then down a dirt road and then there you were, deceptively desolate but still within a reasonable distance for a pizza delivery. A house, adobe-style, with an agave farm attached to it. They negotiated the sale directly with the owner, the concierge's cousin. Victor asked what the cousin did with the agave plants and the cousin responded that he sold it primarily to hipster companies who made organic clothes and paper and alternative sweeteners.

Victor inquired, "What, no tequila?"

The cousin shrugged. "Yeah, tequila, but I don't have the touch I guess. It didn't sell too well, not at all really. So I mothballed the distillery and relabeled the stuff as an all-purpose cleaner to get rid of the stock. Got a few bottles left if you wanna cap the deal with a drink."

Victor looked to Francine then back to the cousin and politely shook his head.

***

The newlyweds fixed up the fixer-upper which included refurbishing the modest distillery because this was their life now, or at least the cover story of what their life was: farmers of agave, makers of hooch. And it took some trial and error, minor explosions, taste tests, but they eventually improved upon the cousin's recipe and reached a point where the product was ready for public consumption or so they hoped.

The mailman, playing the role of guinea pig, after taking a shot or two and his eyes rolling back in pure joy, asked to buy a case of the stuff. And what better marketing than your mailman's word of mouth which in due course reached the neighbors, other mailmen and mailwomen and fellow postal workers and their neighbors and eventually to those running the premier restaurants on the Strip as well as those running the dives on the outskirts, all clamoring for the concoction, recalcitrantly named Fugitive Juice.

The booze biz kept Victor and Francine busy but they had their fair share of free time and so Victor started his novel about the college professor obsessed with a dead girlfriend and driven to insanity and Francine started an all-girl band. She couldn't play strings or keyboard what with her left hand situation but with the new prosthesis, she sure as heck could play the drums, and that's what she did, a quick learner she was, and had a singing voice that wowed despite her sandpaper rasp. The band's sound was of a Blues revival infused with a '70s inspiration and a pinch of Trip-Hop. On the Stratocaster was Kat, the mailman's recently dropped-out-of-college daughter; the keyboard, played by Mona, a 40-something former showgirl married to a cop who was an avid patron of Fugitive Juice; and on bass was Eugenia whose background was unknown because she didn't say much but she sure could spank the shit out of the four tautly tuned strings. Victor loved listening to the band practice in the distillery which by the way had great acoustics. The music energized him, during which time he cranked out his best writing.

This was it, the dream, his dream, their dream.

Wait though, something was amiss. Ah, of course. Though putting one up was not pragmatic and kind of stupid given that this was a farm, it had to be done, the path of the gospel had to be adhered to. He went to the home store, picked up the necessary materials and tools, and while Francine looked on with raised eyebrows, he installed the white picket fence around the adobe-style home.

When he was done, she unraised her eyebrows and said, "I love it," and gave him a smooch.

Victor pushed his luck, said, "All we need now are Jack and Jill."

The shine in her eyes clouded over. "Victor. If I can't be there for them, then—"

"Don't say it. I told you, you're going to be fine, I'll keep you fine. You're not going anywhere."

She did a why-can't-you-just-listen-to-me sigh and headed back toward the house but then seized up, toppled over, landing on her ass. It was the right leg, like rotting on the vine, finally giving out. Within 24 hours, the leg became gangrenous, had to be amputated, which took no effort and the term "amputation" perhaps a misnomer because the leg tore off at the scar with a firm tug. Francine said I told you so but Victor shook his head, labeled it a minor setback, planned to get a healthy replacement leg, and she said oh really? from where? the leg store? Her tone was scornful. Victor didn't have an immediate answer so settled for a prosthetic leg, put in a rush order.

Francine kept on keeping on, living full force, cranking out the Fugitive Juice, getting tighter as a band which was almost ready for prime time, and being a wife to the man she loved. All this in spite of her condition, of her life slowly seeping out of her, God's reclamation project.

On one of their weekly jaunts past the rear property line and onto the adjoining property (which was desert wilderness, a knoll on top of which they laid out a blanket), they got drunk on the Juice and spent quality time under the night sky full of constellations, and Victor blurted out that maybe he was up against it, i.e., God's intent vs. his, but that even if He succeeded this time, Victor would just bring her back, like he did before, despite the fact that he had not figured out the Eunice factor that sparked Francine back to life. But the Eunice part of it, Victor kept to himself. Francine's response was a panic. She begged him please do not do that, just let me die with the memory of us as it is, because what if you bring me back and I'm a clean slate like before with no recollection of our love and of what we had to go through?

"Please, my dear husband. Promise me that."

Victor looked away, said nothing.

"Please? Promise me."

When he turned back to her, he was all clenched and shaky, tears welling. "I can't do that, Francine."

"Listen to me. You got what you wanted. You have my love and you'll have it for eternity. If you bring me back, all bets are off."

He pretended to think about it, blinked away the tears. Said as convincingly as he could, "Okay. Your wish is my command."

CHAPTER TWENTY-SEVEN
Always The Bridesmaid

Las Vegas, not the most populous of cities in the U.S. of A., but looking for two people based on a hunch, even with the resources of the federal government, was at best a wait-and-see proposition according to Bennding. A little over a year since the trail went cold on Victor and Francine, and Ell was bouncing off the walls. Bennding had gone back to D.C. to monitor the data coming in from Vegas. Told Ell to practice patience because it was a rare breed of fugitive who didn't ultimately get comfortable and/or cocky and ended up revealing themselves and becoming part of the data stream. She told Bennding, "Fuck that noise," but what the heck else could she do? She had no access to any of that high-tech data collecting bullshit and she couldn't just up and storm the shores of Nevada because of a thing called "jurisdictional limits."

"Fucking jurisdictional limits," complained Ell as she distractedly waded through paperwork on other files.

"You've been getting more irritable by the day, Ell," said Hobin from his desk. "You need to have faith in what Special Investigator Bennding says about waiting it out."

"Bennding is a dickhead."

"Ell..."

"Can't you see, Hobin? The longer we wait, the big-brained bastard aka Victor Gottenberg aka the Mad Scientist gets further and further away, what with his calculated scheming and planning and—"

"Are you in love with the professor or something or at minimum lusting after him?"

"What kind of stupid-ass shit is coming out your mouth right now?"

"Your behavior is symptomatic of sexual tension compounded by sense of abandonment which equals manic behavior including rage, and in your case, more so than usual, the rage."

"How the fuck would you even know such a thing?"

"My wife, soon to be ex, displayed the same symptoms, not for me, but because I was an impediment to her sexual fulfillment."

"Seriously?"

"She told me as much in our doomed counseling sessions."

"Yikes. Sorry to hear it but you're reading me all wrong, Hobin. This is my usual manic rage. I'm just doing my job."

"That's why I ask because I'm wondering if you can. Do your job. In your condition."

"There is no 'condition.' You're barking up the wrong

phallic symbol. And if you ever question my ability to do my job, I will kick your sorry, soon-to-be divorced, fat ass. You get me?"

"How can you love a criminal and not an upstanding law-abiding and law-enforcing citizen like me?!"

Ell plunged a right hook into Hobin's puffy belly, bent him in half, and he deflated like a balloon with a slow leak, flattening out on the floor. She stood over him, waited for the apology but instead, he grimaced at her, wheezed out, "I'm not sorry. I'm not sorry."

What the? Very un-Hobin like, his non-apology and sass. Ell raised a fist, contemplated dispatching another punch at the head of the Judas but kinda difficult to do when the pathetic fool dripped pain-induced drool and tears. Ell needed a scapegoat, went to the phone, dialed, waited and waited until the dickhead answered.

She tore into Bennding about there having been no results reported by him and that it was enough already with the be-patient bullshit. And then she let loose with her diatribe about the bloat and bureaucracy of the federal government and his being part of the creaking machinery and—

"Chrissakes, woman," said Bennding. "Have you stopped drinking or something? Because if you have, it's not working for you. Get off the wagon and start imbibing immediately."

"Goddammit, Bennding, I'm sick of being a wallflower at this party. Give me something, anything, even a pretext, so I can get you to get my ass into Nevada under the umbrella of federal jurisdiction."

"You sure are demanding for someone who has zero leverage. I take it you're single. Am I right, Detective?"

She slammed the receiver repeatedly against the desktop while spouting invective.

"Ell!" said Hobin. "That's government property."

"Bennding?" she said into the cracked-in-half receiver. When there was no answer, she went to Hobin's phone and dialed again.

"Uh, please don't break my phone," said Hobin.

Bennding answered with, "That was just rude, Detective. But having said that, I am simpatico to your predicament. So I will share with you information that has been trickling in from the target area which may be relevant. Have you ever heard of the Trade in Tequila Agreement?"

"Uh…"

"I didn't think so. You drink it, don't give a crap where it came from. I understand. But here's the deal. Tequila can only be produced in the country of Mexico, but per the Agreement, it may be bottled in the U.S., which means significant economic benefits for U.S. businesses, in the hundreds of millions of dollars."

Ell with an intentional heavy sigh.

"By your intentional heavy sigh I sense you may be thinking that this old geezer is spouting irrelevant cow pie, but listen up, Detective. Because of the Agreement, there is federal oversight and those responsibilities belong to the ATF and to the Treasury Department. You do remember who I work for, right?"

A gurgle of irritation rattled in Ell's throat.

Bennding continued. "All news of tequila gets intercepted, put into the federal data-flow and red-flagged where necessary. Just so happens, the law enforcement in Las Vegas is buzzing about a new product distilled locally."

"Are you seriously thinking Gottenberg and Francine have become bootleggers?"

"Different names but they fit the physical profile. And get this. They've named the tequila 'Fugitive Juice.' Ain't that a big F.U. to us?"

"Have they been picked up by local authorities then?"

"You must be kidding. No one gives a rat's a-hole about nickel-and-dime B.S. like this. They're not buzzing about it because it's a good bust. It's just chatter about how good the product is. In other words, they're satisfied customers."

"So what are we waiting for? Let's move!"

"Down, Detective. I'm in the process of getting authorization from upstairs. Besides, the Zombie and Mad Scientist aren't going anywhere. The freaks are apparently married now. They're nesting."

"Married?" Couldn't hide the hint of panic in the question.

"Yup. Mr. and Mrs. Smythe, Abe and Heloise. Ain't it romantic? Probably planning on having a couple of baby freaks." He laughed until the laughter degenerated into phlegmy coughs.

Ell placed the receiver down onto the cradle of the phone.

"What? What happened?" Hobin asked. "Why do you look like that? Did the Special Investigator find them? Are we headed to Las Vegas? Why are you crying?"

She turned her head away from him.

"Ell?"

If she spoke, the sobs pressing against her diaphragm would for sure escape.

"Ell?"

She made a quick exit to the restroom, made sure it was empty, stepped into the last stall, locked the door and punched it and punched it and punched it until the door was speckled with knuckle-blood, until she felt she had justification for her crying.

CHAPTER TWENTY-EIGHT
The Lovingly Prepared Dinner

In the fading light of the setting sun, they sped down the dirt road that led to the agave farm, kicking up an abundance of dust in a not so generic, government-issue vehicle. A Humvee, the best the local field office could offer on short notice. Bennding didn't give a shit, in fact, seemed to relish the show. Drove like he was freakin' General Custer, late getting to the Last Stand, his Last Hurrah.

Hobin sat shotgun holding on for dear life but giggling like a child whose joy was based on the immediate and with no concept of the potential consequences. Ell, like a harried mother, telling the gung-ho kiddies to calm the fuck down. Pinched the bridge of her nose, trying to will away the onset of the irritation-headache and trying but failing to keep at bay the thought that this excursion was perhaps a very bad idea.

They skidded to a stop in front of the adobe-style house but not in time to avoid the white picket fence. Bashed it pretty good. Bennding and Hobin hopped out, opened the rear hatch, pulled out and quickly strapped on bulletproof vests, retrieved and readied semi-automatic rifles and checked their sidearm. Ell stepped out of the Humvee, put her nose to the air, took in the aroma of freshly baked bread and either pot roast or pork chops. Pan-fried potatoes too, maybe? Obviously dinner-time. It seemed unlikely that Victor had, or cared about, culinary skills, so Ell assumed it was Francine cooking up a meal for her and her hubby.

Ell's mouth watered, her stomach gurgled. Imagined the couple sitting, not in their dining room, but in the kitchen, at a small table with barely enough room for two, overloaded with food that would last them a week in leftovers, and Victor uncorking the Cab Franc, pouring it for Francine into a coffee mug because they hadn't gotten around to getting proper wine glasses yet, and Francine taking a sip and making "mmmmm" noises and saying dig in my love and asking how was your day and Victor answering oh nothing too exciting, still working on my mad scientist plan to make us live forever so we can love forever, and by the way, I've come up with a solution for Ell's infertility because I did promise to help her with that after all. Wonderful, Francine would say, just wonderful because Ell seems like a beautiful person who totally deserves your help. Then they would eat and not have to talk while enjoying the lovingly prepared dinner because it was like that with them — comfortable with each other even in silence.

Ell suddenly got the urge to cook for real, like by way of

a stovetop and oven even though she primarily was a microwave maven. And maybe invite over that guy her mom had been trying to fix her up with, the son of a former teammate of her dad who had washed out of the NFL due to injury and was now selling cars but with ambitions of buying into a fast-food franchise. Per her mom, not the physical specimen he used to be during his playing days but still a pretty good catch.

Ell turned to the jackasses. "Listen to me, jackasses. Stand down. Relax. I'm going to walk up to the door, knock, announce our presence, maybe get invited to the dinner table and have a nice little chat with Mr. and Mrs. Smythe over pork chops and pan-fried potatoes and ask them to peaceably come down to the field office where we can talk about what may or may not have happened, sort things out."

"Pork chops?" asked Hobin smacking his lips. "Please let me come with you, Ell."

Bennding slammed his palm on the hood of the Humvee, said, "Woman, did you leave your balls back home in your panty drawer? You want to talk to the perps did you say? You want to break bread with them? Sort things out? We're talking about a zombie and a madman here, we're talking about a couple who've left a trail of dead bodies. On top of which they are violating an international treaty with their distilling of apparently high-quality tequila. As the lead officer, it is my call as to how this is going to go down and I am going to batter-ram the door, kick the newlyweds facedown to the floor, cuff them and interrogate them until they tell me what I want to hear, and if not, I will beat them senseless until they confess."

Ell was ready to slug Bennding in the chin that he was jutting out when she heard Hobin gasp. He was bug-eyed, pointing a jittery finger at the house. The porch light had come on and there stood Francine at the doorway looking in their direction with hands on hips, head tilted questioningly. She wore an apron that said "Kiss The Sexy Chef."

"Hello?" Francine asked.

"Z-z-zombie!" announced Hobin and took cover behind the Humvee, then opened fire.

The shots strafed across the front of the home, shattering windows, Ell yelling "No no no!" over the rat-tat-tat of the rifle-fire. Bennding also took cover and joined in the shootout, apparently a way better shot than Hobin, hit Francine, collapsing her. Ell punched Hobin in his glass jaw which made him stop shooting and he bounced forehead first off the rear fender of the Humvee. She then turned to Bennding, planted a knee to his boys which caused him to fold over and face-plant into the dirt.

Ell sprinted toward the house, but halfway there, she realized Francine was no longer lying at the threshold. She then heard three consecutive pops of a handgun-discharge coming from the house. The bullets clank-clanked into the Humvee. Ell hit the deck. She stayed there for what seemed like forever but was more accurately something close to 30 seconds. With the gunshots seemingly stopped for now, she hopped onto her feet, and staying crouched, ran toward the house, entered with gun pointed. A smear of blood-trail led down a hallway.

Music played in the background, wafting from somewhere within the house. A familiar tune, lodged in her memory since childhood. A song of the R&B-funk

genre to which she had watched her parents dance a slow dance to in the living room one night when it came on over the radio. Her dad, a strapping young NFL linebacker in his prime, pulled her looker-mom away from her kitchenly chores. They danced, cheek to cheek. Ell was maybe six or seven years old then, but she got it, she understood. And admittedly she's been longing for the same ever since, that magic her parents had.

Crackle of rapid gunfire snapped Ell out of her reverie. The shots came from the Humvee, from Bennding, who stopped firing long enough to yell out,

"Victor Gottenberg aka Abelard Smythe, Francine Styne aka Heloise Smythe. Surrender now. There is no escape. The premises is surrounded. And Detective Lavenza, be advised. The stunt you just pulled in assaulting a federal officer has caused you to be labeled as a Hostile."

More strafing of the house.

Ell mumbled, "Fuck off, Bennding," and followed the blood-smear which led into the kitchen where Victor was kneeling next to Francine's sprawled out body and performing chest compressions on her.

"Come on, Francine," he gasped out. "Almost there. Come on, come on."

With each pressing of her chest, blood seeped from Francine's mouth. A puddle of blood pooled on her torso from the bullet wounds and soaked Victor hands. Francine was clearly dead.

"Victor…"

He looked up. Tears on full gush. "Help me, Ell. Help me. Please."

"Victor," she said, swallowing hard. "There's no helping

her anymore."

"No no, it's still possible. I just need…" His eyes were frantic, searching, grasping for anything. "…need to get her to my O.R."

"Snap out of it, man. Your former residence has been locked down by the Feds, including your so-called O.R. in the garage. Besides, it's like a thousand miles from here. Listen to me. There's a federal officer out there, along with my dumb-ass partner, who are hell-bent on taking you down. The fact that you shot at them has given them even more license to do just that." She knelt down next to him, put a hand on his shoulder. "I'm sorry but it's over. You had your run with Francine. And now, you need to just plain run."

His eyes flickered to life. "You're letting me go?"

"I've never arrested someone for bringing a dead person back to life and I'm not about to start." She reached out to Francine's face and brushed aside strands of hair. "The hard part of my job is that sometimes the difference between right and wrong is not so black and white."

"Ell?!" It was Hobin, inside the house somewhere. "Are you okay? Please tell me you're not dead. And by the way, did we nail the zombie?"

Then, Bennding's voice. "To anyone in here, and I mean anyone, I will not hesitate to use deadly force, and in fact, I challenge you to challenge me because I am up for it. You hear me?!"

Ell stood, said in an urgent whisper, "Victor, you need to get up now and do as I say."

He stayed slumped over Francine. "I cannot leave her here, Ell. I can't"

"Do not complicate things. She is dead. There is nothing more you can do except to save your own ass."

"She comes with me or no deal."

"This is not a negotiation. I've handed you a gift, okay, so you need to be kissing my ass and saying 'sure, Ell, whatever you say, Ell.'"

Victor stood, straightened himself out. "My ass is not worth saving if I can't take her with me." He walked toward the counter, grabbed the 9mm handgun from where it lay next to the sink. "I will die trying."

"Goddammit." She turned her attention to the entryway of the kitchen, heard Hobin and Bennding's shuffling steps approaching. Ell looked at Victor, then back at the entryway, then came to a decision.

"You win. But you must do as I say. Do you understand?"

He nodded.

She holstered her own weapon and confiscated his gun and told Victor to hurry up and get into the pantry. He did as told. Ell hid along with him and left the door ajar just enough to poke the barrel of the gun through.

Victor asked, "You're going to shoot them?"

"It's okay, they're wearing vests. I'm just going to knock the wind out them."

And so they settled in, waited.

Hobin entered the kitchen, pointing the rifle-muzzle wildly about until he saw Francine's body and trained his gun on her.

"Omygod omygod it's the zombie."

"Let's not start crapping our pants, Detective." It was Bennding. "Because she looks pretty dead to me."

"B-b-but she's a zombie. How can you be sure?"

"I'll show you." Bennding walked to Francine and pointed his gun at her forehead.

"Motherfucker," hissed Ell, took aim, shot Bennding's right kneecap off, then put two into Hobin's chest, knocking him on his ass before he could react. Bennding, though wailing in pain, admirably crawled toward the gun he'd dropped. But Ell put a stop to that by shooting him in his left ass cheek. While the jackasses moaned and writhed on the kitchen floor, Ell stuffed the 9-mil into her waistband, told Victor let's move.

They carried Francine to the Mustang, placed her on the back seat. Ell called in and reported that officers were shot and that she herself had been wounded and the suspect was now on the move in a white four-door sedan headed due west.

"You need to haul your ass outta here," Ell told Victor. She handed him his gun. "But first, you need to shoot me."

"What?"

"Right here," she said, pointing at the meaty part of her thigh. "There's plenty there, so shouldn't be too much damage done."

"Ell, I can't."

"Do you want me to get fired? And thrown in jail?"

He shook his head, but asked, "Can't I just tie you up or something instead?"

"No offense, Victor, but no one's going to believe I was overpowered and hogtied by you."

He did a semi-flex of his sad little right bicep and said, serious-like, "I beg to differ."

"Beg all you want but it ain't happening so you need to man-up and do this my way."

Victor did his little-boy-sad-face and hugged her and told her thanks and took aim but she said wait wait wait, then unstrapped the non-company-issue .22 from her ankle and handed it to Victor and told him not to judge her just because she preferred to be shot with the .22 rather than the 9-mil. He said no way would he pass such judgment and expertly shot her exactly where needed. It hurt more than she thought, more so than when Percy had shot her. She planted her ass on the dirt driveway, took off her shirt, balled it up and pressed it against the wound. She popped open the bottle of Fugitive Juice Victor had left for her and guzzled as she watched the Mustang disappear behind the kicked-up dust cloud under the blast of moonlight. Ell let out a long, shaky sigh, put her head in her hands because she could no longer hold it back.

"I'm sorry for your loss, Victor," she sobbed. "I'm so sorry, I'm so sorry, I'm so sorry..."

Body Count Tally: 9.
1. Joseph Cruciate.
2. Joseph's girlfriend Hannah Potemkin.
3. Cheese-on-a-stick-eating guy.
4. Special Investigator Blake Lemmonshire.
5. Percy's receptionist.
6. Special Agent Proll.
7. Dean Hiram Brasz.
8. Henry Clerval, and finally,
9. Francine Styne

CHAPTER TWENTY-NINE
Double Redundancy

Victor drove the Mustang down the freeway with Francine laid out on the back seat rotting away by the second. Took him a great strength of will to keep from exceeding the speed limit to avoid unwanted attention from expected company. Sure enough, here came a helicopter with spotlight ablaze flying toward his farm, the light training on the Mustang for a few seconds then moving on. Soon came the ground force, a bevy of cop cars, sirens and flashing lights, headed in the opposite direction from Victor. He pulled off the freeway few exits later, drove about a mile more on surface streets until he reached the tail end of a shopping mall and parked in front of a defunct dry cleaners. The store was unlit and the glass frontage had been painted white from the inside to create the opaque visual barrier.

It was early evening, fair amount of shoppers still

strolling about. Victor thought better, parked instead at the rear entrance of the store. The interior held remnants of dry cleaning equipment and chemicals, but mainly plenty of medical supplies and instruments. Basically, the place was a replica of the Operating Room Victor had built in his garage. The plan here was to perform triage, to get Francine patched up enough to re-resurrect her, then keep her in an induced coma until full repair and recovery.

But what about the fact that Francine had now been dead for 47 minutes with more dead-time to come with the triage surgery and no way to stop the decay cascade? Most importantly, what about the Eunice factor? Had that been resolved? Because there was no woman named Eunice in this former dry cleaning establishment.

Victor answered these questions by ignoring them and getting straight to business. Rolled up his sleeves and cracked open Francine's thoracic cavity. Even with the bare minimum work, the surgery took 71 minutes. Victor bemoaned his less than stellar surgical skills and almost wished that the bastard Henry was still alive. At least Henry with the magic hands could have been useful in performing the surgery in one-third less time. Victor quickly dispensed with the self-pity and grabbed the aluminum shell helmet from which 10 insulated cables led to the black box which in turn was connected via single cable to a laptop computer. He strapped the helmet to Francine's head, attached the electrodes sprouting from the black box to her ribcage. The EKG monitor on the computer screen currently flatlined. Victor typed final commands into the computer, the question "READY?" pulsed on the screen.

He paused to listen for the telltale sound of God's ire

but he heard no thunder. This did not mean He was asleep at the wheel though. God had thrown Victor a curveball. Instead of taking Francine back by way of the expected slow, physical deterioration, badge-carrying assholes were used as the agents of death. Touché. Now Victor wondered what His next move would be.

He gazed at Francine, her delicate naked body, the mended bullet wounds, jagged surgical scars. Her scissor-cut clothes in a blood-soaked pile on the floor. Victor's defiant energy was sapped and he no longer thought in terms of science and logic nor could he rely on prayer. He was basically down to wishing upon star. Poked his head out the backdoor, looked skyward. Overcast. Of course.

Victor got back to the task at hand, activated the black box which hummed and bucked and the lights lit up on the aluminum helmet and Francine shimmied and shook but she remained flatlined.

Victor stared at the EKG monitor.

"Please, please, please."

And stared. And stared. Nothing changed. He asked imaginary Eunice, "What am I supposed to do here? Tell me what to do!"

"Kiss her, jerkwad," said Eunice.

Yes! The kiss! He bent over and whispered into Francine's ear, then kissed her. A passionate lip-lock for a good minute, with some tongue too for good measure.

There was a blip on the EKG monitor.

Then another. Another and another. Heart rhythm, somewhat erratic just now, but there it was. And the slight rise and fall of her chest, gurgling breaths. Her eyelids fluttered, ever so close to opening.

"Francine!" Victor did elated hops. "Yes yes yes!" He

planted kisses on her face and she opened her eyes but did not seem to register his presence. She did a little cough, which was followed by gagging and choking and spitting up of blood. Then the surgical staples came loose and/or popped out and the thoracic scar opened up, releasing copious mixture of bodily fluids and blood.

Victor was stunned, had never seen such an epic systemic failure. He went into full freakout mode, pressed down on the oozing scar, reached for the staple gun, but Francine started convulsing, which made him miss the mark and plant three staples into his hand. He yelped, dropped the staple gun and doubled over, gripping the operating table for balance. When he opened his eyes, he noticed the seepage had slowed but Francine's body looked deflated, as if nothing more to seep. She was still convulsing, but worse. Her head lolled to the right and stuff started discharging from her neck scar.

"No no!" Victor reached for her neck but slipped on the expectorated gunk pooling at his feet. His shoulder slammed the floor first, then his head bounced, dizzying him for several seconds. There was a clunk clunk, and when his double vision went back to single, he saw Francine's still helmeted head rolling on the floor like a rotted fruit disposed by the tree. The inertia of her falling head had yanked some of the cables from the black box, causing sparks to fly, then the pop pop of firecracker-type explosions, and soon the black box caught fire.

Francine's top-heavy, helmeted head came to rest, upside down, at the stack of containers of dry-cleaning chemicals. She faced Victor directly and her eyes were still open but not focused on anything. Her lips slightly parted as if stopped in mid-utterance. Victor stared at Francine, willing with all his might for her eyes to show a flicker, a focus. Please, something, anything. But there was nothing.

He felt the heat of the fire intensifying, saw the firelight taking over as the primary source of illumination. Heard the sizzle and crackle of various materials being devoured by flames. Victor did not move, didn't really want to. This would be their final resting place. It was thematically fitting, given the disaster that was his love life.

An oxygen tank exploded, sending shards into the chemical stockpile, which then also exploded into a sensational fireball. The sprinkler system was activated but all it contributed against the out-of-control chemical blaze was in making steam. The finer hairs on Victor's body had been singed but otherwise his on-the-ground position kept him from harm's way for the moment, which triggered his delusional optimism, and he took this moment as a sign that maybe he should not die just yet. He belly-crawled and retrieved Francine's head and made it out of the rear door as the place rained heated water and charred debris.

Victor placed Francine's head in the passenger's side seat, started the Mustang and drove around to the front of the mall and parked. The first of the looky-loos were gathering. The flames licked at the glass frontage like a captured animal about to bust loose and bring some hurt on the world. Black dense smoke spewed from around the seam of the entry door. Sirens closed in.

Victor bid adieu to mostly-Francine's body, seat-belted her head in place, put the Mustang in drive, got on the main drag and headed back toward the freeway, toward whence he came.

CHAPTER THIRTY
Them Bones

Victor was tapped out. Had finally burned through the last of the embezzled funds and it wasn't as if he could just resume his teaching position at the University or any university for that matter. On top of which, he was on the lam and his alter ego Abelard Smythe had been outed, and so he once again would require an alternative identity. He contacted Guy who offered condolences after hearing about Francine's demise and said he'd happily do what Victor asked. For a reasonable fee.

First was the new identity and backstory. He was now Wilmar Hoboken, inventor. Home-schooled then self-taught thus no formal education, survived primarily on the funding of his parents while he tinkered and toiled for a "better mouse trap" and toward intellectual property riches. His area of focus was in the medical field, and after multiple failures on trying to improve upon various medical devices, he invented the W-Hobok Fuser (fka V-Gott Fuser) that made it possible to reattach severed nerve endings, which in essence meant a cure for paralysis from spinal cord injuries. It made him a millionaire several times over and then some. Retired young and became reclusive because he could afford to be.

Secondly, Guy acted as the go-between in licensing the rights to the patent of the actual V-Gott Fuser (now known as W-Hobok Fuser) to a Chinese auto parts manufacturer desperate to get into the medical supply business. After the respective lawyers navigated the international bureaucracy and hashed out a deal, Victor was able to factually fulfill his new identity by indeed becoming a multi-millionaire, retiring and disappearing off the grid as a recluse.

***

Victor guided the boat back to shore with a cooler full of his catch of lake trout. On mornings like this, Victor felt rueful for being the culprit of causing the only ripples on the water's pristine surface and for the disturbance of the tranquility by the lawnmower-hum of the outboard motor. His house, the only one on this lake's shore, came into view through the morning mist. The backdrop of the towering Black Spruce forest dwarfed the modest abode.

He moored the boat to the rickety dock. Cinched his yellow slicker, adjusted his beanie over his ever ample 'fro, picked up the cooler, and walked the path toward the house, the mud squishing under the soles of his rubber boots. He stopped, thought he saw something. Scratched at his mountain-man beard, squinted through the mist.

It was inevitable from living in such a remote venue, that there would be whispers of ghost stories, which just a year ago, Victor would have dismissed as another myth, empirically unproven. But now, he wanted it to be true, wanted there to be a possibility of having Francine back in any form, even as an apparition. In the eleven months since he'd been living here though, there had been no otherworldly visitors. Until this moment maybe.

There was no easy way to get to this location except by a floater-plane, or by trekking over a mountain range and then through the aforementioned forest which was feasible only during summer months. The sole floater-plane on the lake was Victor's, parked on the shore. And currently, it was not a summer month.

But there he was. The dude sat on the porch steps, tamping down a cigarette. Did ghosts smoke? Victor resumed walking until he got close enough to recognize this specter. Percy Maplewerm. It made sense that Percy would be dead, what with his criminal-enterprise ways, the price of doing business and all that. But why the haunting? Was he still pissed off about the over-a-decade-ago altercation when Victor beat the crap out of him? So this was a revenge haunt?

As Percy flicked the cigarette butt was when he finally saw Victor. With a big-time grin, Percy said, "Well looky here, it's the miracle worker at last. You are one tough motherfucker to track down." Percy hustled out to meet Victor, laughing at himself as he almost fell twice, slipping on the muddy path. "Check you out, all mountain-man looking and shit."

Victor gawked. This ghost was a very good facsimile of the original, maybe more so in fact. The hunchy posture was now a moderate slouch, no more greasy aura, and also, hair implants. The afterlife agreed with Percy.

"What is it, man?" asked Percy. "What's with the look?"

"Oh. How rude of me." Victor put down the cooler, offered his hand, and when Percy shook it, Victor said, "You feel amazingly real. So what is it like on the other side?"

"The other side of what?"

Victor explained. Percy cackled for like a minute straight. Victor felt pretty stupid for the misperception. According to Percy, he was having zero luck tracking Victor down until he contacted Guy whom he had known through Henry. Guy was reluctant to let Percy in on the whereabouts of Victor but had a change of heart when Percy told him about his mission and after Percy slipped him a few G-Notes.

"How'd you get here though?" said Victor.

With a shrug, Percy said, "I have my ways, man."

Victor said all right and didn't press and told Percy to take a load off, and cooked up some trout for breakfast. As they ate, Percy got around to asking about Francine, wondered where she was, actually concerned about them possibly having broken up or something because "that would be tragic, man, just tragic." Though Percy had yet to mention why he'd gone through the trouble to come here, Victor had figured it out, and so he didn't have the heart to tell Percy the truth. The truth that, all that was left of Francine was her head (which Victor refroze, despite his theory that a human being should not be subjected to multiple freeze/thaw cycles, because what other effin' choice did he have at this point?). The truth that, despite laboring for the past year in research and experimentation in an effort to find another way to re-resurrect her, he had not been able to find a viable solution to undo the cellular degradation. It was akin to overcooking a steak, then trying to come up with a way to reverse the process to where it was a juicy medium-rare. And even if her head could be re-resurrected, there would be the whole ordeal of having to track down and procure a perfect replacement body.

Things had gotten desperate enough to where Victor actually, at least for a moment, contemplated looking into to time travel. And then three and a half weeks ago was the first time he pointed the barrel of the 9mm flush to his temple. Then again a week later. It wasn't the fear of death that kept him from pulling the trigger but the fear that he had not tried hard enough, that there still was something he could do to bring Francine back.

"Francine's fine. I flew her into the city so she could do some long-needed shopping. Gonna pick her back up in a few days. Sorry you missed her." Victor forked up the last bit of the trout and said, "I know you didn't come all the way out here just to say 'hey.'"

"You remember what we talked about the last time?"

"I do." Victor pointed at Percy's backpack leaning against the wall. "Is that her in there?"

He smiled, flashing his no-longer-yellow, oversized chompers. Went to the backpack, pulled out a burlap sack labeled Idaho Potatoes, but its contents clattered, very un-potato like. Percy opened the bag and proceeded to withdraw the various bones of a human skeleton and meticulously laid them out on the floor. A few missing pieces, minor ones (bones of the fingers, wrist, toes), otherwise it was a complete set. There was evidence of bone-decay telling of a long ago burial but the effect was muted by the meticulous cleaning that had been done to them.

"Victor, meet my wife. At least what's left of her."

Victor picked up the bones, studied them, though there was no real purpose for doing so other than making a show of it for Percy's sake.

But Percy wasn't fooled. "Look, man, I know what you're gonna say. What the fuck are you supposed to do with this? How are you gonna bring my wife back with some old-ass bones, right?" Percy paused, contemplated, said, "You know how they say, it ain't like it's brain surgery or like rocket science? Well, what I'm asking for is like those things and then some, but I know if anyone could do it, it's you, man."

"Percy——"

"Hold up. Let me say what I gotta say. Please. So what I was thinking was, cloning."

Victor straightened up in his seat, gave an appreciative smile. "That's actually not bad. The science is still murky where human cloning is concerned, but it's an interesting idea. It's also very illegal. But we don't care about that, do we?"

"No, we do not."

"You have to realize though, Percy, that a cloned version of your wife is not the same as your actual wife. Physically, sure, but characteristically, unless her whole life is replicated exactly the way it originally happened, which is impossible, she is going to be a different person."

"I don't give a shit, man. I just wanna see her again, hear her voice, touch her skin."

"But, Percy——" Then Victor stopped from saying anymore. When Francine was resurrected, she wasn't exactly the same person that he had known, was she? So was it anything different than what Percy was proposing? Not really. "All right. But just know that statistically the chances of finding usable DNA are almost zero."

"Quit being a downer, man, and let's just do this thing."

Victor fetched a hacksaw and went to work on one of the femurs. Not un-expectedly, the marrow was desiccated, so any cells containing DNA were dust. The other femur was cut in half with the same result. Then the humerus, hip bone, ribs, sternum. When Victor picked up the skull, Percy said, "Enough already. Just stop."

"Sorry," said Victor. "It was a long-shot."

"I know. But, fuck." Percy covered his eyes with his hand and cried quietly.

Victor suggested they get stupid drunk. Didn't have to ask Percy twice. As their drunken day rolled into night, Percy's posture returned to extreme hunchiness, his eyes became darkly plagued, and his aura dripped oil. They talked about philosophical and existential stuff, and at one point when Victor mentioned the challenges of going against God's will, Percy practically had a conniption.

"With the whole universe at His feet, do you really think God cares about a couple of nothings like us?!" raged Percy. "So what if we bring back to life a loved one or two out of the billions that have died and the billions that will die. You're flattering yourself, man. God ain't losing any sleep over us." Percy took a moment to unlace his boot, threw it across the room at nothing in particular. He then focused on the bones laid out on the floor and slumped like he was deflating from a slow leak. After 10 minutes of mutual silence, Percy asked for a flashlight and shovel and gathered up the bones, stuffed them back into the potato sack, and with only one boot on, trudged out of the house and into the forest where Victor watched him bury his wife's remains. When Percy was done, he handed the shovel to Victor and headed back to the house.

Victor asked, "Are you going to put up a marker?"

"What for?" Percy's stern answer.

Victor stayed standing there, pointing the flashlight at the desolate grave. Felt himself slipping back toward atheism, a place where he really didn't want to be. Faith equaled reason, even if that Faith was of a God-Fearing type. Randomness was not so appealing at the moment.

They awoke in the morning under the pall of a hangover that ranked among the higher ones on the intensity scale. Victor made some pancakes, which they only picked at, brewed some coffee extra strength and filled a thermos to take with, then flew Percy back to civilization.

On the way there, Victor asked, "By the by, you still in the business?"

"Nah."

"Seriously?"

"Serious shit, man."

Victor laughed.

"What?" said Percy. "You can't imagine me not selling dead chicks?"

"No, I cannot."

Percy did his cackle. "Me neither. But when I dug up my wife's bones, I heard her talking to me, telling me what I'd been doing was some fucked up shit. So I cold-turkeyed it. Got my real estate brokers license."

"Selling real estate? Are you shitting me?"

"Salesman of the month, three months straight."

"Huhn."

"It's all bullshit though, man. Who the fuck was I trying to kid? Them bones of my dead wife? Fuck that shit."

"Percy——"

"Tell me this. If you had failed to bring Francine back, would you have said 'oh, well, I'm just going to resume a normal life now,' or would you be extremely fucked up still?"

"Uh, the latter, I guess."

"No shit 'the latter.'"

"So you're going back to…"

"Selling dead chicks? Damn straight. Besides, the real estate market is in the shits right now anyway."

Percy fumed in silence in juxtaposition to the emphatic buzz of the propeller-engine. Then he asked, "So what about you, man? You gonna stay mountain-manning it forever? Is Francine cool with that? Hard to imagine a chick being cool with that."

Victor thought about it. Blinked away the hangover-haze, and suppressing a grin, said, "You're right, Percy. I don't think Francine is cool with it. So you know what? We will be heading back to the real world."

"Right on, brother."

Right on indeed.

CHAPTER THIRTY-ONE
Like An Orgasmic Acid Trip

Ell got a call from a wannabe confidential informant who said I can be helpful to you, let me be your C.I., and by the by, I come cheap, and she said give me a sampler of what you've got and he said I've got two words and they are Victor and Gottenberg. Ell asked what he wanted and his response was, a stiff drink or two or three, maybe Buffalo wings too. It's a deal she said. He suggested Goode & Gish's Bar & Grill.

"The what?"

"Goode & Gish's. You've never been?"

"No. And it better not be charming, or hipster, or upscale, or—"

"It's a dive bar on the fringes of the industrial sector."

"Oh. Well okay then. Not sure how I missed that one."

"Glad you approve," he said, then gave her details as to how to recognize him, and capped it off with, "See you there, Ell."

"Wait. How do you know me by that name? Hello?"

***

Noon. And the place was crowded. A musty smell combined with the aroma of stale beer and fryer-grease. Clack of pool ball collisions; ping ping ping of the pinball machine; drunken raucous banter; the juke box playing a pop/soul song, a woman singing about a broken heart, sweet revenge. Because of the dim lighting, it took Ell until the end of the song to spot the C.I. sitting at a corner booth. A half empty pitcher of draft, two mugs, two shot glasses, bottle of bourbon. He wore an '80s metal-band T-shirt and a trucker cap, the agreed upon signs of recognition.

As Ell got closer, she noticed that the C.I. was heavily bearded with a flop of 'fro spilling out from under the cap. That fuckin' 'fro was the giveaway. She cracked a grin, slid into the booth. "I should've known. Like a bad penny, you are."

Victor returned the grin. "Hello again." He poured beer into the mug on her side of the table, whiskey into the shot glass.

"My favorite kind of greeting," she said and dropped the shot glass into the beer, gulped heartily. Half-emptied the mug, set it down. "You shouldn't be here, Victor."

"And here I thought you missed me."

"Being accused of shooting cops and a federal agent, then vanishing into thin air, tends to put one on the Most Wanted List. So you need to go back to being off-grid."

"I knew it. You do care, you still love me."

"Seriously, Victor."

"I'm not Victor anyway. I am Wilmar Hoboken, inventor." He pulled out a passport, showed the photo of his bearded face. The moniker was Wilmar Hoboken. "See?"

Incredulous shaking of her head. "Whatever. Have it your way, *Wilmar.*" She drank down the rest the beer, offered up the mug for a re-pour. "So how's Francine?"

"Dead." He fished out the shot glass from the mug, refilled both. "I figured you guys found her charred remains."

"We did. And I must say, that was a cluster-fuck of a situation you left behind."

"What can I say? When I fail, I do it fantastically."

"But we didn't find her head."

A waitress walking by was stopped mid-step by the conversation and gawked.

Ell said to her, "Oh, perfect timing. We'll have the large order of wings, extra spicy."

"Uh huh," said the waitress. Slowly resumed her course, snuck cautious peeks over her shoulder as she walked away.

"Anyway. So where is Francine?"

"Dead, I said."

"Don't believe you. You made away with her head for a reason."

"You're right. But I can't turn a well done steak into medium rare."

"Huh?"

"The decay-cascade..." he said, tone burdened with the weight of defeat.

"So you're just giving up?" As soon as she said this, she knew it was an absurd question, making it sound as if re-

reanimating a woman who was now twice dead was somehow not absolutely improbable, and that anyone not accomplishing the task wasn't trying hard enough. But she cared too much not to ask.

Victor's response was, "I have accepted that I cannot control everything and that there are limits even for me."

A stunning pronouncement. So much so that Ell discounted the fact that the statement sounded rehearsed, a seeming emotional detachment. Instead, the news made her quiver, jaw muscles tightening with an instant welling of tears. Francine was really gone. The miracle was dead. What could have been the most amazing and greatest love story since that true story which inspired *Romeo and Juliet*, was just like that, over.

Ell sniffled, said, "That really sucks for you."

"It totally does."

The waitress returned with a large plate piled high with wings.

Ell said, "Is it wrong for me right now to be thinking that those wings look totally nosh-able?"

"It's called comfort food for a reason," said Victor.

"So it's okay to…"

Victor dug in first, gnawed on a wing, and before you could say damn this is good, Ell was sucking some chicken bones clean. Nothing was said during this nosh-fest and nothing needed to be said. It was understood that the emptiness had to be filled someway somehow and if it was via Buffalo wings, then so be it. And when there was nothing left but spindly chicken bones and full stomachs, Ell and Victor leaned back into the aged and unpleasant smelling vinyl seat, loosened belts, unbuttoned pants, and exchanged belches and some flatulence too, and they laughed about that and then Victor said,

"Wanna get pregnant?"

Ell shook her head, kinda violently, trying to snap out of her stuffed-full-of-wings reverie. "Is that a question or a proposition?"

Victor laughed, said, "Maybe both. Yes, both. The thing is, I made a promise to you, remember, about curing you of the ills of your less than cooperative uterus?"

She straightened up, leaned into the table with arms crossed. A scowl. "What are you up to, Victor? Are you on the rebound from your dead girlfriend, desperate to nuzzle yourself between hot-chick thighs, with your johnson all up in the lady garden, like say, the last time we did the deed?"

"No no, it's not like that at all." He reached across the table and grasped her extra-spicy-Buffalo-sauce-stained hands. "Ell. Look into my eyes and hear me, please. I've learned my lesson. Francine's final death was a turning point for me. I've learned my lesson."

"You said that already."

"Because it bears emphasis, Ell. Em-pha-sis." A drama-queen sigh. "So the lesson learned? Love and obsession should be mutually exclusive. Or else it results in crazy-ass disasters, such as the shootout at the agave farm and et cetera, and I don't need anymore of that crazy-ass shit. What I need is stability and I know I can have that with you. And in being able to help you with your fertility situation? Maybe that just means something like redemption, I mean, I don't know. If I can get you pregnant, that's like, okay so I failed with Francine but I can succeed with you by bringing a life into this world. You know?"

The look he had just then, so damn earnest.

"Are you trying to tell me that you've got a thing for me, on top of which, you've got some kind of super sperm to get me knocked up?"

"Something like that."

"So were you just born with the miracle semen or have you been experimenting on your nut-sack during your fugitive-time?"

"Something like that, the nut-sack thing."

"I'm flattered but it's peculiar. Why not artificial insemination? How about in-vitro?"

Victor did the faux I'm-so-offended look. "Well if you must know, doing 'the deed' as God intended is the best method of delivery. Besides, it's straight from the tap, a personal touch. More romantic that way." A dirty grin, an exaggerated wink.

She kept a poker face but Skepticism sat on her shoulder talking smack into her ear. The whole scheme did seem crazy. Just like that, there was going to be a baby, there was going to be a man. There was going to be a baby with this man. It's not like she had anything against Victor, although the disgusting beard had to go, the 'fro needed to be trimmed, and except for the metal-band T-shirt, his wardrobe was a bit too geezer-ish. Otherwise he was of a decent gene pool and obviously devoted and loving. But now that it was being offered up on a silver platter right this second, she had to take a moment.

But seriously, what else was out there on the horizon? That dude, the former NFL player who worked at the car dealership with whom her mom was trying to fix her up? Yeah, she dated him and he gave it a yeoman's effort but in the end, he came out. And then there was Hobin who would have been a consolation prize at best. He'd attempted to off himself by overdosing on sedatives but failed. Had left a note referencing Shakespeare, something about an apothecary and Romeo. Wasn't clear if it was due to his ex-wife or Ell or the disappointment of life in general. Most likely the ex-wife. But the "attempt" was bullshit. Barely a handful of sleeping pills. It was just a pussy way for him to get attention. But it worked. Hobin and the Department Psychologist, with whom he was mandatorily required to meet before returning to duty, apparently hit it off pretty good, to the extent that they got married last May. It was highly unprofessional of the psychologist, was Ell's thinking. Also in her thought was: Are you kidding me? Hobin gets another shot at happily-ever-after while I'm left cuddling up with the vibrator?

In other words, it was the status quo for Ell. There was jack-shit in her future, nothing to hang her hat on and, on top of which, getting closer to the dreaded four-o. And here was Victor, shoveling his gospel in her face.

"I see that you're thinking about it," said Victor. "Maybe I can convince you by telling you that..." A swift lean over the table, planted a wet smooch on Ell's astonished lips. The beard was gross but somehow a turn-on at the same time.

It went from surprise to "mmmm" noises from Ell. Tongues became involved, exchange of wing-sauce residues. She didn't need anymore convincing. Told Victor to pay the tab and let's go already. After he threw down some bills on the table, she took him by the hand, pulled out of the booth and made haste before she could think about it too much. Out in the parking lot he suggested his place and she was okay with that and they got into their respective vehicles, sped to Destination Sex Fest, or alternatively known as, Project Preggers.

***

It was like an orgasmic acid trip, was how Ell remembered it. After downing the drink-concoction Victor had whipped up as a prelude to the festivities, things got naked and hot and sweaty and juicy and sticky and slippery and there were swirls of colors and the sensation of flying at the speed of light while under water and accompanied by jazzy guitar music, and of the course the orgasms, omygod the orgasms. And then there was the alien probing, hot white lights, insertion of cold metallic devices, space-language. Say what? Okay so maybe that part was something akin to a fever-dream?

Ell woke up and exclaimed, "Sweet mother!" and asked what the heck that concoction was and where could she get more of it? And by the way, "You're pretty awesome in the sack."

Said he, "Aw shucks."

And three weeks later, her pee triggered a plus sign on the plastic stick.

CHAPTER THIRTY-TWO
The Nutsack Conspiracy

The girl was born on the Day of the Dead, the date of irony where births were concerned. She slid out of the chute bellowing like she had something to prove. Had ten fingers, ten toes, and all that good stuff. Mom and Dad, happy as pie. They named her Rosaline.

***

Despite Victor's prodding, Ell did not want to retire from the force. She was on maternity leave but planned to get back into the thick of things soon enough. Ell loved her daughter and was determined to be a good mom but didn't think a woman had to give up on her hard won career to be a loving and capable mother. Besides, the Department allowed for flex-scheduling and Victor had nothing better to do than be a stay-at-home dad anyway. But that one day when she came home from her shift and took Rosaline in her arms and the kid uttered something that sounded very much like "mama" for the very first time, Ell was hook-line-and-sinkered. Told the Department that she was taking a leave of absence then mothballed her sidearm while Victor was being all smug-like.

***

Speaking of Victor. He doted on the both of them, Ell and Roz. He was perfect in that way, almost too perfect. But who's to complain? And content he was, so content, like he had dreamed a perfect dream and was now living it. In fact, the house they now lived in, Victor had custom built to fit the specs of the home he had dreamed of long ago, a split-level Ranch style with four bedrooms, two and a half baths, white picket fence, a fully mature oak tree planted with a tree house and tire swing included.

Ell had never met a man like him, and at times she wasn't sure whether that was good or bad. Mostly it was a wonder, but then an occasional fear-of-the-unknown notion would spark up in some synapse deep in the recess of her cop-trained brain, which she knew was stupid, a knee-jerk thing. She loved him, yes she did. But still. It was like something warding her off from holding on too tight, as if this whole thing was too fragile and would shatter at any moment if not handled with caution. This was how her history informed her. Jesus, thought Ell, am I truly this fucked in the head?

***

The answer to that question was more likely a "yes" after Victor had proposed to her on the eve of Roz's first birthday and offered up an eye-popping ring and she asked are you asking me as Wilmar Hoboken or as Victor

Gottenberg, and he said Victor died with Francine. Ell responded with a guttural noise and said maybe we should revisit this at a later time and Victor shrugged and clomped the ring-box shut.

***

Roz was a runt. Ell was close to 5'9" and Victor was 6'2". So what happened? Victor reassured Ell that Roz would grow into her genetic framework soon enough. That's what he said when she was born. And then, when she turned one. And two. Then three. When Roz turned four, Victor explained nonchalantly that genetics was a quirky thing.

"That's not a very scientific explanation coming from a guy like you," said Ell.

"Science is an imperfect art," he said while holding Roz and doing raspberry kisses on her poofy cheeks and making her squeal with laughter and pretend-begging him to stop daddy stop. "But she's perfect, Ell. So let's just believe in the magic."

"Did you just really say, 'believe in the magic'?"

"Roz, can you tell your mother to stop being a noodge?"

"Mommy, stop being a nuj. Daddy, what's a nuj?"

"Victor, be serious. I'm worried about what effect your super sperm might have had on R-O-Z."

"You mean besides conception?"

"Don't be a smartass. Exactly what kind of experiments did you perform on your nutsack?"

"Mommy, what's a nut-zak?"

Ell took Roz from Victor, nuzzled her nose in Roz's frizzy unruly hair, whiff of fruity-scented baby shampoo. "'Nutsack' is where half of you came from. The weird half, apparently."

"Okay," said Roz.

"Ha ha, good one," said Victor. Kissed them on their respective cheeks. "It's all good. Nothing to worry about. Trust me."

"Uh-huh," said the ladies, warily.

***

But before you knew it, there was a familial rhythm to the Lavenza-Gottenberg universe. Ell back to work on flex-time, Victor cranking out the novel series, Roz acclimating intellectually and socially in kindergarten. The weekday rituals: the harried breakfasts (the Lavenza-Gottenbergs were not morning people); Victor chauffeuring Ell to work and Roz to school and back home again; and in the evenings while Roz watched PBS (the kid preferred the NewsHour over Sesame Street), Ell and Victor performed tag-team cheffing, the meals from said efforts initially sucked ass because they were learning on the fly but they eventually started churning out some gourmet-type stuff, and after the family gleefully polished off dinner, they did their nightly assembly line routine of clearing the table and washing the dishes while singing songs per Roz's pop-tune suggestions. Then the weekend outings: art museum (the Impressionists!), bike rides (tandem and a half!), the mall (the latest fashions, including accessories! and that one place with the amazing pastry and ice cream concoction!), movies (Roz and Victor loved romcoms), parks (the one with the lake with the model sailboats), picnics (at the park with the lake with model sailboats), zoo (pandas on loan!), et cetera. And "et cetera" meaning Ell ended up saying okay to Victor's previously submitted marriage proposal and they got hitched city-hall style, Roz playing the part of bridesmaid. Being so swept up in this familial rhythm allowed Ell to ignore things like her daughter now at the age of six still had not grown into her genetically predisposed height and not looking anything like either of her parents, but what did it matter when Ell was as happy as she'd ever been. Until of course, she couldn't ignore it anymore.

***

You know how with children, one minute they look a certain way, and the next minute they've grown like three inches taller and their features which you thought leaned toward Aunt Petunia were now looking more like Grandma Rose? Something like that happened with Roz, age seven. She was now suddenly recognizable to Ell, not necessarily as a Lavenza-Gottenberg offspring, but someone for sure. But who?

Ell puzzled over this question one Sunday morning at the kitchen table while the family enjoyed French toast and made their way through the Sunday paper. Ell took a moment from the news perusal and watched Roz read the op-ed page. How beautiful she was, her daughter, but in the ethereal sense really, because "pretty" wasn't exactly Roz's suit. Her nose outpaced the growth of her head by a 2 to 1 margin. That frizzy, unruly hair, the ears the size of wings of a small flying animal. Her brows of such angle and bushy-ness, that if furrowed just so, gave her a sinister appearance. Eyes the color of sludge. Lanky-looking despite the below average height. Hunchy posture. Big head.

But there was something to keep one stay looking. The

quirkish features worked together to become a composition exceeding the sum of its parts. And something bone deep, an invisible beacon. Like a prism. Had to know how to look at it to get the translucent piece of glass to emit a rainbow.

It was at that moment Ell recognized her as someone she knew for sure. She flipped through the head-shots in her memory bank but none matched. It just had to be there though. The identity was, like, on the tip of her tongue.

And then, there it was.

Made her jolt to her feet. Heart pounding against her sternum as if wanting to bust loose, make a run for it. But was she sure about this, the I.D.? Not really, but needed to at least disprove it.

"What's wrong, Mommy?" Roz looking up at Ell while her little index finger place-holdered the sentence she was reading.

"Um, nothing." Ell picked up a napkin, wiped powdered sugar off her daughter's chin. "Mommy forgot to do something at work, so gotta go in for a bit."

"What? On a Sunday?" Victor suddenly alert. "But what about our bike ride? And to the mall later for that amazing pastry and ice cream concoction?"

"You guys are gonna have to go without me," said Ell.

"Awww," replied Victor and Roz in sad unison.

***

Ell plowed through the archived files to find what she was looking for. Laid the file on the cold concrete floor of the basement file-storage room. Her hands shook as she thumbed through the pages, eventually getting to the photos. When this missing-person file had been opened, the family had, out of an abundance of caution, provided more photos than were necessary, including those from childhood. Ell found the one with handwriting on the back indicating, "age 7." Couldn't bring herself to flip the photo over to see what the girl looked like then.

"Come on, come on. Just do it already." So she flipped it over. But had her eyes closed. "Please please please please please. Let it not be her." She opened her eyes and saw Roz staring back at her.

After sobbing for about five minutes, Ell told herself to get her shit together, then put the photo back, and returned the tear-stained file labeled "Styne, Francine" to its rightful place.

***

When Ell got home, Victor was cleaning up the kitchen of the detritus of what appeared to have been major takeout-food action.

"Oh, hey," he said. "You sure were gone a long time."

"Is Roz in bed?"

"Yeah. We totally gorged ourselves. There's leftovers if you—"

Ell cracked the bridge of Victor's nose with the butt of her gun, then popped various ligament of his left knee with a swift and brutal roundhouse kick. He collapsed, yelled out in pain until she stuffed the gun barrel into his mouth.

"Shut up! Just shut up or I will right here right now blow the back of your head off."

He bit down on the barrel, grimaced and moaned. After he writhed for a minute, she put the gun away, zip-tied his hands behind his back, and stood over him.

"Okay, asshole. As you can see, I am one pissed off chick with a gun. So when I ask you a question, you damn well better give me a satisfactory answer. Number one: How did you do it? How did you clone her?"

Victor spat out the blood that had dribbled down from his busted nose, said, "The science of it actually turned out to be pretty simple these days really, you just need—"

She kicked him in the ribs.

"Ooof! Okay okay," he gasped. Took a moment to get his breath back. "Okay, so..."

Francine's DNA had come from her head which was currently in a preserved state in a previously undisclosed location. To simplify it, DNA (in the somatic cell nucleus) + unfertilized ovum (with its nucleus removed) = cloned human embryo. The minor issue of Ell's uncooperative uterus was overcome by whipping up a form of uterine super glue to ensure that the egg stayed put. The night of the orgasmic acid trip was when he did it. He had drugged her via the fanciful drink preparation and inserted the embryo. The alien probing which Ell thought she had imagined, now made total sense.

"So it had nothing to do with you tampering with your nutsack?"

"No. That was just a cover story."

"A stupid cover story I believed like a stupid fucking idiot." She sucked air through her teeth, the sound loud and angry. "All right then. Number two: How did you think you were going to get away with this, huh? I was going to eventually figure it out."

"I don't know okay? I mean, I'm just flying by the seat of my pants here. I was just happy to have her back, and happy about what we have here. Our family. You know?"

"No, I do not know. You freak. She is Roz, not Francine. Does that information even penetrate your thick skull?"

"I don't care."

He tried to sit up but she put her heel to his cheek and knocked him back down, planting his face into the nose-bleed puddle.

"Here's number three: did you ever even love me?"

He was about to answer, but stopped, as if knowing that whether he told truth or lie, it wouldn't matter anyway.

She yanked him up by the zip-tied wrists, onto his feet. Marched his gimpy ass out into the backyard. Made him kneel facing the oak tree with the tire swing and impressive treehouse.

"If I had any patience," said Ell, "I would take a cleaver to you and chop you up into one-inch cubes and feed you to the feral dogs and seagulls at the garbage dump. So consider yourself lucky that I'm gonna end it for you quickly with a bullet through your larger than average yet totally lacking in common sense brain."

"I totally deserve it, Ell."

"Shut up." She jabbed the barrel into the juncture of his skull and spine. "You're not going to talk your way out of this."

"I know you'd take her away from me and I'd rather be dead than have to live through that."

"You know what the sad part of that is? It's that you're telling the truth. That's the kind of fucked-up individual you are." She holstered the gun. "I'm not going to waste a bullet on you, Victor. Because I want you to suffer the consequences."

"What? No!"

340

"Yes, Victor. I'll be transferring funds from our account to my own account. Consider it my share of community property. Divorce papers will find its way to you soon enough. Sign it, don't sign it, I don't really give a shit, but you will never see Roz or me again."

"No no, please! Don't take her away from me."

"I'm also going to retrieve Francine's head and give that poor girl a proper burial. So no more cloning for you."

"Goddammit, Ell. Don't do this." He struggled onto his feet. "I am begging you."

She turned her back on him, started walking to the house.

"Ell? Ell!"

He hobbled at her, impressively fast for a guy with a busted knee, but she turned quickly enough, side-stepped him, and lickety-split, re-pulled out her gun and slammed it broadside into his temple. And in slow motion, he toppled like a felled tree, unconscious, onto the dewy lawn.

***

When he came to, shivering under the weight of the morning mist, he knew it. They were gone. Francine, once again, had slipped through his fingers.

341

CHAPTER THIRTY-THREE
The Angel And The Fat Grayish Worm That Turned
Out To Be A Severed Finger

Legally, "community property" meant half of the stuff earned as a married couple. Ell's definition was apparently not the same. When she had transferred "her share" of the funds from their joint account to her own, she left him only enough for groceries and utilities and miscellaneous for the next six months. This was totally not half of what had been in the account, not even $1/5000^{th}$ of it. So then he was going to tap into the investment portfolio but Ell beat him to it, had liquidated the whole thing.

What was that expression? Something about a woman scorned?

He sold the house, which helped, but still needed a job. Shouldn't have been a problem for Victor Gottenberg but he was no longer Victor Gottenberg. He was Wilmar Hoboken, no real work experience, not even a degree in higher education, just some dude who invented a device that revolutionized medical science and made millions from it then lost it all. Had nothing else to show when asked what are you currently working on. Couldn't he have just remade or re-concocted prior inventions within Victor's portfolio, or come up with new ones? Yeah but he had no energy to do so because his sole motivation was gone. And so Wilmar was a one-hit wonder, not exactly bankable, and now a nobody.

Anyway, he still needed to get a job. He was finally able to convince a community college that he was of professorial material, although "convince" was probably too generous a term. This college had a dearth of science-qualified teachers and the dean of the department interviewing him was admittedly, heavily self-medicated (stressed out, something about a scandal involving him and a female student or two or three, possibly a fourth) and was not quite attuned to Wilmar's lack of teaching credentials and Victor not so subtly bribed him with a promise of some excellent prescription medication that would help with the self-medicating what with Victor's connections to the medical community. They closed the deal. Victor started immediately, taking over the general biology classes on Monday, Wednesday and Fridays, which had been temporarily taught by an art history adjunct who had been laid off but brought back due to the science department shortage and was now laid off once again. Upon introduction, the adjunct did not shake Victor's hand but spat on his shoes instead and stomped off, cussing and cussing about the state of the educational system in this country.

Victor bought a used travel trailer and rented a space at

a trailer park located next to a quaint bay of the beach community. It was currently off-season so Victor had the place to himself. In the evenings, if it wasn't too chilly, he reclined in a lawn chair and watched the bay sparkle from the light of the setting sun while he sipped on a bottle of beer and smoked a joint. This wasn't so bad, was it? A decent enough teaching gig, a place on the bay, beautiful sunsets, good weed. Enough to make one forget about stuff. Like, say, Francine. Francine who?

Not really. That was total bullshit. In fact, Victor had hired a P.I. to track down Ell and Roz's whereabouts. But no luck. They had obviously gone through a complete identity makeover, was the explanation. Victor fired that guy and hired someone else. That someone else also accomplished jack shit so was eventually replaced by someone else who was eventually replaced by someone else and so on. Every time Victor heard the term "off the grid," he had the urge to wallop the culprit.

And then, November 2nd rolled around. Francine's, er, Roz's birthday, the first one since Ell took her away. Eight years old she was now. Victor did not watch the sunset that evening and not because it was too chilly. Instead, he stayed in the trailer, broke apart one of his disposable razors, retrieved the blade, and downed a half bottle of generic label scotch, slit his wrists. While blood dribbled down his arms, he stripped naked, sat in the tight confines of the shower and kept drinking until he couldn't.

When he awoke, he was not dead. He found himself sitting in a puddle of blood. Felt lightheaded but the cuts were not deep enough and too high on his forearms to have ensured quick death. Lesson learned: Avoid being stupid drunk while attempting technically demanding suicide. His arms were still dribbling blood but barely because of the coagulation, and besides, the moment had passed. He found some super-glue and sealed the cuts, showered, got dressed, drank a carton of orange juice and went to work.

***

In the summer, the trailer park was at full capacity and Victor was doing his usual sunset routine, when down by the shore, a couple caught his attention. They were young and beautiful and obviously in Love with a capital "L." They wore bathing suits and were frolicking in ankle-deep water. Literally frolicking. The guy with his stupid six-pack abs, her with the not-so-stupid boobs that were coming achingly close to fleeing the bikini top with every successive bounce. What a couple of assholes.

Victor struggled his stoned-drunken self out of the lawn chair and trudged toward the irritating twosome.

"Hey! Yeah, you two. Get a room, as they say."

"Excuse me?" said the dude, who appeared to be a much larger human from three feet away than from Victor's initial vantage point.

But Victor, through courage of the chemically enhanced type, pressed on. "How about taking your little party elsewhere so we in the public don't have to endure the disgusting display. I mean who the fuck do you two think you are, with the stupid frolicking and the abs and the boobs and rubbing it our faces?"

"I don't know what your problem is, man," said the large fella, "but you damn well better leave my wife's body out of the conversation."

"Your wife!? You two are married?" This bit of news made Victor seethe. "That's even worse. And you know what? I will not leave your wife's body out of the conversation." He reached out and clutched the wife's ample left breast which was just the right amount of fleshy firmness, and it made him nostalgically sad and turned-on at the same time until she slapped him ridiculously hard. And while Victor swayed, dazed, the husband finished him off.

The incoming tide lapping at his prostrate body was what brought Victor back to consciousness. Checked his watch. Two in the a.m. His jaw was busted for sure and his cheek still stung from the wicked slap. A little pissed off that no one bothered to get his knocked-out ass off the shore. He could've drowned for fuckssake. He alleviated his ire and bodily aches by smoking a joint and going to bed still sandy.

***

Another November 2nd. Roz, now nine. Victor's ache was bone deep, could barely move. But had enough wherewithal to make his way to the cabinet where he grabbed the bottle of sleeping pills, dumped it into a cereal bowl and crushed the pills into powder form, then tossed the powder into the blender with a goodly amount of generic brand vodka. He guzzled the death-sleep concoction.

But woke up not dead, found himself on the floor with his face in a puddle of vomit. The irony of, once again, not being able to off himself on the Day of the Dead was not lost on him. Shrugged it off, showered and shaved, ate some buttered toast and went to work.

***

New semester, fresh meat. Victor locked in on a student

who kinda sorta looked like Francine. She was a little too tall, too pretty, and not thick enough in the ass to be a perfect match, but still. Nothing that some extensive plastic surgery couldn't remedy. Sustained electro-shock to wipe out her memory and replace said memory with that of the life of Francine Styne. Piece of cake. He set up shop in a rental storage unit and lured the student, drugged her, did the electro-shock thing before the surgery to see if it would take. It took all right but not as planned. She awoke as alter-ego-Greta, spoke with an indistinguishable accent, had a taste for wallop-packing beer, copious amounts of it, and lived for scary violent sex, the advances for which Victor vociferously refused for fear of potential detrimental effects to their health and safety. Victor zapped her and zapped her but Greta would not go away and he came to the realization that this whole thing was a super stupid idea. So he re-drugged her and left her on the steps of the student health center late one night with a note attached to her that said please help. She was written up in the school paper as a cautionary tale of the college party scene, recovered her original persona with no recollection of the events and dropped out of school, never to be seen again. Victor felt like a total douchebag about the whole thing, was inconsolable, at least until he swept the memory under the synaptic rug by way of booze and weed.

***

Summer again already? Apparently so. And that asshole couple was back. The large fella, the husband, had put on a few pounds and the six-pack was now more like a two-pack. The wife had to resort to wearing a one-piece now, no more bikini. Small measure of satisfaction on the part of Victor. Until they trotted out an infant.

Those fuckers had procreated. Victor lost his shit. He charged at the little family while spouting invective wrapped with denunciation and laced with spittle and went on about how they were not superior to him with their love and marriage and adorable little baby girl and any potential future adorable little babies that they may be contemplating and—

Victor was awakened by a stray dog gnawing at his crotch. He shooed the dog away, found himself laid out on the bay shore. Checked his watch. Three in the a.m. Touched his pain-pulsating forehead and felt what he believed to be knuckle dents in his skull. Ah yes, now he remembered, the large fella's large fist hurtling at him, then lights-out.

Victor crawled to his trailer, made it as far as his lawn chair, but couldn't quite make it onto said lawn chair. He took a minute, and while resting, found a roach and promptly smoked it down and fell asleep with his face plastered to the gravelly pavement.

***

November 2nd was again just around the corner. Another year missed in the life of Roz. They called them Formative Years for good reason and it was daggers to his heart that he could not be there as a profound and lasting influence in her life. And two days ago was when Victor fired the latest P.I. whom Victor had warned not to utter the words "off the grid," but the P.I. ultimately reported that the wife and child were far off the grid, and that if he, with his 37 years of P.I. experience, couldn't track them down, nobody could. Even refunded Victor half the retainer.

In anticipation of the Day of the Dead, Victor had to once again choose his poison. So the day after the P.I. gave him the bullshit news, Victor purchased a gun from his weed dealer, a former student. It was a rickety .38 but reasonably priced with a money-back guarantee and couple of bullets thrown in, one more than needed.

On the day of, sometime late afternoon, he took to his lawn chair, settled in with a bottle of generic brand tequila at his side and did the sunset routine then went into the trailer and placed a bullet into the chamber of the gun and stuck the tip of the barrel firmly against his temple. The prior failed suicide attempts, Victor chalked up to involuntary penance. God apparently held grudges. And so Victor, ever defiant, said under his breath, "Try stopping *this*," and pulled the trigger. But the rickety piece of shit exploded, launching gun-part projectiles every which way.

He found himself on the floor, not dead. Fierce ringing in his ear. Touched his temple, no bullet hole, but he noted that his ear was a pulpy shred. And there was something else that felt wrong. Checked his right hand. Beaucoup blood and no more index finger. Victor wadded up some paper towels and duct-taped it to his hand to stanch the bleeding, then looked for his digit. Found bits of ear, no finger though. At least he would get his money back on the gun.

He rummaged up his handy dandy surgery kit, went outside, retrieved the bottle of tequila, toasted yet another defeat, guzzled, and made quick and sloppy stitch-work of the finger stub. Passed out on the lawn chair and dreamed of having a conversation with an angel who looked like Roz as a twenty-something adult. The angel told him to stop being a dipshit already.

"It's like you have blinders on," she said. "I don't know if it's on purpose or because you're stupid. Either way, you need to get with the program. And FYI, look for a sign."

"I'm not sure what you're saying, but okay, Roz."

"I think you have me confused with someone else."

When he woke up, he was not in the lawn chair but lying on his back at the threshold of the trailer, upper body inside, legs splayed on the steps. In his grip was the tequila bottle, about an eighth full. At the bottom of the bottle was a fat grayish worm that was not there before. Actually, no. It was his index finger.

"What the?" Stared, thought about it. "Oh, wait. Is this what you meant, Angel, the sign?" Didn't wait for an answer and called the P.I. he had just fired and re-hired him and told him to follow up on a lead.

CHAPTER THIRTY-FOUR
Love Your Fate

The severed finger indeed pointed the way. The tequila. Which equaled agave. And what did that mean to Victor? His former farm in Vegas, that's what. The P.I. found Ell and Roz there, hiding in plain sight. The property was now owned by Justine Moritz aka Elizabeth Lavenza. Ell's alter ego's background was a blank slate, no connection to any law enforcement agency but appeared to be involved in illegal hooch-making, some excellent tequila called Fugitive Juice.

Victor told the P.I. to tell Ell that he wanted to meet her and the P.I.'s response was you don't tell someone who's been hiding from you that you've found them and want their permission to come see them, you just effin' show up! Victor said just tell her that she owed him. All right, whatever, said the P.I. and went forth as commanded and regretted ever doing so.

"That woman is crazy!" he reported back. "All I did was knock on the damn door."

Ell had effortlessly wrangled him to the ground, stuck a gun barrel down his throat, warned him that next time she was going stick it up his ass, pull the trigger, and blow his shit out of the top of his skull. He believed her, took it as a sign and hung up his P.I. license, retired that very day. Called Victor from his Florida condo.

"She clearly wants to be left alone."

"But did you tell her she owed me?"

"Did you hear the part about where she had me gagging on the gun barrel?"

"But did you tell her?"

"Yeah. It seemed to be the thing that triggered her."

"Oh…"

"But. In the end she told me to tell you to go ahead and show your sorry ass there if you were so inclined, but that you would be doing so at the risk of severe death. Her words exactly. I'm assuming you don't want to die severely."

Victor wasted no time, hitched the trailer to the Mustang and hit the interstate.

***

The dirt road that led to the agave farm was now paved. But otherwise the place looked the same. Even the white picket fence had been rebuilt. Victor parked, got out too quickly and stumbled, his trick-knee stiff from the long drive. When he got up off the pavement, he saw Ell strolling from the house. She wore aviator shades which reflected the late morning sun, her face evincing nothing. But the shotgun she was toting evinced plenty. She

352

stopped a few feet in front of him, leaned the shotgun against her shoulder. With hip tilted one way, and her head the other way, she seemed to be studying him.

He asked in a jokey ice-breaking way, "Do you always greet guests with a show of deadly force?"

"Only the unwanted ones," she said, not smiling. "You look like shit, Victor."

"*You* don't. You really don't."

"Save the flattery."

"It's not," he mumbled.

"What the fuck happened to your ear? And is that a finger you're missing?"

"Um. A mishap of sorts, heh heh."

"Uh huh."

"So. Why *this* place?"

"The Feds had it on the auction block. It was a good deal, especially with the rumors started by Hobin about zombie bacteria. And I heard it was the place to be if one wanted to be off the grid."

Victor smiled, nodded.

"On top of which, I've got tequila growing in my backyard. What's not to like?"

"You do know that's illegal, right, the tequila-making?"

"It's okay. I've got connections. And frankly, people would only give a shit if I stopped making it."

"How are sales?"

"Sales are great how did you find us?"

"The P.I. that you scared the crap out of."

"I doubt that joker could find his own asshole. So how'd you do it?"

He rubbed at his stubbly chin for a leisurely moment. Eventually fessed up, said, "An angel."

She scoffed. "An angel, of course. Ever the romantic, huh, Victor? It's going to be the death of you, you know."

"You would think. But so far, that theory's been proven wrong."

"What?"

"Nothing."

A pause, one of those that seemed way longer than actually was. Chit chat petered out. Shuffling of feet, kicking of pebbles. And then,

"Okay, so. About me owing you one," said Ell, wiping a palm against her thigh, holey jeans. Took off the aviators, hooked it onto the collar of her size-too-tight T-shirt. She couldn't quite meet his eyes. "You're right. Francine died because of me."

"I wouldn't go so far as saying that."

"Bennding would never have found you and Francine if it weren't for my giving you guys up."

"But did you know that he was going to do what he did?"

"No," she said, kinda pissed. "Of course not."

"All right then."

The drone of a prop-plane in the distance caught their attention. They watched it fly by, probably headed for the Strip, dragging one those banners behind it that said, "Will You Marry Me, Eunice?"

Victor said, "By the way, I never did get those divorce papers."

"Didn't know where to send them."

"Uh huh."

They exchanged smirky smiles. Then Ell stopped suddenly with the smiling, got all serious like, angry even, as if catching herself doing something embarrassingly stupid.

"Anyway. I let you come here, so now we're even," she said.

"But, wait. I haven't—"

"Those were the terms."

"I didn't realize specific terms had been negotiated."

"Don't start sassing me, man." She unshouldered the shotgun, held it with ease, like it was an extension of her body, like shooting it would be about as difficult for her as spitting on the ground, and with about as much remorse.

He swallowed hard. And then,

"Mom, please?" A girl's raspy voice. "No bloodbaths today. You promised to take me to the mall."

Victor followed the voice to the doorway and mouthed the words oh my God. It was Roz, all grown up, slouching on the porch, and "all grown up" meaning the kind of grown-up-ness that a parent sees in his child whom he hadn't seen in over three years which is a super long and huge difference-making time where children were concerned. He floated, pulled toward Roz via her gravity. That was until Ell slammed the butt end of the shotgun into his chest, stopping any and all forward momentum, forcing a gurgling grunt out of him.

"Why are you here, Victor?!"

"To see my daughter."

"Don't lie to me, you sonofabitch. I know you're here to see Francine." She head-pointed at Roz. "But that kid is not Francine. Get that through your thick skull."

"I know that, Ell. I really do."

"Bullshit. I want you outta here now." She shoved him toward the Mustang.

"Dad? Is that you?" asked Roz.

"No," said Ell.

"That is so totally him, Mom."

The shotgun barrel was all up in Victor's face now. "Leave or die," said Ell.

Roz hopped off the porch, fast-walked toward them. "Mom! Do. Not. Kill. Dad."

"Are you really going to shoot me in front of Roz?" said Victor, being all pseudo-ballsy.

"Yeah, I really am gonna." Click-clack went the shotgun as she cocked it. "Because her witnessing my blowing your brains out is, I'm guessing, going to be less traumatic than her having to grow up with a supposed father trying to turn her into his dead girlfriend. Sorry, dead *wife*."

Victor watched Roz approaching. "Ell. Please let me see my daughter."

She shot just above his head, the blast reverberating through the desert air.

"Mom!" Roz, frozen in mid-step, hands covering her ears.

Victor uncrouched, shook off the tinnitus, swiped a backhand at his sweat-drenched forehead. Took a few seconds to calm his breathing. Said, "I renounce her."

"What?"

"I renounce *her*, whose name shall never be uttered again, all right? But please. I can't lose my daughter too."

The light in Ell's eyes flickered, softened, but only momentarily. Kept the shotgun trained on him.

"Okay, Ell." He grabbed the barrel, held it to his head. "Pull the trigger. Because if you deny me my daughter, I've got nothing. I'm done. And God knows I've tried to end it myself but apparently I'm to suffer to the bitter end.

So here's hoping that this is the end."

He stared her down and she glared back his stare and he stared back her glare and so on until,

"Shit," she said and pulled away the shotgun. Moved aside, allowing for a path between him and Roz. "Victor. So help me, if you fuck this up..."

Victor looked at Ell, then to Roz, back to Ell. "Thank you," he sighed out. "I will not fuck this up."

He jogged to Roz, knelt down on one knee in front of her. "Hi," he said.

"Jeez, you guys," said Roz. "Are we done with the drama now?"

"Sorry. Your Mom was kinda P.O.'d at me."

"Well, she didn't shoot you so that's good."

He laughed. "Yeah, that is good."

"And you're back. Finally. That's good too."

"So you don't hate me?"

"Maybe a little."

"Oh."

"But, Dad, you were gone like forever. I know it was for a good cause and everything but it was a really super long time," she said with a sad raspiness.

"Wait. Why do you think I've been gone?"

"I know it was top secret but I asked and asked and asked and Mom finally told me. About the Amazon? Looking for a new medical miracle from the rare plants? Because you haven't done 'jack shit' since inventing the W-Hobok Fuser?"

He turned to Ell. She gave a little shrug as if to say okay so maybe I left open the possibility of reconciliation or most likely I was going for a convenient story whereby I could kill you off, i.e., eaten by piranhas, and give you a redemptive death for the sake of your daughter. Either way, he smiled a thanks-for-not-telling-her-the-truth smile, turned back to Roz. Hot tears of happiness rolled down his face.

She said, "Jeez, Dad. You're crying. Okay okay I don't hate you."

"You don't?"

She clamped her hands on his wet cheeks. "No haters here."

Victor hugged and hugged his daughter and she was like, you're hugging me kind of tight and it's hard to breathe but it's okay I missed you too.

"I love you, Roz." said Victor.

"Love you too, Dad." Planted a kiss on his chin. "Um, Mom? Can Dad come to the mall with us?"

Ell propped the shotgun against the Mustang. Crossed her arms, legs shoulder-width apart, assumed the this-momma-ain't-taking-none-of-this-shit stance.

"Pleeeease, Mom?"

"Yeah, pleeeease, Mom?" tried Victor.

Ell almost busted a blood vessel holding back a laugh.

Then child and father simultaneously: "Please please please please please please please!"

Ell to herself, said, "God help us."

***

Eight years later and there's Roz packing up the hand-me-down Mustang with stuff to stuff her dorm room with. Got accepted to her first-choice school, but was headed instead to a different university. "I'll be closer to you guys that way," was her excuse. Nothing wrong with the school she chose except Roz's reason, her real reason. Because Ell and Victor knew better. It was Benson Bicklebaum. The other university was *his* destination and *he* was Roz's destination. On-again off-again high school sweethearts. Currently somewhere between on and off. Mom and Dad were reluctant to apply the term "obsessed" to their daughter for obvious reasons, but still.

Ell and Victor had dutifully put up the parental resistance: You're doing this for all the wrong reasons; you're too young to know what love is; focus on your studies instead of something fleeting as a schoolgirl crush; there's plenty of fish in the sea; you've got your whole life ahead of you; blah blah, etc., all of which Roz shrugged off and chuckled at as if to say, are you serious you two die-hard romantics with your crazy history, of which Roz shouldn't have known anything about but she was all attitudinal as if she did.

After the Mustang was packed, there were hugs and kisses and the obligatory our-little-baby's-going-off-to-college tears and sniffles and then Ell and Victor watched Roz drive off.

"She's actually doing it," said Ell. "Giving up her dream school to chase after Benny."

"Where did we go wrong?" said Victor.

"There should be no 'we' in that question. She inherited your genes via osmosis or something."

"Good one," he said, not really meaning it.

They sighed contemplatively. Victor put his arm around Ell's waist, reeled her in. She leaned into him, clamped her arms around him.

"Well," he said. "Here's what I think. We need to just love our fate."

"Huhn," Ell said. "That's actually not bad. Because

359

why fight it?"

"Right?"

"Yes. Let's do that. Let us love our fate."

They were all smiles and even high-fived each other. Then took a moment as they looked down the road. The longer they stared down that road, less and less their smiles became until Ell and Victor were downright frowning. They turned to each other.

"On second thought, 'love your fate' is stupid."

"I know."

They stared back down that road. Then, said in unison, "God help us."

EPILOGUE

'Twas was eight years later again when one of those couldn't-be-anything-but-bad-news-middle-of-the-night phone calls jolted Ell and Victor awake. Victor picked up, and sure enough, it was Roz, frantic, calling from the Arctic.

The Arctic?

Here's the backstory: Roz and Benson, wife and husband team, working on their Ph.D. thesis research — Hers: "Creating a Super Human - A Matter of Enhancement at the Cellular Level"; His: "A Super Human's Super Babies - A Matter of Genetic Transference of the Enhancement at the Cellular Level." In lab experiments, Roz had created super-rats that were stronger, resisted disease, tolerated extreme temperatures, and/or healed quicker. All accomplished by tweaking the mechanics of cells via a viral trigger. But the process needed a more stable trigger, of embedding the tweak into the genetic code, which was where Benson came in. Roz hadn't yet been able to get all of the super-traits to manifest in one rat but the results were good enough with minimal side effects to where they wanted to start human trials. But where did one go to acquire said humans who would be up for being guinea pigs to be experimented on at the cellular and genetic level, that if something went wrong, there was a good chance that this "someone" would be seriously screwed?

They actually didn't have to go anywhere. The Department of Defense showed up at their doorstep. Of course. Their holy grail, the super-soldier and all that. They apparently had sniffed out Roz and Benny's research even before it was presented as a thesis proposal and had been keeping tabs ever since. So voila! They had their human "volunteers." And step-one was to test extreme environmental effects on the viraled military personnel. And lo and behold, the DOD already had a research station up and running at an environmentally hostile location. Hence, the Arctic.

So, back to frantic Roz. She blathered between sobs and vice versa about a blizzard and some of the men being lost during the field test, including Benny. Eventually they were found, but frozen to death.

"Holy crap," said Victor.

"What? Is she okay?" asked Ell.

"Benny's dead."

"Jesus," said Ell.

"I'm so sorry, Roz," he said.

"I need your help, Dad."

"Of course, anything."

"I need you here."

"Um, okay."

"I need your help to resurrect Benny."

Victor cleared his throat. "Say what?"

"I know about your girlfriend, the one who committed suicide, the one you brought back to life."

A long moment. "I'll call you back in five." Hung up and squinted at Ell.

Ell said, "What'd she say? Why are you looking at me like that?"

"How is it that she knows about Francine?!"

Ell looked confused, thought about it some, then her eyes sparked as if with recollection. Chewed on a nail, contemplating how to explain it.

"Ell?"

"Copious drinking plus being pissed off at you during your exile years equals me blabbing to our then eight-year-old daughter about your mad scientist exploits."

"You told her I was a mad scientist?"

"Not directly, but it was implied."

"That really hurts."

"Get over yourself. Roz thought it was cool. Why do you think she became a scientist?"

"Oh." He smiled a proud-father smile, which lasted like three seconds. Looked at her askance. "But wait. You didn't tell her about the—"

"The cloning? Are you fucking insane? And what I told her about Francine, I made her promise never to utter a word of it unless there was an emergency."

"Like when her husband gets caught in an Arctic blizzard and freezes to death and she needs me to resurrect him?"

"Exactly. So are you going to—"

"Absolutely not."

"Victor! Of all people, you know what she's going through."

"Yeah, maybe. But you know what else I know firsthand? God's wrath, okay? I am not going to mess around with the natural order of things because that is how one gets royally screwed. So, rest in peace, Benny."

"Victor! Go help your daughter."

"No."

"You know whose wrath is worse than God's?"

He gulped. "A woman's?"

She tapped index finger to nose-tip, the international sign for "bingo!"

***

Victor arrived at the research station 48 hours later with the cover story that he was Roz's thesis professor to help iron out some quirks. In front of the DOD staff, Roz and Victor were like, nice to see you, professor, and nice to see you, Ph.D. candidate Roz, and can we go to the morgue and check out the bodies to try and determine why their extreme weather resistance didn't kick in, that is except for your husband who was not part of the sample group, so sorry for your loss.

Roz kept it together until they were left alone with the frozen bodies in the makeshift morgue, at which point she bawled her eyes out while saying she thought she'd been all cried out but apparently not and Victor took her into his arms and told her "there there" and held her until the sobs resolved to sniffles. Then, straight to business. They stood over the three bodies laid out on the floor, covered with white sheets. Victor pulled the sheet off of Benny's face. He looked peaceful, maybe even a faint smile.

Flicked at his forehead. Plink plink was the frozen-solid sound of Benny's skull.

"Poor, Benny," rasped Roz.

"Honey, are you sure about this? I mean, look at him. He seems pretty happy in death."

"Dad!"

"Okay okay. But hear me, Daughter. There may be immense consequences for what we are planning to do, i.e., barging into God's realm."

"But it worked for your girlfriend so it should work for Benny. I think you're just bitter because she ended up dumping you and marrying a hunky NFL quarterback."

"Wait, what? Is that what your mother told you, because it's totally not true."

"It's okay, Dad. People get dumped."

"Do you want to know what really happened to Francine?" He was about to lay it all out re: the utter cluster-fuck at the dry cleaners, but then Roz stared at him with watery eyes and he thought better of it. "You're right," he said. "I am a little bitter. Who can compete with a hunky NFL quarterback with a hunky one-syllable first name?"

"Don't worry. Two-syllable first names and geeky professor types are making a comeback. So her name was Francine? It's a nice name. I bet she was amazing and beautiful to have inspired you to do what you did."

He wanted to tell her, just look in the mirror, but instead kissed her cheek and smiled and said, "Let's do this."

***

The black box that was used to resurrect Francine was a no-go, didn't want a repeat of the aforementioned dry cleaners incident. Besides, the black box technology was antiquated, going on 30 years old. So on the flight over, knowing full well he would cave to Roz's imploring him, Victor brainstormed hours straight for alternatives to jump starting brain function to bring Benny back.

While Victor was configuring a better version of the black box via the holo-app on his tablet computer, the generic-business-class-looking passenger next to him stirred awake, noted said hologram and asked,

"Is that some kind of brain reviving machine?"

"Something like that."

"Hmmm. Seems kind of old-school." He reached into the seat-pouch, pulled out couple of bottles of mini-booze, handed one to Victor. "What I mean is, there'd be more efficacy by way of organic medium rather than mechanical. Deliver what you need to the source by the most reliable method. I'm just spit-balling here, but for example, pharmaceutically, or better yet, biologically."

Victor stared at his own reflection in the passenger's unfashionably oversized and thick-lensed glasses, said, "That *is* a better idea. And I think totally doable nowadays. I've been out of the game for a while, so thanks."

"Glad to help." He finished off the mini booze.

Victor asked, "Are you in the bio-med biz? An M.D., maybe?"

"Nope. But I have played both on TV."

***

Victor didn't tell Roz that the core idea came from some dude on the plane who had zero credentials except for playing roles of those with actual credentials. The fleshed-out plan was to use Roz's viral transport methodology to deliver to key points in the brain the energetic pulse needed to get the engine cranking so to speak. But instead of the host cell carrying a virus, it would carry the energy source, tiny nuclear nuggets, mini power generators.

"That sounds a little crazy," said Roz.

"Not in my universe," said Victor. "But what I'm worried about is, where to get the radioactive source."

"Um, Dad. We're on a military base. In the Arctic. Where secret experiments take place. Do I need to spell it out?"

"So what you're saying is, there is available radioactive —"

"Yes, Dad, yes." She rolled her eyes and pulled him by the parka sleeve and they schlepped across the compound to pay a visit to the lead-lined storage facility under the mess hall where they "shopped" for what they needed, then headed back to Roz's lab. It took them a few months to perfect the process to where they felt confident enough to start experimentation.

"Where are the lab rats, by the way?" asked Victor.

"Dad. We're on a military base. In the Arctic. We don't need to use lab rats."

"So what you're saying is—"

"Yes, Dad, yes."

Roz had one of the dead personnel, Test Subject No. 3, brought to the lab. After No. 3 was thawed out, a teeny tiny hole was drilled into his skull through which "magic potion" batch-21235A was injected. Two minutes and 17 seconds later, No. 3's body began trembling ever so slightly, then built up to full-blown convulsions which continued for 38 seconds. Until his head exploded.

Brain and skull bits plastered Victor and Roz. She stared at the exploded-head Test Subject in utter horror, had her mouth covered with both hands to either suppress a scream or prevent from blowing chunks. Victor wrote in his notebook: "Side effects - exploding head. May need to reduce radioactive material." Told Roz, "You might want to rethink the whole lab rat situation."

***

It was another month of tinkering and experimenting (yes, with lab rats this time) before confidence level was back up as high as it could go for now at 99.8%. During the time when the bodies of Test Subject No. 10 and Benny were thawing out, Victor sat Roz down and had a chat over coffee and pie at the mess hall. It was about 2:00 a.m. and the place was deserted, lit minimally, and quiet except for the howl and rattle caused by the wind intent on blowing the base to Kansas.

Victor said, "Are you hearing that?"

"The wind you mean?"

"Uh-huh. The weather's been clear and calm for weeks." He nervously fiddled with the pie crumbs left on the plate. "And suddenly this?"

"It happens, Dad. This place is the wild west of weather events. Is this what you wanted to talk about, the weather?"

He said nothing. The pie crumbs crushed to dust.

"Dad?"

"Francine didn't run off with a hunky one-syllable-first-name NFL quarterback. She suffered physically through a resurrected life, would have eventually deteriorated to death but got shot dead instead, and I stupidly tried to resurrect her again and her head fell off and her body was incinerated in a dry-cleaners." He put his head in his hands. "The whole thing was not pretty."

"I know what you're trying to do but things will work out. The experiments went off without a hitch. Benny will be fine, I'm sure of it. As for you, I don't know, what with your crazy stories."

"You don't believe me? I still have Francine's head in a cryogenic state in an undisclosed location if you want proof. Okay, that's not 100% true because your Mom forced me to give up the location and gave Francine a proper burial in a location undisclosed to me. But otherwise it is all true. Ask your mother."

Roz laughed and laughed. "Thanks for lightening the mood. That much I did need." She slurped the rest of her coffee and got up from her seat and took Victor by the arm and stood him up. "Come on, Dad. Time to perform some more miracles."

He let out a weary sigh.

"Chin up," she said. "After all, I love my husband. And love conquers all. In fact, that should be our family motto."

Victor took a long look at her, said, "No. It really should not be."

***

The "magic potion" worked! Test Subject No. 10 was resurrected! Benny too! They came to as if waking from hibernation but otherwise they were physically and mentally without adverse effect it seemed. Both were understandably freaked about the fact of their deaths but thankful for being resurrected. Roz on Cloud Nine, Victor, cautiously optimistic. Even the weather had cleared. The

DOD, ecstatic about the magic potion.

No. 10 and Benny were kept under periodic observations but free to join the herd in the meantime, go about their business. But No. 10 came down with an intense fever a week later. Benny the same, a few days after that. Flu-like symptoms, severe enough to be bed-ridden. Complaints of big-time headaches, and their skin being super painful to the touch.

Then on one of those nights at the infirmary, No. 10 was found feasting on the cracked-open skull of the on-duty nurse. The Marine M.P.s were called. No. 10 did not respond to verbal commands and when the M.P.s attempted to physically restrain him, they were tossed aside with little effort. So they took up their sidearms and shot him repeatedly in the torso which had zero effect. Then they tried blowing his brains out. That worked.

The M.P.s reported that there were no physical manifestations to provide clues as to what exactly caused No. 10's behavior. But they noted the opaque eyes, superhuman strength, and skin the color of late stage meat rot. They also reported sustaining some injuries, but only minor ones, such as contusions, scratches and some bite-marks. And when they checked on Benny, he was not in his room. The M.P.s instead found an orderly crumpled in a heap under Benny's bed with his brainpan licked clean.

The bitten Marines contracted the "infection" and Benny was running amok among the science-research personnel, all of which helped to spread the infection rapidly, and by morning the place was crawling with zombies, and brain-eaten corpses were littered about. A handful of survivors, including Victor and Roz, with M4 carbine rifles blazing, made it to the helipad where two Huey UH-1's were filling up quickly, readying for takeoff. Victor clambered into the helicopter, offered a hand to Roz but she just stood there.

"Come on, Roz!" yelled Victor over the engine noise.

She looked over her shoulder past the Marines holding up the rear with their M4's, picking off the fast approaching horde. She turned to Victor. "Benny's still out there. I think I can turn him back, save him."

"You need to worry about saving your own ass."

"My ass is not worth saving if I abandon my husband."

"He is a zombie! He has eaten human brain! Thinking that you can change him back is crazy."

"Not in my universe. I can't leave him, Dad."

And with that, she sprinted past the Marines, did an end-around the hungry mob by ducking behind the mess hall, past the motor pool, and toward the three-story dorm building.

Victor grabbed a couple of M4's, and cussing like crazy, ran after his daughter. He found her on the roof of the dorm building, looking over the mayhem with binoculars.

"Dad!"

They hugged.

"I haven't found Benny yet," she said.

"We'll find him."

They watched the Hueys taking off, zombies hanging all over the helos. One of the helicopters fishtailed 180 degrees, losing control, veered into the other, both exploding and crashing to earth in a fiery heap.

"Omygod," said Roz.

There was banging at the roof door. Victor and Roz turned, watched. He handed her one of the M4's. Still banging. Zombies apparently did not know how to use a doorknob. After about the 100th bang, the steel door flew off its hinges. The zombies poured out onto the rooftop. The M4's were aimed at the oncoming swarm, ready to unload, ready to—

"It's him!" yelled Roz.

She pointed at the zombie leading the charge. Benny. Roz dropped her rifle.

"Benny! Benny, it's me. Roz. Your wife. I love you. Let me help you."

He growled incoherencies, got more agitated. Seemed very hungry for wife brain, as well as father-in-law brain.

"Benny, please!" She picked the rifle back up. "Dad, I don't think he's hearing me."

The horde was close enough to where one could smell zombie B.O. Victor and Roz shuffled backward until they reached the edge of the roof.

"Dad," Roz rasped weakly. "I could use some ideas right about now."

Victor took a good long look at his daughter, soaking her into his retina for all eternity. He then turned to the zombie horde, lowered his rifle. Gripped Roz's hand. "Repeat after me," he told her. "Love conquers all. Love. Conquers. All."